# Losing Faith

## The Hale Series

# Janiah Benitez

# Trigger Warnings

Addiction
On Page Overdose
Suicidal Thoughts
On-Page Self-Harm
Bipolar Depression
Mention of Abortion
Post-Abortion Depression
Mention of School Shooting
Mention of Child Abuse
Mention of Sexual Assault
OCD (including intrusive thoughts
and compulsions)

To those battling their mind,
you're stronger than you think;
Don't lose faith in yourself.

# Part I

# *Chapter One*

## LISETTE

THE SMELL OF MIXED LIQUOR engulfs me. I can practically taste it in the air as swarms of bodies move around the crowded bar. I watch people regularly spill their drinks as they move, and as desperate as it sounds, I never wanted to be a tile on a bar floor as bad as I do right now. A simple life of having alcohol thrown on you to be cleaned up at the end of the night.

I glance around the room again because people-watching at a bar when you're sober is a lot more fun than doing so while drunk. At least I keep telling myself that so I don't down the double shot of tequila in front of me.

Forcing my eyes to stay off of my drink, I focus on a couple in the corner who are clearly in a heated argument.

"Do you want me to make you something else?"

My eyes snap forward to the bartender. "I'm good," I tell her as I grab my glass and watch the drink swirl around.

I feel a pair of eyes on me, but when I look up, the bartender only gives me a nod before someone calls her over. I bring the glass to my lips, and when the sour scent assaults me, reminders of what I will need to wake up to tomorrow if I drink this nearly suffocate me. I place the cup back down hard enough that some of the drink splashes onto my hand.

My eyes zone in on the cool liquid, and before I can change my mind, I lick it off my hand. My eyes fall shut as the slight burn surges through my blood and I quickly realize that was a *terrible idea*. My mind runs wild as I realize having a few hours with a blank mind will feel a lot better than the worry of tomorrow's what-ifs.

*If you drink this, you'll be another disappointment.*

I'm already a disappointment, what's one more?

Grabbing the cup, I watch the tequila swirl, taunting me for one sip. I rest the cup on the counter before reaching for the coin in my back pocket.

I pick a side before flipping it in the air, but before it can land in my hand, someone snatches it out of the air. I look up and the bartender shakes her head as she examines the coin. I feel my brows pull together and almost reach over the counter to snatch it back, but she opens her mouth.

"Flipping for a drink with your sobriety chip?" She rolls the coin between her knuckles causing my previous annoyance to be halted by her little party trick. "We're supposed to carry these around as reminders to *stay* sober, not to decide whether or not we should drink."

"I'm aware." I reach for my six-month sobriety chip, but she turns her hand palm side up, and it disappears.

I send her an unamused look. "Cute." I lean back in my seat and she doesn't seem moved by my glare as it settles on her.

Instead, she slides my drink off the counter, trading it for a cup of ice and a can of club soda. "When you hit rock bottom, I'll let you have that double shot of tequila. Until then, you keep fighting."

I rub my finger around the rim of my new cup as my eyes settle on her again. "And how do you know I'm not already at rock bottom, Houdini?"

She seems to let out a low chuckle I can't hear over the music. "Because you're flipping coins to decide your fate. Rock bottom doesn't look like that, blondie. Trust me." The seriousness in her tone looms over me and my eyes land on my new drink.

I may not be at rock bottom, but the pain in my chest doesn't care how low I am. I want a drink *now*, not when I'm desperate enough to sniff leftover oxy off the ground.

"Change your face," Houdini calls out to me again, but as my eyes drag up to hers, I can't find the energy to obey her wish. Her shoulders slightly slouch before she swipes someone's card and walks over to me. "You're doing great."

I have no idea why the sobriety gods sent me this stranger who's clearly desperate to be someone's sponsor, but my nice chips are almost used up.

"I'm not." I bang my knuckles on the counter a few times in thought. It isn't until she takes my hand and rubs away the redness in them that I notice how hard I was hitting myself.

"You're sober," she reminds me before turning my hand palm side up and my sobriety chip is laying there. It's dim in here, but the blue coin shines just enough in my hand to see the big six in the middle of the triangle.

"How long have you been sober?" I ask and a somber smile touches her lips.

She reaches for her back pocket before setting a red chip on the counter in front of me. I turn it over, expecting something different than the number that correlates with the color of the coin, but the number one stares back at me.

"I was sober for seven years before a month ago."

My eyes meet hers and she gives me a weak smile as she shrugs.

"That doesn't mean those seven years don't count for nothing," we both voice at the same time, and her smile turns more genuine.

"You meet with Winter?" She mentions the Chair of my AA group and I nod with a small smile.

"She's annoying as shit but some of the stuff she says is tattoo worthy." I lift my sleeve to show her my upper forearm.

Her eyes slightly widen before she breaks into a laugh and lifts her cropped top just a bit. On her ribs is my identical tattoo. It *wasn't for nothing.*

My smile grows before my eyes narrow on her. "Okay, who the hell sent you here, Houdini?" I glance around the room, expecting to find my brother somewhere, but he isn't in sight.

Her laugh touches my ears again. "I could say the same about you."

I turn back to her and she holds her hand out to me.

"The name's Erin."

I take her hand in mine. "I like Houdini better," I tease. "Lis."

She nods in thought before someone shouts an order at her. "On it." She grabs a bottle and cup but keeps her focus on me as she works. "How come I've never seen you at a meeting?"

I open my soda and pour it into my cup. "I only go on sandwich days."

She tilts her head back with a laugh before her face morphs into pleasure. "Ugh, those sandwiches are so good."

"Right, and that asshole refuses to tell me where she gets them from because she thinks I won't go to meetings anymore." I roll my eyes at the reminder, and while Winter may be right, she doesn't have to withhold such valuable information.

Erin sets down the drink she's making before immediately preparing another one. "I had to switch my schedule so now I can only go on donut days." She lets out a sigh as if it physically pains her but I bet it does. Those donuts are always stale as shit.

"Of course, you have a schedule for your plans." I shake my head at her as I take a sip of my soda and she looks offended before she plasters a smile on her face for the girl who hands her a tip.

"Thank you, baby." She blows her a kiss before putting the money in the tip jar and turning to me.

"What's that supposed to mean?" She places a row of shot glasses in front of a group beside me.

"Just that you have perfect French tips as a bartender which tells me you're very organized."

A smile touches her lips as she pours a rainbow drink into all of the shot glasses in one swift move. The group of girls she's serving record her pouring the shots before saying some sort of chant and throwing their heads back.

They each squeal as their faces scrunch and envy seeps into my blood at their freedom.

Two knocks on the counter in front of me has me turning my attention away from them and onto Erin again. "It was great talking to you, but you should call your sponsor and go grab food or something." The sympathy oozes off of her and if it wasn't for us being in the same AA group, I would've stayed.

I know AA is anonymous, but everyone in our group is like family. Even if Erin and I somehow have never met until now, I refuse to relapse in front of her.

She walks off to take another order as I text my brother.

> You awake?

It's only 1:00 a.m., but he replies immediately.

**Biggest Loser**

No.

I roll my eyes before sending him a middle finger emoji and he replies by reacting to it with a laugh.

You good?

Peachy.

I text him the code word we came up with because neither of us have the balls to tell the other, *I'm at a bar, come save me.* When he likes the message, I know he's on his way since he has my location. While I'll never admit it to him, I appreciate Sire more than anyone on this earth. He'll drop the world and come to me when I need him without making me feel like the burden I am. It is one of my favorite things about him.

The next ten minutes I sit with my soda and wait for my brother as I talk to Erin when she's free.

"Is this seat taken?" A husky voice reaches my ears before a strong whiff of cologne hits me and I don't know much about perfume, but I know whatever *that* is, is expensive.

I turn to the side and a tall guy in a three-piece suit smiles down at me. It's clear he's not from here since he's wearing *that* in the cheapest bar in LA.

"No, go ahead," I say in my best British impersonation before nodding for the seat.

He sits before holding a hand out to me. "Connor."

I take his hand with a smile. "Lucy," I lie.

He kisses the back of my hand. "That's a beautiful name."

*They always say that. Where are you from, Lucy?*

"Where are you from, Lucy?"

*See?*

I pull my hand away as I offer another smile. "Originally from Bloomsbury, but I moved here just over a month ago."

Erin catches a part of my sentence and lets out a loud snort which she fails to cover with a cough.

Connor nods as if he's paying attention, but his eyes are on my chest. "And what brings you to LA?" His eyes meet mine again for a brief second before they're on my thighs, seamlessly pulling my jeans down with his eyes.

"She's a Dodgers fan." A familiar voice sounds from behind me and I shake my head when Connor looks up and practically drops dead at the sight of my brother.

"Sire Griffin?" He looks around the room as if to check that the rest of the bar also sees the LA Dodgers star pitcher. He stands from his seat and holds a hand out to my brother with a nervous laugh. "Holy shit. I'm a huge fan, dude."

"Thanks, man." Sire shakes his hand before his eyes settle on me. He focuses on me, analyzing my features before he leans over and grabs my drink.

"You could just ask, you know." I point out, my fake accent still in play and a furrow grows in his brows.

He takes a whiff of my drink, the proud look on his face hard to miss. "Not asking saves you from needing to come up with excuses if you *did* drink." He sets my cup down. "You're welcome."

I let out a scoff before hopping down from the stool. "You know I wouldn't come up with excuses; I'd just tell you I simply wanted to drink."

He lets out a low laugh as he sets down a fifty bill by my drink. I already paid, but I let Erin have the tip. "You have all your stuff?"

Before I can respond, Connor, who I forgot was still there, cuts in. "Sorry, do you mind if I get a picture with you?"

Sire looks like he's about to agree when I cut in. "He can't take pictures with fans after midnight." I roll my eyes. "It's some weird thing his agent is making him do, but if you're here tomorrow say"—I glance at Sire—"5:00 p.m., you can get a picture and autograph?" I look back over at Connor and his mouth is agape, as if I just announced he won the lottery.

"Yeah, yeah, of course, five is perfect."

"Perfect," I exclaim. When his brows furrow, I realize my accent slipped. "You have a great night, Connor love." I slip back into it and he only looks more confused but I grab Sire's forearm, walking as drunk as I can a few steps away until someone calls me.

"Hey!"

I turn at the sound of Erin's voice and walk back to the bar.

"Your sponsor is Sire Griffin?"

"He's my brother, but yeah, the loser is also my sponsor. Please don't befriend me for him, he's married." He isn't, but with the way he talks about his girlfriend, they may as well be married with kids.

"Brother?" Erin glances between me with my pale skin and blue eyes before looking back at Sire who's the opposite.

"We're adopted," I clarify with the short version of the very long story.

She nods in understanding before reaching behind my ear and revealing a piece of paper with a phone number on it. "I must stick to my strict schedule so we won't see each other at AA, but we should hang out. Walk the strip with our best Bloomsbury impersonations."

I let out a soft laugh as I take her number. "I'll text you, Houdini."

She nods in response before someone calls her attention. I walk out of the bar with Sire, and when the fresh air hits me, the reality that I was, once again, so close to relapsing hits me.

"Is Vidia awake?" I quickly take the lead of the conversation before he wants to *talk about it.*

Since the topic is his girlfriend, he easily goes along with it as we walk to his car. "I woke her up to let her know I was coming here. I promised to keep her in the loop."

I glance up at him and, for once, don't tease him about being madly in love. I'm glad he has the support system he does. It's not easy dating an addict, or so I've been told by countless exes, but Vidia sticks by him like no other.

"Why the hell did you tell that guy I'd come back here tomorrow? He's going to be waiting all day." He glances down at me, amusement playing in his eyes.

"That's the point." I shrug. "I didn't like him. He was gross."

He slightly pauses. "Did he do something to you?"

"No, caveman. Do you think he would've been smiling about autographs if he had?" I voice before he can turn around and pick a fight in my defense.

He nods in response, but when I look forward, I feel his eyes on me and I know what's next. We reach his car and he leans against the hood before saying, "We're going to talk about it eventually so let's skip the I *don't want to talk* part."

I look over at him before tilting my head to the side. "But that's my favorite part." I pout and when he remains serious, I roll my eyes. "It's the same reason as always. I wanna leave Earth and I'm not talking about traveling to the moon."

He doesn't laugh, and at times like this, he makes it hard to cope since he won't laugh at my dark humor.

"Be happy I only *almost* chose alcohol over actually choosing this." I pat my thighs, silently gesturing to the scars under my jeans.

This time he breaks and a smile slips. "I'm glad you're staying safe, but—"

"Everything before but is bullshit." I point at him.

He rolls his eyes before trying again. "I'm glad you're staying safe," he states. "What happened to our system? You could've called me before coming here." He gives me a pointed look, and I walk around the car for the passenger seat, but when I pull on the door, it's locked.

"Come on," I plead.

"Answer me," he counters gently and the concerned look in his eyes makes my skin crawl because he's being too nice for comfort. Bullying each other is our entire relationship, but he's too into his sponsor role right now.

"Open the door."

"I just want one answer. Tell me or walk home." He sounds annoyed now and I know he's not actually upset, but the niceness is gone which I appreciate.

I let out a defeated breath as I run my thumb along the handle of his door. "You know that voice you get? The self-doubt. The constant reminder that you're a bother to everyone in your life. That calling a friend or sibling is just going to annoy them?"

My eyes meet his but he doesn't respond.

"That voice was extra loud today and when I picked up my phone to call you, all I felt was that you hated me, so I went to drink."

Sympathy seeps into his brown eyes and I pull on the door for an escape. He unlocks it as promised, but before I can close the door, he grabs it.

"That voice is lying to you," he reminds me. "It always will." He shoves my shoulder, forcing me to look up at him. "You're never a bother and I could never hate you."

I bite back a smile and pretend to gag. He lets out a laugh before closing the door and a smile spreads across my face when he isn't looking.

# Chapter Two

## JACKSON

I TAP ON MY STEERING wheel impatiently as I sit in traffic. My eyes keep darting to the time, and I remind myself that I'm only five blocks away from my daughter's school. I almost get out and walk because I *hate* being late to get her, but a few cars start moving.

*You're already ten minutes late, what's three more?*

When I finally make it in front of the school, my eyes quickly find my kid's pink dress as she sits on the steps of her school. My annoyance quickly fades at the sight of her smile as she looks up at her teacher but then I notice the dean standing with them.

"Great," I mumble as I turn the car off and step out.

"Daddy!" Isabelle rushes over to me, and as soon as she's in reach, I lift her and throw her in the air. Her laugh captures every ounce of my attention and I pull her in for a hug.

"How was your day, penguin?" I set her onto the ground again and she grabs my hand, but I don't walk off because I feel her teacher and dean watching me like they have a lot to say.

"It was perfect. I got a *great* student sticker." She shows me the back of her hand which has a huge gold star.

"Good job, baby." I fix the bow in her hair before walking over to her teacher. "Hi, I'm so sorry I was late. There was an accident on the highway."

Neither of them looks like they believe me, although I'm not lying. "No problem," her teacher, Rose, says, and her tone alone tells me it's certainly a problem. "*Another* reminder though, her tardies are accounted for and we want all of the kids to be a part of that ice cream party at the end of the year." Condescendence drips from her tone as she offers me a forced smile.

*You shouldn't punish kids for their parents being a few minutes late at pick-up, but okay.* "Thanks for the reminder, Ms. Rose." I offer her a smile and before she can respond, Dean Carmen joins.

"Do you have some time to come in and speak with us regarding Isabelle's grades?" She looks down at my kid with a smile, and when I look down at her, she doesn't look nervous or guilty, so I'm assuming they didn't tell her whatever problem there clearly is.

"Yes, of course." I follow them inside and we slow down as we reach a group of kids building Legos.

"Isabelle, why don't you wait here while we talk to your dad?" Carmen smiles down at her.

She looks up at me for approval and I give her a smile as I nod for the other kids and she takes off.

"Is everything okay?" I ask once she is out of earshot. Both of them share a glance as we continue walking and my mind begins to run wild with the worst-case scenarios.

"Not really, Mr. Carter," Carmen starts. "We had our first assessment earlier this week and her test scores were concerning." She opens her office door for me and as I walk in, I turn to her instead of sitting.

"I thought you were working with her after seeing her score for her entry exam?" I look between both of them and Rose raises her brows unamusingly, but I bite my tongue.

These private school people have their heads so far up their asses. Being that we're moving soon, I enrolled my daughter into this school since it's closer to our new home, but a part of me is having serious regrets.

Carmen gestures to the chair in front of her desk and I take a seat as she sits in front of me. "We usually like to have these talks with both parents," the dean starts, her gaze carefully watching me. "Mom hasn't made an appearance and we think her involvement would be beneficial."

I force a smile. "Mom won't be making an appearance. It's just me," I remind them. We vaguely spoke about this at registration and like before, their nosy gazes are apparent.

"Well," Carmen continues, her judgmental gaze clear as day. "We've noticed a delay in Isabelle's development and things like this can happen after divorces. I heavily suggest Mom—"

I cut off her assumptions. "The separation wasn't recent so I doubt that. What exactly is she delayed with?" I switch the topic, my concern peaking again.

Rose hands me a folder before standing beside her boss. "We have been working with her, but she hasn't been making much improvement, especially since her uncle is constantly pulling her out of school during her tutoring hours."

I open the folder and the first paper is how many times she's been taken out of school early. A bright red *ten* stares back at me, and while that doesn't seem like a lot, it certainly is considering school has only been in session for one month. She's practically missed half of her tutoring sessions.

I swallow my anger and decide I'm killing Isabelle's *uncle*. The next few papers are a few of her assignments and her last development test. I read through her scores as Isabelle's teacher speaks up again.

"We can't stop her from being pulled out of school early, but let's be honest, there can only be so many family emergencies. She needs to be in school and I think Mom will agree."

"I agree." I close the folder and let my eyes meet their harsh gaze. "She won't be pulled out of class anymore," I assure them. I was aware she was being taken out of class for her ice cream dates with her uncle since the school calls me whenever someone picks her up, but I didn't think it was this bad. Either way, I already told him to stop doing this.

"Jackson." The dean folds her hands together on her desk. "Isabelle's promotion to the next grade is in doubt. Considering she's a new student and on probation, like all new students are in their first year, failing will unfortunately get her kicked out of the school."

I stare at her for a beat, but she's being serious. "She's five," I point out. "Five-year-olds aren't necessarily reading novels." I try to hold back my defensive tone but fail.

"No," she drawls. "However, she isn't reaching milestones we like to see in kids her age, which could be for a number of reasons." She raises her brows as she focuses on my frame.

I keep my initial response to myself. "She has the entire semester to catch up. Children develop at different ages."

She nods in understanding before leaning back in her seat. "I'm aware, however, we have high expectations for all of our students and she's currently not meeting them. I just don't see her catching up in three months. I told you this would be a concern when she tested to get into our school considering her score was borderline passing. I'm aware five-year-olds aren't reading *novels*, but if you look over the assessment, you'll find she struggles with separating facts and opinions. She has a hard time conveying the meaning of passages that are read to her. She shows little interest or throws in the towel completely when she's having a hard time in class—"

"And her math score was in the ninety-nine percentile," I remind them. "I doubt you'd show interest in things you struggle with, it's our job to help her."

She looks offended, but I continue to defend my kid.

"She's also bilingual as your requirements state. Her speech is amazing for her age and her tuition for the *year* was paid in full long before her first day. A comprehension test and failing to separate facts from opinions are going to get her kicked out?" I glance down at the assessment. "Giraffes have pretty fur?" I read one of the questions she got wrong where she should have answered giraffes have long necks. "Can we not agree why a five-year-old would think that's also a fact?" Sure, she struggles with some things, but not enough to be kicked out.

"No, considering she was the only one in the class to get that wrong," Rose cuts in. "With all due respect, an unstable household can be a direct result of her low performance in school."

I lean back in my seat and I'm sure my face shows just how much her words offend me, but she has the nerve to continue.

"Why is it that Mom can't meet with us?" She pries *again* like a starving lion.

"I'm sorry, do you all not accept students with single dads?" I look between the both of them and now it's their turn to look offended, but the second they found out Isabelle's mom wasn't in the picture, it's like I can't make a single mistake without being labeled a bad dad. As if my kid is suffering because she doesn't have a present mom and her struggling in school is a result of that, which isn't true.

"Of course we do." Carmen laughs nervously. "We're going to keep working with her, but I highly advise a personal tutor for after school. We have great ones here."

"I'll look into it." I stand from my seat, but she adds more.

"The next exam is in December and if she doesn't pass, I suggest transferring her for the spring semester. You wouldn't want an F or summer school on her record."

"With all due respect, Dean Carmen, I'm not transferring her in the middle of the year, especially since mid-year transfers are nearly impossible in private schools."

Rose raises her brows again in disapproval as she collects Isabelle's folder. "I'm sure a public school transfer would be a piece of cake." She holds out the folder to me. "Our expectations are not just for our students."

I bite my tongue so hard, I can taste the copper in my mouth. I could buy the property we're standing on three times over, but because of the narrative they made up in their mind for the reason Isabelle's mom isn't in the picture, I don't deserve to be here.

"Have a good day," I bite out before taking the folder from her and walking out. As I pass by the group of kids, I find Isabelle adding a Lego to the top of the building they're making that is nearly her height.

"Let's go, princess." I keep my tone light, refusing to let my annoyance affect the way I speak to her.

We're walking to the car when she glances up at me. "Did Ms. Rose tell you about my reading test?" She looks down at her feet. "It was so hard, but she said I did good. I don't think I did." Her head hangs low, and I lift her into my arms as we cross the street.

"You did your best and that's all that matters. I'm proud of you, penguin." I kiss her nose before opening the back seat. "We'll keep practicing." I put her in her car seat and she nods in return as I put her seat belt on.

As soon as I slip into the driver's seat, she asks for my phone to play music.

"Let me text Abuela, you're going to go to her house and I'll meet you there later." I text my mom and Isabelle speaks up from her seat.

"Do you have to run errands?"

"Just one."

"Hello Isabelle's dumb ass uncle," I voice as he opens the door.

Sire looks confused at first before a smile tugs on his lips, and I know he finds it funny when people are mad, but I might punch him in the damn face.

We met in college, and when he and his brother were signed with the Dodgers, they also signed me to be their agent. When my daughter was born, Sire was always around us and she started calling him *Uncle Sigh*. Since we are as close as we are and I don't have any family in the States besides my parents, he's on my kid's blue card, but that's changing today.

"What's up your ass?" he teases.

"Read this." I shove the paper I received from Isabelle's school.

"Don't shove shit at me." He tries to shove it back at me, but I push the paper into his chest again.

"Read about how my kid most likely won't be promoted to first grade thanks to your dumb ass always pulling her out of school early."

"What?" He glances between me and the paper.

"What I just said." I walk into the apartment and his huge rottweiler walks over to me. I pat her head before she walks over to Sire's girlfriend, who's making her way to us.

"Hey, Jackson." Vidia treads lightly as she glances at the paper he is reading. I say hi in return as I watch the realization slowly hit him.

"They can't do this." He shakes his head in annoyance as he hands the paper to his girlfriend.

"Yes, they *can*. She isn't meeting the requirements to be moved up. Do you expect them to let her struggle in the next grade?"

He remains silent.

"Exactly, you pulled her out of school *ten* times this year and I told you to stop doing it. Now look." I gesture to the paper.

I can tell he feels bad, but his sympathy isn't going to help my kid. I'm more mad at myself for not putting my foot down and taking him off her blue card like I said I would.

"It was not—"

"It was, Sire. They showed me her record, she's barely been in tutoring. Aside from you fucking up my kid, do you know how bad of a father I look now?" I read with Isabelle every chance I get but of course, they don't know that nor do they care.

"Oh, please. You're not a bad dad, Jack—"

"To them I am. It was hard to get her into this damn school and all of them doubted me from the second I signed her up because they think she's suffering with one parent. Now she's failing and it's proving all of them right that I can't do this." I let out a long breath before running a hand down my face. I feel my head pounding and I don't think today could get worse.

I turn to leave but stop short at Sire's words. "Wait, Jackson, I'm sorry, okay? I shouldn't have pulled her out of class so much but you're far from a bad dad, man. You're the best damn parent I know and everyone who doubted you can go fuck themselves."

I shake my head at him before turning around and he goes on. "You *can* do this. You're already doing it. You're kicking ass at raising Isa."

"And we'll make sure she doesn't fail," Vidia voices from his side before grabbing a hold of his hand.

"Yeah." Sire nods encouragingly. "Bring her over for a few hours after school and I'll work with her, get her up to speed."

Vidia offers me a smile as she continues for him. "If that doesn't work, then we'll find the best tutor and pay for everything." She smiles up at me and I decide not to decline their offer only because she's smiling at me like she thinks this will work and I need it to work.

"Fine."

They both nod but I look over at Sire again.

"You're off her blue card."

He must sense the seriousness in my voice because his entire face drops. "Jackson, come on." When I don't respond, his shoulders drop slightly. "Who are they going to call if there's an emergency and you don't answer? I swear—"

"They'll call Vidia."

Her head snaps over to me and she looks confused before her face softens and a smile grows on her face. "Really?"

"Yeah, I know you two are always together, so you'll most likely be with him in the event of an emergency, or you'll call him." I give her a shrug as her smile grows. "Either way, I trust you." She also went to college with us, and while we weren't as close, if Sire is dating her, I trust her with my kid.

"Thank you. I won't be pulling her out of class, promise."

Her boyfriend playfully shoves her away and her laugh fills the entire apartment. "Smartass." He rolls his eyes at her with a smile before turning to me. "August is going to be offended. You told him he was your third option after your mom and me."

I let out a soft laugh as I imagine his brother's dramatic reaction. "I lied. I love your brother and I'm sure he's great with kids, especially mine, but he's one of the last people I'd trust if anything happened to Belle."

He wouldn't be able to stay calm or focus very long in an emergency, which isn't his fault, but still.

"I'm telling him you said that."

"I'm sure you will, asshole."

Sire laughs and I ignore him as I hug Vidia goodbye.

"Bring Isa over anytime so we can tutor her."

"Okay." I have serious doubts about this, so I'll be looking for actual tutors. I pull away from her hug when my eyes land on someone sitting on their couch.

She ties her hair into a bun and as if she can sense me watching her, she turns to me and I realize it's Sire's sister. In the last few years I've known Sire, I've hung out with Lisette in group settings a few times, still, she doesn't offer me an inch of a smile.

She turns back to her phone and I turn back to Sire just as he offers me his hand.

I mindlessly do our short handshake as I glance back at his couch. "Your sister okay?" I nod towards her, noticing she looks *off*. She's usually always smiling or making a joke.

"She's gonna be okay." He musters up a smile and I decide not to push for information as I turn my full attention to him.

"If Belle gets kicked out of this school, I'm seriously not letting you around her anymore."

"She's going to pass the next exam," he assures me, and she better.

# Chapter Three

## LISETTE

WHEN THE FRONT DOOR SHUTS, I stand up from my seat. "I need to go." I turn on my heels and Sire's face drops.

"Why?"

I bite back a smile at how disappointed he sounds. "Aww, are you going to miss your favorite person?" I tease.

He rolls his eyes at me now as he settles on the couch. "I've been missing August for hours." He mentions our brother who he not so secretly favors.

I throw a pillow at him but he catches it.

"You feeling better?" He watches me carefully.

"Yeah," I voice honestly. "I told you I just needed to sleep the urge off." I offer him a smile, and when he nods in understanding, I'm glad he doesn't force me to talk about my feelings again.

"Thanks for listening earlier, I'll repay you with a drink."

He stifles a laugh.

"I'll probably come by tomorrow to bother you." I take one step before he sticks his foot out to trip me. I catch myself before I can eat shit and he's laughing up a storm from beside me.

Vidia stifles a laugh as she settles next to her boyfriend and I flip them both off as I head for the door. "Maybe I won't come back at all."

"Ugh, thank god," he mumbles loud enough for me to hear.

"We love you," Vidia calls out.

"Mhm." I slip out as Harmony texts me again. I quickly reply and let her know I'm on my way down as I step into the elevator.

As I'm leaving the building, I spot her with her back to me. I walk up behind her quietly before grabbing her waist. "Whatcha looking at?"

She jumps with a yelp before turning on her heels.

I let out a laugh at the terror on her face. "Who had you so distracted?"

She turns back around as she nods across the street. I follow her line of sight to Jackson. He talks into his phone as he sits in his car. His short blond curls styled perfectly, complimenting the charcoal gray suit he's in.

"He's hot," she whispers as if he can hear from all the way over there.

"I'm sure he's twice your age." I flick her forehead before pulling her to my car by her school bag.

She rolls her eyes at me as she pushes me out of her grasp. "You're the one who said older men are better."

An older lady glances at us, her eyes wide, and I plaster a smile on my face as I shove Harmony in front of me.

"You're making me look bad. Get in." I unlock my car and she only laughs at me.

"Since when did you care about being perceived as the good and responsible older sister?" She raises one brow and I falter as she calls me her sister.

I'm aware that's what I technically am to her, but it doesn't feel that way considering we didn't grow up together.

I ignore her before walking to the driver's side.

"Speaking of your responsible sister, where does Satan think you are?" I steal a glance at her and a guilty look covers her face.

"She knows I'm here." She keeps her eyes forward and I simply stare at her until she caves and turns back to me. "Okay, that's a lie, she thinks I'm at a friend's house."

I nod in return. I know I don't have the best relationship with my biological family; I haven't spoken to most of them in years, but it still hurts when I'm reminded just how much they hate me.

"What did Ana say when you got home yesterday?"

Harmony is quiet for a beat as she picks at her nails and a smile touches my lips as I stop picking at my own nails. Ana is the middle child between us and she makes it her whole personality that she raised Harmony and is a twenty two year old mom to a seventeen year old.

"She asked about you."

I roll my eyes at her lie as I start the car. "Stop trying to make me feel better." I can see her shoulders slouch in the corner of my eyes before she tries again.

"She mentioned something... something I actually wanted to ask you about."

I prepare myself for her to bring up my addiction, knowing Ana loves to throw that one in my face. I can feel Harmony watching me and after a beat, she builds the courage to speak up.

"She said I shouldn't hang out with you, but I reminded her about what my therapist said about mending my family."

I steal a glance at her and I hate that she even needs therapy.

"Ana said we're not family because you chose the Hales..."

I let out a scoff as I grip the steering wheel tighter. I'm about to open my mouth and say every awful thing I can about a girl that lost her title as my sister a long time ago, but I bite it all back. Up until a few months ago, I hadn't seen Harmony since she was a baby, and it wasn't until she wanted to *mend her family* that we started to get closer.

No progress has been made with her family because our bio mom is still using and I'm not going back there. I told her she could mend *her* family and get to know me separately but we aren't a part of the same family anymore, and I don't think she's come to terms with that just yet.

"Is it true?"

"What?" I steal a glance at her as I snap out of my thoughts.

"Did you leave us with mom when we were babies to go live with the Hales?" She sounds torn and a bitter feeling takes over me as I realize this is the narrative her sister has of me.

"I was a baby, too, Harmony." I look over at her at the red light. "I was *four* when I met Sire. When I met August and Sage, the twins, you had just been born and your dad was beating me upside the head. I was *seven*."

She flinches.

"You and Ana were always with your grandma and I was with the Hales. I grew up with them and when I moved in with them at fourteen, it wasn't because I hated you, I just—" I cut myself off and someone honks behind me before I can continue.

"You just what?" she voices as if she desperately needs to know.

"I didn't leave you and Ana. I was escaping that house. It had nothing to do with you. You were fine with your grandma, and if she wasn't such a bitter old hag, maybe I would've stayed."

I let out a frustrated breath before slowing down the car. I remind myself that I answer her questions because I would also want to know if I were her. She was a baby when our lives were falling apart and I'd want to know what happened, so that's why I put myself through hell and answer everything she wants to know about my childhood.

"I just don't understand why Grandma didn't take you in with us. Why did it matter to her that we had different dads?"

I shrug in return.

She takes my phone and I sit in silence as she puts a song on, keeping the volume low.

It isn't until I'm parking in front of my apartment that she turns to me. "I'm supposed to hang out with Mom again next week." She watches my reaction carefully, but I don't give her one.

Ana has custody of her, but Harmony insists on bonding with her mom. If this is what she wants, I'm not going to let my relationship with her get in the way.

"Is she sober?"

She shakes her head gently. "She's on and off."

I hold back a bitter laugh. "There is no on and off with her, babe. Don't get your hopes up. She's either on or trying to be off and failing." I know I sound hypocritical since I'm also struggling with my addiction, but I'm not the one who had three little girls begging for her attention and *still* has one daughter who wants her in her life.

Harmony's eyes dull slightly as she looks down at my phone. I follow her line of sight to my home screen of a picture of Sire and me with the twins.

"Who's birthday was it?" Harmony has a small smile on her face as she stares at the four of us around a cake.

"It was mine and Sire's first soberversary."

She steals a glance at me, a somber smile on her face. "How old were you?"

"Fourteen."

She nods as she looks between me and the picture. "How are you doing?"

I know what she's asking, but I don't answer as I study her. I was just four years younger than she is now when I started using drugs to cope. As my eyes roam her gentle features, I can't help but think she's too pure to belong to the family she was born into.

I'm flawed beyond repair. Ana is filled with too much hate to feel an ounce of happiness. Her parents are a piece of shit, but Harmony... She's perfect. She's so understanding and too forgiving. She's bubblier than my sister Sage, which I didn't think was possible. A part of me understands why Ana doesn't want her bonding with me.

"Your sobriety I mean," she clarifies when I don't answer.

"I know what you meant, baby girl." I muster a smile. "I'm six months sober."

Her entire face lights up. "That's so good!" Her smile nearly lights up my car and I can't help but smile in return.

"And how are you and Sire?"

My smile grows at her great memory or maybe she just pays attention to me which is refreshing.

When she reached out to me, Sire and I were still silently fighting over some harsh words that were exchanged a few years ago. We were close, but there was a tear between us for a while.

"We're good," I voice. "Ever since he apologized to me earlier this year we've been good. It's like a weight is off my shoulder having him back." I shake my head at my words. "He was never gone, but we weren't talking to each other about our sobriety—now we do."

She watches me and slowly, her smile drops. "You talk about him like he really is your brother."

"He is." My brows slightly furrow at her words as a short laugh escapes me.

She nods softly before she musters up a smile. "Do you think I could ever be a sister to you?" She glances down at my phone again. "Like you are with your other sister?"

I glance down at my phone and my eyes immediately land on Sage's bright smile as she slides a finger full of frosting across my cheek.

"No one can compare to Sage, but you can get a close second." I shove Harmony's shoulder and she lets out a laugh in return. "You have nearly eighteen years to catch up on though, so don't get your hopes up."

She rolls her eyes at me as we step out of the car, but I don't miss her hopeful smile.

# Chapter Four

## LISETTE

I STARE UP AT THE ceiling before letting my eyes fall shut. A minute barely passes before I sit up in my seat. "This is so stupid."

Sire throws his hands up in defeat as he slouches in his seat. "I'm telling you, this worked when I did it with my therapist. Give it a chance."

I restrain from rolling my eyes at him. "And I'm happy you're doing well with your shrink, but I can't close my eyes and *locate where my feelings are manifesting from.* I'm depressed, there's nothing more to it."

He gives me a bored look. "There's probably more to it."

"Or maybe I just have clinical depression because it runs in my shitty genes? Or maybe it's because I'm an addict? Nothing *triggered* me. I woke up sad and I wanted to drink. You're my sponsor, help me feel better." I lean back in my seat again.

He watches me before getting up from his seat. I let out a defeated breath as he walks away, but he's back less than a minute later. He drops a tiny bottle of vodka on my lap, and I feel my brows furrow as I sit up in my seat.

"This is an exercise I do with Kayden," he mentions his sponsor. "When all else is failing, it makes me feel accomplished when I have my temptations close and still resist it. Keep that bottle with you for a few days. If it's too much, call me and we can try something else, but keeping it will prove to yourself that you're not doing as bad as you think."

I keep my eyes on the bottle before I take it in my hands. I can feel the pull in me to take a small sip, but I simply squeeze it in my hand before tucking it away.

When the door swings open, Vidia's dog comes running in and a little girl chases after her.

"Come here!" She laughs behind the dog and I study her for a beat, trying to figure out whose offspring this is. When she turns and I see her big gray eyes, I quickly recognize her.

Isabelle yanks Athena's tail, and when she lets out a bark, she jumps back. I laugh at the panic in her face as she runs over and climbs the couch next to my brother.

"She's going to bite you," I whisper to her, and when Athena comes closer, her teeth showing in innocent excitement, Isa hides behind Sire.

"NO!"

I slightly jump at how loud she screams, but when she starts crying I roll my eyes before rising from the couch.

"Lisette, what is wrong with you?" Sire pulls Isabelle into his arms and she clings to him as if Athena already bit her. "She's nice, princess. She's not going to bite you. Look at her."

Sire bends over to pet the dog, but Isa squirms in his arms, begging him not to be put down. I laugh at them and when Vidia looks over at me, she rolls her eyes.

"Jackson is going to kill you if she tells him you made her cry."

I don't tell her I don't care because I'm sure she knows, but when I look back down at Isa, it always surprises me how much she resembles her dad and it's more than just his blond curls and gray eyes.

"He has *such* a cute kid"—I shake my head at myself, skipping over her threat—"When she isn't screaming and crying." I walk into the kitchen. I pour myself a cup of juice as I watch Vidia wipe away Isabelle's tears.

"She's mean," Isabelle tries to whisper but fails terribly.

"She can hear you," I whisper loud enough for her to hear, and take a sip of my juice, but when she looks over at me, the little asshole sticks her tongue out at me.

Vidia clearly bites back a laugh before Sire puts her down and she walks over to me like her name is on the building. "I do *not* want to be your friend."

"Well that hurts my feelings," I voice dryly as I walk past her. I think she says something behind me, but she stumbles over her words so I ignore her and head for the couch.

Laying my head on the pillow, I keep my eyes shut as my head runs with a million different reasons to drink the bottle that's burning a hole through my pocket.

A weight settles in my chest the more I think about it and I *just* want to sleep. For like, a few months. I think a six-month nap will help me reset.

I feel someone soothing my hair and I think it's Vidia, but when I open my eyes Isabelle is looking down at me. "I like your hair."

I focus on her for a beat and she just keeps her eyes on my hair. "Remind me how old you are, kiddo?"

"I'm five." She puts up a hand.

I nod slowly as I study her. She's on the smaller side for a five-year-old.

"Did I really hurt your feelings?"

I smile at her. "No, honey. I'm sorry for making you cry. I was only kidding."

She nods appreciatively. "I'm giving all my friends a nickname and I said I don't want to be your friend, but"—she pauses for dramatic effect and puts a finger up—"You get *one* second chance. I have the perfect nickname for you." She nods like she's proud of herself and I bite back a smile.

"That's very kind of you."

"Yeah, I know. So, how do you like *Lissy?*" She smiles down at me hopefully.

"Okay," I entertain her. "And what's your nickname?"

"Well, my name *name* is Isabelle Faith Carter, but Daddy calls me Belle or Faith when he's mad or just Carter when he's *really* mad." Her eyes widen a bit, and I bite back a laugh.

"Uncle Sigh and Titi Vid call me Isa and Grandma calls me Bella." She continues.

I catch the way she says *Bella*, like beautiful or pretty in Spanish. "What do *you* want to be called?"

She turns her head to the side as she twirls my hair through all of her tiny fingers. "I like Belle 'cause that's the princess's name." She looks down at me. "You know Belle? With the Beast and—"

"Yeah, I know her. So you want to be called Belle?"

She nods, but it doesn't seem like she was even listening to my question as she does something in my hair.

"Can I braid your hair?"

"No, thank you, kiddo. Go ask Titi V if you can braid her hair." She's cute, but I'm not letting her tangle my hair after it took so much of my energy to get out of bed and wash it today.

"Titi doesn't want her hair braided." Sire quickly saves his girl-friend from having a knot in her pretty curls. "Let's finish reading, Isa."

Sire wraps an arm around her waist and pulls her closer to him as she lets out a laugh.

At the reminder of the conversation I overheard the other day, I sit up and watch Isabelle sound out the words in her book.

After a minute of her trying, Sire reads it for her and that's how their *tutoring* session goes for the next five minutes before the teacher in me can no longer take it.

"She's not going to learn if you just tell her what word it is."

When Sire glances over at me, it's clear he's about to mess with me and tell me to mind my business but he glances at Isabelle before clearly remembering something.

"You have an education degree." He smiles as he hands me the book. "Help us."

Vidia flops onto the couch, her brows slightly furrowed. "You studied education?"

I nod as I pick up the book. "I was a special education teacher." *Before I relapsed and got fired for going to work hungover one too many times.*

I glance at Sire and he offers me a small smile. I naturally went to him when I lost my job, simply to vent, but then he said I didn't need a job and he'd take care of everything for me. I didn't want to let him do that, but he *is* a trillionaire or something, so I let him and he paid for my rent for the rest of the year before transferring me more money than I'll ever need.

I tried to pay him back, but we made a deal: As long as I fight my depression and make myself the priority, he'll help with everything else. So that's what I've been doing.

Not having the stress from having to work has been a huge weight off my chest. I loved my kiddos, but I was depressed that I needed to work, then I was depressed because I got fired. Now I have enough money to not work for the rest of the year and somehow, life still sucks.

Pushing my thoughts away, I sit on the edge of the couch so I'm closer to Isabelle. Since I'm not sure where her standing is, I grab Sire's laptop to do a short assessment.

I have her make letter-sound associations but after the first two, she turns to me as if I offended her. "I'm five, I know my letters. C-c-cat is with a C. This is too easy."

I bite back a laugh at how annoyed she is but from what I overheard from her dad, her school thinks she's really behind.

"Easy means you're doing good. Let's continue."

She shrugs before she turns to the laptop. Instead of simply doing what I said, she cracks her knuckles and pretends to crack her neck before starting, as if this was a competition of a lifetime. Sire and Vidia let out a low laugh before she associates each sound with all the letters in the alphabet with close to no issue.

It isn't until we start working on CVC words—consonant, vowel, consonant—that she struggles to recognize and pronounce them, but the school year is still very early, so I'm confused as to why her school is blowing this out of proportion.

"Good job." I give her a high five when she gets one right and her smile lights up the room.

We work on some other things, and Vidia and Sire join here and there, but after a while, they get up to go do something in their room.

We're in the middle of a new set of words when there's a knock at the door.

"Let me get that. You're so close, keep sounding that one out and use the clues in the picture." I rise from my seat, and when I open the door, Isabelle's dad is clearly surprised to see me.

"Hey," he starts slowly, his brows slightly furrowed as he looks into the apartment, most likely for Sire.

"He's helping V with something in their room." I take a step to the side so he can enter, and when he does, I expect him to go walk to his kid, but he stays in front of me.

"Hey," he voices again.

"You already said that."

A smile grows on his face as a light blush meets his cheeks. Before I can tease him about it, he gets a phone call. I let the door shut as he brings the phone to his ear.

"Jackson Jones."

I feel my brows pull together but don't say anything.

After a beat, he says, "Okay, I'll check when I get home." With that, he ends the call and turns back to me. "Sorry about that."

I tell him it's fine with a slight head shake. "Is your full name Jackson Jones or do you have two first names?"

"The latter." He shakes his head, almost like he's had to explain this plenty of times.

"Mom and Dad couldn't decide?"

He lets out a low laugh that sounds rich as shit and I'm quickly reminded he's Sire's agent, and with the suit he's in, he's most likely rich as shit. "That's actually exactly what happened, which was silly since they only ever call me Jackson."

My eyes scan the rest of his face and I almost ask how old he is because Harmony was right; he's hot, too hot to be a dad to a five-year-old unless he had her young, but I know he didn't.

"How was she?" He gestures behind himself.

"Good," I tell him honestly. "Your kid's cute."

A warm smile touches his lips. "Thanks, Lisette."

"Demeter." I act as if I'm correcting him.

His brows slightly furrow. "Last time we spoke it was Lisette?"

"That was months ago, you have shit memory. Lissy is my middle name," I lie and he nods in understanding.

When I see Sire walk up from behind Jackson, he's shaking his head at me. "What do you gain from constantly lying about minuscule things like that?"

I shrug in return and he shakes his head at me with a smile as he does a short handshake with Jackson who turns to me.

"Your name isn't Demeter, is it?"

"Nope." I walk back to the couch and Isabelle jumps up before I can sit.

"It says lid."

I give her a high five before I sit down. "I told you you could do it."

She runs over to her dad who scoops her into his arms. "How was your tutoring?"

"Pretty good." She shrugs. "I think I like Uncle Sigh teaching me more, but Lissy's not like really bad." She shrugs again and I know she's only saying that because it's easier with Sire, who's not benefiting her, but I'm offended.

"He can help next time then." I lean back on the couch, but Sire quickly counters.

"No, you were great. You're going to help us."

"Says who?" I mess with him, just to see what he's going to offer.

"*You* were supposed to tutor her," Jackson points out to Sire. "You seriously passed this on to your sister?" He rolls his eyes at my brother and I watch as if this was a TV because he looks pretty bothered and I know Sire doesn't like being told what to do. It's like an alpha fight.

"I didn't *pass it on* to her." Sire rolls his eyes at him now. "She's a teacher and offered to help."

"It was barely an offer. I said you were a bad teacher," I remind him.

Before Sire can counter, Jackson turns his attention to me. "Where do you teach?"

"The Milton Academy."

His brows slightly raise and Sire laughs from beside him. "Please don't believe a word this girl says, she's as unemployed as your *child*."

I let out a loud laugh before slapping his leg.

"I have a job." Isabelle pipes up between us. "I own a bakery and I'm a ballet *star*, Uncle Sigh. You know that." Her brows furrow as she looks up at Sire who is quick to apologize profusely to the five-year-old.

When I turn back to Jackson, his attention is on his daughter as he ties her shoe but I still say, "I *used to* work there. It was my first job."

His eyes meet mine as he nods in return. "I heard really good things about them. Did you like the job?"

"Yeah, it was hands down my favorite school to work at. I only left to work at a school that was in desperate need of special education teachers."

He glances at Sire and I hold back a laugh. "That part was true, Jackson Jones."

His eyes meet mine again and amusement fills them before a ghost of a smile touches his lips. "We have to get going, but it was nice seeing you, *not* Demeter."

I bite back a smile, offering a small nod in return as he looks down at his kid.

"Say thank you to Demeter Lissy for helping you with your work." He gently pushes Isabelle in my direction and a snort escapes me at his words.

"Thank you, Lissy." Isabelle pulls me into a hug and I pat her back twice before she lets go.

"No problem, kiddo."

# Chapter Five

## JACKSON

"A RE WE READY?" BELLE LOOKS up at me with her big gray eyes as I pat my pockets for the car keys.

"Yeah, let's go, penguin." I take a step for the door but stop short. "Wait, is the water off upstairs?"

Belle lets out a quiet sigh as she turns to me. "Daddy, you already checked if the water was off. It's okay." She takes my hand. "Let's go before I'm late for school again."

I nod to myself as I take her hand, but as I take another step, I physically cannot leave the house. "Wait, let me just check that the faucet isn't running."

She smiles up at me as she lets go of my hand. "Okay."

I turn on my heels but stop short as I pass the kitchen.

"Dad!" Belle calls out before I can walk in. "The oven is off, you checked already."

I keep my eyes on the oven and I want to let the obsessive need pass, but I can't.

Isabelle comes next to me and taps my leg gently. "I'll check on the oven and you run upstairs to check the water."

I smile at how understanding she is. "Only tap the outside to see if it's warm, don't turn the nobs." I voice before running upstairs. After checking my bathroom and hers twice, I head for the stairs. In the corner of my eyes, I see the guest bedroom and I tell myself that no one used that bathroom. It makes no sense for that faucet to be running, but I quickly check anyway.

Like I was hoping, the water is off, but I tap the nob shut four times and a sense of ease passes through me. When I reach the bottom of the steps, Isabelle is standing in front of the kitchen with a smile.

"The oven is off. Come on." She holds her hand out to me and I take it while glancing behind her.

"Are you sure you checked well?"

"Yes, Daddy." She pulls on my hand and I walk with her, my eyes still trained on the stove. "It wasn't warm. It's okay, I promise."

I nod in return, but my heart rate quickens as we reach the door. I keep telling myself it's fine, but everything else in me tells me it's not and the house is going to be burned to the ground by the time I get home from work.

I force myself to let the feeling pass and hurry out of the house. Isabelle stays standing beside me as I lock, unlock, then relock the door.

"Okay." She takes my hand before I can check the lock. "That's enough. Come on." She pulls my hand and I bite back a smile as I walk with her.

Scooping her into my arms, I kiss her nose and hug her close as the guilt begins to seep in.

"I'm sorry I'm making you late, penguin."

She hugs me in return as she kisses my nose. "It's okay, Daddy. I think your OCD is getting a lot better." She kisses my cheek before tapping my head four times and I stifle a laugh at how sweet my girl is.

"How did I make such a nice baby?"

Her brows furrow as I open the back seat for her. "I'm not a baby."

Holding back a sigh, I nod in agreement as I strap her into her car seat. "Right, sorry." I kiss her one more time before climbing in.

"Do you want to see a quick surprise?"

I glance in the mirror and her eyes light up as she watches me.

"Is the new house ready?" She's practically jumping in her seat and I stifle a laugh as I nod yes.

We've been building our forever home for some time now. I wanted everything to be perfect, so it took longer than needed, but everything is complete. While I haven't taken Belle to the property, I feel bad for this morning and want to show her.

I pass her my phone and she gasps at the first picture. "You made a *pink* door?"

My laugh fills the car. "I sure did. That's what you wanted, right?"

She actually does scream this time and my laugh only grows as I put the car in drive.

"Wait, can we please go see it really really fast?"

"I wish we could, baby, but a minute more and you'll be late."

She nods in understanding, but I can see the disappointment on her face.

"Look at the rest of the pictures and when you get out of school we'll go see it," I promise her.

She nods in agreement and squeals at every other picture as she picks out which room will be hers. "The one next to mine can be for Lola." She mentions her baby doll, who she very seriously claims is her daughter.

"I think that's a perfect idea." I indulge her for the rest of the drive and by some miracle, we get to the drop-off line right on time.

I walk up to the school with Belle's hand in mine. As soon as she sees one of her friends, she's ready to take off running, but I hold her back. "You're forgetting something."

She turns to me with open arms and I kneel down to hug her. "I'm sorry again for this morning, penguin."

"Daddy, I *promise* it's okay. I wasn't even late." She kisses my cheek twice before hugging me again. "I love you. Bye!" She runs off before I can even respond and it makes me miss the days she used to refuse to let go of me when I dropped her off at school.

"I love you too," I mumble to myself as I watch her. When I see her teacher greet her and mark her attendance I walk for my car but stay leaning against it until they go into the school, and only then do I head off to work.

# Chapter Six

## LISETTE

I WATCH MY PHONE RING again and again until it goes to voicemail. My shoulders sag in relief and I open my car door to escape upstairs, but she calls back.

Sinking into my seat, I bring my phone to my ear and decide to get this over with.

"Five missed calls is a bit much don't you think, Ana?" I rest my head back as I stare up at Sire's apartment.

"Oh, sorry. Were you sleeping off a hangover? I know 3:00 p.m. is usually when you're getting out of bed."

A scoff escapes me, but I refuse to let her words hurt me. "You don't know anything about me. Don't be so bitter you missed out on growing up with such a great person."

She lets out a humorless laugh on the other end. "I know you well enough. You're the same girl who only came looking for your family for money so you could do whatever drug it is you're on now. You're just an addict."

I open my mouth to counter but nothing comes out.

"Right." She voices and I can hear the smile in her voice. "I saw your messages with Harmony. You think *sex* is an appropriate conversation to bond over with a teenager?"

I roll my eyes at her words and I nearly hang up on her, but I have enough built-up anger to last me two lifetimes so I keep the line open.

"She's old enough to know how babies are made and if you read the conversation you would've seen the part where I told her she should *wait* to have sex with him." I tap my steering wheel as I try to rein in my anger.

"I also read the part where you told her about sex toys and *lube*?" She nearly shouts and I lose it.

"Oh my god, stop being such a prude. She's turning eighteen soon. I told her to wait, but she's persistent about not wanting to. Did you want me to take her phone away and yell at her for wanting a regular teenage experience?"

"That's not a regular teenage experience. She's not *you*, Lisette. She doesn't need to have sex at such a young age."

I can't help but laugh at her words. "Now I'm a whore. Wow, it was really great catching up with you." I almost hang up but instead go on. "Did you stop and think about why she suddenly wants to sleep with this boy? On the day she's supposed to go hang out with your bitch ass mom."

She doesn't answer.

"She's looking for an escape and when she told you she wanted to hang out with *me* instead of you and your mom, what did you tell her? You said no, and now she's resorting to male validation, and why? Oh! Because your dad's a bitch too."

"At least they're here. They're trying to do better."

*Unlike me*, she doesn't say and I give up.

"You're her guardian, Ana. I don't have to deal with this shit."

She lets out a scoff at my words. "Yeah, I'm her guardian because I'm the one who stepped up for her while you ran and you're running now."

Harmony shouts on the other end for us to stop fighting and they go back and forth, but I don't say anything else as I end the call.

Storming out of my car, I head up to Sire's apartment. It isn't until I'm in the elevator that her words hit me. She's the one person that can make me feel truly worthless.

Every inch of my skin feels disgusting and I'm crawling out of my clothes as I step out of the elevator.

Sire's door is ajar and when I step in, my eyes land on Isabelle's smile as she talks to Sire and her dad. My heart only sinks at the reminder of her tutoring session.

"Lissy!" She rushes over to me and I muster a smile.

"Hey, kiddo." I glance over at Sire and immediately, his face drops as he closes the distance between us.

"What happened?"

I shake my head in response before Isabelle pulls my hand.

"You *have* to see my test score." She pulls her bag off her shoulder.

"This was the weekly spelling test we were practicing for?"

She nods excitedly as she ravages through her folder. Sire has officially passed her on to me for her tutoring and we've been working together for the last few days. I didn't mind since she's a good kid and easy to work with, but I mentally cannot sit and work with her today.

I feel Sire watching me, but he doesn't say anything as Isabelle holds up her test to me.

"Three out of five?" I look down at her before offering a high five. "Nice job, kiddo. We're going to aim for a four next week." I try to add as much enthusiasm into my voice, but she barely notices the lack of it as she gets distracted with Athena, who walks over to lick her face.

"Sire is going to work with you today, okay?"

"Okay." She giggles as the dog licks her hand.

"What?" Sire takes a step towards me. "You're not staying?"

I shake my head before turning to leave, but Jackson is standing there.

"What happened?" Jackson voices now.

Keeping my eyes down, I simply walk around him, but I only make it two steps before I notice he's following me. "Were you crying?"

"Why do you care, Jackson?" I press the elevator and keep my eyes forward, but I feel his gaze on me.

"Is it illegal to care?"

I don't answer and he's quiet for a beat before he says, "Is it *just* Jackson now?"

I let out a tired breath as I turn to him. "What do you want from me?"

His eyes scan my face before his brows slightly furrow. "Nothing." He shakes his head as he takes a step back, the teasing tone nowhere in sight. "I was just trying to make you feel better. Thank you for helping Belle study for her test. I would appreciate it if you'd continue tutoring her until her next assessment in December, but if you'd rather not, I understand."

I roll my eyes as I turn to the elevator. "I didn't say I was going to quit tutoring her. I just can't today." The doors open and I don't bother waiting for his response as I step in.

I press the button for the lobby. My mind is finally blank as I walk to my car, but every step feels so pointless. Slipping into my car, I take out the small bottle of liquor Sire gave me last week.

I stare at the liquor in my hand, clutching it like a lifeline as the need for a drink becomes nearly suffocating. I'm about to twist the top off when Ana's voice rings in my head. I go still as I soak in anger rather than despair.

"I'm not *just* an addict," I tell myself, but I don't believe it.

Resting my head back, I keep my eyes on the liquor as my mind starts to go numb.

I snap out of my thoughts when I get a text and I only check it because the ringtone tells me it's one of my siblings.

**Biggest Loser**

> I know you're not okay. I can reschedule Isa's tutoring if you need a meeting.

> No, don't reschedule with her. She looked so happy to see you.

> She was happy to see you too.

A smile touches my lips. but I don't even consider going back up there.

> I'll go to a meeting on my own. Don't cancel on her.

He likes the message and I call the one friend I know will make me feel an ounce better. After a few rings, she answers.

"Did you call me by accident or are you in grave danger?"

I roll my eyes at her and I really wish she could see my face right now. "Hello to you, too, Bay."

She laughs on the other end. "You sound like shit."

I let out a groan as I put her on speaker and start the car, not wanting to be in this space anymore.

"Damn, that bad?"

"Yeah," I admit. "What are you doing right now?"

"Honestly? I was going to go play our favorite game of Fate."

I let out a laugh as she voices our game where we sit in a bar on a bad day and if a guy offers to buy us a drink, we say fuck it and relapse because at that point it's just *fate.*

We're both very aware of how bad that is, but we only ever go and *actually* drink on very dark days which was only once for each of us. A huge part of me wants to join her, but I refuse to let Ana be right about me.

"Come to a meeting with me."

She lets out a groan on her end and I can't help but laugh.

"Let's go play Fate instead." She sounds excited, but I can hear the hurt behind her joking tone.

"If you come with me I'll spill the recent tea about Satan."

She lets out a gasp now. "Bio family drama? You should've led with that."

I stifle a laugh and I'm truly grateful for friends that can make me forget about how badly I want to throw my life away.

# Chapter Seven

## LISETTE

"BLONDIE?"

I turn on my heels and lock eyes with Erin.

"Houdini?"

A smile grows on her face as she looks between me and Bay. "Of course, you're friends with Bay. She has a thing for damaged goods." She teases before hugging Bay who laughs.

"*She's* damaged goods, you're just damaged," Bay counters, pulling a laugh out of us both.

I've known Bay for nearly eight years now; we met in college and she knows me better than most people, so it feels good knowing she thinks I'm damaged *goods* and not just damaged. Joke or not.

When Erin pulls away, she nods for the donut table. "It's not sandwich day." She brings up our conversation when we met at the bar.

"It's been a long day, but if there's not at least one good donut in that pile, we all get to drink tonight."

Erin lets out a quiet laugh, and the man beside her glances between us, his brows pulled together.

"Winter lets us have a cheat day," I whisper and he only looks more concerned. "Oh, are you not at that stage?" He's clearly new here and this is too good to pass up.

"She's joking." Winter shoves my back before coming beside me and giving me a *look*. She tucks her white hair behind her ear before serving a donut on a napkin and handing it to the guy. "I love to see new faces, please"—she gestures to the circle of chairs—"Sit wherever you'd like."

He walks off after thanking her and she turns to me accusingly, but I offer a smile in return. "Hello there, December."

She rolls her eyes playfully as she turns to make a cup of coffee. "You don't usually come in today." She peeks at me before turning to add sugar to her cup. "Should I be worried?"

"Of course, you should," I say with as much enthusiasm as I can, and a smile she's clearly fighting appears on her face.

"You're always the light of my day, Lisette." She stirs her drink with a small smile, the wrinkles near her eyes more prominent.

"I'm glad someone is benefiting from my crippling depression." I tap her shoulder twice and head over to the circle with Bay and Erin before she can respond.

I turn to Bay as she takes her seat. "Since I already gave you the recap in the car, do I have to share?"

"You don't *have* to. If you just needed to be in this space, then you know you can sit silently and soak it up." She shrugs before a smile touches her lips. "If you don't share, at least talk to Winter at the end. I think it'll be good for you to hear whatever advice she has to give."

I nod in return as Winter makes her way over to start the meeting. There are a few familiar faces and they look worse than I'm feeling, which makes me feel better.

I know that sounds bad, but nothing is worse than coming to a meeting and everyone is doing good. It's rare, but I came in hung over once and had the courage to share first. Everyone after me spoke about how their life was getting better. I drank again once I left.

"Hello everyone," Winter starts with a bright smile. "I see a lot of new faces which makes me so happy. If you're up for it, I'd love for you all to introduce yourselves."

The newbies share their names and sad stories as my anxiety begins to eat at me. I zone out and my call with Ana is on a loop in my mind. I slip my hand into my pocket and hold onto the bottle of liquor, letting myself feel good about *not* being hungover like she thought I was.

When I hear sniffing, I look up and Bay is fighting back tears. I feel my brows furrow as I look around the room, but one of the new guys is still sharing and he's just talking about being from Washington.

I lean into Bay as I whisper, "Remind me not to take you to Seattle."

A smile appears on her face as she looks up to the ceiling and blinks away her tears. "Sorry, I know you don't like feelings." She faces forward again, her eyes still glassy.

"I'm not going to hold your hand or hug you, but don't let me stop you from crying." I shrug and her smile grows as she wipes a tear.

Winter notices her struggling, but waits for the new people to finish before focusing on her again. "Bay," she starts, her somber smile on her. "What's going on, dear?"

Bay takes in a deep breath before smiling over at Winter, but she's still fighting back tears. "I feel like ever since my abortion, I've been seeing so many things that remind me of it. I don't think I made a mistake, but it *hurts*, and seeing pregnant women, or baby bottles in the chip aisle because people don't put shit back where they found them in Walmart, isn't helping."

She starts crying again and a laugh escapes me. "I'm sorry." I cover my mouth with my hand when a few people look at me. "I laugh when I'm uncomfortable," I clarify.

"I hate you." Bay lets out a laugh that mixes with a cry. "Ugh!" She looks up at the ceiling and wipes her tears. "Okay, I don't want to cry anymore, so Lisette needs to share, and since she interrupted, we can all laugh at her together. I promise it's good."

The group lets out a laugh, and I smile around the room as they give me a minute to collect my thoughts. "I have a little sister," I start. "Two of them." My eyes fall to my hand as I pick at my nails.

"My birth parents were both addicts and absent when I was a kid. The boy next door also had a shitty mom, and we became best friends," I say, not wanting to say Sire's name. "Then we met these twins at school, and they had a *perfect* life."

I shake my head as images of August and Sage's huge childhood home come to mind. I thought they were royalty when I first went to their house.

"They became my family, and we called their parents mom and dad. Then they adopted the boy next door, but couldn't adopt me since my parents had rights and shit, and they couldn't take my sisters." I feel myself getting bitter, but not at the Hales, it's the reminder of my birth parents that puts the sour feeling in me.

"Although they didn't adopt me, they were still my family and I practically lived with them, but as the years went by, I started using drugs in middle school, and Ana, my bio sister, hated me for becoming my parents. She treated me like shit and I couldn't face her, so I officially moved in with my other family."

I feel everyone watching me as I continue. "My relationship with her was never good, but I went to her for money after not seeing her in years, and that was the nail in the coffin for us."

My throat tightens at the reminder of one of my lowest points.

"Ana just has so much resentment for me because I moved out of that house. She thinks I abandoned her, but I was a kid too. Why is it my fault for not giving up my childhood to raise them? Yes, I feel like shit about it, but they had their grandma who was basically raising them and refused to take me in. I had no one but the Hales."

I look over at Winter for an answer and she nods in understanding.

"It wasn't your job to raise your sisters. Don't burn yourself for your parents' sins."

Her words lift every guilty feeling off of my shoulders.

"Ana is great for raising her little sister, but she has no right to belittle you because *she* resents her parents for making her feel like she needed to step up and be the parent. I think she's jealous that you escaped. It's completely fine to be angry, but to blame you? What they endured wasn't your fault and your presence wouldn't have made much of a difference because you were a *child*."

I nod in return as I blink my tears away, refusing to cry because of Ana, of all people.

Beside me, Bay shoves my arm. "Tell them about how you told your seventeen-year-old sister to buy sex toys and lube."

"Oh my god." I look up at the ceiling as I let out a laugh.

"She's bonding with her younger sister," Bay tells the group and I shove her as they laugh at us.

Turning to the group, I defend myself. "She's looking for male validation, as I once did. I told her she doesn't need a useless man for an orgasm, and Ana thinks I told her to go become a damn pornstar." I roll my eyes at the reminder and the entire group seems to appreciate the lighter mood before the rest of the sob stories begin.

Naps after a meeting are the *best*, but being awoken by someone knocking on your door isn't. A yawn escapes me as I open the door. When I see Jackson, I blink a few times to make sure my eyes aren't playing a trick on me.

"Hey," he starts softly. I take a minute to take him in, but it only adds to my confusion. He's in a navy blue suit and I'm realizing he's almost always in a suit.

"I needed to go into the office," he says, and I'm going to assume that explains the outfit. "These are for you." He holds up a bouquet of flowers and I squint my eyes, trying to make sense of what's happening.

"What are you doing here?" I finally say.

"I'm on my way to pick up Isabelle."

I wait for him to add more, but he takes too long, so I say, "Okay? This isn't Sire's house."

A smile appears on his face and my eyes land on his one dimple. "I'm aware. It was obvious you weren't okay when I asked earlier, so I got you feel-better flowers." He holds them out to me, but I don't take them.

"How did you get my address?" I cross my arms as I look up at him.

"I asked August for it." He shakes his head now. "He told Sire, who threatened to tell my daughter the Tooth Fairy isn't real if I flirted with you or entered your house so"—he pushes the flowers further to me—"I am here strictly 'to give you these feel better flowers and state that I am not interested in you.'" He mimics Sire's voice and I let out a quiet laugh as I shake my head at how annoying my brother is.

I take the flowers from him, and by some chance, he got my least favorite ones.

"Sire told me irises were your favorite."

I let out a scoff as I examine the blue irises and white lilies. "Of course, he did."

"Do you not like them?" He looks between the bouquet and me, his brows pulled together.

"I don't like things that don't last."

He studies me for a beat before glancing back at the flowers. "That's the beauty in them though. We learn to appreciate them while they're here."

I shake my head at his words. "I'd rather not get attached to things that are just going to die."

He goes still.

"But thank you," I voice, trying not to sound completely ungrateful and pessimistic.

I can see his mind running with different thoughts, but he instead changes the topic.

"When I went to pick up Belle today, her teacher told me she did really well during popcorn reading."

My eyes meet his and he looks as grateful as he sounds.

"They're 'thank you' flowers *and* 'please keep tutoring my kid because I'm desperate' flowers."

I shake my head at him as I lean against the door frame. "So they're feel better flowers, thank you flowers, and a bribe? The math isn't making sense, Jackson Jones. One bouquet equals one reason. I'm afraid I can only accept one, and since I feel like shit, these are my feel-better flowers." I shrug.

He smirks down at me. "Fair enough."

I nod in return. "Find another tutor and find another way to say thank you."

His smirk grows into a smile. "I'll get you another bouquet as my bribe and find another way to say thank you," he counters.

His eyes search mine and slowly, his smile fades. "Your brother wouldn't tell me what upset you, but I hope the flowers make you feel better."

I nod in return as I take a deep breath of the bouquet. I plaster a smile on my face as I let out a relieved breath. "Ahhh, I can already feel the sadness seeping out of me. These are great."

He laughs softly before turning more serious. "I don't like burning bridges with people my daughter likes, so I'm sorry I kept pressing you about it earlier and upsetting you."

I shake my head at him. "I'm sorry for being a bitch."

He quickly counters. "It was none of my business, I should've left you alone."

"Yeah, but you care and I appreciate that. My brothers have good friends."

A smile touches his lips.

"I told Belle you'll get her ice cream if she passed her spelling test. Don't make me look like a liar." I point at him.

"We wouldn't want that." Before turning away he adds, "Thanks again, *not* Demeter Lissy."

A laugh escapes me, and I close the door on him. I rest the bouquet on my table and shake my head at the sight of the irises before grabbing my phone.

The first ring barely goes through before Sire answers the FaceTime and I can't help but smile. "Sitting around and waiting for me to call, huh?"

He rolls his eyes at me, but I can see the smile he's biting back. "Talk to me."

I flop onto my couch as I give in. "Harmony and I have been hanging out."

His brows furrow. "Harmony as in—"

"As in my baby sister."

He nods slowly as his gears start turning and I catch him up on the last few months of my life I've been keeping from him. He looks shocked by the end of it and I know it's because I usually tell him everything. When I add what happened today with Ana, I can see his annoyance growing.

"I still hate them." He rolls his eyes and I hold back a smile.

It truly makes me feel good knowing I'm not the only one who still holds resentment towards them, but it makes me feel even better because he gets it. His bio mom is worse than mine, so he understands every loathing ounce within.

"I know Harmony was a baby when we moved in with the twins but if bonding with her is causing this much commotion, just leave."

I shake my head at him, knowing he would say that. "She's a kid, Sire. When we moved in with the Hales, I didn't know any better. Now I do and *she's* the one who wants to be in my life. Ana is a bitter bitch, and her mom is still using. I can't shut her out."

He gives me a knowing look. "If it's costing you your mental health and sobriety, yes you can."

"Harmony is not the problem," I counter. "I know what I'm doing. Plus, I like her. She's like a mini-me."

He rolls his eyes now. "So she's an annoying brat? Love her already."

I stifle a laugh at him. "It's weird because she's the youngest and I know I'm technically the oldest to them, but with *our* family, I'm the youngest so she really is just like me. She looks like me too, it's weird."

A smile grows on his face as he watches me. "You like her," he voices as if he's just realizing.

"She's cool, I guess." I brush him off but the truth is, I can totally see myself being an older sister to Harmony.

At the sound of princess music and Isabelle singing along, I change the topic. "You told Jackson not to flirt with me?"

Sire watches me carefully before asking, "Did he?"

I roll my eyes at him. "Why would he, you weirdo? We *barely* know each other since we only speak for two seconds when he picks up and drops off his kid."

Sire thinks about it before nodding. "True, but I don't care. I already have to suffer through someone I hate dating Sage," he mentions Liam, his *rival*, who our sister is madly in love with. "I don't need my best friend with my other sister." He rolls his eyes, but I know deep down, he's happy our sister is happy.

Per usual, I decide to mess with him. "Well, if it bothers you so much I'll be sure to add him to my to-do list."

"Lisette," he warns and I offer him a smile before setting my phone up so he can see me write on the paper in front of me.

"Fuck Sire's DILF best friend." I add an exclamation point, and when I look back at Sire, he doesn't look amused. "Put his offspring on the phone," I say with a laugh.

Sire rises from the table before walking to the living room, and when I hear the movie playing, I know they didn't read at all. He hands her the phone and she smiles when she sees me.

"Hi, Lissy. Are you feeling better?"

I smile at her. "Yes, I am," I answer honestly.

She nods before a guilty look covers her face. "We didn't work today."

I shake my head and she bites back a smile. "If your dad asks, just blame it on Uncle Sigh."

She quickly agrees and laughs at something Sire says.

"I heard your popcorn reading went well. I'm proud of you, kid."

She quickly gets comfortable as she tells me about it. "I kinda cheated." She giggles and a smile touches my lips. "I counted how many people was in front of me, then I counted the lines and practiced mine in my head, so when it was my turn, I read it fast."

I let out a laugh and when she throws her head back and holds her stomach as she laughs with me, I laugh harder.

# Chapter Eight

## JACKSON

I'M IN THE MIDDLE OF proofreading an email for the third time when my work phone starts ringing. When I see it's a blocked number, I feel my brows furrow as I bring it to my ear.

"Jackson Jones."

Someone lets out a relieved breath on the other end.

"Jones, thank *fuck* you answered." Rome Booker's voice sounds through the other end and a million bad thoughts run through my mind as to why he would be calling me through a blocked number.

The only downside to being a good agent is all the damn spoiled kids want me. I work for the sports agency, Athletics Prime. When Sire and August signed me as their agents and my first check cleared, I was ready to quit since I didn't even need the job anymore, but I love what I do and the Hale brothers were my friends long before my clients, so quitting wasn't an option.

This kid, however, makes me question how much I love this job.

"What's up, Booker?" I lean back in my seat as I prepare myself for today's bullshit.

"I got arrested. I'm at station—"

"Why are you calling *me*?" I pinch the bridge of my nose. "I'm your *agent*, not your criminal defense attorney." I shake my head at my words. "Why did you get arrested?"

He lets out an annoyed breath before yelling at someone. "Back up!" He shouts a few foul words and I bury my face in my hand. *I can't catch a break with this kid.*

"You there?" he says to me now.

I look around for where the fuck I would've gone. "Yes, I'm here, Rome. What did you do?"

"I got in a bar fight," he says as if it's absurd to get arrested for such a thing when I'm sure he was at fault.

I glance at my watch before shaking my head. "It's not even 2:00 p.m., Rome. You're not even twenty-one." The disappointment seeps out of me as my mind runs through what I'm going to do with him.

"Why did you call me?" I ask again.

"First of all, it's 5:00 p.m. somewhere. Second, I don't have anyone's number memorized, and had your card in my pocket for some reason. Third, the legal age to drink is subjective."

"It's quite literally *not*."

"Agree to disagree. Listen, come pick me up, my cell smells like a pig's pen."

I rub my temples as I decide whether or not I should leave him in there and he must hear my thoughts through my hesitation because he goes on.

"The people in here already recognized me. Do you want word to get out that I got arrested? You said we needed to work on my image."

"Yeah, that doesn't mean to go—" I decide to stop wasting my breath and shut my laptop. "I'm on my way."

He tells me where he is and I hang up on him as I stand from my seat and walk out of my home office.

Belle and I officially moved into our new house and my first day working from home *was* going great, but I can never have a perfect day with clients that behave worse than my five-year-old.

THE ENTIRE RIDE TO THE police station I go over in my head what I'm going to say to this kid to make him listen, but as I imagine his response, none of them are what I want to hear.

When I walk into the police station, a few officers stand straighter at the slight glance at my suit. I walk to the front desk and the officer stands from his seat. "What can I do for you?"

"I'm here to pick up my client, Rome Booker."

It's clear he knows exactly who that is as he gets the necessary paperwork. I head out when I'm done and lean against my car as I wait for him.

After a few minutes, he strolls out of the police station carefree with nothing more than a busted lip. I let out an annoyed breath as he smiles when he sees me.

He throws his hand up. "Jones."

"Rome," I mumble disappointedly.

He tilts his head to the side with a knowing look. "Aww, come on. Cheer up."

I stare at him for a beat and when I don't *cheer up*, his smile fades from his face.

"You get arrested again, and we will no longer be working together."

His brows furrow as he searches my eyes. "We have a contract?"

"Sue me," I deadpan before nodding for my car. "Get in."

He does and I walk around for the driver's seat. While I'm bluffing about quitting as his agent, he doesn't know that and seems to believe me.

When I slip into my seat, he's glancing around the car. "I didn't know they had pink interiors in Durangos." He nods to himself.

"They don't." I start the car and he doesn't say anything as we drive off. I had the car customized because Isabelle wanted us to have a pink car, and while I'd drive a pink car, I was able to negotiate with her so we have pink seats that match the two pink stripes on the outside of the car.

Rome looks around the back seat and he must notice Belle's car seat before his head snaps to me. "You have a *baby*?" He says it as if I kidnapped my own kid.

"A daughter, yes," I reply dryly and I feel his eyes on me as he tries to figure something out.

"How old are you?"

I glance at him as he gives me a once-over.

"Thirty-two." I turn back to the road and in my peripheral I see his gears turning.

"That's a big car seat."

"It's the perfect size for a five-year-old."

"She's *five*?" His eyes bulge again. "You had a kid at *twenty-seven*?"

I let out a short breath in annoyance as my brain tries to figure out what's so hard to grasp about that.

"I can't imagine having a kid in eight years." He shakes his head to himself and I don't tell him to not have a kid because, at this rate, he's doing the opposite of everything I say. "She was an accident, wasn't she?"

"Excuse me?" I turn to him now and he puts his hands up in defense.

"I'm just saying." He shrugs. "I don't see a ring on your hand, and you're definitely the marrying type. Considering you're not with your baby mama makes me think she was an accident." He shrugs again as he looks out his window, his head laid against the seat.

"At least you only have to worry about her on weekends."

I feel my eyes narrow as I study him and right about now, I wish those buttons in cars that eject people through the roof were a real thing.

"I don't *only worry about her on weekends.* I have full custody. And just because she wasn't planned doesn't mean I didn't want her." I shake my head at him. "Twenty-seven isn't even insanely young to have a kid—you know what? Stop talking about my baby." I shut him up.

I keep driving, and when I get an email with his name in the subject, I quickly read it at the red light. I let out a scoff at the end of it before tossing him my phone. "I hope this is a lesson learned."

He scans the email from a brand stating they no longer want to work with him and I can see him shaking his head in my peripheral. "They can't do this."

"They can and they did." I shouldn't feel as good as I do, but I do. He was really excited to work with *Lululemon* because he was apparently attracting more girls, but this is a great punishment after his arrest clearly made the headlines so quickly.

Rome is the hottest topic right now in college baseball around the country. He gets a lot of press, but I'm not one of those believers in bad press being good press. Sure, we love his name getting out there, but not when every single thing that's said about him has been bad for the last *month.*

"Can't you do something to get them back?" he pleads.

"I can." I shrug. "I'm not going to, though."

"Why?" he asks as if he wasn't in handcuffs less than an hour ago and I have no reason to not want to help him.

"Because you don't deserve it. Get your act together and maybe you won't lose brand deals." When I steal a glance at him, he looks pissed, and considering I'm a dad to a kid who had a *very* long tantrum phase at two years old, I know he's about to throw a fit.

"Well, you're my agent and you work for me, so I'm telling you to fix it."

I let out a scoff at his tone. "And I'm telling you no."

He lets out a huff in defiance, and when he starts breathing harder, I put on my dad face and try my hardest not to laugh. After a minute of him huffing and puffing, he turns to me.

"Can't I pay you more to fix this for me?" *Brat.*

"Your money doesn't talk to me, kid. Until you get it together and start listening to me, I'm not doing anything for you."

He crosses his arms before turning to look out his window and I really wish I could take a picture of him and show the girls who want to sleep with this childish *boy.* The drive to his campus is silent, and when I pull up in front of his dorm, he turns to me.

"I'm sorry I got arrested." He doesn't add more, but it's clear he's only apologizing because he wants his way. Isabelle has pulled this card way too many times for me to not notice.

"You should be." I unlock the door for him but he doesn't step out, instead, he changes the topic, another stunt that isn't going to work.

"How's it going with the Red Sox's contract? Were you able to—"

"They're not going to offer you more money, kid. We upped the deal twice," I interrupt with the same thing I've been telling him all week. "A one hundred and ten million dollar contract for five years is a great deal."

He opens his mouth but I beat him to it.

"There's no news from the Dodgers. I know you want to sign with them, but they don't want you. They didn't make any offers. Maybe you should *listen* to me and stay in school. Recruits aren't going anywhere, but once you sign, you're less likely to get the team you want as a trade." I could've delivered my words a bit nicer, but I need to pick up my kid from school soon and he doesn't deserve my good mood after annoying me with his comments about my baby girl.

He nods before his eyes meet mine again. "You're close friends with the Hale brothers, right? Like more than just their agent."

"Yes?"

He nods in thought. "Can you get them to come watch me play?"

I study him but he seems very hopeful about this. "What is them seeing you play going to change? They don't recruit for the Dodgers, they only play for them."

"Right." He nods. "They're the best on the team and got recruited from this school." He nods to his campus. "Maybe they can give me tips on what I'm clearly missing."

I don't tell him it's discipline and brain cells and instead say, "I'll talk to them. In the meantime, lay low. I'll draft a statement for you to post on social media about what happened today. Don't talk about it with anyone."

He nods hopefully before thanking me and stepping out of my car.

I PULL INTO BELLE'S SCHOOL just as they're walking out, which means I'm early and it makes me feel good. It's like the nicest fuck you to stick in the mud Ms. Rose.

As I'm walking over to the class, Isabelle is talking to a friend and doesn't notice me.

Just as I reach her, Ms. Rose steps beside us. "Mr. Carter." She gives my outfit a once over before her annoyed face meets mine again. "In Isabelle's folder you'll find a red card." It nearly sounds like she's *happy* about the news.

I glance down at Isabelle who has guilty written all over her face. Holding back a sigh, I look back over at her teacher. "What happened?"

"She was using inappropriate language today." A smug smile grows on her face and I'm sure it's because this is feeding her delusions that I'm a horrible father. "The first time this happened, last week, I gave her a warning, but since this was the second time, her red card needs to be signed and brought back to me. On the back you need to fill out the action plan for how we're going to reduce the foul language."

She gives me another once over. "Maybe reducing such language at home will help."

I bite my tongue before finding the right words. "We don't use inappropriate language at home." That's partly a lie but it's not like she'd know. "I'll talk to her."

"That'd be great." She holds her clipboard to her chest. "If it continues, maybe Mom can come in for a meeting?"

I force a smile. "It won't continue." I don't remind her that Belle's mom isn't in the picture, *once again*, but I can see her nosy expression from a mile away as to why. That's an explanation she doesn't need, and since she's so desperate to know, I make it my mission to not enlighten her on the details of my life.

"Have a great day, Ms. Rose." Taking Isabelle's hand I keep my gaze on her. "Do you have all your things?"

She nods quietly, and without sparing her teacher a second glance, I walk over to the car with her and strap her into the car seat.

When I'm in the driver's seat, I let out a defeated breath before turning to her.

"I'm sorry." She beats me to it, her eyes watering.

"Baby girl," I start gently. "I *really* need you to be mindful of how you speak in school." I focus on her, and while I can't explain to her that I'm already on thin ice with these people, she seems to understand the sincerity in my voice.

"I just dropped my lunch and said *oh shit*, but I apologized right after." She wipes her tears. "Are you disappointed?" she nearly whispers.

Taking a hold of her hand, I kiss it gently. "I know it was an accident, and I'm not disappointed," I reassure her because I care more about the fact that her teacher heard and is going to give me hell for it. "Let's just remember next time to not speak that way in school or at all."

She nods before kissing my hand in return.

"Is Ms. Rose ever mean to you?" I watch her carefully, but she quickly shakes her head, her brows pulled together.

"No, she's always so nice." She shrugs. "She was even nice when she gave me a warning about no cursing."

I focus on her for a beat before deciding to believe her. I'm starting the car when she quickly changes the topic and tells me about her Good Writer sticker.

"I can't wait to show Lissy. She says I can have ice cream when I get stickers."

I smile at how much happier she sounds and I can tell it's for Lisette and not just the ice cream or the sticker she received at school.

At the reminder of Lisette, I stop by the store to get her my 'please keep tutoring my kid' flowers because I forgot them the last few times I dropped off Isabelle.

I know she was joking when she said she'll only accept the last bouquet as her feel-better flowers, but why not keep the joke running? I do have to find a real way to thank her for working with Isabelle though, because she refuses to let me pay her.

Since Sire had an away game today, she's coming to our house for tutoring and it's all Belle talks about on our way home.

# Chapter Nine

## LISETTE

I DRIVE THROUGH JACKSON'S GATED community slowly, marveling at all of the huge houses. When I make it to the end of the street, a beautiful house stares back at me, and I almost think I have the wrong address until I see the pink door he told me I won't miss.

I marvel at the sleek black two story house. All of his windows are tinted so the clear sky stares back at me, and while I can't see the inside, I'm sure it's just as nice as the exterior.

Tall palm trees are planted on either side of the house with five steps leading up to the door. There's a balcony on the right side and under that is a tall gate, blocking off what I'm sure is a lavish backyard.

"Yup." I nod to myself as I drive up his long driveway. "He's rich as shit."

I try to shake off the shock of how big this house is as I step out of the car. When I ring the doorbell, I fully expect to hear church bells or something, but it's a standard bell.

A minute passes before the door opens slowly. When I hear a loud grunt, I look down and Isabelle is struggling to open the big door, so I help her with a push.

"Excuse me," Jackson yells angrily and she jumps as she turns around. "What did we talk about yesterday?" He comes up behind her, and she takes a step away from the door as she looks up at him.

"Not to open the door," she mumbles, and he gives her a stern look, but doesn't say anything for almost a full minute. A short laugh escapes me at how awkward it grows and Isabelle looks up at me before she covers her smile with her hand.

"It's not funny," Jackson tells her and her smile is gone. "Don't open it again."

"Okay, Daddy." She turns to me and her smile is back. "Hi, Lissy. Sorry about that." She waves at her dad, and I bite back a laugh at his face, but he doesn't reprimand her again. "Let me give you a tour of our new castle."

"It definitely looks like a castle." I look up from the marble floors to the high ceiling in awe before looking over at Jackson. "Hello, Jackson Jones."

"Hello, Lissy." He smiles in return and I roll my eyes at him. Before I can remind him that only his kid is allowed to call me that, she drags me around the house for the tour.

"THIS IS MY FAVORITE PART." Isabelle races me back down the stairs after the tour upstairs. At the end of this hall are two sliding doors. "Ready?" She turns to me.

"I don't know," I tease. "I'm still trying to process the indoor arcade upstairs."

Her dad laughs from behind me and she ignores me as she opens the sliding doors to reveal what I'm assuming is her dad's office. It's a standard office, but the entire wall in front and beside his desk is a window to the backyard and the yard somehow seems bigger than the house.

"This is my favorite part," Isabelle exclaims, and I expect her to be pointing at the pool, but she's sitting in a smaller version of Jackson's desk with a pink chair. "This is my office." She gestures in front of her and I break into a laugh.

"What's your job?"

She folds her hands on her desk as she looks up at me. "I'm a gymnastics sports agent."

I smile at her words and behind me, Jackson mumbles, "And the bakery."

"Oh." She looks back over at me. "And I own a bakery *and* I'm a mother, of course, you met Lola."

"Yes, I did." I nod in thought as I remember her doll. Looking around the office, unlike the rest of the house where pictures of both Isabelle and Jackson fill up the walls, here are just pictures of Isabelle from a photoshoot when she was a newborn. "Now I understand how you're able to afford such a big castle."

She nods like she agrees with me and I turn to Jackson with a smile. "Nice castle, JJ." I nod once and he tilts his head back with a laugh.

"Now it's JJ?"

"Yup." I smile over at him. "Or would you prefer just Jones?"

His face scrunches as if that will pain him. "Please no."

I let out a soft laugh and he turns more serious. "Thanks," he says for my earlier compliment.

"Lissy, let me show you my gymnastic moves." Isabelle jumps to press a button on the wall, and what I thought was a floor-to-ceiling window slides to the left, letting her out to the backyard.

I nod in amusement. "You better live here long after you retire," I mumble.

Jackson lets out a soft laugh as he steps beside me. "Yeah, that's the plan. I know it's a bit over the top, but I wanted her forever home to be perfect. Something she can sell when I'm gone if she needs to."

I look up at him and he watches his daughter flip around the grass. As his eyes follow her movement, I'm certain he'd commit inhumane crimes for his kid.

"Considering you could afford all this, I think she'll be okay without selling the house when you're gone," I say with a laugh and he looks down at me with a smile.

When I look back around at all of the pictures, I turn to him in thought. "Are you self-absorbed and obsessed with your kid or are pictures of her mom not allowed?"

When his face drops, I realize I hit a nerve.

"The few I have of them together don't match our aesthetic," he jokes, but it's way too bitter for me to even fake a laugh.

"I'm going to take that as pictures of her aren't allowed."

A smile forces itself onto his face.

"Damn." I offer a smile. "If I knew you two hated each other so much, I wouldn't have brought her up." I put a hand up in defense, and he doesn't even offer a smile as he looks over at his kid, who's playing in her pink playground a few yards from us.

"She's the mother of my kid. I could never hate her," he clarifies, and for some reason, I believe him.

Since I'm nosy and don't care that curiosity killed the cat, I ask, "How often does she see Belle? You seem to have her all the time. Belle also never talks about her."

"She doesn't see her."

I nod in understanding. "That's even better." I smile brightly when he turns to me. "Bad moms help build character in kids. At least she'll be funny, look at me."

I get a small smile now as he looks back over at Isabelle.

"Let me guess." I desperately keep trying to lighten the mood. "She found someone with a bigger castle?"

Jackson lets out a scoff but a smile grows on his face. "Close." He turns to me now. "Belle got sick as a baby, and when it became *too much* for her, she turned to another man and then left without warning."

"Oh." The word slips past my lips.

He nods once.

I glance off to the side before nodding slowly. "That sucks. Isabelle won't gain a great sense of humor since she left without traumatizing her."

He stares at me for a second before a laugh escapes him. "Are you always like this?"

I take a second to act like I'm thinking before turning to him. "Yup." I shrug. "At least when I'm sober I am. Drunk me is a bit emotional and not funny at all. Then high me is just really happy and telling everyone in sight I love them; it's gross."

He laughs harder before shaking his head. "Well, in that case, come over the next time you're intoxicated so I can see those two personalities and decide who I like more."

I pause for a beat when I realize he's being serious and knowing he doesn't know I'm an addict is so damn refreshing. "If I'm lucky, you won't ever meet those sides of me."

He still smiles at me, but his brows slightly pull together at my somber tone. Before he can question me, his phone starts ringing. He glances down at it before looking up at me.

"I have to get to work. I'll be in here if she needs anything. You two can work in the living room or on the patio. Help yourself to anything in the kitchen while you're here."

I nod in response before walking out to the backyard. "Let's get this party started, kiddo."

Isabelle slides down the slide one last time before running over to me. "I almost forgot to show you." She tugs on her shirt to show me a sticker that says *Great Writer!*

I offer a high five and she jumps up to reach it. "You are just on a roll, huh? Do you even need me to tutor you?"

"Of course I do, silly. Stickers don't make school easier." She sounds a bit sad and I squeeze her chunky cheeks as we walk into the house.

"Good thing practice makes perfect."

Her smile is back as she tells me about the short rhyming sentence she read in class, and when she shows it to me, I explain to her what she spelled wrong, and for practice, I read it back to her and she writes it again, this time, everything spelled right.

We work for the next two hours and Jackson walks past a few times, nearly every half hour. He doesn't say anything, he just walks over, ruffles Isabelle's hair or kisses her head, as if he's making sure she's still here.

I'm in the kitchen pouring Isabelle a cup of juice when he walks over *again* and sticks his head into the living room. I watch him walk over and gently touch Isabelle's arm. She doesn't even glance at him as she traces her vowels and he walks back out, his eyes locking on mine.

"Do you have separation anxiety or am I not trusted to be alone with your kid?"

A guilty smile tugging on his pretty face. "Sorry." He watches me like I should be offended and he feels horrible for whatever's in his head.

"What is it?" I let out a soft laugh, but his eyes dart to the ground.

"It's nothing." He musters up a smile as his eyes meet mine.

I feel my brows furrow as I watch him. "Well now I feel like you really *don't* trust me with her, which isn't the worst thing, you barely know me, but if it's something else, just say it." I cross my arms over my chest and as I study him, I begin to question if maybe he does know about my addiction.

His shoulders slouch before he forces a smile. "I have OCD, it's an OCD thing and it's dumb, ignore me." He brushes me off and I nod in understanding.

"It's not dumb. Don't do that." My arms fall to my side and his eyes dart back up to mine. "Trust me, I'm far more screwed than you and your OCD. I also had a roommate who had OCD, so to some extent, I get it. You don't have to brush it off. I'm aware it's more than just being a neat freak and it's *not* dumb," I reassure him.

His eyes scan my face carefully before he stands a bit straighter. "Thank you." His words come out more like a question, but I nod in response as he continues. "I told myself I would only check on her every hour, but it's clearly not going well." He forces a smile before his eyes scan the kitchen.

"Is it because you don't know me that well or..." My voice trails off as I try to understand.

He's quick to shake his head no. "It's not you," he reassures me. "I'm stressed with work. I have this client that's driving me up a wall. The stress makes the intrusive thoughts worse, and I worry about her a bit more."

"So you like checking on her." I nod in understanding, but falter when he shakes his head.

"It's nothing." He tries to brush me off again.

"Jackson, I'm in *your* house and watching *your* kid." A smile grows on my face at how much he's beating himself up about telling me whatever it is. I don't know what a filter is when it comes to personal stuff, so him holding back is very foreign to me.

I try again more gently. "I don't want you to feel awkward in your own home. If you need me to do something a certain way to put you at ease, let me know," I suggest, remembering my roommate who needed me to do her compulsive rituals with her.

His shoulders sag before he explains. "I don't need you to do anything. When I get an intrusive thought that she's going to get hurt while I'm working, I need to tap her, and I feel bad coming in and bothering you both." He quickly shakes his head. "I know she's physically okay, but my brain convinces me she's going to choke or drown in the pool the second I turn my back, so I just need to undo those thoughts by touching her."

My eyes dart down to his hand as he taps on the island four times.

I grab the juice for Isabelle. "Don't feel bad."

His brows furrow.

"About constantly checking on her. You're not interrupting us or bothering me so don't feel bad and don't apologize." I nod firmly, knowing the guilt comes with the disorder.

Slipping past him, I meet Isabelle on the couch again. I rest the cup of juice next to her and she thanks me. When I notice she's done tracing the vowels, I set a new paper in front of her.

"I don't like this one." She moves it aside and grabs a different sheet as she takes a sip of her drink.

"Thanks for letting me know." I grab it again, knowing she's only saying that because she struggles with these. "We're still going to try," I tell her and she looks surprised by my words, but I gesture to the paper.

"I'm saying the *really* honest truth." She puts a hand up in defense as she tilts her head to the side. "I don't really care about the main idea of this story. It looks boring." She shrugs and I bite back a laugh.

"I appreciate your honesty." I gesture to the paper. "I think you're just saying that because you have a hard time focusing on the main idea and that's okay. There's a lot of details in the story, but practice makes perfect and once you get better, I think you're going to really like figuring out the main idea."

She lets out a sigh as she looks up to the ceiling.

I try my hardest not to laugh. "Come on." I pinch her fat cheeks. "Try to figure out what the story is going to be about based on the pictures, then I'll read it with you and we can figure out what they're doing with this money."

She caves and turns to the paper.

At the sound of footsteps, I turn just as Jackson walks in with a bouquet of flowers. I shake my head at him as I bite back a smile.

"Belle, we forgot to give Lissy her flowers."

She puts a hand up as she focuses on her paper. "Daddy, you're diracting me."

"Dis*tract*ing," Jackson corrects her and she only nods as she examines the pictures.

I get up from my seat and walk over to him as he holds out the flowers, and I notice they're crocheted.

"You said you don't like things that don't last." He nods to the bouquet. "These will."

My gaze meets his as a smile touches my lips. This is probably the nicest thing anyone has done for me, but there's no way I'm going to say that and make this a sappy moment.

Instead, I take the flowers with a smile and say, "Is this the bribe or the thank you flowers?"

I look back up and a smile grows on his face. "The bribe. She doesn't like her in-school tutor, so now I'm really desperate."

"Don't lose sleep over it." I turn more serious. "I honestly like working with your daughter, you didn't need to get me these."

He shrugs. "Well, consider them a thank-you gift."

I look down at them again, and a smile stretches on my face.

"I'm done with work, so I'm going to start cooking. You should stay for dinner. Consider it a part of my thank you gift," he offers and I give him a knowing look as I tease him.

"Flowers and dinner?"

He shakes his head as he sees where this is going.

"I'm totally telling my brother you're head over heels for me, JJ. I hope your daughter doesn't have any more loose teeth." I give him a stern look and he lets out a quiet laugh.

"Please don't." He rolls his eyes now. "He already told her about Santa and I'm still pissed about it. I need her to have the Tooth Fairy a little longer."

My jaw slightly drops but he's clearly serious. "He spoiled Santa for her?"

He nods before rolling his eyes again. "It was a while ago because I didn't tell him Vidia was his new physical therapist. It was back when they weren't on good terms."

He reminds me of how Sire and V couldn't stand each other when they were broken up, and with how they behave now, you would've never guessed they practically hated each other for four years.

"He's such an asshole."

I turn at the sound of a gasp and Isabelle has her eyes on me. She looks like she's waiting for something, and when nothing happens, her brows furrow as she looks over at Jackson. "Daddy, tell her."

I turn back to Jackson and he bites back a smile before he puts his dad face on, and I try my hardest not to laugh at whatever is happening.

"We don't curse in this house, Lissy."

I bite back a laugh. "I'm sorry." I glance at Isabelle and she's watching her dad for more.

"If it happens again, you can't watch TV before bed."

I nod in understanding. "I prefer doing other things before bed, but since I don't want you to withhold that from me either, I'll behave."

His jaw slightly drops before he closes it and I bite my tongue when his cheeks slightly blush.

He turns more serious now, his voice low. "I don't want the Tooth Fairy to be ruined for my kid. Don't say things that'll get us both in trouble, Lisette," he warns before walking to the kitchen, leaving me stuck in place.

What is that even supposed to mean? Sire said he'll retaliate if *he* flirts with *me*. Are my inappropriate jokes going to provoke that?

I bite back a smile as I settle onto the couch with Isabelle.

I thoroughly enjoy doing the opposite of what I'm told, especially if it's going to get me in trouble or piss off my brother. While I'm sure my flirty jokes won't be reciprocated, I'm interested in seeing how many buttons I can press before Jackson, and his *follow-the-rules* self entertain me.

# Chapter Ten

## JACKSON

I GLANCE INTO THE LIVING room at the sound of my daughter's laugh. A smile reaches my lips when she covers her face with the paper she's working on and beside her, Lisette laughs before tickling her side.

"You *know* that's not what that says." She takes the paper from her before sounding out a few words with her. "We can be done for the day since you gave it a try."

Isabelle races over to me as I turn to grab some seasoning for the meat.

"Daddy, can we start baking for KC's tea party?" She turns to Lisette excitedly. "KC is our new neighbor. She goes to my school too. Daddy, did I tell you that?"

She glances at me before whipping back to Lisette before I can answer. "She made a *big* order with my bakery today."

Lisette raises her brows amusingly as she sits at the island counter.

Isabelle races off to the fridge before she can reply. She's grabbing the clear container we keep the eggs in, but I swiftly take it from her.

"Let's do it when I finish putting everything on the stove."

"Why not now?" She grabs the eggs again, but I put them back in the fridge.

"Because I can't bake and prep dinner at the same time."

"Well, duh, that's why *I'm* going to bake." She turns back to the fridge, but I lift her into my arms, and she fills the kitchen with her laugh when I flip her upside down and rest her on my shoulder.

"What did I say about saying *duh* to me?" I poke her side and she laughs up a storm as she wraps her arms around me. "Now you have to stay like this forever."

I let her go and she holds me tighter as I season the meat.

"I'm going to fall," she voices with a laugh, and when I look up at Lisette, she's biting back a smile.

"Whenever you set her free from her upside-down punishment, I can bake with her," she teases, and in a quick move, my kid raises her head in excitement. I quickly bring a hand to her back before she can fall.

"I can bake on my own, but you can help with the small stuff."

"You can't bake on your own." I set Belle down and mess up her hair. "Stop it with the duh," I tell her more seriously before looking up at Lisette. "You don't have to bake. I'll get to it in a second."

"It's fine." She shrugs. "I don't mind and I literally have nothing else to do."

Before I can convince her otherwise, Isabelle is handing her the eggs. "Let's get to it."

"Someone's bossy," Lisette mumbles and a crease grows between Isabelle's brows.

"Well *duh*, I'm the boss of *my* bakery."

"Faith," I deadpan and she turns to me slowly. "It's *rude*. Enough with the duhs."

"Okay." Her brows slightly raise. She's about to take a step away when she lifts a finger. "Is that a fact or opinion?"

I hold back my smile, using all my strength to keep my face neutral. After I spoke to her dean, we've been working on what's facts and opinions in our day to day life. Clearly she's a smartass.

"What do you think?"

She taps her chin, a small smile on her face. "I need to get my notepad with the order for KC's party."

"That is a fact." I nod once.

She goes off to get it in her bag, giggling quietly.

"You're so strict with her." Lisette bites back a smile and I get back to making dinner.

"I don't think I'm necessarily strict. I'm parenting her."

When I glance back at Lisette, she shrugs. "What would I know?"

My eyes squint as I study her before I turn to put the food on the stove. "Do you disagree with my parenting?" I voice, not offended, but simply wanting her opinion.

I think I'm doing just fine raising Isabelle alone, but she doesn't have a woman figure other than my mom. I'm always open to parenting advice, especially from women.

"It's not my place to disagree. I'm not her mother and I wouldn't *know* anything about parenting since I didn't have a good one. I wasn't judging if that's how you took it."

"I didn't," I clarify. "I just appreciate insight from women." I turn back around and she nods.

"That's great but my insight doesn't count for much. Ask Vidia, she has a great relationship with her mom." She shrugs.

I study her for a beat, and while I don't know her very well, she seems to not care about much. I find myself envying that of her. She carries herself like she doesn't have a care in the world, and granted, she doesn't have the responsibility of a kid or job to worry about but still, the world feels so chaotic and she sits here like she's just floating by.

"Okay." Isabelle walks back in, pulling my eyes away from Lisette. "Should we start the cookies first or the cupcakes?"

Lisette uses her hands to gesture that she doesn't know. "Well, *duh*, you're the boss. You decide."

I shake my head at her and she bites back a smile when Isabelle turns to me.

"What? So *she* can say it?" She looks between the two of us and I let out a defeated breath.

"You're just like your brother, making my life hard."

Lisette tries to bite back a laugh but a snort escapes her.

"She was joking," I tell Isabelle. "Go ahead and tell her what to do, boss."

She thankfully lets it go and starts bossing Lisette around the kitchen.

I don't get more than fifteen minutes of peace when I hear Isabelle gasp and knowing it isn't anything serious, I turn around slowly to peek at wherever they're doing.

Lisette runs her finger along the edge of the bowl they're mixing the cupcake mix in before dragging her tongue up her finger and as my eyes watch her movement, my heart rate quickens.

My eyes fall on her throat as she swallows. After a beat, her tongue darts out of her mouth, and again, she licks the last bit off her finger and I feel my face heat when her eyes meet mine, a smirk growing on her face.

"You're looking at me like you want some." She dips her finger in again before holding it out to me, and as I register she's eating raw batter, I quickly wipe her hand, careful not to touch the batter with my bare hands

"You're going to get sick." I turn on my heels and I drop the napkin in the trash.

"Does it taste good?" Isabelle voices, and as I turn on my heels, she dips her finger in the bowl. I feel my eyes bulge as she tries to eat it and I quickly grab her hand to stop her.

"No!"

She slightly jumps and immediately my heart sinks for yelling.

"Sorry." I kiss the top of her head before picking her up and rushing her to the sink. "I don't want you to get sick, penguin. Please don't touch or eat the raw batter."

I wash her hand twice and as I'm about to add soap to her hand a third time, she pulls away.

"Daddy, they're clean. I don't need to wash my hands so much. Remember?"

I bite my tongue as I watch her turn the water off. "Just two more—"

"Daddy, I promise they're clean. No more."

I remain holding her, my eyes on her dirty hands. "Penguin—"

"The deal was two times, Dad." She pushes away.

Setting her down reluctantly, I watch her carefully as she walks back to the kitchen island and climbs the stool.

"Now, where were we?" She looks down at her recipe sheet and with every second that passes, I'm sweating more and more.

"Isabelle, can I please just wash your hands two more times?"

She looks over at me and gives me a knowing look, and as much as I want to leave her alone, I can't push it aside. Understanding crosses her face as she lets out a soft sigh.

"Daddy, let's practice happy thoughts. My hands are very clean." She smiles at me, but her words only make me more uneasy.

"We can practice after, baby. *Please*, okay?" I grab her before she can object and finish cleaning her. After the fourth wash, I let out a calming breath before setting her down.

"*That* feels better." I nod to myself before kissing her. "Thank you."

Her brows slightly furrow as she looks up at me. "Daddy, we were only washing our hands two times. What happened?"

I feel like shit as I watch her confused face. "I'm sorry." Kneeling down to her eye level, I take hold of her small hands, kissing them gently. "Nothing happened, penguin, it's just the raw food..."

She looks like she doesn't understand, and it only makes me feel worse for putting her through this.

"Okay." She shrugs before walking off, but I pull her back.

"I'm sorry."

She smiles at me before leaning over to give me a light kiss. "You don't need to say sorry, Daddy." She lifts her hands. "Now they smell extra good. Thank you." She walks off and I smile to myself as she climbs her stool again.

When Lisette walks past me, I somehow remember her presence and I feel my face heat in embarrassment. She heads for the sink and I cook beside her silently as she washes her hands.

"May I ask why the raw eggs didn't bother you?" she voices gently before washing her hands again.

I steal a glance at her as I watch her wash her hands. "They did... that's why I cracked the eggs for her and then washed my hands."

She adds more soap to her hands and my heart rate slowly lowers.

"I keep them in the clear container because the ones they come in bother me." I don't know why I explain, but I feel the need to.

She nods in return before I notice her washing her hands for the fourth time.

Biting back a smile, I turn to meet her eyes. "Thank you."

She nods once before walking back to Belle and I want to tell her to drink something to wash out the batter she ate but I bite my tongue and mentally repeat to myself that she'll be fine.

"So," Lisette starts, and I turn to her before leaning on the counter. I wait for her to make a joke about my obsession with food contamination or for an excuse that she has to leave after that show, but it never comes.

"I need to have more..." she pauses as she searches for the right word. She settles on, "structure."

"Structure?"

"Yes, I need a routine. A reason to get out of bed and tutoring fits perfectly into my empty schedule, so what days should I come over?" She pulls out her phone, I'm assuming to add it to her calendar, but her words make me falter.

"You don't have another reason to get out of bed?" My voice comes out softer than I intended, and she steals a glance at me before she focuses on her phone again.

"Perks of depression."

Before I can say anything, Isabelle raises her head from what she's doing and sets the measuring cup down. "What's depression?"

Lisette looks over at me for an answer and Isabelle looks between the two of us. "It's when you're really sad," I say.

"Why are you sad?" Isabelle asks softly and Lisette's smile seems more sincere now.

"I wish I knew, sweet girl."

I can see the confusion on Belle's face, so I better explain. "Sometimes when someone is depressed they don't know why. It's like when I don't know why I need to wash my hands so many times, I just need to in order to feel better. Until it feels *right*."

She nods slowly and I can see her understanding as I go on, knowing she's more than smart enough to grasp my words.

"People who have depression feel lonely, and the things that usually make them happy don't. You don't have the energy to do anything and their mind is mean to them."

Belle looks over at Lisette, her brows furrowed. "Even ice cream doesn't make you happy?"

Lissette and I stifle a laugh before I kiss Isabelle's cheek.

"You know how I have my OCD?"

Belle glances back at me and nods in understanding.

"Well, depression is a disorder too." I shrug. "Some people have it and the same way we have extra patience with Daddy, we give extra love to people who are depressed. We remind them of how important they are in case their brain tricks them into forgetting."

I personally think it's good explaining these things to her. She's a curious and very smart kid. With my OCD being impossible to hide, she picked up on every little thing I did. Rather than letting her grow up confused, I taught her why I am the way I am. She's going to find out about these things eventually, and if I can make her compassionate to people who are different, then I will.

When I glance over at Lisette she smiles at Isabelle, but I can see now that she's just hiding behind her smiles and jokes.

Isabelle nods before leaning over and hugging Lisette. "You're so important," she exclaims. "Without you, I would fail my test."

We all break into a laugh before Isabelle kisses her arm. "Do you feel better yet?" She peeks up at her, her arms still around her and Lisette lets out a quiet laugh.

"Almost." She squeezes her tighter before kissing her curls. "You're great at giving hugs."

"So are you." Isabelle pulls away before tapping her arm four times. "I won't let your brain trick you." With that, she turns back to her cupcake tray and Lisette watches her, almost in awe.

## Chapter Eleven

# JACKSON

"**A**RE YOU SURE IT'S FRIDAY?" Isabelle reads the date on my phone *again*, her tiny foot tapping impatiently.

"Well yesterday was Thursday and Friday comes after Thursday. That's a fact." I try to convince her I'm right for the *third* time. "Unless someone changed the order of the week."

She looks up at me like I just grew three heads. "Who could change the order of the week when Lissy was coming over today?"

I bite back a smile as she watches me like she's ready for war. "I was joking, baby."

She hums. "Lisette was supposed to meet us here when I got home from school. Why is she late?"

I stifle a laugh as she paces the living room with her arms crossed. On the table in front of us are the books and worksheets Lisette made for their tutoring sessions, and I've never seen her so eager to do her homework.

We decided Lisette would come over the three days I work from home. She's taking this tutor thing very seriously and I appreciate it. Belle also looks forward to seeing her every Monday, Tuesday, and Friday, but she's so impatient.

At the sound of the door ringing, she lets out a gasp before taking off running. I follow after her and she grabs the handle before turning to me. I give her the green light and she pulls the heavy door open.

When she sees it's a package, she looks up to the ceiling with a sigh.

The mailman looks between the two of us. "People usually have the opposite reaction when seeing me."

I quickly apologize for my kid. "Sorry, she's waiting for someone." I sign for the package as Isabelle pulls it in.

"If you see Lisette out there can you tell her to hurry?" She looks up at our mailman but before he can respond, a car pulls up. She looks past him, a smile so damn big on her face as she waves Lisette over. "You're here!"

Lisette laughs in return as she climbs out of her car. "Well it's Friday, isn't it?" She passes the mailman on her way to us before leaning down to pick up Isabelle. "Oh wow, you're heavier than you look." She adjusts her on her hip before turning to me.

"Hey, hot stuff." She gazes up at me and I find myself admiring how clear of a blue her eyes are. She playfully flutters her long lashes at me and I take in just how pretty she is.

Even with the tired bags forming under her eyes, the rest of her face is one that makes all her flirty comments fuck with me. She doesn't have soft features but sharp ones instead.

Strong cheekbones and jawline. Dirty blonde brows that look as though she hasn't had to pluck them a day in her life. Full pouty lips.

Her whole face just makes it so much harder to ignore every flirty comment she's been throwing at me. Every other word that comes out of her mouth is a joke, so I don't take anything she says seriously, but her words never fail to make my face heat. Even though I know she's just looking for a reaction out of me, my body doesn't know that and it's giving me the wrong reactions.

"You're late."

Her smile morphs into a smirk as she steps into my house. "So you waited for me by the door? Did you miss me, JJ?"

I roll my eyes at her just before she turns back to me. "Belle is just impatient."

She nods like she doesn't believe me before she turns to my kid. "Did he miss me?"

"Yup, we both did," Isabelle voices cheerfully and I let out a laugh as I walk past them.

"She has no idea what she's talking about."

"I know what I'm talking about, Daddy," Belle counters.

"Right," Lisette joins. "So just say you missed me, Daddy."

I bite my tongue, but no way in hell do I turn around. I can hear Lisette's soft laugh from behind me and I shake my head at myself when my cheeks heat. She's my closest friend's sister and I can't go there. I know that and I don't think I even *want* to go there, but her looks and words are messing with me.

"I need to get to work. I'll be in my office." I keep my back to them as I disappear to my office.

In an attempt to distract myself, I read over a contract for a client one more time before we get on a call. I'm in the middle of answering one of his questions when my phone starts ringing. I steal a glance at it, but when I see it's Rome, I send it to voicemail.

"Sorry about that." I turn back to the camera but I can barely open my mouth when it starts ringing *again*. I hit decline just as a text comes in.

**Rome B**

> stop ignoring me. this is important.

> I'm in a meeting. I'll call you back.

> are u meeting with chase rhodes???

I don't reply as I turn back to Chase and my phone rings *again*.

"Is everything okay?" Chase looks around, his brows furrowed in concern.

"Yeah, kid, I'm sorry. Give me five minutes." I quickly mute the call and turn my camera off before answering Rome's call. "What the hell is your problem?" I bite out.

He lets out a scoff on the other end. "Why are you meeting with the *enemy*?"

I feel my face morph in confusion as I glance over at Chase's innocent smile. "What are you talking about? You guys are team-mates," I remind him.

Rome lets out a huff as he tells me about them fighting for the same girl and how Chase wasn't being a team player at last night's game.

"Rome, are you kidding me right now? He's my *client*. I don't care if he outshined you yesterday for a chick's attention. If this girl wanted you, you'd have her." I rub my temples when I feel a headache coming.

"He did *not* outshine me. I got the game ball and I do have her. *He* can't take a damn hint."

I'm truly at a loss for words.

"Did you know the Dodgers sent him an offer? Is that what you're meeting with him about right now? Did you *help* him?" He nearly yells now.

"You're joking right?" I can feel the veins in my temple about to burst. "I cannot discuss this with you because he's my *client*. This isn't a competition."

"It quite literally is. The Dodgers are only taking one person this year."

"Who told you that? That's not how it works, Rome."

I can hear him pacing from how loud he's walking around his dorm.

"Don't let him sign with the Dodgers. I just—"

I hang up on him before blocking his number and returning to my meeting with Chase. His mom is on the call with us and she looks so proud of her son as we discuss his offers.

"You don't have to decide now." I step in when he asks his dad for his opinion. "You all can take a few days to think about it."

His mom turns to me, tears in her proud eyes. "What do you think he should do?"

"Well, it depends on what you care more about. Everyone wants the Dodgers, but if we're being realistic, with the lineup they have now, you won't see much pitch time. Griffin and Cane never see the bench." I know Rome would probably do a backflip if he heard my words, but I don't voice them for him.

Chase lets out a short laugh. "I think I'll gladly be a bench warmer for Sire Griffin and Noah Cane."

A laugh escapes me at his words. "The Yankees are—"

"No." Chase shakes his head. "I'd be such a hypocrite if I played for them."

I nod in understanding. "I get your loyalty, but in a few months you won't be a fan cheering in the stands or booing the Yankees, you'll be playing beside these guys. If their pitcher really is injured, there's no doubt you'll be pitching half the season."

His shoulders sag as he weighs his options.

"The Cubs are lowballing you though," I admit. "You said you wanted to move back to Chicago for your grandparents and you'd have a great season with them, but I can get you a better offer and you can have everything you want."

His parents express their gratitude, and I'm emailing Chase about a brand deal when my eyes land on an email from Rome.

**Subject: DID YOU BLOCK ME?**
**Jones I need you're head in the game right now. I understand he's your client but I was you're client first. Do you know no loyalty??? I thought we were closer then this? Your being so selfish!**

I genuinely can't help but laugh at him. "It was great talking with you Chase. I just emailed you a few endorsements to look over. I'll see you on Tuesday. Keep in touch." I end the call before replying to Rome.

**Subject: Yes, I blocked you.**
**Then= Sequence. Ex: You were being a brat and *then* you pissed me off, so I blocked you.**
**Than= Comparison. Ex: I prefer Chase rather *than* you.**
**You're= You + are. Ex: *You're* the one being selfish.**
**Your= Ownership. Ex: *Your* attitude is getting old.**
**We are not close. Hope this helps!**
**Coldest regards,**
**Jones.**

He doesn't reply for a while and I let myself believe he's working on his grammar rather than sitting in his anger.

When I hear the door open quietly, I can see Belle peek her head in from the corner of my eye.

She walks over to me quietly and I feel a smile grow on my face as I pretend I don't see her sneaking into my office. She walks over quietly, her hand covering her smile as she laughs.

I look up from my laptop but don't turn to her, and she goes still. I glance to the side she isn't on before shrugging and looking back at my laptop and she giggles harder.

When she gets closer, she crouches in front of my desk before popping up. "Hi, Dad!"

I jump back in surprise, and she fills the room with her precious laugh.

"Where did you come from? You scared me."

She laughs harder and I smile down at her as she folds her hands on my desk and rests her head down. "Watcha doin'?" She fiddles with a paperweight as her pretty eyes gaze up at me, and I want more than anything to shut my laptop and go hang out with her.

Instead, I raise my brows at her. "The real question is whatcha doin'? I thought you were supposed to be working with Lissy?"

She lets out a sigh as she rolls the paperweight between her hands. "We're taking a break 'cause she's on a phone call." She shrugs. "So whatcha doin'?" She gets on her tippy toes as she tries to pull my laptop into her view, but I gently push her hand before she bends the screen back.

"I'm working on a proposal to negotiate a client's pay with a contractor."

Belle nods in understanding. "Yeah, I was working on that yesterday. It's a lot of work, huh?"

"Not really. Writing the proposal is easy, but the back-and-forth negotiating is a lot of work sometimes." I know she doesn't understand what I'm talking about, but watching her pretend she does is my favorite thing.

"Yeah," she shakes her head this time. "That part is a stress."

I bite back a laugh and she peeks up at me from the side of her eyes.

"What's negoate?"

"Negotiate." I correct her and she tries the word on her tongue twice before she gets it right. "It's like when I say it's time for bed and you say one more movie and we agree to ten more minutes."

She nods.

"That's us negotiating."

I see it click in her head as she stands up straight. "Oh, well, that reminds me of a negotiate I have." She turns to her small desk in the corner of my office and sits in her pink chair before opening her toy laptop.

She types a bunch of nothing before nodding to herself and turning to me. "So how do I write the prosal?"

"Proposal." I help her again. "You just say what your client wants and what you're willing to agree to. Then talk about how this will be a good agreement for the other person."

She nods before typing. "Okay." She grabs her laptop and puts it on her lap as she turns to me. "My client wants to have a sleepover at KC's house." She looks up at me as she waits for my reaction. "This will be a *great* agreement for you because you can scream

at the TV with her dad. You guys had fun doing that yesterday."
She smiles proudly as she shuts her laptop.

"That was a great proposal."

She nods excitedly.

"I'm going to have to decline your offer, though." I shrug as I
turn back to my laptop.

"*What?*" I see her shaking her head as she opens her laptop
again. "You can't do that."

"I actually can. You can write another proposal, and if I like it
better than that one, I'll agree." I look over at her and she looks like
she doesn't understand. "This is when we negotiate and come to
an agreement in the middle. You can have another playdate with
KC but you're not sleeping there."

"Why?"

I look back at my laptop as I see her getting upset. "You know
the rule. No sleepovers. You can have a playdate. That's my proposal. Final offer."

At the sound of footsteps, I look up and Lisette is walking in.
At the smile on her face, I know she heard most of that.

"I'm her business partner and we'll be drafting that *prosal*
together." She rolls her eyes at me playfully. "Shame on you for
taking advantage of my rookie partner."

I bite back a smile as I lean back in my seat. "She shouldn't be
in this field if she doesn't have the experience." I shrug.

She leans down to my daughter and whispers loud enough for
me to hear. "We're going to get you that sleepover."

Belle lights up and my smile is gone as I turn to Lisette. "No,
she isn't. I'm being serious." I turn to Belle when I see her pouting.
"Don't start," I warn.

She pouts her lip further and it *truly* pains me, but I stay strong
and look at my laptop.

"Please, Daddy?" she pleads.

I don't respond and I feel my chest tightening when she walks
closer to me.

"Daddy, *please?*"

I look down at her and she bats her long lashes at me.

"We can get ice cream with her, then have a playdate by the
pool, but no sleepover."

She smiles at my words. "Okay!" She skips out of the room, and when I look up at Lisette, she's shaking her head at me with her arms crossed.

"She just played your sorry ass. She was talking about getting ice cream with KC earlier."

"No, she wasn't."

"She sure was." Lisette laughs at the shock on my face, and I shake my head at myself.

I notice Lisette glance at my laptop before her eyes meet mine. "Are you busy?"

"Nope." I lean back in my seat. "I sit at this desk for hours on end to get away from my manipulative child."

She breaks into a laugh as she walks over to my desk. "My sarcasm is rubbing off on you."

"Eh, just a bit." I give her a shrug.

"Well, this is serious."

I focus on her for a beat. "Is anything ever serious with you?"

"Nope."

I bite back a laugh as I push my laptop aside. "What's up?"

She sits in the chair in front of my desk before looking down at herself.

"Uh uh." She shakes her head before standing up. "I don't like this, let's switch."

"What?"

She's already walking towards me and gesturing for me to stand. "Switch." She pulls my arm, and I rise to my feet before she sits in my chair. I watch her as she spins to face forward and folds her hands together at my desk.

"This is a big chair." She glances down at it.

"I'm a big guy."

Her eyes cut up to mine, and when a smile grows on her face I shake my head at her.

"How many inches are we talking?" She glances between my legs before looking back up at me, and I bite back a laugh as I take a seat in front of her.

"What is wrong with you?"

"Surprisingly, a lot."

My eyes cut to hers and she's just sitting there with a gorgeous smile.

"You really believe there's something wrong with you?" I study her for a beat and her smile doesn't waver, but I see how she forces it more.

"You haven't seen what's in here." She taps her head. "Back to what I wanted to talk about."

She continues before I can counter and keep the conversation on her and I notice she does that a lot, deflects when I ask about her.

"It's about Belle."

I feel my brows furrow as I slightly sit up in my seat, but she puts a hand up, her smile slowly returning.

"Chill, Daddy bear. She's fine," she tries to reassure me. "She had a red card in her folder though."

I let out a groan as I cover my face. "Jesus Christ," I mumble.

"Yeah," she treads lightly. "She was apparently being disruptive during quiet time and wouldn't stop laughing, but coming from a teacher and knowing she isn't a disrespectful child, that's a ridiculous reason for a red card."

I throw my hands up. "*Thank* you," I exclaim. "I feel like I'm walking on eggshells with these people. God forbid a child behaves their age." I understand needing to correct her behavior if she was truly being disruptive, but a red card for laughing? These cards are apparently a last resort, and her getting two in one week is absurd to me.

"I also read over her assessment and I think they have something against you."

Hearing her words are incredibly reassuring because I was starting to feel like I was going crazy. "So you don't think she's behind?"

She takes a beat to respond and I study her closely before she shrugs. "I don't think it's fair to label her as *behind*. Kids develop at different ages," she says exactly what I told them. "She *could* be more advanced, sure, but she turned five in August which was barely two months ago. She'll reach the milestones soon enough."

I nod in return.

"What exactly did they tell you? I don't understand why they're giving you such a hard time. She's honestly a great kid."

I sink in my seat as I rant. "They're incredibly invested as to why her mom isn't in the picture and it's not in a mandated reporter kind of way. They're simply nosy." I roll my eyes as their comments come to mind. "When I was registering, I overheard them comment about how I probably cheated on her."

Her brows raise before she lets out a scoff. "I hate private school teachers, especially those kind." When she smiles this time, I know a joke is coming. "On the bright side, you can go to their higher ups if they kick her out of school for failing her next assessment. I know private schools have different rules, but it sounds like they're breaking some."

I offer her a smile, but her words don't make me feel better.

"She's not going to fail," she reassures me. "Change your face and have more faith in me, asshole."

I let out a low laugh. "What did I say about the language?" I tease.

"Right." She nods before giving me a once-over. "We wouldn't want you withholding the big guy from me."

"*Lisette.*" I feel my face heat and her loud laugh fills the room as she rises from *my* seat.

"You seriously need to stop with the inappropriate comments, especially in front of my kid. I don't care if she doesn't catch onto them," I tell her more seriously.

She rolls her eyes at me as she makes her way around my desk. "Your blush is so cute though." She ruffles my hair. "I'll stop saying them in front of your kid since she's a sponge."

"Stop them all together."

She studies me for a beat before leaning against my desk with her arms crossed. "If I don't stop, will this count as sexual harassment?"

"What?"

"Well, you're telling me to stop, but I can't tell if you *really* want me to stop because I'm making you uncomfortable or if you want me to stop because it's simply inappropriate."

I almost tell her they're making me uncomfortable to put an end to this, but I don't want her to stop. Her comments get more creative each day and they're harmless, but it's messing with my head and making me see her as more than Sire's little sister.

"It's not sexual harassment."

She nods once before opening her mouth, but the sound of something loud falling has us both going still. I wait for a beat, but when I don't hear anything, I race out of my office.

"Belle?" My heart is fighting to get out of my chest as I search for her because the house is *still* silent, which is scarier than hearing cries after a crash that loud.

"Isabelle!" I call out to her, and when I don't see her in the living room, I turn on my heels.

"I'm okay," she voices and I let out a breath of relief when I see her in the kitchen unharmed.

"Jesus *Christ*, kid." Lisette holds her chest as she walks into the kitchen. "You gave me a damn heart attack. What the hell are you doing?" She helps Isabelle stand from where she is on the floor before looking at her head and a smile touches my lips at her worry for my kid.

"So you *are* serious about things." I pick up the two chairs Belle managed to knock over and Lisette turns to me with her brows pulled together.

"Well, your petrified face scared me more than she did, but yes, I take some things seriously." She rolls her eyes at me and I bite back a laugh before turning to Belle for an explanation.

"I fell and the other chair fell with me when I grabbed it." She rubs her head and I move her hand to examine it, but she's fine. "We should get new chairs, those aren't safe."

"What were you doing to fall?" Lisette asks for me, and I keep my gaze on Belle, but she doesn't answer.

"Right," I start. "The chairs are safe. Please don't do whatever it was that made you fall." I kiss her head before scooping her into my arms.

"Daddy, you don't have to carry me. I'm fine."

"Well, you scared me, so let me carry you." I hold her tighter and she doesn't fight me on it as we settle on the living room couch. She's in my lap for half a second before she's crawling away.

"I'm not a *baby*."

I scoop her into my lap again. "You're *my* baby."

"I'm a big girl," she counters as she pushes me away harder and I let her go this time.

"You look like a baby to me," Lisette voices from beside us and Isabelle turns to her slowly before staring at her like she's a terrorist.

"You must not know what a baby looks like."

I break into a laugh.

"Whatever." Lisette flops beside me on the couch. "I'm not arguing with a *baby*."

"You're *not*. I'm a big girl." She raises a brow, and when Lisette doesn't have anything else to say, triumph covers Belle's face.

"Your kid's a brat," Lisette mumbles as Isabelle turns to her worksheet.

"You know she's not," I counter before turning to Isabelle. "You were red carded today?" I watch her carefully, but her brows furrow.

"No, I had such a great day. We're having a pizza party next Friday. I also think it's Sofie's birthday. We *have* to get her a present."

I have no clue who Sofie is, but I grab her folder and when I pull out the card she genuinely looks confused. "Did you not get a warning?"

"No?" She sounds even more confused. "Will I still get to go to the pizza party?"

"You will, kiddo," Lisette reassures her. "Are you sure Ms. Rose didn't give you any warnings today?" she asks from beside me, but I know my kid isn't a liar and I make a reminder to call her school.

# Chapter Twelve

## LISETTE

I LET MY EYES FALL shut as I raise the volume on my speaker, desperately trying to get the music to drown out my thoughts. I focus on the lyrics and beat of the song while ignoring the weight in my chest and the desperation eating at me for a drink.

I look back at my canvas and get back to the painting I'm working on. Glancing at the crocheted flowers Jackson got me, I mix some more white into my paint to match the shade of purple of the yarn.

After another half hour of trying to drown my feelings in my work, the painting is complete. I set my brush down and tilt my head to the side to examine it. I glance at the flowers beside the canvas, and both are nearly identical.

"Not bad." I nod to myself as I rise from my seat, but a second later, the weight is back in my chest again.

Walking into my room, I head for my turtle tank and Piglet swims over to me. "I need you to support my emotions right now, bud." I put my hand into the tank and he swims into my hand. "You're such a good turtle." I smile down at him as I scoop him out of the water.

Settling with him in the living room again, I place him in a bucket with some water. Grabbing an older incomplete canvas, I sit at the easel with it.

After a few songs, the painting looks more put together. A faint banging at the door catches my attention, and as I pull my headphones off to listen, it sounds like the damn police are outside. I tread to the door lightly before going still at the sound of someone crying.

"Open the door!"

"Harmony?" I quickly swing the door open and when her eyes meet mine, her tears are traded for anger.

"If I didn't think you'd beat my ass, I would slap you right now."
She storms past me before throwing her school bag at her feet.
It's still early in the morning, so she's cutting and I roll my eyes
as I imagine Ana's call.

I shut my door before turning to her. "Yeah, I'd kick your ass,
so keep those manicured hands to yourself."

She looks at me like she's going to hit me anyway and my smile
doesn't waver.

"What is your problem?"

"Me?" She nearly shouts. "I've been knocking for ten minutes.
Why were you ignoring me and why did you block me?" Tears
start to form in her eyes again, but I'm beyond confused.

"I had my headphones on. I didn't know you were knocking
my door down and I didn't block you. I was calling you all day
yesterday."

Her brows furrow before she pulls her phone out of her pocket.
She looks over at something as her shoulders sag. "It says I have
you blocked..."

I let out a scoff as I take a seat in front of my canvas again. "Ana
took your phone didn't she?"

Harmony mumbles a few curses, and since I'm not the responsible older sister between the three of us, I don't say anything
about her language.

I pick up my paintbrush again as she settles on the couch
beside me.

"Who got you these flowers?" She touches them gently, but I
don't miss her numb tone.

"My sugar daddy." From the corner of my eyes, I can see her
go still before she steals a glance at me. I stifle a laugh and she
visibly relaxes.

"Hey, I wasn't judging."

"Mhm." I roll my eyes at her. "I'm tutoring a family friend. Her
dad got them for me."

She nods in thought as I return to working on my painting.

"You kept them, so I'm assuming he's hot and not a creepy older
guy you're working for."

I bite back a smile. "He's the guy you said was hot a few weeks
ago." I turn to her. "Nice car, expensive suit, and tie."

Her brows furrow before her eyes widen and she sits up in her seat. "No way. I've been stalking him all week and now you tell me he's a *family friend?*"

I'm about to answer her when my brain catches up to what she just said. "What do you mean you've been stalking him? You saw him for five seconds, how did you find him?"

She lets out a scoff as she leans back in her seat again. "I can find anyone, Lis."

*That's not concerning.* Choosing to change the topic, I tell her how I know Jackson, and she's far too invested in this man.

"So he likes you?"

I let out a laugh. "The flowers were a joke. He does not like me."

She looks like she believes otherwise. "He paid attention to what you said about not liking real flowers and went out of his way to get you crocheted ones? He likes you."

"He does not."

She shrugs before focusing on my painting, and when I see her brows furrow, I turn back to the canvas. I keep my eyes on the drowning girl, but nothing looks wrong with it.

"What?" I look between her and the painting as I watch her smile disappear.

"You told me you paint as escapism."

The pain in my chest intensifies but I don't say anything as I continue adding more detail to the water on the canvas.

"Are you having a hard day?" she voices gently.

"Every day is a hard day; it's an addiction."

I can see her nod in the corner of my eyes. "Are you still sober?"

I can feel her watching me as if her life depended on my answer.

"Yeah, Harmony, I'm sober."

Her shoulders ease as she nods again. "Mom isn't."

I don't respond because I have nothing nice to say and she clearly already feels like shit.

"When I went to hang out with her that day Ana called you, she was high as a kite." She pulls her legs onto my couch as she watches me paint. "She thought I was you."

I go still.

"We don't have any pictures of you at the house, but Ana says I resemble you a lot when you were my age."

"Yeah." I clear my throat before straightening my back. "It's creepy."

She goes quiet again and I swallow my feelings as I turn to her. "What happened?"

Her eyes meet mine before she sits up. "She yelled at me. She kept calling me your name and yelled about how I need to stop hanging out with those lawyers and how they're snooping around her life."

Dread begins to eat at me as my heart sinks. Memories of my childhood come in flashes and I force myself to look back at the painting, picking up the brush instead of the bottle in my pocket.

"What lawyers were you with?"

"Mom." When I notice her brows furrow I try again. "Kathrine Hale is a lawyer and Isaac is with the Bureau. When they adopted Sire, they were looking into adopting me. She was never their biggest fan."

I steal a glance at Harmony and I can see her confusion. "Why didn't they adopt you?"

"Your mom still had her parental rights over me. If she signed them away, the court would question her ability to care for you and Ana. Your grandma wasn't giving you up and it was just too messy. Kat didn't want to break up the family more than what it was, so I just lived with them without court permission."

"And Mom... *let* you leave?"

The reminder adds a simmer of anger inside me, salt in the fucking wound. "Yup." I turn back to the painting, but as I add blue in the wrong place, it pushes me over the edge. I shove the canvas away before standing up, my breathing heavier.

Pressing my palms to my eyes, I take a minute to calm my breathing. "Sorry." I voice when I register Harmony's silence.

"It's okay."

I pick up Piglet from the bucket of water and settle on the couch beside Harmony.

"I'm supposed to hang out with her again tomorrow." She picks at her nails and I shake my head at her.

"Why are you doing this to yourself? These visitations aren't court-mandated. Ana is your guardian and your therapist is an idiot for suggesting you bond with her."

"I'm the one who wants to see her... my therapist didn't suggest it."

I feel my back straighten when her eyes fill with tears.

"I know you hate her, but she wasn't always like this. She was sober when I was younger. It wasn't until a few years ago that she relapsed." Her eyes meet mine now. "I want my mom back."

I feel my brows furrow as I focus on her. "When was she sober?"

Harmony wipes her tears before sniffling quietly. "When I turned seven Grandma got sick. Mom got clean, and we lived with her again."

I shake my head at myself. Angry that I'm letting her words hurt so much.

"What?"

I swallow the lump in my throat. "If she was clean when you were seven, that means I was fifteen..." *She was clean and never came back for me.*

I muster up a smile as I sit up. "You're cutting school and I'm not in the mood to hear your sister's mouth." I rise from the couch. "Get your bag, I can drop you off."

She lets out a sigh and remains sitting. "Can't you let me stay?"

"And stand in the way of your education? I'm a drug addict, but I'm not an evil person, Harmony." I walk over to her bag and scoop it up. When I turn to her, she doesn't even crack a smile. "My offer to drop you off is standing for the next ten seconds. Get up or walk to school."

She rises from her seat before snatching her bag from me. I put my turtle back before heading down with her and the car ride is silent as I shove all of my feelings down. With each red light, my eyes fill with tears as images of her with a sober mom come to mind.

It isn't until we pull up in front of her school that Harmony turns to me, her eyes soft and the clearest of blues. "I'm sure she had a good reason for not going back for you. Maybe she knew you were happy with the Hales."

I plaster a smile on my face as I unlock the doors. "Don't cut class for useless boys. They're not worth your education."

She keeps her gaze on me for a second before climbing out. I watch as she disappears into the building before my shoulders sag and everything in me breaks. My eyes begin to water as a lump too big to breathe forms in my throat. I rub the scars on my thighs, but it's suddenly all too much and I feel like I can't breathe.

Rushing out the car, I lean against the door as I gasp for air. I can barely see as my vision blurs, but I don't let myself cry, I don't let myself feel any of it. Instead, I pull the bottle out from my pocket and let the burning liquor force the lump down my throat.

# Chapter Thirteen

## JACKSON

L ETTING MYSELF INTO MY PARENTS' house, I head for Belle's room and lay her in bed before going in search of my mom, who I find in the backyard.

"Mi querido." My mom lights up, her Puerto Rican accent thick. A small furrow grows in her brows when she notices my face. "What's wrong? Y la bebe?"

"Sleeping upstairs." I muster up a smile. "She had a nightmare last night and barely slept. She's beat."

My mom nods in understanding but keeps her concerned gaze on me. "Is she the only one that's beat?"

I let out a defeated breath before following her to the patio to sit. "I had a meeting with her school today." I roll my eyes at the reminder. "I feel like I made everything worse. They clearly can't stand me and going in today was probably their last straw."

My mom lets out a huff. "Don't pull her out of school because of them. They push and you push harder." Her stubbornness shines through her words.

"I'm not transferring her out, but I'm tired of the back and forth, Mom. When she first started they were worried that she was too quiet when she was simply shy, now she's coming out her shell and she's disruptive. She isn't reaching milestones, she speaks out of turn to answer their questions. Nothing is enough for these people." I cover my face in my hands as my bigger issue comes to mind. "I think she has my OCD."

My mom sets her watering pot down and turning to me. "Why do you think that?"

"Because she was tapping my back, like this." I tap her arm the way Belle was before she fell asleep.

"I'm confused, querido." She looks down at my hand. "Why is this tapping concerning you?"

"She did it in sets of four, Mom." I lean back to look at her better. "I do things in fours."

Her eyes narrow. "Maybe she's just copying you? She's a kid, bebe. Kids copy their parents."

I shake my head and I get up to pace, thinking better that way. "She's been doing this for a while and I didn't think much of it until today," I mumble a curse for not noticing sooner.

"You didn't notice until today... when you were extremely stressed with this meeting?" My mom rises from her seat before closing the distance between us to take my hand. "Your OCD is just obsessing over this because you're stressed. She's too young to have—"

"Early onset begins showing at six. She's turning six soon." I take out my phone for a Google search.

"No, she isn't. She *just* turned five, and—"

"Do you think I gave it to her?" I search her eyes before continuing in Spanish for her. "I can't always conceal the compulsions. I try not to do it in front of her, but I just can't help it sometimes. What if she started doing it to copy me but it manifested into OCD and I *did* give it to her?"

Her brows furrow further and I let out a frustrated breath as I run a hand through my hair. She doesn't understand and I need her to stop looking at me like I'm crazy because I'm not.

It took my mom a long time to come to terms with my OCD. I could have gotten diagnosed a lot quicker, but she brushed it off, claiming my disorder wasn't real. My grandma said the same and I think it was a cultural thing, especially when they tried to fix me with remedies, but my dad put his foot down and got me the help I needed. She's still coping with how to deal with it and I wish she understood.

"Jackson, baby, you know your OCD is not contagious," she treads lightly.

"She's afraid of contagious things, too," I voice at the reminder.

"She's a *child*. Children are afraid of deadly contagious diseases. OCD is not one of them." She sounds like she's reminding me but I already know that.

"You don't get it." I sink into a chair, burying my face in my hands. "I feel like I have no idea what I'm doing sometimes, Mom. Like I'm the worst fucking dad. I'm *ruining* her."

"What?" She takes hold of my hand, but I pull away.

"Do *not* say that," she starts again. "You're an amazing father to that little girl. Those teachers are just giving you a hard time but once they realize you're not going anywhere, they'll leave you alone."

"I'm sure they'll blame me for her possible OCD. Me or her being motherless," I mumble.

My mom takes my hand, understanding covering her face. "You only get like this when one thing happens," she starts quietly although Isabelle isn't around. "Did she ask about her mom?"

I nod in response, a weight growing in my chest. "I don't hate her. I hate myself for not hating her, but I *do* hate that she makes my daughter question herself because of her absence."

My mom nods in understanding as she squeezes my hand. "You just need to keep doing your part to make sure she doesn't feel like there's anyone missing."

"I know that. Playing the role of two parents isn't hard. When she looks around at her friends and notices she doesn't have a mom; or when we go to the doctor and they ask for her mom's medical history in front of her, *that* part is hard."

A sympathetic look crosses her face before she forces a smile. "Have you thought about when you're going to tell her more about her mom? You don't have to tell her why she left, but talking *about* her will help so she doesn't feel clueless."

I shake my head as I think of how that'll go. "It'll be too hard."

"Para ti o ella?" my mom asks gently, but I don't answer and instead pull out my phone and for the next two hours, I research whether or not Belle has OCD.

I'm in the middle of reading another article when my dad walks over and rests his hand on my shoulder. "Jackson, why don't you get on a call with your therapist?"

I let out a defeated breath as I shut my phone off. "I meet with her once a month," I remind him. "I'll talk to her next week."

He watches me carefully before putting his hands up in surrender. Rising to my feet, I go find Isabelle. She's still sleeping but I decide to lay with her.

# *Chapter Fourteen*

## LISETTE

"**Y**OU'RE DRUNK," BAY DEADPANS.

"I'm tipsy. Very different," I counter but her eyes only narrow. "Let's talk about you. How's the post-abortion depression going?" I smile over at her as I sit up on the couch.

"No, Lis." Her eyes drown in understanding, forcing me to look back at my wine glass. "We're talking about you right now. Why did you feel like you couldn't call me or your brother before making this choice?"

I lay back on the couch, biting my cheek as I try to find the right words.

"We can sit here in silence all day, babe," she nearly whispers.

I pull in a deep breath before turning to her. "Sire is just going to tell me to stop hanging out with Harmony or to limit our time together and eliminate all talk about her mom because of how it makes me feel, but I can't do that to her."

"Oh." Bay nods in understanding. "So instead, you've been sipping on wine all week, letting her mom be the reason you throw away six hard-earned months of sobriety?" Sarcasm drips from her tone as she whips her dark curls over her shoulder.

I look up at her, giving her a knowing look.

"Do you think I'm wrong?" she asks and it doesn't sound rhetorical; it's as if she really wants to know.

"Yeah." I shrug. "Those six months don't—" I cut myself off as I try to find the right word. "I'm aware that they *matter*. I'm glad that I was clean. It just doesn't feel like it's worth anything."

My eyes meet hers. "Like... in the grand scheme of things, six-months sober compared to eleven years of addiction doesn't seem like an accomplishment." I shrug. "It makes me feel dirty thinking about it."

"Like you hate yourself," Bay voices my exact thoughts before sitting beside me. "You're not dirty, though. It's not six-months clean compared to eleven years of addiction. You were six-months sober *period*. When we go to a meeting we don't say 'Hi, I'm Bay and I'm six years sober but I've been an addict for nine years, so fuck me, I'm worthless' do we?" She shoves my shoulder with hers.

I look over at those deep blue eyes and her pretty smile. "No..."

"Exactly." She shrugs. "You're not dirty. The world thinks we suck for having shitty genes and generational trauma, but screw the world. You definitely need to wash your hair and trim your ends, but you're not dirty."

I stifle a laugh as I shove her away but she goes on, more serious.

"I know you think you deserve to feel like this. You think you deserved being abandoned as a child, so you're letting yourself soak in all this hurt but you don't deserve this shit."

I swallow the bitter taste in my mouth as I look forward and I almost reach for my glass until it hits me that maybe she's right. I think a part of me deserves this, but I use every bit of my strength to think of the part of me that doesn't deserve this.

The me who makes my siblings laugh. The me that Isabelle loves being around. The me that Jackson trusts around his kid. The me that Bay isn't tired of yet, even after eight years of friendship.

I look over at her again and her eyes are on the wine glass. When I met Bay my freshman year of college, she shocked me with how much I ended up liking her. At the tour they, told us we'll find our lifelong friends on campus and I didn't believe them for a second.

I was never good at keeping friends. I became friends with Sire because we were neighbors and hated being home, so we sat outside together for hours on end. Then we met the twins because of him, but with Bay, I did that all on my own.

She sat with me during lunch at orientation and I thought I made it clear that I wanted to sit alone, but she either lacked social clues or outright ignored my glare because she sat right next to me with her big smile and frizzy curls.

It was way too hot to wear long pants that day, but while everyone took one glance at my scars and stayed away, Bay sat with me. When someone was staring at my leg and she cursed them out, I knew I'd be trying to keep her around for a while. All these years I've been waiting for her to wake up and be done with me, but the day never came.

She pulls in a deep breath, dragging me out of my thoughts. "The post-abortion depression is still depressing." She rests her head on my lap.

I pat her head. "Want a glass of wine? No baby means you can drink."

She stifles a laugh before it slowly fades. "Do you think I could've raised a baby?"

"Absolutely not." I tap her head again. "Didn't you just learn that newborns can't drink water?"

"*How* was I supposed to know that?"

I stifle a laugh as I smooth out her long dark hair. "Assuming you had the money to pay your rent yesterday, you now have less than two hundred dollars in your bank account. You still live with a roommate whom you have a very toxic relationship with and the man who got you pregnant didn't even give you money for the Plan B and then left you."

She looks up at me, her eyes torn, but I can see the understanding in them.

"Anything is possible so, yes, you could have raised that baby but at what cost? You know you're not mentally stable to raise a baby. And postpartum? Ugh." I shake my head at the thoughts. "Motherhood seems like a shit show."

"Maybe that's why your mom left you." She smiles up at me and my jaw drops before I break into a laugh.

"Too soon." I shove her off my lap and she laughs harder in return.

When our laughs sober, we both lean back on my couch before she speaks up. "Maybe a baby would've made me get my life together. Give me something to live for and shit."

I rest my head on her lap this time. "Key word being maybe."

She looks down at me.

"I think you're going to be an amazing mom one day, but what if you didn't get your life together?"

"I would've." She shakes her head at herself before a tear spills from her eyes.

Reaching up, I wipe her freckled cheek. I take hold of her hand before squeezing it. "Your hormones are all fucked up," I remind her. "You sat with your options and thought very hard about the choice you made. You can't change the choice you made, but you can change what you do now to make sure you're not in that position again. Our actions are only mistakes if we don't learn from them. Don't let the abortion be a mistake. Get your shit together so you can be a good mom."

She nods in return before wiping her cheek. "You give great advice when you're drunk."

I roll my eyes at her as I push her hand away. "I'm tipsy," I counter.

"And you've been tipsy since *last week* when you found out your bio mom was sober for half your childhood."

I pull in a deep breath as I sit up. A very small part of me is proud I've been able to avoid my family long enough for them not to notice, but I quickly feel like shit for making up lies and avoiding my brother.

"I just needed some time to sit in it." I turn to her now. "I'm done feeling like this. Why do you think I called you today and told you?"

She watches me carefully as I continue to convince her that I'm fine.

"I'm going to go to a meeting tomorrow and I'll be back on track."

She nods in return before my phone starts ringing. I lean over her, and when I see it's Jackson calling, I bring my phone to my ear.

"What do you want, Jackson Jones? I'm trying to plead my innocence here."

His deep laugh sounds through the other end and it surprisingly makes me feel a little better. "Nice hearing from you, too, Lissy," he replies and I roll my eyes at him.

"How many times am I going to tell you, only your kid can call me that?"

"I still don't get why the nickname is exclusive to her."

I don't answer but he goes on as if he wasn't expecting me to.

"Who are you pleading your innocence to? And please don't tell me it's a cop." He sounds exhausted and I can't help but laugh.

"It's not but don't worry. My mom is the DA, so I think I'll be okay."

He chuckles on the other end. "I'm just calling to let you know you don't have to come over for tutoring today. We're going out."

"What? What do you mean?"

"Is that an issue?" He sounds confused now.

"Yes, it's an issue. I need to get back to my routine or I'll fall off the deep end and I'm not having a good week. Do you want me to fall off the deep end? Do you want my cause of death to be *Jackson decided to cancel the highlight of Lisette's week?*"

He chuckles before going quiet, then: "Is tutoring really your only reason to get out of bed?"

"No," I partly lie.

"But it's the highlight of your week?"

"Yeah," I answer truthfully this time. His daughter is a handful but that just means she's a good distraction. I haven't been drinking on days I tutor her, besides today, but that's only because I was nervous about confessing to Bay.

I can't have my three-hour distraction cut from my day, especially not now.

Jackson hums in thought. "Well, I'm not canceling my afternoon with her so she can study with you. She'll see it as punishment and it's a tradition that we go apple picking, so just come with us and you can read with her for a bit when we get back."

I almost make a joke about them having a corny *tradition* until my brain catches up to where they're going. "Did you say apple picking?" I sit up.

"Yeah, I can pick you up in ten if you're free now."

"Yeah, I'll be ready." I rise from my seat before hanging up, *desperate* for an escape and a distraction because if I leave myself to think for more than five minutes, I'm going to want to drink.

"Woah." Bay looks between me and my phone. "Who got your mood changing so quickly?"

I roll my eyes at her before wiping my smile. "Not who. *What.*" My smile returns despite my efforts. "I'm going apple picking."

Bay shakes her head at me as she follows me into my room. "What is your deal with apples?"

"It's the tree," I clarify. "They symbolize many things, but—"

"The redemption and love sticks with you," she finishes for me. "Yeah, you talk about this all the time. I still don't get it. You're so spiritual for someone so depressed."

"Screw you." I let out a laugh as I walk into my closet for a change of clothes.

"Are you going with your brothers?"

"No. One of their friends."

"Hold up." Bay is leaning against my closet door now. "You're *fucking* your brother's friend and he's still breathing?"

I tilt my head back with a laugh as she watches me, her mouth ajar. "I am *not* sleeping with him."

She looks like she doesn't believe a word I'm spitting.

"Trust me, you'd know if I was sleeping with him because I wouldn't shut up about it. This man is a hot dad. You'll be the first to know when he's in my pants."

"He's a *dad*?" She lights up at my words. "Of course, you and your daddy issues want to sleep with him." She shakes her head as she squints her eyes at me.

I'm hysterical in my closet and I hear her laughing behind me. "I never said I want to sleep with him, I just said I'll tell you if I *do* sleep with him." While I'm constantly making flirty comments to Jackson, I don't mean any of them and he knows that. I just like getting a reaction out of him, and since I have daddy issues, I also like when he tells me to stop doing it. I like when he tells me what to do in general.

"You said *when* he's in your pants."

I pause, replaying my own words—and damn, she's right.

"I don't blame you. You say he's hot. He has an offspring. He's your brother's friend, which makes this whole thing dirty and forbidden. Ugh." She lets out a sigh as she fans herself. "I think I want to sleep with him. You should share."

I roll my eyes at her with a smile as I change my shirt. "He's so type A, he probably doesn't even do threesomes." I turn to her. "Now that I think about it, he's probably not good in bed. I can totally see him being all soft and kissing my scars and shit."

She rolls her eyes at me. "God forbid a man be kind to you in the bedroom and show affection." She turns more serious and I flip her off.

"Have you met the mom?"

"His or his offspring's?"

"The kid's," she clarifies.

"She isn't in the picture." I shrug my pants off before holding a different pair in front of me in the mirror. I tilt my head to the side and decide to try the shorts on.

"This is actually perfect. There'll be no baby mama drama. What are you waiting for?"

"Did you ignore the part where I said I *don't* want to sleep with him?"

"You don't want to, but you don't *not* want to." She sends me a knowing look.

I don't disagree because she's right. If the opportunity presents itself, I certainly won't turn it down. Jackson is hot, and I'm sure after a while he can get the job done.

"How many kids does he have?"

"Just one girl."

Bay smiles at my words. "A girl dad. It keeps getting better."

"What's so good about girl dads?"

"They're soft," she says as if she's stating the obvious. "He'll spoil the shit out of you."

"Well, he's rich as shit, so I'm sure he can afford to."

Bay shakes her head at me as she throws her hands up in defeat. "You are wasting so much potential right now, Lisette. I am demanding you give this man a chance."

"He has not said he wanted a chance with me." I break into a laugh as I grab my shoes and walk past her. "Back the hell off playing Cupid. I thought you of all people would suggest I steer clear of relationships in the state I'm in. Especially with a kid involved. We *just* decided motherhood was scary."

"No," she counters. "You and your mommy issues decided motherhood was scary." She follows after me and flops on my bed as I work my boots on.

"You're right, though," she continues when I don't reply. "This can go up in flames very quickly... the fire might feel good though." She says the last part more to herself.

"Yeah, when doesn't it feel good when it's a man who's good to you?" Relationships ending because the man is too good and you're not in a good mental space will *always* be worse than ending it because he treats you like shit.

It hurts so much more when they're perfect and you're the problem. You have no one to blame but yourself.

# Chapter Fifteen

## LISETTE

I 'M WALKING TO JACKSON'S CAR when I see Isabelle looking out her window. When her eyes meet mine, her entire face lights up as she starts wiggling in her seat.

"Lissy!"

I let out a laugh as I reach into the car to give her a high five. "What's up, kiddo?" I squeeze her fat cheeks and she giggles in her seat.

"Dad said we were coming to pick up a surprise person, but I'm so glad it's you."

I glance over at Jackson, but he's not paying us an ounce of attention as he aggressively types into his phone.

When I look back over at Isabelle, she holds up a bouquet of blue crocheted flowers and a smile touches my lips.

"Daddy said you were feeling sad again."

I take the bouquet from her, and she reaches over to grab something else. She holds out a box to me now, and I take it from her. When I open it, I realize it's fried Oreos.

"Did you make these?"

"Yup." She smiles proudly. "We had some leftover and I was going to give it to KC, but Daddy said we should save them for you."

"That was really nice of him, thank you." I glance over at Jackson just as he lets out a defeated sigh and turns his phone off. He turns to look at us and he's clearly annoyed with something, but his eyes soften as he looks at his daughter.

"I wanted to give her the flowers."

I look back over at Belle and she sticks her tongue out at him. "Too slow."

I hold back a laugh and Jackson sticks his tongue out at her in return. He looks over at me and nods for the passenger seat. "Come on."

I climb in and hold the flowers out to Jackson. "You look like you need them more."

He smiles down at me before putting the car in drive. "I'm fine."

I nod to myself as I put my seatbelt on and rest the bouquet on my lap. "Considering you told me you were fine when I didn't ask, makes me think otherwise. Don't tell me you caught my depression." I hold my heart in faux fear and Belle speaks up from behind us.

"Is depression *contagious*?"

I glance up at her in the mirror and she holds the front of her shirt over her nose.

I laugh to myself quietly as I decide to mess with her. "Yup, you have approximately five days left."

Her eyes widen, but before she can freak out, her dad steps in. "She's *kidding*. I wouldn't let her near us if she was contagious, penguin." He looks over at me and shakes his head. "Do you ever know when to stop?"

A soft laugh escapes me as I open the box of fried Oreos. "You have so many chances to mess with her and never do."

"I know how to pick my battles. We're trapped in this car with her for an hour, do you want to hear her cry about being contaminated with depression for an hour?"

"Fair enough." I nod to myself before taking a bite of the Oreo and they taste amazing.

Jackson's phone goes off again, and he glances down at it before rolling his eyes.

"Let me guess," I start, wiping the corner of my mouth of Oreos. "Girl problems?"

A smile grows on his face, but he doesn't answer me as he keeps his eyes on the road, so I go on.

"Is she not taking the hint?"

Jackson shakes his head at me, clearly biting back a laugh.

"I can totally act like a crazy girlfriend and call her if you want."

"Let's not." He shakes his head at me, a short laugh escaping him. When he turns to steal a glance at me, my jaw drops.

"Don't tell me you were being irresponsible and got her... *pregnant*," I whisper my last word. "You're not ready for a kid, Jackson Jones."

He bursts with a laugh and I can't help but laugh beside him.

"I'm afraid you're five years too late with this speech." He lets out a long breath before turning more serious. "It's not girl problems, but at this point, I wish it was. I would gladly deal with an accidental pregnancy than this kid, right now."

My brows raise at his bluntness. "Wow, what the hell did she do?"

His brows furrow, and when he glances between me and the road, realization crosses his face. "Wait no, I wasn't talking about Belle. I meant one of my clients, oh my god. That sounded so bad." He steals a glance at the mirror and I can't help but laugh at his face, but Isabelle is watching something on her tablet, not hearing a word from us.

"I love you, penguin." He sounds so sorry and I bite back a laugh.

When Isabelle doesn't reply, I turn to look at her and her jaw drops as something happens in the movie she's watching.

"I still can't believe Scar kills his *brother*." She shakes her head in disbelief before looking up at us and her brows pull together. "Did you say something?"

"Daddy said he loves you." I fill her in and she smiles before looking back at her screen.

"I love you both, too."

I look back over at Jackson and his cheeks have a light blush to them.

"What?" I ask when I notice him gripping the steering wheel.

"You need to stop calling me that." He keeps his voice low, and I feel my confusion grow before it hits me and I bite back a smile. "I'm being serious."

I hold back my laugh as I look forward. "Whatever you say, Da—"

"Lisette," he warns, and my laugh escapes me. "I will gladly leave you in the car while we go apple picking."

I turn to him, and he glances between me and the road, his expression completely serious.

"Not the kind of punishment I was hoping to receive from you, Daddy." I slowly run my hand down his arm before breaking into a laugh. "Okay, that one was a bit much," I admit, but when I focus on him, his jaw ticks before he shifts in his seat.

I glance down between his legs when he shifts again, and it's my turn to blush when I see him getting hard. I face forward and decide, for once, that I need to shut my mouth.

# Chapter Sixteen

## JACKSON

FOUR YEARS I'VE KNOWN LISETTE. In all that time, I barely interacted with her, we simply had nothing to talk about and no real reason to cross paths, but now she's in my car and I want to risk everything. I want to ruin Easter and the Tooth Fairy and every other special thing her brother is going to spoil for my kid in retaliation for touching her.

"Isabelle." I put the car in park before turning to her and desperately trying to get my mind off of the woman in the seat next to me. "When we get in there, please do not ask me for a pet pig. We're not getting one." I warn her before we even see them because two years ago, she threw a very big fit in front of everyone. I gave her the same warning last year and she was pretty good, but she was asking about the pigs before we left the house today.

She swings her feet back and forth as she smiles at me. "How about we *negotiate*?"

A smile grows on my face although I try to fight it.

"I think that's a great idea," Lisette starts and I silently curse myself. "How about Isabelle gets a pig and Daddy can get something he wants?" She turns to me, and when I see that smile, I know I'm in trouble.

"What do you want?" She keeps her voice low and it's as if all the air is sucked out of the car.

"Stop it," I warn her.

She holds my gaze before her eyes cut down to my lips. "Stop what?"

"Stop looking at me like that. *Stop*." I whisper my last word more sternly before forcing myself to look at my daughter. "It's either a pig or a candy apple."

"What?" Her brows shoot up to her hairline as she stares back at me. "That's a hard choice."

"This is us negotiating."

"No, it's not," Lisette cuts in. "This is an ultimatum. Don't trick her."

"Are you tricking me?" Isabelle raises one brow and I can't even take this seriously.

"You know what? I'm the boss and what I say goes. No pig." I climb out of the car before either of the girls can disagree.

I'm really starting to regret letting Lisette tag along and not because I suddenly want to kiss her, but because I'm afraid I'm going to have to deal with a tantrum over a damn farm animal before I leave this fair.

My windows are tinted, so I can't see the girls talking, but when I open Isabelle's door and see her innocent smile, it's clear they were discussing something.

"Are we ready?" I help her out of her car seat as she glances at Lisette and giggles.

"Yup." She climbs out of the car with my help and as I turn to get the door for Lisette, she opens it herself.

She smiles over at Belle before holding her hand out to her and the pair walk ahead of me. I take them in and you would've thought our outfits were planned with the way Lisette coincidentally matched our western boots and black shirts.

I pay for all of us when we get to the front and they hand us each a basket.

"We should pick apples last so we don't have to carry the heavy basket all day."

Lisette agrees and Isabelle pulls her hand to the table of people bobbing for apples.

"Lissy, you go and I'll record." Belle pulls my phone out of my pocket before turning the camera on.

Lisette looks between the people at the table and I give her a push. "Go ahead."

It's clear she doesn't want to but after pinning my kid against me, I'm giving her a hard time.

She rolls her eyes at me before flipping me off. I step in Isabelle's line of sight before she can see. I keep my eyes on her as she lines up with the two other people and the old man at the front explains the rules to them.

Everyone puts their hands behind their back when he tells them to, but, of course, Lisette keeps her hands on the table.

I shake my head as I take a step behind her and lean into her ear. "Cheater."

"Shut up."

I let out a low chuckle before glancing over at Belle. When I notice she's recording the cotton candy machine, I turn back to Lisette. Taking both her hands in one of mine, I hold them behind her back.

She glances over her shoulder at me, her eyes focused on my lips and there my heart goes again, speeding up.

"You didn't say anything in the car earlier." She leans back, pushing her ass to my dick. I suck in a breath of surprise, but neither of us move.

"What do you want?"

I look between her eyes as they trail down to my lips. "What do *you* want?"

A smirk grows on her face. "I asked first, JJ."

My breathing gets heavier as I become more aware of every inch of her pressed against me. My eyes cast down her frame, and with the way she's angled, I can see into her shirt. Her pink lacy bra changes the entire meaning of the color for me.

"Say it," she taunts.

Before I can admit I want her, someone blows a whistle and the two people beside us dunk their heads in the water.

I give Lisette a push and she follows suit, bobbing for the apples, but as she bends over, she pushes against me harder. A low grunt escapes me, but I don't move and she doesn't try hard *not* to rub against me.

One of the contestants finishes and when Lisette notices, she shakes her face of the water, a tired breath escaping her.

"You're not going to finish?" I almost call her a sore loser, but she leans her back to my front before looking up at me with those damn eyes.

"I'll finish another time."

My cock twitches at her words, and when she glances down, I know she felt it. I quickly unhand her and take a necessary step away. Just as I do, Isabelle tilts the camera to the red and orange trees above us before turning to us.

"Oh, did you win?"

"She gave up like a sore loser," I answer for Lisette, and when I turn to look at her, she's drying her face with a towel someone hands her.

My eyes follow the water dripping into the front of her button-up shirt and I swallow the dryness in my throat at the sight of a bit of cleavage showing. Her pink bra is on the front of my mind. She has the bottom of her button-up tied and my mind runs wild at the bit of skin showing.

*Fuck.*

I can *not* be thinking about half the things running through my mind regarding this girl. My eyes don't hear those thoughts as they scan down the rest of her frame. I take in the way her shorts hug her waist, but then my eyes land on her thighs and I notice the scars on both of them.

Her jokes about being depressed ring in my mind, but *that* clearly isn't a joke.

My eyes meet hers and she's already watching me, catching me staring.

"Sorry," I shake my head at myself, feeling like an asshole for being one of those people who stare at someone's scars.

"That was a horrible apology." She pouts and I know she's joking, but I also know she's just hiding behind her humor. "You should find a better way to say sorry." She gives me a once over but I don't entertain her flirty comment.

"If you ever need a reason to get out of bed, you always have one with us."

She meets my eyes, her smile slowly fading. I nod once, silently telling her I mean it.

She opens her mouth, but I stop her from making a joke. "Don't," is all I say before taking her hand and dragging Isabelle over to hold her. "Come on." I guide them forward and Lisette doesn't say anything as she walks ahead, holding hands with my daughter.

I watch them as Isabelle records the fair and occasionally me and Lisette. My phone starts ringing, but she ignores it as she takes a picture of the biggest apple tree on the field. When someone calls again, she lets her head fall to the sky with a sigh and answers, but I snatch the phone from her before her smartass can say something.

"Daddy, tell them you're not working." She rolls her eyes and instead of reprimanding her for the attitude, I try my hardest to be understanding. I told her I won't work today, but I've been getting calls all day and she knows it's work.

When I look down at my phone, I realize the last one was my mom, but I don't answer, knowing exactly why she's calling. "They won't call again." I put my phone on Do Not Disturb and hand it back to her.

"This girl just won't back off, huh?" Lisette teases.

I shake my head of my thoughts but decide to rant. "One of my clients is my living nightmare. He just got into a really bad fight and the other guy, who's my other client, is now in the hospital. He's making my life hell. His offers are being pulled from under him left and right, and if I don't clean his image and secure him on a team, I'm going to be losing a lot of money."

Lisette's brows raise but she understandably doesn't look all that interested. "I'm sure you won't go broke. Worst case scenario, sell your castle or one of your cars." She shrugs and a laugh escapes me.

"I know it doesn't seem like a big deal, but this is my job and—"

"Hey, I was kidding." She shrugs again, turning more serious. "He sounds like a pain, but I'm guessing you don't have him saved as *ma* in your phone." She gives me a knowing look and I feel my shoulders sag.

I glance down at Belle and decide this isn't a conversation she needs to be a part of. When we reach the tree house, I ask Belle if she wants to go play in it, which she does.

I keep a close eye on her, but when she's out of earshot, I turn to Lisette. "Rome was who I was texting in the car and he's been calling me all day, my mom is a whole other story."

She raises her brows. "Does everyone have mommy issues or is that what I attract?"

"I have a great relationship with my mom," I clarify. "The last few days, she's been bugging me about *Isabelle's* mom. She wants me to talk to Belle about her, but I don't want to and I know I'm being selfish, but it's hard for everyone. I feel like shit and I really don't want to talk about it."

I watch for Lisette's reaction, but she simply nods slowly as she thankfully changes the topic.

"I guess this week is just a feel like shit week for everyone."

I keep my gaze on her as she settles onto the bench beside us. "I did something really really stupid this week." She shakes her head at herself, her tone in complete despair.

I settle beside her before shoving her with my shoulder. "Do you want to talk about it or sit in silence?"

She glances over at me before looking over at the tree house in thought. "You know Sire and I are adopted, yeah?"

"Mhm." I hum in response as I lean back on the bench.

"My sister recently reached out to me, and every time she talks about our bio mom, I actually want to jump off of a roof, especially when she talks about how *good* she is. I didn't have that good mom she had, and I hate myself for being jealous, but I think I am. She just made me feel so unworthy of love and I hate her so much."

Her shoulders sag as if a weight was physically taken off of her.

When she looks over at me, all I can see is how broken she feels and I do the only thing I know how to make someone feel better. I hug her.

She goes still, but as I hold her tighter, her tensed shoulders slowly ease.

"I think you're very worthy of love."

She doesn't say anything as she pulls away. "Rome is the client you were telling Sire about, yeah?" She changes the topic and I let her.

"Yeah."

She nods in thought as she faces forward.

"To clean his image, why don't you make him do some sort of charity event or something with kids? It can be a long-going thing so the public doesn't think it's to cover up everything going on. People love kids."

"You love kids," I correct her and she takes a beat to look back at the tree house.

"I love your kid," she corrects me, and hearing her words does something to me because my one rule was to not get involved with the women in my daughter's life, but hearing she loves Belle makes me want to break that rule.

# Chapter Seventeen

## JACKSON

I OPEN MY DOOR FOR Rome and he has the nerve to look as pissed as I feel.

"Don't look at me like that," he grumbles as he rolls his eyes at me. He attempts to walk into my house, but before he can pass me, I grab him by the arm more harshly than needed.

"You're in my damn house, little boy. You'll respect me or you'll leave and find a new agent." I stare down at him and he watches me for a beat before silently nodding. I let go of his arm before walking into the house with him.

We're heading for my office when Isabelle hops down from the steps. "How about this one?" She poses as she shows me her third costume option, and I don't understand why my mother bought her every costume idea she's had the past two weeks.

I examine her Tinker Bell outfit. "I think this one is my favorite."

She looks down at herself before turning to Rome. "What do you think?"

He gives her a once over before turning to me and I raise my brows, silently telling him to agree with me so she can stop trying on all eight of her costumes. "I agree with your dad. This one looks very nice."

She hums in thought before turning to me. "Can you put my hair in a Tinker Bell bun so I can see if I really look like her?"

"I have to talk to Rome, but when I'm done I'll do your hair... again." I force a smile but when she smiles in return, I can't even be annoyed because she's too damn cute.

"I just had a better idea." She lights up. "How about I take all my costumes to Uncle Sigh's house and he can help us?"

"Okay." I take a step for my office but she speaks up again.

"But"—she puts a finger up—"Everyone needs to help, so can you make sure Uncle August and Sagey and Titi Hazel *and* Titi Vid *and* Lissy will be there?"

My smile widens at her excitement. "I'll call them and make sure they're all there."

She nods in return before taking off to change and I quickly escape into my office with Rome.

"She's taking Halloween very seriously." Rome raises his brows at me, amusement in his tone, but I'm too pissed at him to even crack a smile.

"You've been blowing up my phone for days, so now is your chance to explain to me why a video of you beating Chase to the brink of death is circling the internet."

He opens his mouth, but I yell before he can finish.

"Over a damn *girl*? I cannot have my clients pinning against each other. Tell me now if this is all a game to you because I won't try to save the last contract you have. *One*, Rome! That's all you have left because no one wants to fucking work with you anymore."

He shakes his head at me before his temper clearly rises. "You think this is just because of a girl?"

I pace the office. "Your coach told me—"

"Our coach is covering for him," he snaps. "If you answered my calls and had a bit more faith in me, you'd know he was forcing himself on her."

I go still before I turn to him.

"Our coach didn't add that part, did he?"

I let out a defeated breath before running my hands down my face.

"We were at a party," he starts. "And I know you told me not to go to any more parties after videos of me acting like a drunk fool were circling last time. Spare me on that speech."

I settle in my seat as he explains.

"The minute I noticed your *precious* client was there, I was saying my peace and about to leave, but when I went into the living room I saw him in the corner with a girl on his lap."

He paces as he continues.

"Now *yes*, I was already mad because I was sleeping with her first, so Coach had that part right, but he had his arm wrapped around her extremely tight and she looked uncomfortable, so I went over and I heard her tell him *countless times* to let her get up, and what did he do?"

He doesn't let me answer.

"He ignored her and kept trying to kiss her. She kept saying stop, and when he put his hand up her skirt, I lost it." He throws his hands up in defeat. "I grew up with five sisters and if it was any of them on his lap, I would want someone to stand up for them. I wasn't going to just stand there or leave. If that cost me my future, then so be it, but you have a baby girl and I thought you'd understand. If you want to defend a *rapist*, then I'm fine with getting a new agent."

He storms off, but I stop him before he can leave.

"Wait." I lean back in my seat as I pinch the bridge of my nose. "In no way am I defending him."

Rome turns on his heels before focusing on me. "I can't believe you preferred him over me." He crosses his arms now.

"That was before this information came to light," I defend myself but his face drops.

"You *really* liked him more than me?"

I let out a scoff. "Kid," I deadpan. "You are my only client who makes my job hard. I like everyone better than you."

"Even Chase the sexual assaulter?"

"Please do not call him that."

"Why?" he pushes. "Because it'll make it harder for you to clean his image?"

"Because it'll be harder for me to clean *your* image. As of five seconds ago, he's no longer my client."

His arms drop as he focuses on me.

I rub my forehead as I weigh my options. "I need you to make a video addressing this. I'll give you a loose script to follow, but you need to focus more on how the situation made you feel and shine light on the girl needing help rather than painting Chase as the villain." I put a hand up when he opens his mouth.

"I know he's the bad guy here, but the media is going to pick apart your statement. You can't spend five minutes talking about how he's an asshole. You need to take accountability and defend yourself. This isn't about him," I tell him more sternly.

"I'll give a statement to our PR team announcing we're dropping Chase from Athletic Prime and why. I'll make sure they highlight you and maybe we can get some of your offers back."

His shoulders slouch as he settles in the seat in front of me. "Is your boss really going to let you drop him that easily?"

"Without a doubt." I sink into my seat. "The company is run by women and there's a zero-tolerance policy for these kinds of things."

Rome nods in thought.

"Who is this girl?"

His eyes meet mine. "Her name's Izzie. We've been messing around for a few weeks, but it's nothing serious. I met her in my chem class." He shrugs and the fact that her name is so close to my daughter's hits a nerve.

"Is she okay?"

He nods in return. "Shaken up but she's fine. I think me nearly killing Chase scared her more than he did, but she's still talking to me, so I guess that's a good sign."

There's a knock on my door before Isabelle walks in wearing a new costume. "Can we make my hair black for this costume?"

I open my mouth but quickly shut it when I realize she cut her damn hair.

# Chapter Eighteen

## JACKSON

"Alright, penguin." I tuck my wallet into my back pocket as I hand the bag to Isabelle. "Are we missing anything else?" She peeks into the shopping bag as I guide her towards the exit. "Candles, pumpkin carving kit, trick-or-treating bags." She nods at my bag. "And the pumpkins. I think that's everything."

"Okie dokie. Did you pick a movie or is it my turn tonight?" I take a hold of her hand as I walk across the parking lot.

"You can pick." She shrugs before kissing my hand and my heart melts.

"My sweet girl." I lift her into my arms, blowing a raspberry in her neck. She laughs up a storm as I reach the car.

"We should invite Lissy to our date night." She lights up as I slip her into her car seat.

I smile at how obsessed she is with Lisette. Recently, everything she does she wants to do with her.

"It's not a tutoring day, princess." I strap her into her seat.

"Do we only get to see her on tutoring days?"

I pause as I realize she's right. "Touché." I shrug. I almost make up another excuse, but she looks so damn excited and like always, I cave. "I'll call her."

"Perfect." She takes the pumpkins from me before hugging them and I kiss her fat cheeks.

Shutting the door, I let out a defeated breath. I haven't seen Lisette since apple picking when she shamelessly rubbed her ass on me before saying she *loves* my kid.

I'm never *not* in control of my feelings. I always have a plan for things, and I certainly never break the rules, but Lisette and all of her damn laughs are knocking me off my axis.

When I climb into the front seat, Belle is quick to make me call Lisette before driving off. I'd be a liar if I said I didn't also want to see her and spend all night carving pumpkins while listening to her jokes. I do. Desperately so, I just don't like not being in control and Lisette... she makes me *want* to lose control.

I realized at apple picking that being around her is so refreshing. For a long time my world has been so chaotic. My OCD makes it feel that way, and being a dad before all else sure doesn't leave room to take in the small things outside of my daughter's life. I didn't mind that until I realized the small things I wasn't noticing; Lisette reminds me of them.

Her beauty is the kind that makes you do a double take when you're walking down a busy road. Her inappropriate comments are the kind that are worth getting in trouble for. And her smile stops the chaos.

*I'm fucked.*

I squeeze my eyes shut, pressing my palm against my forehead as I realize just how fucked I am and just how badly her brother is going to kick my ass.

"Daddy?" Belle pulls me out of my thoughts. "You okay?"

"Yeah, I'm calling right now, penguin." I shake my head of my thoughts and pull out my phone. I hit her name before I can think twice about it.

After a few rings, she answers. "What's up, JJ?"

I smile at her nickname for me. "Hey, what are you doing?"

"Oh, you know..." she drawls. "Thinking about how hot blondes are."

I roll my eyes at her, but a light blush heats my face. "You're very full of yourself."

"Ugh, I know right? Want to fill me with something else?"

I open my mouth but nothing comes out as the tips of my ears heat. On the other end, she barks up a laugh.

"Dirty, dirty mind you have. I meant *food*. I'm starving."

"Right." I clear my throat. "Listen, Belle and I do these date nights every week. Today we're carving pumpkins and watching Halloween movies. We wanted to know if you're free to join? I'm picking up pizza." I tap my steering wheel as I wait for her answer.

"You do daddy-daughter date nights every week?" It sounds like she's smiling on the other end.

I shrug as I sink into my seat. "Yeah, I'm raising a girl in a world filled with bare minimum boys. I want her to have high standards and be unimpressed by little boys who believe in splitting bills."

She takes a beat to respond and I find myself tapping my steering wheel again.

"That's... so damn sweet. I'm free tonight, but I don't want to bother by intruding?"

I roll my eyes at her. "We're *inviting* you. Don't be silly, you could never bother us. Should we pick you up?" I put my seat belt on before starting the car.

"I'll meet you at your place."

We end on that and as soon as I hang up, Isabelle speaks up from behind me. "Is she coming?"

"Yes, ma'am."

"Yes!" She fist bumps the air and I can't help but laugh.

I'M ADDING A FEW MORE spider webs in the kitchen as Isabelle inspects my every move.

"Here you go." She holds a bowl of plastic spiders to me. "Add some right there." She gestures to the cabinet above me.

"Baby, you know Halloween is in five days, yeah?" I really don't see the point in adding more decorations when the month is nearly over, but she's a little crazy over holidays, so I don't voice my thoughts.

"I know, we're *so* behind." She shakes her head at me. "These spiders should've been up October *first*." She rolls her eyes. "I can't believe you forgot them." She holds the bowl closer to me when I don't take the creepy things.

I didn't forget them, I hid them because I hate spiders. All my life I've been able to avoid hanging them up, but earlier this month, she snuck them into the shopping cart and swiped it when I wasn't looking at self checkout.

She looks like she's waiting, but I'm saved by the bell when someone knocks. I literally jump off of the counter. "I'll get it." I move around her and the bowl of nasty insects.

When I open the door, Lisette smiles up at me. "No suit and tie?" She gives my jeans and T-shirt a once over before nodding in approval.

"No oversized hoodie?" I glance down at her cropped top and plaid pajama pants.

"Well, I was under the impression that this was a date. These are my best pants." She rolls her eyes playfully and I bite back a laugh. "Or does daddy-daughter dates plus me no longer make it a date?" She walks in before turning to me.

I close the door instead of answering her, giving myself time to figure out if she's really flirting or joking. "It's still a date." I turn on my heels and take her hand. "I appreciate the pants." Slowly, I bring it to my mouth and when I kiss her, she breaks into a laugh before pulling away.

"Well, now I have to burn my hand." She rubs my kiss away on her shirt.

I watch her with a smile as she walks further into the house.

"Is that Lissy?" Isabelle calls out before her head pops out from the kitchen.

"The one and only." Lisette calls back. "What's up, kiddo?"

"I *love* your shirt." Belle walks over and hugs her side. "We're putting up decorations." She tries to hand the bowl of spiders to me again, but I don't take them.

When I hear Lisette giggle, my eyes pull away from the fake bugs and up to her.

"Are you afraid of spiders?" she teases.

I narrow my eyes at her. "I'm a grown man." I roll my eyes at her. "The only thing I'm scared of is harm coming to my child and torture interrogations... and raw food. And hospitals, but—"

I don't get to finish my sentence as Lisette plucks a spider from the bowl and flings it at me.

"Stop!" I take a few steps back in a hurry, pulling my shirt over my head to get it off of me. In front of me, both girls are literally crying from how hard they laugh. "Very *funny*." I roll my eyes at the pair.

"Fine." I kick the plastic spider further away. "I don't like spiders. Stop bullying me."

Isabelle smiles up at me as she slowly walks closer while holding the bowl out.

"I mean it." I step away. "Please respect my boundaries. Making me uncomfortable isn't funny."

Immediately, Isabelle pulls away from me. "Oh, I didn't know you were actually scared. Sorry, Daddy. We don't have to put the spiders up. They're kind of ugly anyway," she reassures me as she walks back to the kitchen.

Lisette smiles as she watches her walk off. "You are doing such a damn good job at raising her." She shakes her head before looking back at me.

"Thank you." I smile proudly.

She nods in return, her eyes falling on my bare chest. Slowly, a pink blush meets her cheeks and I bite back a smile in return. "You should keep your shirt off. Pumpkin carving is messy."

My smile widens. "You think so?"

"Mhm." She hums, her eyes meeting mine.

Before I can tease her, Isabelle walks back out. "How are we feeling, people?" She smiles up at us. "I don't want to see any sleepy heads. We have a long night ahead of us." She treks into the living room like she's on a mission.

"You mean we have two hours ahead of us since your bedtime is eight o'clock and you have school tomorrow," I correct her as we follow close behind.

She gives me a knowing look that I return.

"Let's *negotiate*." She smiles and I'm so proud of her vocabulary constantly expanding but I wish I didn't teach her that one. "Eight thirty," she starts.

"Eight." I smile down at her.

"Ten?" She tilts her head to the side.

I break into a laugh. "That's a big jump. How about eight fifteen?"

She pretends to think. "Nine fifteen. Final offer." She holds her hand out to me and it's cute that she thinks she has the final say.

"Eight thirty. My final offer on the condition that you're in the shower by eight." I hold my hand out and her smile returns.

"Deal." She holds her hand out but pulls away before I can take it. "On the condition that I get to have two more pieces of chocolate cake." She keeps her face stone cold, but I see she's holding back a laugh.

I give her a knowing look, silently reminding her that she already had two pieces. "Half a slice." I take her hand.

"Deal." She shakes my hand firmly, her smile on full display. "I already showered and I had *three* cupcakes at school," she reminds me and I shake my head at how well she just played me. She's going to have a sugar rush, but I only hope she crashes quickly.

She giggles to herself proudly as she sits in front of one of the pumpkins.

"You're raising the future POTUS," Lisette whispers from beside me and I stifle a laugh.

"You said you were hungry, yeah?"

She nods in return and I walk over to the pizza and serve her.

We settle on the couch and as she eats, I draw the face I'm going to carve out on mine and Isabelle's pumpkin. Beside me, Lisette watches a Halloween cartoon with Isabelle who's stuffing her face in cake.

When something happens on the screen, Isabelle holds her belly as she laughs. A smile touches my lips and I watch Lisette as she looks down at my daughter, a bright smile on her face.

She leans over, kissing her cheek before wiping her mouth clean. "Pretty girl." She kisses the top of her head and I watch in awe as she watches my kid.

We remain like that until Isabelle finishes her cake and I'm snapped out of my thoughts as both girls turn to me.

"Ready to carve?" Belle askes before chugging her water like she's been lost in a desert all day.

"Yeah, let's start." I cut the bottom of Belle's pumpkin first. When I set it in front of her, she starts carving out the insides with a spoon, dumping all of the waste in the bag between us.

"How'd you get such a clean cut?" Lisette voices from beside me. When I turn to her, I let out a laugh at how she's holding the knife like an axe murder.

"Okay, have you heard of the word *gentle*?"

She rolls her eyes at me, not sparing a glance my way as she stabs the pumpkin.

I jump in my seat before sliding closer to her. "You're going to cut off a limb. Let me help you."

She pulls the pumpkin away from me. "I can cut a vegetable on my own."

"Fruit."

"What?" She turns to me.

"Pumpkins have seeds. Technically it's a fruit."

She rolls her eyes. "If it's not sweet, it's not a fruit."

My brows furrow now and she immediately looks like she wants to take that back. "So... there's these things called pineapple—"

"The last thirty seconds didn't happen. I have a college degree." She waves me off.

I quickly put my hands up in defense. "What do I know? I'm just a man and you're a smart, independent woman with a college degree. It probably is a vegetable." I smile over at her.

Her eyes narrow further before she grabs the knife. She tries to pull it out of the pumpkin but struggles and a snort escapes me. Her brows rise now before she swipes the knife I have in front of me.

"Are you being smart?" She holds the knife out to me.

I bite back a smile. "Never." I shake my head.

"Carve the vegetable for me and speak when you're spoken to."

"Yes, ma'am." I hold my hand out and she places her stabbed pumpkin in my lap. I pull out the knife with ease and bite back my laugh when I see her roll her eyes.

In silence, and with her pointing a knife at me, I carve the bottom of the pumpkin. When I'm done, I grab a spoon and turn to her.

"Here you go, reina."

Her eyes narrow again as she slowly takes the pumpkin. "Belle, what'd he just say? Is he calling me bad names in Spanish?" She keeps her eyes on me.

"No silly, reina is queen," Isabelle voices from behind me, immersed in her pumpkin. I smile at how perfectly she rolls her R's.

I keep my eyes on Lisette and I don't miss the small smile on her face before she *shoos* me.

"Thanks, I guess." Her smile is on full display now. "This is a competition in case you didn't pick up on that."

"What do I get if I win?" The words fly out of my mouth before I can think of a more appropriate response, my eyes scanning down her frame.

When I look up at her, her eyes are already on mine. "If you ask nicely and behave, you can have whatever you want."

I let out a low laugh before shaking my head at her. Her brother sneaks his way into my head and the guilt seeps into my pores when I see her smile.

As if she read my mind, she simply nods before looking down at her pumpkin again. "This feels familiar," she teases. "Are you going to voice what you want?"

"Nope." I face forward, focusing on my pumpkin.

THE NEXT HOUR AND A half consist of the three of us carving our pumpkins while I steal glances at Lisette. She pretends not to notice and smiles to herself. In return, when I'm not looking, her eyes find their way to my biceps and the rest of my shirtless frame.

Stepping outside, we set our pumpkins on the doorstep, the electronic candles under them.

"Okay, let's see." Belle jumps off of the steps and stands a few feet away to get a better look. We follow after her and I shake my head at the overachiever Lisette is.

While Belle and I have a standard face carved out of our pumpkins, Lisette managed to perfectly capture Ghost Face and it's not just his iconic mask, but he's holding a knife too. With the way she carved it, she managed to add shadows and it looks incredibly realistic.

"You're really talented." I nod to myself. "You paint and stuff, too, right?" I glance down at Lisette, remembering some canvases in her apartment the first time I went over.

"Yeah, it's the only thing I'm good at." She shrugs as if her talent is no big deal.

"That's not true." I bump her arm gently. "I'm sure you're great at a lot of things. For starters, you know the difference between fruits and vegetables."

She breaks into a laugh before shoving me. She uses a lot more force than I was expecting, forcing me to step away from her.

"I should get going." She smiles at me before kneeling to hug Isabelle. "Good night, princess. Thank you for letting me crash." She kisses her cheek and Belle immediately wraps her arms around her neck.

"You weren't crashing. We wanted you here." She kisses her nose and Lisette's entire face softens as if she desperately needed to hear that.

She musters up a smile as she rises to her feet. Glancing down at her phone, her brows raise. "It's only seven thirty." She pinches Belle's cheek. "Hurry, you have just enough time to start a new movie."

Isabelle lets out a gasp before running into the house quicker than I've ever seen her run, leaving us laughing behind her.

When Lisette looks back over at me, I find myself not wanting to say goodbye. "So," I tuck my hands into my front pockets. "What are you doing tomorrow?"

Being that tomorrow also isn't a tutoring day, I won't be seeing her until Friday, which is a bit disappointing.

She rolls her eyes as she thinks of something. "I was *supposed* to go to a pottery thing with my friend, but she canceled."

"We can go with you." I shrug.

She shakes her head. "It's in the morning. Belle will be in school."

I nod in return. "Oh... well then I can go with you."

Her brows furrow now. "Don't you have that fancy job that requires you to wear a suit at home?"

I bite back a smile. "I'm off tomorrow." I'm most certainly *not*. "What time were you supposed to go?"

"Eleven."

"Perfect." I have a meeting at eleven then two more right after. Eleven is indeed not perfect. "I can pick you up after I drop Isabelle off at school if you're up early enough? We can get breakfast then head over."

Her eyes slowly narrow as she watches me. "Are you asking me out on a *date*?"

I swallow the sudden nerves at her offended tone. "Is that against the law?"

"My brother sure does think so."

Right... her brother who I'm best friends with and certainly should not do this to since it goes against every bro code.

"Well, it's not a date." I shrug again. "You stay over for dinner all the time and we just went apple picking the other day," I point out. "We're just hanging out on my day off."

She doesn't look like she believes me as a smirk grows on her face. Slowly, she takes a step towards me. Tilting her head up to look at me, she cocks her head to the side, her ponytail swaying from side to side.

"If you admit you want me, then we can hang out tomorrow. As a *non* date."

I bite down and when her smirk appears, I know she notices my jaw ticking. "Fine." I take a step towards her. Slowly, I run my hand down her ponytail, slightly tugging so her eyes are on mine rather than my lips.

"I want you," I admit. "But I can't have you just yet, so this needs to remain rated G until I talk to your brother."

Excitement seems to flash through her eyes. "Let's negotiate." She trails a finger down my chest and my breath gets caught in my throat at the contact. "Rated X."

"Uh uh." A low chuckle escapes me. "G."

Her finger trails lower. "Rated R?"

"G." I say more sternly, my jaw clenching at the feeling of her nail trailing dangerously lower.

She keeps her eyes on mine as her finger lands right above my belt. "PG-13." She smiles up at me now, her eyes squinting. "Final offer with no conditions from both parties."

I should probably do some research as to what exactly PG-13 consists of, but considering I only let Isabelle watch *some*, I shouldn't be agreeing. "Deal."

# Chapter Nineteen

## LISETTE

"H ELLO?" HARMONY WHISPERS ON THE other end of the call. I take in her surroundings and I think she's in her school bathroom. "Is everything okay?" Her eyes scan my face and surroundings.

"Yeah, sorry to call while you're at school. I forgot they don't let you use your phone." I roll my eyes at the stupid charter school Ana put her in. "Where do you think I was going based on how I look?"

I lean my phone against the bathroom mirror and take a step back so she can see me. I watch her carefully as her eyes scan my frame. Slowly, a smile appears on her face.

"You look so cute when you actually try to. Why do you always wear baggy clothes?" Her eyes cast lower. "Your legs look so good in those. Wait, turn around, I don't think I've seen you in tight pants. I need to know if we have big butt genes because this *can't* be my adult body." She glances down at herself.

I shake my head at her as I angle myself to check out my ass in my new jeans. "We have big butt genes. Eat more and stop following Ana's new vegan diet. You hate it and I don't know why you listen to everything she says." I roll my eyes at her as I get back to the point.

"I don't want to look like I tried to dress up." I tug at my tight long sleeve. It's cropped since all of my tight shirts show my belly and I know I look good, but I don't want to look like I *tried*.

I woke up today in a really good mood which I'm trying to take advantage of. I had enough energy to wash my hair *and* style it. I wore something cute and did some light makeup in case my mood shifted throughout the day. Look good, feel good, and all that mojo.

Then I remembered Jackson, and I are hanging out today and I'll be damned if I let a man think I got cute for him.

When he called me last night, I was in the middle of drowning my loneliness in a painting. As desperate as it sounds, hearing both he and Isabelle *wanted* to hang out with me made my whole night.

I don't like inviting myself places—the fear of being unwanted or bothering is too great. Everyday I hold my breath when I call my friends or family, afraid they're going to wake up and decide they don't want to deal with me.

Then Jackson called me and all night he made me feel... important. He didn't necessarily do anything, but him wanting me around made me feel like my presence mattered. Like I *don't* take up too much space. Like I'm *not* too loud and annoying.

When men make me feel that way, it's usually when I'm naked, and while I always tease Jackson about taking it there, he doesn't look at me like a piece of ass. He doesn't want me around for that, which I'm still trying to wrap my head around.

I'm aware that I can get that reaction out of him. That much was obvious at apple picking, but... he smiles when he sees me in my two day old baggy clothes. He laughs when I make sexual jokes rather than attempting to take me up on my empty offer.

I take pride in surrounding myself with people who make me feel good. It took a long time for me to recognize bad influences and will myself to stay away. No matter how badly the addict in me wanted them around; simply so I can have someone to blame my fuck ups on.

Jackson is a part of those people I surround myself with who make me feel good. He makes me think he'll miss me if I disappeared off the face of the planet tomorrow.

"Well." Harmony snaps me out of my thoughts. "I can spot a no makeup-makeup look from a mile away. If you didn't dress like you don't care about your health every day, I wouldn't notice how much you tried."

I bark up a laugh as I flip her off. She laughs in return before my phone goes off with a message. Grabbing my phone, I notice it's from Jackson.

**JJ**

> Good morning. I just dropped Isabelle off, are we still set for breakfast?

"Who are you smiling at?" Harmony teases and I quickly wipe my smile. The second I do, she lets out a gasp. "Do you have a date with *Jackson*?" She gasps again.

"It's not a date."

As if she heard me say the opposite, she literally squeals. She starts shooting a ton of questions at me but I ignore her as I reply to him.

> Hey, yeah breakfast is still a go on one condition.

> *sighs*

> LMAO

> Fine, I'll just cancel.

> I'm joking! What are your conditions?

> Breakfast in bed, preferably yours.

I bite back another smile as his text bubbles appear then disappear. This happens a few more times before a picture comes through. It's clearly a definition, and when I tap on it, I realize he Googled what PG-13 consists of.

> Breakfast in bed can happen on the condition that our clothes remain on. I don't make the rules.

> That'll make for a boring movie.

> With you as the star? Doubt it.

This time, I can't hide my smile if I try.

"Hello!" Harmony loudly reminds me of her presence.

"Go to class. Senior year is important." I hang up on her before sending one more text to Jackson.

> True, you'd bore the crowd though so let's save breakfast in bed for when we make this rated R. I'll see you when you get here, hot stuff.

He doesn't reply, but with the sudden energy to clean, I decide to pick up my room, starting with the pile of cups and water bottles.

I finish my room fairly quickly and get halfway through with the living room when someone knocks on my door. Not expecting anyone, my brows pull together as I set the trash bag down and head for the door.

"Hey." Jackson stares back at me, a bouquet of blue crocheted flowers in his hands.

I give him a once over and shake my head at how good he looks in casual clothes. Don't get me wrong, he's hot in everything, but now he's in a black sweatsuit and this is my favorite look.

"You're so beautiful." He sounds out of breath and my defense response is an eye roll.

"I'm going out later today," I lie, refusing to let him think this was for him when really, I'm just having a good day. "You didn't need to get me flowers. We agreed this wasn't a date."

My eyes meet his and he simply smiles down at me before shrugging.

"I made it clear that I wanted you last night. We're keeping it casual until I speak to your brother, but until then, I'm going to show you a glimpse of what you're in for."

I bite my cheek so hard, I can taste the copper in my mouth. "Flowers in a color I hate are what I'm in for?"

He stifles a laugh now. "I'm not ever going to win with you, huh?"

I shrug as I grab my keys from beside my door. "Why would I *ever* make anything easy for the male species?"

JACKSON OPENS THE DINER DOOR for me before I can reach it and I shake my head at him. He just paid for our breakfast and while I'm not considering this a real date, he's earning all of the brownie points in my book.

He steps beside me before looking down at his watch, and I can see the diamonds in it glisten against the sun. "We have two more hours before we have to head to the pottery shop. Is there anything in particular you want to do?"

"Do I have a budget?" I smile over at him teasingly.

"Not at all. What do you want?" He doesn't even hesitate and I realize he thinks I'm being serious.

"I'm not letting you buy me—" I cut myself off as my eyes land on his wrist and I remember he's rich. My smile widens as I fully turn to him. "Can we make a trip to Apple?"

Thirty minutes later, we're at the mall. The people at the front greet us and I smile in return as my feet take me to the iPad section.

"So." I grab the one I want as I turn to Jackson. "Look at how pretty and huge this one is." I let him see the back before explaining all of the digital art I want to try on an app the iPads come with.

When I finish my rant, he's still standing like he's listening in great detail. "You didn't have to convince me, I was getting it either way."

"Oh, I know."

His smile grows as I look down at the device.

"I just have no one to talk to about my art. I think I want to start going out and drawing in public. Like at cute parks and stuff, soak in the sun or what not. This will just make that easier." I shrug, knowing I probably won't have the energy for that on most days, but it's about setting intentions, so I let myself believe my words.

"Well, I like hearing you talk about things you enjoy, so you can always tell me all about it."

My eyes meet his and he watches me for a beat before nodding behind me.

"So we should get the pen thing, too, right?" He goes in search of them and I follow behind him with a smile.

"If you insist." I shrug. As we pass the new AirPods Max, I stall in my steps. Closing the distance between myself and the table, I grab a pair and when I press the noise cancelling button, the busy room goes silent. My jaw drops.

I play a song on the phone that's connected to it and my jaw drops further. One of the employees in front of me laughs at my reaction. Pulling them off, my hearing comes back. "These are pretty cool," I admit with a laugh as I set them back down.

"Is there anything I can help you with?" She nods at the head-phones.

"Yes." Jackson steps up beside me. "Can we get the new iPad and the pen?"

She asks us which one specifically and Jackson tells her we'll take the newest version of both.

"Would you like to add WiFi and cellular data to the iPad?" The employee looks up from her tablet. "You'll be able to make calls without having your phone near you."

I glance over at Jackson and he nods. "Yeah, can you also add the two year Apple care to both?"

She types into her iPad and after I put in my information, she asks if we want anything else. Before I can say no, Jackson speaks up.

"Can I also get the headphones and a case for everything?"

I almost tease him into also getting the cool headphones for me, but the iPad is what I came for, so I don't push it.

After he sorts through the colors and also requests two new chargers, she gets the products for us.

"Alright, your total is $4,159.03."

My brows slightly raise, but when I turn to Jackson he simply hands her a black card without blinking.

"You two have a good day." She hands me the bag and we thank her before bidding her goodbye.

"Thanks, sugar daddy." I smile up at Jackson as we walk out.

He lets out a low laugh as he shakes his head at me. "Anytime, sugar baby."

I bite back my smile as I look back down at the bag, my eyes landing on the headphones. "I'm totally going to be borrowing these whenever I'm at your house." I take them out of the bag to admire them through the box.

"What do you mean?" He lets out a low chuckle. "They're yours. The chargers too. I didn't need anything."

"What?" My eyes snap up to his.

"Why would I need *headphones*? I wouldn't be able to hear Isabelle burning my house down." He laughs again, but I can't shake my shock. "She'll actually just steal them from me, so please don't let her use them. The minute she realizes she likes them, she'll want them, and she doesn't need those."

I gaze up at him, a smile I can't shake on my face. "The iPad and pen are appreciated, but you did *not* need to get me anything else."

He looks down at me before shrugging. "Want to return them?" He stops in his tracks, throwing his thumb over his shoulder.

"Hell no." I shove them back into the safety of my bag and he laughs from beside me. "They're all appreciated. I owe you some sugar later tonight."

He laughs up a storm as I quicken my steps to get my own door.

I LET OUT A FRUSTRATED sigh when my pot plummets. My shoulders sag as I brush the hair from my face, but I go still as I feel the wet clay on my forehead.

At the sound of Jackson's giggling, I slowly turn to him. I keep my glare set on him before my eyes cast down to his perfect vase.

"Why are you so good at this?" I'm supposed to be the artistic one here and I'm failing miserably, which feels like a huge hit to my pride.

Jackson only shrugs, as if he's not even trying. "I took a pottery class in college."

I let out a scoff. "Yeah, like a hundred years ago."

His jaw drops before he splashes some clay water at me.

Glancing back at my blob of clay, I take a minute to appreciate us being alone and I'm only failing in his presence. Bay was supposed to be here with me and we booked the couple session since it was longer than the group one, but Jackson isn't the worst pottery companion. He'd be the best if he wasn't kicking my ass at this.

"You're so cute when you mope," Jackson voices with a laugh before rising from his seat.

"Screw you."

"Mhm." He doesn't entertain my jab as he drags his stool behind mine. "Here, we can do it together." He brings his chest to my back and I unconsciously melt against him, soaking in his warmth and manly scent.

He brings his arms around mine before dipping my sponge in water, soaking the clay. "You just need to have patience." He keeps his face so close to the side of mine, his beard prickles my cheek. When I take in a breath, I can smell his aftershave and I almost tease him about cleaning up for this *date*, but he speaks up first.

"Here." He guides my hands to the clay. "Step on the peddle."

I give it a light push and the wheel under our hands begins to spin. His hands engulf mine entirely as he helps me shape the clay. I feel my heart pounding in my chest as he dips our fingers into the center, creating a hole in the clay.

This should *not* be as intimate as it is and I'm not sure if it's just my mind finding ways to make everything sexual, but his veiny hands look hotter now as they're dripping in wet clay.

"What shape do you want?" His warm breath touches my ear and I try to reply but my voice doesn't come out strong enough so I simply shrug in return. "Flower pot or vase?"

I shrug again, and this time, his deep chuckle sends shivers down my spine.

"Are you actually upset about struggling with this?" He presses closer against me before I feel his face in my neck. I suck in a breath of surprise as he places one soft kiss on my neck.

Turning my head, our faces are incredibly close, our noses practically touching. My heart rate quickens and my eyes cast down to his lips just as he licks them.

"I'm not upset," I find myself saying.

"No?"

I shake my head in response, my eyes on his mouth. A smirk tugs at the corners of his lips before he leans forward. I do the same but before our lips can meet, he kisses my cheek.

"PG-13, sweetheart." He faces forward again and I use the rest of my strength to get my heart rate under control.

# *Chapter Twenty*

## LISETTE

WHEN I NOTICE SAGE'S BOYFRIEND sulking in the corner, I walk over to him with a bright smile. After shoving Liam's shoulder, he slowly looks over at me.

"Yes?"

My smile widens at his monotone voice. "Do you not like your costume?" I glance down at his outfit and he does the same before rolling his eyes.

I stifle a laugh when he lets out a sigh.

"Sage likes it."

"Do *you* like it?"

He looks over at me again. "I just told you Sage likes it."

I tilt my head to the side as I study him. "So you like it because she does?"

He doesn't answer.

"Is there anything you *wouldn't* do for her?"

His brows furrow as if he can't understand me. "Why would I not do any and everything she wants?"

I don't get to tell him that's absurd as my sister walks over, a bright smile on her face. "You look so cute." She fixes his shirt and a smile grows on his face as he looks between her eyes.

"Beautiful," he mumbles as he watches her like she's the only thing he can see and it physically hurts my heart to watch.

I glance over to the couch and August is on top of Hazel. He whispers something in her ear that makes her smile before she buries her face in his neck. Across from them, Vidia sits on Sire's lap as he helps her apply her lip gloss, his eyes drowning in awe.

I'm surrounded by couples and if I wasn't so lonely, it wouldn't feel incredibly suffocating. Jackson suddenly pops into my mind, the perfect day we spent together and how much I miss being so close to him hits me like a truck.

"Okay, so are y'all going to have an orgy or are we going out?" I look around the room and we all look too good to sit here any longer.

"Sire can't make up his mind," Hazel says as she looks over at my brother.

"Hazel can't mind her business," Sire counters.

The room breaks into a laugh and Hazel opens her mouth to voice a harsh reply, but August distracts her with a kiss.

I turn to Vidia for an answer but she shrugs. "The line for the haunted house is going to be ridiculous if we don't leave soon."

I turn to August next and he also shrugs. "I want to go to the party, but you're adamant about this haunted house, so I guess we can go there."

Sage remains quiet and I give her a knowing look. "It won't be that scary, Sage, come on."

She looks around the room before shaking her head. "It wouldn't be named the scariest haunted house if it isn't *that* scary. I don't want them touching me. They like to separate groups." She takes Liam's hand and to no one's surprise, he agrees with her.

The room goes back and forth *again* when the door rings. I let them debate as I walk off, and when I open the door, Jackson stares back at me.

He smiles down at me before his eyes drop down to my outfit and I feel a smirk creep onto my face as he stares at the cut on the top of my dress, perfectly tugging my boobs.

"My brothers are here," I whisper and his eyes dart up to mine before he glares down at me.

"Where are you going like that?"

"You look so pretty," Isabelle greets me before I can reply. She pulls my leg in for a hug and I pat her back.

"I think Daddy agrees." I smile up at him but his glare doesn't falter.

"What are you even supposed to be?"

"Diane, Sin of Envy." I raise a hand as I flaunt my short orange dress. Taking a step back I gesture to the living room. "August is into anime and wanted us all to be the Seven Deadly Sins. Sage got one of her designer friends to make our outfits and they are incredibly on point."

He walks in after his kid skips into the living room and she heads straight for my brothers.

I turn to Jackson as I shut the door and his eyes are on my chest again. "Are you going to tell me how hot I look or are you going to keep staring at my titties?" I keep my voice low as I watch him carefully.

We haven't seen each other since the non-date and as he watches me like a starved man, the butterflies from having his arms around him are back like they never left.

His eyes meet mine and I bite back a smile when I notice his jaw clenching. He glances into the living room and I follow his line of sight to Sire who's distracted with Isa.

Jackson shifts his body so he's standing directly in front of me with his back to my brothers. "You look hot," he whispers and I open my mouth to tease him, but nothing comes out.

I go still when he takes a step forward. My breath hitches as he reaches for my top. He grazes my boobs every so slightly and holds eye contact as he puts his fingers in the front of my dress before pulling my top up. "Where are you going in this?"

I cock my head to the side. "Is your room an option?"

His eyes narrow as he pulls my top higher. He doesn't say a word as he walks off and I bite back a smile as I pull my dress down again before following him into the living room.

"So you don't have time for me anymore?" Isabelle glares up at Sire. "I thought we were best friends?"

"We are." He scoops her into his arms before kissing her cheek. "I can go trick or treating with you for a little while, but August wants me to go out with him too."

I realize his predicament when I remember he told her they'd spend the night together.

"If you want to hang out with him, then *fine*." Isabelle pushes him away as she crawls out of his lap.

"Don't be like that, princess."

She whips her head around, her curls swinging in Sire's face. "Lissy will come with us." She marches over to me. "Right, Lissy?" She looks up at me with those big gray eyes and I'm about to agree simply because she's so damn cute, but my jaw drops.

"When did you cut your hair?" I kneel down before turning her around to examine her curls that were once down to her butt and now only a few inches past her shoulders. She's had her hair up the last few times I've seen her, but now I notice it's dramatically shorter.

I look up at Jackson for an answer and when he rolls his eyes, I stifle a laugh as I realize she did this without his knowing.

"I swear I stepped into my office for *five* minutes and she chopped half of it off. I tried saving it, but that's the longest I could go without it looking botched." He shakes his head at her and I break into a laugh before kissing her precious head.

"I'll go trick or treating with you, but no more playing with scissors, my sweet girl."

"Deal!" She turns around before throwing her arms around my neck. I let out a laugh as I rise while carrying her.

August quickly sits up in his seat. "But the group will be incomplete."

I roll my eyes at his genuine worry. "I'm sure you all will be recognized with two sins missing. Sire will join you all later." I look over at Isabelle before kissing her nose.

"Am I your favorite now?" I glance over at my brother with a teasing smile.

"Yup, I don't even know who Uncle Sigh is anymore." She rolls her eyes as she turns away from him.

His jaw drops and I break into a laugh as I walk backward with her while waving goodbye.

When we reach the door I whisper in her ear. "Say, so long fuckers."

She stifles a laugh as she turns to the living room. "So long fuckers!" She flips them off and her dad's jaw drops before I take off running with her and I can hear all of my siblings laughing behind us.

We're both a laughing mess, but when I see Jackson marching towards us, our laughs quickly sober. Beside him, my brother and his girlfriend are hiding their smiles.

Jackson steps in front of us, his dad glare on. "I'm not going to say anything to both of you because I know that won't happen again, right?"

Behind him, my brother watches us with his brows raised, a teasing smile on his face.

Isabelle nods quietly and a shiver runs down my back at how *hot* he sounds when he's being commanding.

"Get in the elevator." He nods to the side when the door opens and in silence we all step in. When the door shuts, I grab my phone.

> Aren't you going to call me a good girl for getting in without a fuss?

I steal a glance at Jackson. He pulls out his phone and I don't miss the way his jaw ticks. Peeking over at Sire, he isn't paying us an ounce of attention.

> Will I get punished if I make her curse again?

> If you want me to punish you there's other ways you can accomplish that.

> Noted.

He shakes his head at me, but I can see him biting back a smile.

## Jackson

WE'RE AN HOUR INTO TRICK or treating and I still can't get used to Lisette's little dress. Every single time I look over at her, it's as if I'm seeing her for the first time. Her words from before are like a song stuck in my head and I can barely string together a thought that doesn't consist of her wearing that in my room. Her brother following after us is only adding shame to every thought I have of her.

"Oh, isn't this so cute?" An elderly woman smiles at my fire-fighter costume before she focuses on Isabelle's flame dress.

"I'm perfect, right?" Belle spins for her and I shake my head at her huge personality.

"You are," the woman agrees. "Your costume deserves a double scoop of candy." She digs into her bucket before giving Isabelle more candy than needed.

We bid her goodbye and when I turn, I expect to find Lisette behind us, but she isn't. My eyes scan the front yard and at the other house, I spot her short orange dress standing in front of a guy wearing a sheet that barely covers him.

He looks around Lisette's age, and when she laughs at something he says, I roll my eyes at the pair. I catch him shamelessly gaping at her boobs and swallow my annoyance. I know I sound like a hypocrite since I've been stealing glances at her all night, but this kid is... he's not me.

"I feel like we're walking too slow," Belle complains before grabbing her uncle's hand. "Chop chop." She takes off marching and Vidia follows close behind them with a laugh.

"I need to grab something from the car. I'll catch up with you guys," I call out and they nod in return before they turn the corner. Spinning on my heels, I walk over to Lisette.

"Okay, I need a hint." She laughs as she gives his body a once over. "Sexy mummy?" She tilts her head to the side as she guesses his costume.

He smirks down at her. "You think I'm sexy?"

I roll my eyes at how pathetic he sounds.

"I think sexy is what you were going for," she teases and he holds his heart as if she wounded him.

Before either of them can say anything else, I step beside Lisette. "What did Daddy say about talking to strangers, sweetie?"

The guy in front of us takes a step back, his eyes wide as he examines Lisette again.

Lisette lets out a scoff as she turns to him. "I'm a grown woman. That sounded really bad, but he is *not* my dad."

He visibly relaxes as I smile down at her.

"No, but she *does* call me Daddy."

Her jaw drops now, and when I face forward, he takes off without a word.

Beside me, she slaps my forearm. "That was so unnecessary."

"Did I lie?"

"I thought I was the one wearing the sin of envy costume."

I let out a scoff. "You thought that was jealousy?"

"Well, it surely wasn't affable."

I ignore her.

After a few seconds of me glaring at her, she stands in front of me with her arms crossed. "If that wasn't jealousy, then you won't mind if I leave early to go with him? He invited me to a party."

I don't say anything and she shakes her head before turning, but as she takes a step, I wrap my arm around her waist and drag her back to my front.

"You don't even know him." I glare down at her. "He could be an axe murderer."

She keeps her back against me as she tilts her head back to look up at me. "Maybe I have a knife kink." She shrugs and I'm about to respond before my eyes trail down to her outfit.

I feel my jaw clench as I let her go to shrug my jacket off. "Put this on." I hold it out to her, but she takes a step back.

Her eyes fall on my bare chest before she shakes her head. "Kiss me."

"What?" I scan her face but she only smiles.

"You've been giving me that look all night."

"What look?" My brows furrow.

"That I *want to kiss you*, look." She crosses her arms again and as her boobs are pushed together, all of my blood rushes south. "You were also fighting a boner in the car and that's the second time your body has had that reaction to me. Not to mention, you look hot in suspenders, so cut the PG-13 stuff. Kiss me."

I watch her for a beat but she's being serious. I shove my jacket closer to her. "Put it on."

"Kiss me and I'll cover up my perfect tits."

"You're Sire's little sister," I remind myself.

"I'm Sire's little sister who you said was hot, boobs you stared at, got jealous over, and got a hard-on to." Her smile widens. "My ass also felt all that junk in your pants, but you draw the line at our lips touching? It's just a kiss, JJ."

She takes a step closer. "Are you scared you'll like it?"

"I just want to talk to Sire first. It's the decent thing to do." I hurry past her.

"Well, when do you plan on talking to him?" She steps beside me.

"We should catch up with Belle and your brother." I change the topic, desperately needing a buffer between me and this woman.

"Hiding behind your daughter? *Coward*," she whispers.

"Shut up," I bite out before trying to move around her, but she steps in my way.

"I won't say another word if you kiss me, but if you don't, I'll have no choice but to believe you *weren't* jealous because you no longer want me and I'll talk back to every guy who looks at my titties because I won't be covering them and—"

I wrap a hand behind her neck before my lips come down on hers. She doesn't miss a beat as she melts against me, her hands wrapping around my neck.

Everything in me feels at ease as I slide my tongue against hers. I take a step closer, needing more and she backs away until she's pressed against the car behind her.

A whimper escapes me as my other hand trails down her side and it's as if my entire body ignites. I slip a hand in her hair, pulling at it and she moans in return before biting my lip.

She trails a hand down my chest and just as I grind against her, a car alarm goes off, pulling us apart. I'm practically gasping for air as she brings a hand up to her lips, as if she were checking that they were still there.

"What are the chances we could do that again?" she asks breathlessly.

Reality hits me and I take a step back before turning on my heels and grabbing my jacket from the ground. I hold it out to her and she simply shrugs it on without a word.

"Good girl."

Her entire face is beet red and I bite back a laugh as we catch up to her brother.

# Chapter Twenty-One

## LISETTE

"I HAD SEX WITH KALEB."

I go still before looking at Harmony in the mirror, and she's looking at me as if she wasn't supposed to tell me that.

"It was so bad." She buries her face in her hands before quickly looking up at me. "I mean at first it was good," she clarifies. "Like when we had our clothes on, it was *really* good. Then we were naked and it was still good when he was touching me, but then he put it in and it was just awkward, and it hurt and it was just *bad*."

I shake my head at her as I turn back to her hair.

"Aren't you going to say you told me so?"

I steal a glance at her and she looks like she's holding her breath.

"Did you use a condom?"

She nods slowly.

"Good." I return to combing her hair. "It will get better when you're with a guy you like instead of the first boy who calls you pretty when you're sad." I give her a knowing look and her guilty eyes cut to the side.

"Ana and I got into a fight and I invited him over. But he's my boyfriend now."

I don't answer, although she doesn't really give me time to.

"Ana overheard me telling my friend you were teaching me how to drive and she was being such a *bitch*." Her eyes quickly cut to mine, but when I don't comment on her language, she continues. "She said really mean things about you and I think she was more mad that I defended you."

My eyes trail to hers now. "What'd she say?"

Her eyes cut to the side again. "Is this Sage? I wish I could model like her." She changes the topic as she focuses on the Polaroid I have on my mirror of Sage on the runway.

"What did she say about me?" I push harder.

She lets out a defeated breath as her eyes meet mine. "The same stuff... you're a drunk and I shouldn't be in a car with you. You're not family to us." She shakes her head. "Nothing that's true."

I nod in return as I gesture to the picture of my sister.

"Yeah, that's Sage." I smile to myself as I focus on the good in my life. "Her boyfriend is so damn obsessed with her. I love them together."

Harmony takes the picture off of my mirror to get a better look. "She's so pretty."

"Right?" I lean over her shoulder to look at Sage. "She deserves the world."

A smile touches Harmony's face as she steals a glance at me. "You sound so proud of her."

"I am." I stifle a laugh as I turn back to the mirror to finish my hair. "Success came naturally to my brothers. I mean, *sure*, Sire had a shitty start, but the second he met August and picked up a baseball, his life started falling into place."

I shake my head at my thoughts. "Sage doesn't talk about how she fought tooth and nail to make it in the industry. I was up with her most nights as she cried about how hard it was, especially being a black girl. There were countless castings I had to literally drag her to. She has come *such* a long way. I feel like it was just yesterday that August and I were teasing her for sucking her thumb in her sleep at *ten* years old. She's older than me, but she's still my baby sister in my head." I laugh at the memories but falter when Harmony's smile fades.

I realize my mistake, but she only musters up a smile as she picks up the other picture I have on my mirror, this one of all of my siblings and me at the twins' birthday.

"You're happy with them." She tells me rather than asking. "Can you be honest with me?" She looks over at me.

"I won't start lying to you now," I tease but she remains serious.

"This is your life and this is your sister." She picks up the picture. "If I'm not what you want, I can go and take my Ana drama with me."

I roll my eyes at her as I take the pictures from her. "If I didn't want you around me, you wouldn't be here." I stick the picture back onto my mirror.

A small smile touches her lips, but she doesn't look convinced. I shake my head at her as I open the drawer in front of us. She looks down and a genuine smile touches her lips as she picks up a picture of us eating ice cream a few weeks ago.

The next picture she grabs is of her driving for the first time in my car. She stifles a laugh as she grabs a picture of her sleeping with Piglet on her forehead.

"You're my life too." I pick up an older picture and she lets out a gasp as she grabs it.

"Is this us?" She pouts as she focuses on younger me holding her as a baby.

"I never forgot about you, Harmony, and if I knew you were back at that house after your mom got clean, then I would've gone back for you. I didn't see you after this day because your grandma took you and I had no clue where she lived."

She keeps her eyes on the picture. "Why did you print all of these?" She looks back at the drawer and shuffles through more pictures of her and my other siblings.

"I like to keep my reason close."

"Reason for what?"

"To stay sober."

Tears build in her eyes before she pulls me in for a hug.

"Don't ruin your makeup after I just spent an hour on it." I shake my head at her and she lets out a laugh as she pulls away to fan her eyes. She looks back in the mirror with a smile as I continue working on her hair.

"Jackson kissed me," I voice when the brief silence starts to feel too heavy.

Her brows furrow before a smile touches her lips. "I *knew* he liked you."

"It wasn't just *any* kiss." I shake my head at myself as images of his hands on me come in flashes. "It was a fuck me against the hood of this car, kind of kiss. Like, please keep kissing me, I'd rather this than air."

"Oh." She nods as she smiles at me in the mirror but she looks worried. "I didn't know kissing was that good?" She looks down in thought now. "Am I kissing wrong?"

"Kissing him is that good," I say more to myself.

"Am I a bad kisser?" Her brows furrow as she looks at herself in the mirror. "What am I doing wrong?" she nearly whispers.

"But that was a few days ago and he's ignoring me." I shake my head at my reflection, more disappointed by how annoyed I am by this.

She lets out a gasp as she looks up at me. "What an asshole."

I roll my eyes at myself. "Okay, he's not *ignoring* me, but I was supposed to go over yesterday for tutoring and he canceled at the last minute via *text*."

"Well, what'd he say?"

I recite the message from memory since I've been picking it apart for the last twenty-four hours. "Canceling tutoring today. My mom wanted to see your favorite student. Sorry for the short notice."

Her face scrunches. "Sorry for the *short notice*?" she mocks. "Is this a fucking email? Ew, why is he being so formal?"

"Formal is bad, right?"

"Uh, yeah." She shakes her head at me. "You're going over today, right?"

I nod in return as I finish up her hair.

"Okay well, wear a cute outfit and act like nothing happened. Don't even bring up the kiss or the text. Just walk in, say hi to him if you normally do, and go straight for the kid."

I hum in thought, and I probably shouldn't take advice from a seventeen-year-old, but I go into my closet and change my baggy clothes into something cuter.

After I get her stamp of approval, I drop her off at her friend's birthday party before heading over to Jackson's.

When he opens the door for me, I smile up at him like I normally do. I'm about to voice a flirty hello but decide against it.

"What's up?" I walk past him and he nods in return as he lets the door shut.

"My mom is going to drop Belle off in a few, but we should talk." He walks into the kitchen and I follow after him.

"Don't tell me you're ending things." I hold my heart. "I told my mom about us."

A smile grows on his face as he shakes his head at me. "About Halloween," he starts, but he doesn't add more.

I raise my brows, gesturing for more.

"That can't happen again."

I nod in understanding as I lean against the counter in front of him. "I understand. Trick or treating can be very detrimental. I'll find a different hot firefighter to go with next year."

He gives me a knowing look, but I don't make this easier for him.

"The kiss," he forces out. "No more of it... If I kiss you again, I don't know if I can stop."

I bite back a smile. "Who says we have to stop?"

He gives me a slow once over before letting out a frustrated breath. "I'm hanging out with Sire on Tuesday. I'm going to tell him, then this can continue."

I nod before pushing off of the counter.

"I mean it," he says when I take a step away.

"You sound very convincing." I'm about to walk off when he takes hold of my hand, turning me back to him.

His eyes scan my face before he pushes off the counter, but he doesn't make another move. "Your brother and I are very close friends."

"Best friends some might say." With his hand still holding mine, I rub my thumb along his.

He nods as his eyes trail down my frame again. "And my daughter likes you."

"She actually told me she loves me," I correct him before cocking my head to the side and he watches my ponytail swing from side to side before his throat bobs.

"Right." He nods to himself. "So if this goes south, I'll be ruining multiple relationships."

"You're that big of a heartbreaker, huh?"

He shakes his head as he takes a step towards me. "No, but I don't bring women around my kid. I know you already knew her, but we've been too risky around her."

I nod in understanding, that part making more sense. "So no more kissing."

"For now."

I nod and his eyes follow the small movement. His breath grows heavier as he watches me and I can see the fight in his eyes. I feel my heart rate pick up and my entire body heats as his eyes slowly focus on every inch of me.

"You don't normally wear this to tutoring." He closes the distance between us, bringing us inches apart, his fingers threading through mine.

"I don't." My eyes land on his lips now as he licks them. "But I like it when your eyes are on me like that."

He smirks as he trails his eyes back up to my face. "You didn't have to wear those shorts to get my eyes on you." He steps between my legs, forcing me to walk backward. "That pretty face gets my attention on its own."

I smile up at him as my back hits the counter. "You think I'm pretty?"

His arms come beside me on the counter as he cages me in. "You already knew that, baby."

My stomach does that *thing* as his eyes focus on my thighs. "It's called a praise kink, JJ. Humor me."

He looks between my eyes before leaning down. Rather than kissing me, he rubs his nose along mine. "You always look pretty, and right about now, you'll look very pretty on your knees, but that can't happen, so I need you to walk away for me." He squeezes his eyes shut. "Right now."

My chest rises and falls quicker as his lips brush against mine feather soft.

"*Please* walk away, Lissy."

"What if I don't want to?" I whisper, my lips grazing his. "What if I get on my knees instead?"

"Halloween won't be happening again until Tuesday," he replies, his eyes burning into mine.

"I know that." I rub my nose against his. "No more kisses until you talk to him... on Tuesday."

"Right." His eyes fall to my lips before he shakes his head. "But *fuck*, I want more." His lips crash into mine as I pull him in by his shirt.

My knees practically go weak as he brings his hands to my waist. Without much effort, he lifts me onto the counter and I wrap my legs around him, pulling him closer. My stomach is doing cartwheels as his hands snake up the sides of my shirt.

I'm moaning into his mouth, begging for more with my tongue as I grind against him shamelessly.

He pulls away and leaves a trail of kisses on my throat before he buries his face in my neck. A suck in a breath when he kisses and sucks just where I like it. I run my hand through his hair before guiding his hand to my pants, but he stops, leaving me breathless.

He keeps his face in my neck, his hands on either side of me as he catches his breath.

"Why'd you stop?" I rub his head and he brings his hand to mine as he rests his forehead against mine.

"Because I'm going to come in my fucking pants if you keep making that sound."

I feel my face heat and he kisses my neck twice. He's sucking on my neck again, but when the doorbell rings, he pulls away quicker than light.

I hop off the counter, escaping into the bathroom to avoid meeting his mom. By the time I come out, she's gone and our kiss is the only thing I can think about as I work with his daughter.

# Chapter Twenty-Two

## LISETTE

"WHAT ARE YOU SMILING AT?" I snatch Sire's phone, but I only get to read two words of a sexy text attached to a very pretty picture of his girlfriend before he grabs his phone back.

"Ugh, I love her." I shake my head at him. "You're lucky I'm straight or I would've taken her."

He lets out a scoff as he leans on his elbows. "You couldn't handle her attitude if I gave you a play-by-play script." He looks up at the sky as I lay my head on his chest.

We watch the dark sky in silence before I voice the reason I came out here with him. "I had a glass of wine a few weeks ago."

He tries to sit up, but I push him back down as I keep my eyes on the night sky.

"It wasn't one glass... it was a bottle of wine I drank throughout that week because I had just found out Harmony's mom was sober nearly her *entire* childhood." I shake my head when that feeling settles in my chest again.

"I'm a month sober today." I lift the coin I got in this morning's meeting. I focus on it before sitting up and throwing it across the field with every ounce of strength in me.

I pull my knees to my chest as I bury my face in my arms.

"Go get your chip, Lis." He shoves my arm gently.

"I don't want it." I shake my head at myself. "I woke up feeling like absolute *shit* and being one month sober means nothing. It doesn't matter when I wake up chasing a high I can't fucking have."

I swallow the lump in my throat as I look up at the sky.

"Harmony got a different version of her, but this"—he shoves me again and I look down at my phone—"This is our mom."

I nod in agreement as I focus on a picture I have tucked in my phone case of us with Kat. We're about nine, but she carries me on her hip like I weigh nothing as Sire climbs her back.

"This is who raised us. She's the woman who taught us that love was *safe*. Our surrogates brought us into this world so Kat could find us. Don't give them an ounce of credit more. They're not worth feeling like shit over."

I wipe my tears as I face forward again. "I want to get high *every time* I think about her."

"Yeah." He sits up as he pulls in a deep breath. "I used to feel like that too."

I turn to him now. "Used to? What changed?" I asked, desperate for a cure for this pain in my chest.

"It was something Vidia said," he starts. "She said I was dealt a shitty hand, but I still came out on top in spades. I started remembering that whenever I thought about her, and eventually, the feeling went away because in the end, she put me through hell but I won."

I look forward again before hugging my knees. "This doesn't feel like a win." I rest my chin on my arm before Sire leans his head against me.

"It will soon."

I try to believe him. Believing him is all I have, so I force myself to believe that eventually I won't feel like this.

"I'm so tired of these highs and lows." I bury my face in my arms, feeling physically exhausted. "I can't have more than two weeks of happiness before it's taken away."

"Focus on the things that make you happy and when you feel like this you can turn to them."

I know he's trying to help and it's good advice, but I feel so hopeless that nothing sounds worth it.

"I don't want to do this anymore," I whisper, afraid of my own words.

His entire face drops and I shut my eyes, not having it in me to face him.

"Please don't look at me like that."

"You can't even see me," he mumbles.

My eyes meet his now. "Like that... like I'm selfish for wanting to give up." I look between his eyes carefully. "I'm trying. I swear

I am, but on days like this, I don't want to try. I don't think I have much fight left in me."

He shakes his head, and I can see it in his eyes that my words physically hurt him. "You're not selfish. I'm selfish for wanting you to stay when you're suffering, but I need you, Lis."

I squeeze my eyes shut so my tears don't fall again. "I don't want to…" Sniffling quietly, I lift my head. "I need you to promise me you'll be okay without me. Don't relapse like an idiot."

"What?" He pulls away, his eyes scanning my face frantically. "I won't be okay."

"Sire—"

"Lisette, please, okay? I *swear* it's going to get better. I don't know when, but I'm not promising shit. I can't let you kill yourself; I won't make it." His voice breaks, and I bite my tongue to conceal my cry.

We sit in silence for a few minutes before I start plucking the grass mindlessly.

"Remember how you told me to walk around with that bottle of vodka?"

"Don't beat yourself up for drinking it, Lis." His voice is vacant of all emotion. "It helped when it was supposed to. That exercise works better for me, but now you know your limits. You can blame that one on me if you want."

"I'm in control of my sobriety." Digging my hand in my pocket, I take out the bottle of pills. "That exercise was actually helping, but this doesn't feel the same."

I feel Sire go still as he watches our kryptonite. We don't say anything for a while. We simply stare at the pills of oxycodone I've been carrying all day, not a single word being spoken.

I feel like it's burning a hole through my palm, but I'm too scared of what will happen if I move, so I don't.

"What are you thinking about?" he whispers.

I chew on my lip nervously, trying to think of what he wants to hear.

"The truth." He gently shoves my arm.

"I want one." I keep my eyes on the bottle, the despair eating at me.

Beside me, Sire is so still; I'm sure he's holding his breath. "So what are you going to do?"

I recognize the sponsor talk from a mile away, but it's not what I want to hear right now. I'm sure it's what I need, but I want the bad influence. I want someone to indulge me. Someone I can blame all of my faults on, so I can hate them rather than myself.

"We both know what choice you need to make, Lis. Walk over to that trash can and throw them away. *Right now.*"

I rise to my feet at the urgency in his voice, dragging myself to the trash. Snapping the cap off, the soft light from the lamppost above me illuminates the five pills. I close my eyes as I imagine myself picking one up and placing it on my tongue.

The rush of adrenaline I'll feel as my mouth salivates just before I swallow it. I'll lay right here on the grass as I wait for the high to come and numb me. I'll let it drift me where it pleases. The warm sun will wake me and I'll *still* feel good. I won't wake up the way I did this morning.

When the high wears off and the guilt begins to eat at me, I'll swallow the rest of them and go out as peacefully as I know. It'll be painless. Easy even, and I won't feel the way I do now. I'll be free.

Opening my eyes, I look back down at the pills and wait for the guilt to come. That voice telling me why this is bad, but it doesn't and it scares me, so bad I drop the pills.

Taking a step back, my eyes land on one that landed on the ground. I stare at it for a beat, willing myself to step on it, to pick it up and put it in the trash, or simply walk the hell away, but I can't.

Leaning over, I pluck it off the ground and pretend to throw it away before burying my hands in my pocket and squeezing it in my palm.

Sire keeps his eyes on me as I make my way back to him, a smile on his face. "You're stronger than you think."

*No, I'm really not.*

I settle in the grass beside him, but when he looks up in a hurry I turn to him. He's still looking up at the sky, and when I glance up, my eyes land on an airplane. A smile grows on my face as I turn to him.

"I call it," I voice before he can but by the smile on his face, I know he let me have it.

When we learned about shooting stars and making wishes on them, we would fight for every star we thought we saw in the sky. Being that the city had so much light pollution, we couldn't see shit, but our mom told us we could pretend airplanes were shooting stars. Every single plane we saw at night, one of us would call it before making a wish.

It probably sounds silly, but when he wished on a plane to be adopted and then got his wish, we never stopped believing in it.

I close my eyes as I tilt my head up to the plane. I *wish for a reason to fight.*

I keep my eyes shut as the plane gets quieter with distance.

When my phone vibrates, I slightly jump out of my thoughts. Pulling it out of my pocket, my eyes land on a text from Jackson. I stifle a laugh at the picture of Isabelle. Her shirt is tied with something, making it look like a crop top; her hair in a loose knot on the top of her head. She makes a kissy face in the mirror and behind her, Jackson rolls his eyes.

Suddenly, the knot in my throat is gone as I read over his messages.

**JJ**

> She said she wants to be like you. I'll be starting a petition for you to only wear hoodies when you're near her. She forgets she's five and not twenty five.

> She did not say she wants to be like me.

His text bubbles disappear and after a minute, a video pops up. He keeps the camera pointed at Isa who's still admiring her reflection.

"Remind me why are you wearing that?" Jackson asks from the couch behind her.

Isabelle fixes her bun. "I'm changing my style, so we need to go shopping." She tucks her shirt further, showing more of her belly and I can hear Jackson's faint sigh.

"Who inspired this new style?"

She smiles brighter in the mirror as she tucks her hands in her baggy pants. "Uh, Lissy." She voices as if it were no brainer. "She's so cool. I want to be like her with her cool big clothes and tattoos."

"Oh, are those drawings on your arm tattoos?" Her dad sounds worried and I stifle a laugh as I notice the maker all up her left arm.

"They're cool, huh?" She flexes her arm and Jackson mumbles a "Jesus Christ."

The video ends and I can't wipe the smile from my face.

"Was that Isa?" Sire asks. "She's so damn perfect."

"Right?" I shake my head as I type out a response.

> Stop itttt, she is SO cuteee! I'm going to buy her a few crop tops.

> Lisette… please. I thought I had ten more years before this stage. Stop.

I quietly break into another laugh, the weight in my chest slowly easing.

"What are *you* smiling at? What else did he send?" He tries to snatch my phone but I'm quicker than he is.

Holding it to my chest, I bite back a smile. "Your friend is sending me nudes."

He rolls his eyes before he leans on his elbow. "If he likes his dick, he better not be," he grumbles.

As I watch him, I slowly realize he's serious about Jackson needing to stay away from me.

"What if he and I were a thing?" I voice out of curiosity.

He lets out a scoff. "What if he and I fought for even thinking about it?"

I keep my smile in place, not giving him a reason to believe I'm being serious. I know this is just him being an older brother, but I keep my lips sealed before I can tell him just how badly I want his best friend.

Sire looks between my eyes carefully and I think he can see all of my thoughts until he looks away. "He's a good guy, great even, but we're best friends. It's code; you don't do your friend's sister. It's fucked up."

I nod in return. Laying on my stomach next to him, I rest my head on my arm as I look over at him. I keep my eyes on him for a beat, mindlessly watching him as he watches the sky.

"I never tell you how much you mean to me, but you really are the most important person in my life," I whisper, reminding myself to tell him more often.

A small smile touches his lips as he gazes down at me. "Come here." He opens his arm to me and I let him hold me. "Everyday you wake up and fight is another day I'm proud of you. Even on the days you rot in bed, I'm still proud."

My nose starts to burn as all of the feelings come to the surface, but I keep the tears at bay as I bury my face in his chest.

"You matter, Lis," he whispers against my hair. "So much."

I nod in return, not trusting my voice.

After a beat he says, "Movie at my place tonight?"

I almost tell him I'm too tired for a movie and I'll fall asleep on his couch; then I realize he knows that. "Yeah..." is all I say, appreciating the subtle approach he takes to keep an eye on me. I would've denied, but his company is more comforting than the feelings that'll come when I'm home alone.

I don't know how long I stay in his arms, but after a while, I feel a drop of water land on my head. I look up at Sire, but his eyes are on the sky. In an instant, it begins to pour down on us.

I break into a laugh as he shakes his head disappointedly.

"Come on." He tries to stand, but I pull him back down.

"No, let's wait." I watch the sky as my hoodie gets heavy with the rain. A smile touches my lips as I feel it soak into my shirt. "You know, I read somewhere that rain in the desert is a sign of blessings that'll come after hardship."

I glance over at him and he gives me a bored look.

"We're not in the fucking desert." He pushes his wet hair off of his forehead.

I break into a laugh as he stands to his feet.

"I love how much you love all the spiritual signs from the universe. I hope you accept this as a sign that it's going to get better, but let's accept it from my dry car." He starts walking away, but rather than following him to warmer shelter, I lay on my back, soaking in the comfort the cold brings.

# Chapter Twenty-Three

## LISETTE

S TEPPING OUT OF SIRE'S BATHROOM, I dry my face with a towel as I walk into his living room.

I stop in my tracks as my eyes land on the couch where Vidia straddles Sire. My eyes widen as she deepens the kiss and I'm surprised they're fully dressed with the way her tongue is all over him.

"You two just can't *wait* for me to leave, huh?" I tease. I'm glad I slept here last night, not trusting myself to face my mind alone. However, now I'm starting to think I'll be overstaying my welcome if I spend the rest of the day here.

Vidia attempts to climb off of my brother, but he keeps his arms around her tightly.

"We don't want you to leave," Sire calls out before looking behind the couch at me.

"Well, I'm certainly not joining."

They both break into a loud laugh as I set my towel on a chair.

Vidia is still smiling at me while fixing her smudged lipstick. "He doesn't know how to keep his hands off of me. It's concerning."

Sire's head snaps back to her. "Me?" He starts tickling her and I can't help but smile at the sound of her laugh. Flipping her, he pins her onto her back before climbing over her.

"You two are gross." I shake my head at the couple, but secretly, I'm obsessed with them and so glad they are happy.

Glancing at the clock in the kitchen, my mood plummets when I notice the time. I still have two hours before I need to go tutor Isabelle.

I glance back at the couch where Sire and Vidia whisper to each other and laugh quietly. Vidia is on her lunch break and I start to feel bad for interrupting their alone time, so I collect my things.

I'm nearing the door when they call out to me.

"Hey, I meant what I said," my brother calls. "Stay."

"You're good," I reassure him. "I need to go tutor Isa soon." I muster up a smile, desperately not wanting to be alone for the next two hours. If my pride wasn't such a bitch, I'd tell him that.

"Isa is off from school today," Sire says with a laugh before pushing Vidia's hand away from inside his shirt. "Jackson and I were going to head to the park with her. She wants to play with Athena and he wanted to talk to me. He said he texted you?"

I pull my phone out of my pocket and notice a missed call from him. Opening our messages, he tells me what Sire said before inviting me with them. When I glance at the date, I realize it's Tuesday and he wants to *talk* to him.

I tuck my phone away. "Alright so let's go. Stop trying to get her pregnant."

The couple laughs at me before rising from the couch.

We head down stairs with their dog and as we make it outside, Vidia gets on her tippy toes to kiss Sire goodbye. "I'll see you after work, mi amor."

She starts to pull away, but he pulls her closer.

"For fuck's sake." I roll my eyes at him. "I'll meet you there. Come on, Athena." They laugh from behind me as their rottweiler follows beside me. She stays close the entire walk to the park without a leash. I'm aware she's a trained guard dog, but it's pretty cool.

With the warm sun being out, it doesn't look like the sad patch of grass I was laying on last night. Jackson and Isabelle are already here and I feel my mood skyrocket when Isabelle runs to me.

"Lissy!"

I kneel down with my arms open and she jumps on top of me. "Hello, pretty baby." I kiss the top of her head before setting her down.

She barely spares me a second glance as she starts chasing the dog around. With a laugh, I walk over to her dad.

Today, he sits on the grass in a gray sweat suit.

"You almost look as good as you did in that fire fighter costume."

A smirk grows on his lips as he rises to his feet to hug me. "I prefer you in this." He gestures to my shitty outfit.

I hug him in return as I look down at my hoodie. "Liar, you can't see my perfect tits."

He barks up a laugh as we settle on the grass, leaning against a huge tree.

Jackson lets out a groan from beside me before standing up. He pulls his hoodie off and I feel my brows furrow as he shakes it out before sitting back down only to stand and shake out his hoodie again.

I'm incredibly confused until he does it two more times and I realize it's a compulsion.

When he sits back down next to me, he stares at the patch of grass as if he's *feeling* for something and it must feel right because he lays on his back again.

"How often do you do that?"

He glances over at me before shrugging. "Whenever I get an extremely scary intrusive thought."

He must see my confusion because he explains.

"When I sat down, I thought about Athena literally biting Isabelle's arm off. It all played out in my head. Her screaming, the hospital, her prosthetic arm." He rolls his eyes at himself. "Laying down with that thought solidified that it's going to happen, so I need to shake the bad thoughts away and sit back down while thinking of a good thought to replace it with."

He shrugs. "Sometimes the first shake is okay, but other times it takes a while before it feels right and I get the perfect good thought."

I simply nod in thought as I try to understand and he lets out a sigh before sitting back up.

"It doesn't make sense," he voices my thoughts.

"No, but I know it's not supposed to make sense. Logic doesn't help you so you do the compulsions."

"Exactly."

I nod before shaking my head. "But Athena has never shown signs of aggression. She's the sweetest dog, especially with Isa. It's like she knows she's a kid and she needs to be gentle with her. Why was that your intrusive thought?"

He shrugs as he looks over at his daughter. "They're unprovoked and random. Sometimes even if I truly know something deep down isn't true, it manifests anyway, like the dog hurting Isa for no good reason. My thoughts just take my biggest fears. Before it was my own safety, but now, it's my daughter's."

He watches his kid and there's a protective look in his eyes every time he looks at her.

"How often do you get those intrusive thoughts? That Isabelle is going to get hurt if you don't do the ritual, I mean."

He shakes his head as his eyes follow her across the field. "Countless times a day. It's exhausting and I try to let them pass, but the anxiety from *not* doing it makes me feel like I could die. I *know* she'll be fine if I don't shake out my clothes or hold my breath for thirty seconds while I run to touch her, but it doesn't feel that way... it's like an itch you can't scratch. It's just on the front of your mind and it eats at you."

When he looks back at me, I see him in an entirely new light and not just because of what he said, but because I couldn't imagine having those intrusive thoughts every day. My addiction is a bitch and most days it feels like that itch, but I'm not strong enough to handle zero quiet days.

Before either of us can say anything, Sire makes his way over. "What's good?" He smiles down at his best friend. They do their cute little handshake before Jackson nods over at Isabelle.

"Her ballet classes started and they gave me the schedule for all of her recitals. Please clear your schedule because that little girl won't be on stage if you and your brother aren't there. You know how the last show went when you were late."

Sire laughs as he smiles over at Belle. "Send it to me and I'll move some things around."

Jackson nods in return before tapping his knee. "Listen," he clears his throat before glancing over at me. "I wanted to talk to you about something."

I bite my tongue as I look between the pair.

"Yeah, let me just go say hi to Isa." He doesn't give Jackson a chance to respond as he runs off to Isabelle. When he reaches her, he grabs her from behind before throwing her in the air.

"I don't think you should tell him yet."

Jackson looks over at me, his brows furrowed. "Why?"

I pluck a piece of grass. "I jokingly asked him what he'd think about *us* and he made it clear that he'd be physically hurting you."

He lets out a sigh before burying his face in his hands. I leave him to his thoughts for a beat before he looks over at me. "If I tell him nothing happened yet, he might not be as mad. I can make him think I'm asking rather than telling him this is happening whether he's on board or not."

I shake my head at the sincerity in his voice. "Do you not think you can take him in a fight?"

He laughs. "I think I have a pretty good chance, but I'm not going to beat him up and then sleep with his sister. I'm not an asshole."

I bite back a laugh. "You wouldn't fight to the death for me?"

His eyes dart to mine, a smile on his pretty face that makes his one dimple pop. "I find it concerning that you want me to. Would you fight to the death for me?"

I shake my head in disappointment. "And to think men used to go to war for their country."

He throws his head back with a laugh. "Am I less of a man for not fighting to the *death* for you?"

I shrug.

"Does it make it better knowing I'd do it for my daughter?"

"Fair enough, I *guess*." Playfully rolling my eyes at him, I glance off to the side. I watch as Isabelle and my brother run past us, the tree blocking my view. Facing forward again, I feel Jackson watching me and when I look at him, a smirk is on his face.

His eyes cast down Sire's hoodie I'm in before they land on my bare thighs. "How are you?"

I glance down at the scars on my leg before looking up at him. "Is that your way of asking if my crippling depression is pushing me to hurt myself today?"

He shakes his head as he brings a hand to my thigh. "That's my way of saying I'm mad at myself for only scheduling tutoring for three days a week because I haven't seen you in two days and I want to kiss you, but your brother is right behind you."

A smile stretches across my face.

"But since you brought it up." He turns more serious. "How are you feeling?" He rubs his thumb along on my scars and I'm surprised when it makes me feel better.

I open my mouth to voice a joke but stop short. Maybe it's because he shared such a vulnerable part of himself earlier, but I consider letting my walls down just a bit.

At the sound of his daughter's distant laugh from somewhere behind us, a smile touches my lips. "I was having a pretty shitty few days, but today just got better."

He moves his hand from my leg before plucking a flower from beside us. "Here you go." He holds it out to me with a smile.

"Why do you think flowers are going to heal me?"

He takes my hand before placing the flower in my palm. "I don't think flowers will heal you. I just like seeing that smile on your face whenever I give you one."

I try to wipe the smile off my face, but I'm failing. He leans over and plucks a bigger flower before tucking my hair behind my ear with it.

He looks between my eyes as he shakes his head in thought. "You're so damn pretty."

I stifle a laugh as I turn away. "I look like shit." I gesture to Sire's clothes that I dirtied during breakfast. Picking up a few strands of greasy hair, I show him my split ends, but he's still smiling.

"Well, you're the most gorgeous piece of shit I've ever seen."

I break into a laugh, and when I look over at him, he's still watching me.

"I accomplished something pretty big yesterday," I start. "You haven't unlocked that side of me, so I'm not telling you what it is, but if you knew, you'd be proud."

His gaze softens as a smile touches his lips. "I'm proud of you, sweetheart."

I falter at his name for me and it might just be the praise kink talking, but if he said that to me more often, I might actually stay clean long enough to finally get my year sober chip.

"Do you really mean that?" I find myself asking.

His brows furrow as he squeezes my leg. "Of course, I do. Are you not proud of yourself?"

I shrug as I look down at my nails. "I've made this accomplishment before and I'm tired of being at this stage. I want to accomplish more."

He grabs my chin before tilting my head up to meet his gaze. "Just because you have to go back to the start doesn't mean you're never going to see the finish line. Learn from your setbacks and push through whatever is keeping you down."

I smile up at him as I gently push his hand away. "Is Isabelle in any sports because that was very soccer dad of you."

He laughs beside me as he leans on his elbow. "Just ballet and gymnastics. She was up so early today, twirling and flipping around me. Demanding I record her back handspring at 7:00 a.m."

He sounds exhausted and I can't help but laugh at his fake misery because I know deep down, he loves watching his daughter twirl in a tutu at the crack of dawn.

My eyes land on his biceps as my laugh sobers. He's always in a suit and tie, but as he sits here in sweats and a white T-shirt that perfectly hugs him, he somehow looks hotter? I didn't think that was possible, but tired, ruffled hair Jackson is dreamy.

"You mentioned wanting to kiss me earlier?"

His eyes cut up to mine and I don't miss the smile that tugs at his lips.

"You said no kissing til Tuesday... come here." I nod him over, but he doesn't move as he looks past me.

He sits up and leans over to look behind the tree I'm still leaning against. After a beat, he quickly leans forward. He presses his lips against mine and I just barely kiss him back before he pulls away. When he looks behind me, I realize he's watching out for my brother.

I look over my shoulder and lean over to catch a glance behind the huge tree. When Sire takes off running after Isabelle with his back to us, I turn back to Jackson and kiss him harder, knowing the tree covers us even if they did turn around. Just as my tongue grazes his, he pulls away before leaning on his elbow again.

"No more," he whispers, his gaze shifting to the side. I bite back a smile, watching him struggle not to look at me.

"Not to ruin the mood with the *what are we* conversation, but what the hell are we doing? I can only take so many kisses, so if you're scared of my brother, say it now because this feels like a high-risk, low reward situation."

He opens his mouth before his brows furrow. "I'm a *low reward*?"

"Are you offering me more than secret kisses behind his back? Sire said he'll kick your ass for this, but I think this will be worth his anger if you at the very least fuck me."

His chest rises faster as he gives me a once-over. "Do you have to voice every thought that enters your head?"

"Only the ones that involve us naked and you fueling my praise kink."

He shakes his head at me, his eyes falling shut. When he opens them again, his *dad face* is on, and I wonder if he knows he does that when he's being serious.

"I'm not scared of your brother."

I bite my cheek so hard, I nearly cut myself. Crawling over to him, I rest a hand on the grass next to his head and the other on his chest. As I lean in, he inches away as if I were contagious. I stifle a laugh when he looks over my shoulder.

"A man of true bravery you are."

His eyes narrow on me. "I'm *not* scared of him," he says strongly. "We've known each other for a long time and I respect him *and* our friendship. I'm going to tell him about this before it goes any further."

"So you *do* plan on having sex with me?"

He ignores me.

"Well, go tell him right now. You said you'll tell him today." I lean back on my arms but he doesn't move and I can't help but laugh.

"Shut the hell up, Lissy."

I bite my tongue as I rein it in. "Well." I lay on the grass beside him. "You have fun growing a pair big enough to tell my brother you like me, but I personally suggest telling him after we sleep together since he can't kill you twice."

Jackson lets out a scoff from beside me. "Why are you so confident I want to sleep with you?"

"Because you're not blind."

He chuckles quietly.

"Your dick is also hard right now and I barely touched you."

He goes quiet and I bark up a laugh since I was shooting in the dark there.

# *Chapter Twenty-Four*

# JACKSON

I 'M SITTING ON MY DOORSTEP as I watch Lisette's car pull up, and for the first time all day, a smile touches my lips.

Her head hangs low as she steps out of her car, and when she notices me, she sends me a smile.

"Yes, I'm waiting by the door for you," I beat her to it as I rise to my feet. "I would say I missed you, but I'm really hiding from my responsibilities."

She lets out a laugh as she slightly limps over to me; her laugh dying at the end.

"Hey." I reach for her arm before she can pass me. "You okay?" I glance down at her foot.

"Yeah." She pulls away. "Can you maybe not touch me?"

"Oh." I take a step back as my hand falls to my side. "Sorry..."

"You're good." She nods at the end of her sentence before walking inside and considering we were just sneaking kisses yesterday, I have no idea what I missed.

I follow behind her before shutting the door. "Do you want to tell me what's wrong?"

"I would've if I wanted to." She takes a step, but I swiftly stand in her way rather than grabbing her to keep her from walking away.

Leaning down, I catch her eyes with mine. "If you're having a bad day, that's fine. And if you want to have an attitude, then okay, but my day hasn't been great, so I'd appreciate it if I wasn't on the receiving end of your bad mood."

Her shoulders sag before she looks down at her feet. "Sorry."

"What's wrong?" I reach for her face but stop myself.

"It's been a hard week and—" She cuts herself off before shaking her head of her thoughts. "And you don't deserve my bullshit. Sorry." She forces a smile now as she looks up at me. "Where's my favorite student?"

My eyes scan her face and she looks exhausted. "You don't have to force a smile for me. You're allowed to have a bad day."

She looks off to the side, not saying anything. I decide to let her have her way as we walk further into the house, giving her the space she needs.

When I walk into the living room, the pile of laundry I was folding stares back at me.

"Woah." Lisette stares at the load of clothes. "Did a tornado hit?"

I let out a defeated breath as I escape for the backyard. "I was stress cleaning, but then I got tired." Sliding the back door open, Lisette follows behind me.

"Where's Belle?"

"She's spending the day with my parents." I turn to see her reaction but she doesn't give me one. "They picked her up from school after I told them about my day and by the time I remembered to update you, I figured you were already on your way here and we could just spend the afternoon together."

A small smile grows on her face and I choose to believe it isn't forced. "So you *did* miss me?"

Hiding my smile, I shrug. "I plead the fifth."

She laughs quietly before trailing further into the yard. "Is this glass?" She gently taps her foot on the retractable safety cover on the pool.

"Polycarbonate or something like that," I correct her. "I'm paranoid that Belle will fall in. She can swim, but you never know." When I feel the hot sun on my neck, I pull out my phone and a few buttons later, the pool cover is being pulled back.

"Want to swim?" I glance over at Lisette, but she only shakes her head. I nod in return before pulling my shirt off. Stripping down to my underwear, I slip into the pool and as my body cools down, the pressure in my head eases.

I sit at the bottom of the pool for a few seconds, soaking in the quiet. When I breach the surface, I shake my hair out before swimming to the edge.

I feel Lisette watching me, and when I steal a glance at her, she simply smiles at me as she sits with her feet in the water.

"What?"

She shakes her head. "You're nice to look at."

I feel a blush cover my face and her smile widens. Stepping in front of her, I rest my arms on either side of her. "How much do you like your outfit?"

Her brows furrow as she looks down at her baggy clothes. When it clicks in her head, she looks back up at me. "Don't pull me in there."

I grab her waist but she inches backward. "No, seriously. I really don't have it in me to wash my hair and I *hate* pool hair. Please don't."

I leave her be at the sincerity in her voice. "At least take these off." I tug at her sweats she pulled up to her knees.

She looks down at her legs, her shoulders slouching.

I almost ask her what's wrong before a smile is forced on her face. "Just say you want to see me in my underwear."

I roll my eyes at her, a smile tugging at my lips. "I really just wanted to rest my head on you without getting you wet, but I'll let you continue to believe I want to see you naked."

"I appreciate that." She nods as if she really is grateful. She toys with the drawstring of her pants, her eyes low. "You don't get to see them, though."

I hold her waist, a smirk on my lips. "Please?"

She only shakes her head, her smile gone.

Immediately, I move my hands from around her. "I'm sorry." I take a step back, remembering she doesn't want to be touched.

She shakes her head at me. "No, it's okay." Her eyes land on her pants again. "I just... don't want to take them off."

"Okay." I nod in return. "I was only teasing. You don't have to do anything you don't want to."

A smile touches her lips. She holds her hands out to me. "You don't have to be so far."

I take her hand and she rests it around her waist again. "Why are you having a bad day?" I keep my eyes on her, rubbing her leg, but she winces. My eyes snap down to her thigh and through her sweats I can feel something wrapped around her thigh... a bandage.

She keeps her eyes to the side as she slightly pushes my hand off of her.

We're quiet before I find my voice. "When was that?" I ask gently.

She keeps her face turned to the side, remaining so quiet, I think she isn't going to answer. "Yesterday," she answers after a while, her voice just above a whisper.

"I was with you yesterday." This wasn't there and she said she *wasn't* cutting herself.

"After I got home..."

I look between her eyes, her words from before about having a hard week loud in my head. "You're lovable."

Her brows slightly furrow as she glances over at me.

"At apple picking you said you felt unworthy of love." I gently rub her leg. "Don't let your dark thoughts consume you. You're worthy of everything life has to offer." I watch her carefully and after a beat a small smile touches her lips.

"Thank you for saying that."

I keep my eyes on her before nodding in return. Wrapping my arms around her waist, I rest my head on her lap, careful to avoid her cut and she immediately runs her hand through my curls.

"Do you want to talk about what happened after we left the park?" I ask quietly, feeling for if she stiffens or shifts uncomfortably, but she doesn't.

"I'm an addict, Jackson."

I feel my brows furrow as I look up at her and she looks like she hates herself. "You're sober," I voice, her words from yesterday making sense.

She nods, her eyes low.

Tilting her chin up, I force her to look at me. "You should be proud of that."

She doesn't say anything, but she looks exhausted, so I lay my head on her again and hug her close. This girl is full of so much life. She lights up every room she walks into, and it physically pains me that she hurts enough to hurt herself.

"Nothing happened," she speaks up again. "I'm just an addict. Everything chronically hurts and I can't take anything for the pain."

"You're not just an addict."

She doesn't respond, but I can hear her suck her teeth.

"You're *not*," I say more sternly as I hug her waist close. "You're funny. You're beautiful. You're smart. You care about the fucked up shit in the world. You're a good person. You're an amazing sister and friend. You're a talented artist. You're a *recovering* addict, but that's not all you are."

She rubs my back gently now. "I'm also great in bed."

I shake my head at her, but I don't let her brush her pain under the rug with a joke. "Say it." I pick my head up to look at her. "You're not just an addict."

She meets my eyes before pushing my wet hair off of my forehead. "I'm not just an addict."

I give her a knowing look. "Like you mean it."

She looks like she's being tortured, but after a minute, she sits up straighter and holds her head high. "I'm *not* just an addict."

"Good girl." I kiss her hand and a blush slowly covers her face. Biting back a smile, I kiss her stomach before laying my head on her lap again. "I think you want to have sex with me more than I want to with you."

She lets out a scoff, but I can feel her breathing faster. "So you're admitting you want to have sex with me?"

I shrug. "Take your shirt off so I can see what we're working with."

She doesn't miss a beat as she pulls her top off. I keep my head on her lap, not trusting myself to look at her.

"I hope you're wearing a bra."

"No, you don't."

When I don't reply, her laugh touches my ears.

"Look at me." She pulls my head up, and reluctantly, I let my eyes roam over to her. She's in a sports bra and her perfect smile is on display. "Tell me I look pretty." Her tone is as serious as ever although her smile is teasing.

"You look pretty."

"And I'm the most gorgeous girl you've ever seen," she adds.

I lean forward and kiss her chest. "You're the most gorgeous woman I've ever seen."

She pats my head. "You're so well trained. Who's a good boy?"

I break into a laugh before splashing water on her.

When our laughs sober, she runs a hand through my hair. "Why are *you* having a bad day?"

I feel my shoulders sag before wrapping my arms around her again, wanting her closer. "Belle's school."

"Oh, god," she drawls. "What now?"

I stifle a laugh, appreciating her shared annoyance. "You know how they work on five different words every week for the little spelling test?"

She hums in response.

"Well we were practicing the wrong ones this week, so she 'failed'," I say in air quotes since I refuse to call my five-year-old a failure in anything. "They had a lot to say about it and apparently I'm an irresponsible father. I kind of got into it with them and lost my temper." I roll my eyes, more upset with myself than them.

"They need to fuck off already." She leans back on her hands. "Whatever you said was deserved."

I shake my head at her words. "I told them not to call me unless it was an emergency." I cringe at the reminder. "I need to call them back and apologize."

"No the hell you don't," she counters. "Isn't this the third time they called you this week? Enough is enough, stop being so nice and you better not call back."

When I feel my headache returning, I rest my head on her lap again. "What made you get into teaching?" Shutting my eyes, I soak in the hot sun.

"It was honestly very impulsive."

That doesn't surprise me one bit, but I don't say anything as she goes on, her voice easing the tension in my shoulders.

"My major was undeclared my first two years in college. I was dating this guy at the time and he said his job as a special ed teacher was hard and I didn't believe him."

She stifles a laugh as she thinks of something. "I really just did it to prove to him I'd be better at it than him." She quickly goes on. "But I also have always loved kids. I was babysitting in college to make extra money and after working with a few special needs kids, I knew I'd love my job and I did."

I can feel her mood shift and I kiss her leg gently. "Would you go back?"

She takes a beat to think. "Maybe. I just saw a post about a school shooting in Florida and that shit is sickening."

A chill runs down my back at the mention. I also saw that on the news and I nearly enrolled Isabelle in homeschool on the spot.

"That's actually the reason I got fired, so maybe I wouldn't go back."

I lean up to look at her. "What do you mean?"

She shakes her head before explaining. "My school had a new protocol for that situation. Rather than boarding the door and hiding, we would listen for how far the shots were and if we thought we could get out of the building, we'd run with our kids or remain hiding."

"*What?*" I feel my eyes bulge as I watch her. "They made you practice that with *kids?*"

"No, no." She quickly explains, "Only faculty did it a few weeks before school started."

I thought that'd make me feel better, but it doesn't in the slightest.

"Unless the shots sounded like they were in my direct hall, I was making it out of that fucking building, especially since I knew I only had five or six kids, but when the year started, I had a wheelchair baby and that drill was all I could think about."

I keep my eyes on her and she looks scared of the thought.

"I kept going over it in my head and there was no way I could make it out with five kids and a wheelchair, and I sure as shit wasn't leaving her. On top of that, I had a nonverbal autistic kiddo who wouldn't let anyone touch him. Majority of my plan depended on me carrying my smaller kids who wouldn't run with me, but..."

She takes a deep breath as she shakes her head. "It was overwhelming and when I started drinking, I just spiraled. Then my depression was really bad."

"That shouldn't have cost you your job."

She musters up a smile as she looks to the side. "The board didn't think so."

My heart sinks. "They reported you to the *board?*"

She nods and I hate the disappointed look on her face because I know she feels that way about herself. "I thankfully didn't lose my license, but I was fired and suspended from teaching for the school year. I was cleared for this fall but never got around to applying."

When she looks up at me, a more genuine smile is on her face. "It worked out, though. I'd take tutoring your kid over public school teaching any day."

As I focus on her, I physically can't bring myself to look away from that smile.

# Chapter Twenty-Five

## LISETTE

"**Y**OU KNOW YOU DESERVE BETTER than this, right?**"** I keep my eyes on Harmony as she looks out the window. Her eyes bore into the house that her boyfriend's location led us to.

"What do you think he's doing with her?" She sounds so defeated and it really does crush me.

"He's probably cheating on you, babe." I rip the bandaid right off. "No one goes to their ex's house at midnight for a chat. This is weird and we shouldn't be camping outside her house; just end things. The sex wasn't even good."

When she sniffles quietly, I roll my eyes before pulling in a breath for strength. Tapping her back softly, I channel my inner Sage. "It's okay, babe. You're going to get through this."

She turns to me slowly, her brows furrow. "I know I will, he's just a boy who can't kiss." She rolls her eyes before wiping her tears. "I'm just on my period and pissed off that I let him take my virginity."

"Oh thank God." I let out a breath. "I was really hoping I didn't have to tend to your broken heart."

She stifles a laugh before glancing at the back of my seat. "You'll bail me out of jail if anything happens, right?"

I watch her carefully. "Of course, I will."

She nods once before grabbing the bat in my back seat. Without another thought, she climbs out of the car and marches for his car. I know a baseball bat plus a cheater's car equals a lot of damage, but when she bashes his windshield my jaw drops.

His passenger window is next and the blaring car alarm doesn't slow her down. She reaches into the car, and when I see the pocket knife she pulls out from the glove compartment, I put the window down.

"Don't slash all of the tires," I warn. "Insurance will cover it. Pop three of them and we'll come back for the fourth when he gets it fixed."

A smile grows on her face.

The lights to the house turn on, but Harmony doesn't flinch and I can't help but smile at how badass she is. I guess Ana did something right with her.

Standing at the hood of his car, she pulls out her lipstick before writing xoxo- H.

I stifle a laugh and she climbs back in just as someone opens the front door. They yell something at us, but I'm driving off before they can see us.

"That felt good." She's bouncing in her seat and I can't help but laugh at her.

"Let's get you home before your sister notices you're missing."

On cue, her phone goes off. When she pulls it out, her face falls. "Fuck."

I shake my head at her, but we don't say anything as I speed to her house.

When I pull up, Ana is standing outside. She looks so different and I know I haven't seen her in nearly ten years, but I was envisioning her as the twelve-year-old I last fought with. Her hair was so long growing up, nearly down to her knees but she has it cut to a bob now, making her look so much older.

She looks tired, like she's been up all night looking for her sister, and a part of me feels guilty until her eyes meet mine and I register her anger.

"Don't tell her where we were. Just say you had cravings and I took you for milkshakes." I unlock the car, but before Harmony can climb out, the house door swings open.

My eyes lock on those blue ones and I'm stuck in place. The wrinkles on her face are more prominent than when I last saw her and the years of drug use are obvious as half of her face droops.

"I didn't know she was here," Harmony whispers and I think she turns to me, but my eyes are locked on the woman we shared a womb with.

She marches for my car and with every angry step she takes, my heart exhilarates.

"Harmony, get the hell out of my car." I reach to unlock the door again, but my hand lands on the lock as Harmony pulls on it. She unlocks it, but the minute she opens the door, her mom is in front of us.

I break into a sweat at the smell of her. The liquor and cigarette scent drowning me with memories I wish I could forget.

"Where the hell did you take her?" She bites out and a voice I haven't heard in over a decade sends a chill down my spine.

I try to say something, but when I open my mouth, nothing comes out.

"Are you drunk or stupid?" she drawls before looking in the back of my seat. "Where's that rich family you're always with?"

Harmony steps out before grabbing her hand. "Mom, come on…"

Elaine snatches her hand as she steps closer to me. "Did they come to their senses and cut you off?" She looks around my car before her eyes land on the water bottle on the door.

She snatches it and I feel my hands start to shake as she watches me. Images of her beating me come in flashes, the phantom pain aching through my back.

Unable to pull my eyes away from her, I watch as she takes a whiff. A smirk grows on her face before her eyes meet mine.

"You have some nerve drinking and driving with my baby girl in the car."

I shake my head in response, willing myself to deny it, but nothing comes out.

Beside her, Harmony's eyes dull as she looks between me and the bottle. "What? No, she's sober."

Ana steps between them, pulling Harmony's hand. "She's a liar."

A knot grows in my throat as I shake my head again. "I'm clean." I surprise myself with how strong my words come out.

Elaine looks over at me again and the anger in her eyes shakes me to the core, forcing my eyes to fall. "Do the Hales know you're driving around *drunk* in their car?"

I shake my head, a tear falling on my cheek. "This is my car."

She lets out a bitter laugh. "Who'd you fuck to get it?"

"Mom!" Harmony steps in and when I glance over, she's pulling at her arm. "She's your daughter too. What is the matter with you?"

"She is no daughter of mine." She shoves Harmony away so hard, she nearly falls.

"Hey!" I sit up in my seat. "Keep your hands off of her." I snatch my seatbelt off, but Harmony quickly steps between us.

"I'm fine." She looks at me, silently begging me to stay put.

Elaine shoves her out of her way again and I bite my tongue. "You ruined everything." She takes a swig of my liquor before throwing the empty bottle at me and as the small drops land on me, they nearly burn like acid.

"You couldn't stand being a part of this family." Her words slur as she leans against my car. "You ran after that little boy every chance you got, but you know what? I'm glad you were off getting high with him rather than doing that shit in my house. You have no one to blame but yourself and him."

My vision blurs but I hold my tears back. "Sire isn't to blame for my addiction. You are."

She reaches into my car so fast I barely have a chance to defend myself as she grabs a chunk of my hair.

"Get off of her," Harmony cries.

I don't know what comes over me, but I finally snap out of the shock and grab her hair in return before punching her head.

She pulls me harder and I think someone is dragging her out of my car, but I keep my grip on her hair as I keep hitting her. Even when she releases my hair, I still keep a strong hold on her.

"If you lay a finger on my sister again, I'm going to kill you." I swing at her one more time, the blow landing on her mouth.

She stumbles out of my car, Ana's arms around her as she spits out blood.

"This is who you want to give another chance?" I point at her sorry excuse of a mother. "You hate me so much, but she gets to walk in and out of your life? You're pathetic, Ana."

"Don't throw stones from a glass house, Lisette." She looks at me in pure disgust. "You really expect us to believe you're sober with a bottle in your car? Where are the pills?"

"Close my door," I bite out.

"You're no better than her."

I go still.

"I let her back in because she's my mom and she's sick." When I notice the tears in her eyes, I realize she's the same little girl I last saw all those years ago, desperate for her mom.

"You left us," she continues angrily. "You don't deserve to be saved. Not by us at least. Go with the Hales, you chose them, right?"

"They don't want her either." Elaine lets out a bitter laugh.

Harmony steps forward, tears trickling down her face. She tries to climb back into my car, but they both pull her back before shutting the door. I focus on her teary eyes, but they pull her away from my car.

I don't want to leave her again, but when she nods, I drive off.

I STARE AT THE PILL in my hand, my stomach turning when *nothing* comes to mind as to why I shouldn't just swallow it.

*Don't swallow it. Crush it and sniff it instead.*

Looking up at the ceiling of my car, my leg shakes in anticipation. Sniffling quietly I wipe my tears before focusing on the building beside me. I almost look down at my hand again until my eyes focus on the brunette sitting on the ground.

I can spot a drunk person from a mile away, but my eyes narrow as I realize it's Erin and she's *high*. Slipping out of my car, I close the distance between us.

"Long time no see, stranger." I kick her foot, and when she looks up at me, dread pulls at me because she looks really bad and I don't want the responsibility of helping her. Not because I'm a bad friend, but because I want to sit next to her and get just as high.

"You here for a meeting?" I nod at the building behind her. "Come in with me."

She laughs to herself and I force a smile as I pull her up to her feet.

"Fuck off, blondie." She shoves me away with the bit of strength she has.

I take a step back. "I'm not going to knock your ass out for hitting me just now because you're high, but I'm not going to let that slide twice so watch it, Houdini."

She rolls her eyes before stumbling. I catch her and walk with her.

"Is this why I haven't seen you in weeks?"

She nods in return as she leans her head on me. "Do you want to smoke?" She shuffles in her pocket but I force myself not to look down.

"I don't smoke, Erin."

She laughs again as she hangs her head low. "Right... you're an oxy girl."

I swallow the bitter taste in my mouth as I pull the door, and I struggle to do so while holding her up, but I get us inside.

"Have you tried smoking it? It's *way* better than sniffing."

I plaster a smile on my face, really wishing I slept off the urges and just stayed in my damn bed. "I haven't..."

"You should."

"Erin, please stop." I scan the room for Winter, frantic to get the hell away from this girl. When she gets too heavy, I sit her on a nearby chair.

"Why are you here?" She glances up at me, her skin pale, and her lips dry.

"Winter holds night meetings."

"Why are *you* here?" she asks again before leaning to the side and I catch her before she can fall.

"I feel myself spiraling," I find myself admitting.

She smiles and as she looks at me, it's as if she sees right through me. "Bay said you found a new boy toy."

I roll my eyes as I sit in front of her, and by some miracle, she doesn't fall over. "Bay is full of shit."

Erin nods to herself before pushing her hair out of her face. "Don't fall in love, blondie." She seems to be warning me. "It hurts."

I focus on her and my heartstrings pull for her. "What happened, Erin?"

She stares behind me, zoning out as a single tear silently falls on her face. When she starts leaning over again, I pull a chair over and let her lay on both of them.

I catch Winter behind her and rush over. When she sees me making my way over, her eyes fall on Erin before her shoulders slouch. She opens her mouth, but I beat her to it.

"I have a pill of oxycodone in my pocket," I blurt. "I need you to tell me why I shouldn't take it." I search her eyes, desperate for the wisdom and fucking strength.

"I can't tell you that." She shakes her head.

"Please, Winter." My voice breaks.

She takes my hand, but I pull away.

"No." I take a step back. "No. I don't need your riddles right now. I don't need you to tell me I need to find my reason to stay clean on my own. I don't have one, okay? I can't think of one, so I *need* you to tell me not to do it. Tell me I matter to at least you."

She tucks her white hair behind her ear as she slowly takes a seat, rubbing her old knees. "Sit with me, child."

"Winter." I look up to the ceiling as tears start to fill my eyes. "I can't do this anymore."

"You *know* what your reasons to stay clean are." She tries to remind me. "You print out pictures of your reason every time you get the urge to get high."

I shake my head at her, my eyes still on the ceiling as I command my tears not to spill.

"Whose picture did you print last?"

I squeeze my eyes shut.

"Whose picture, Lisette?"

"Isabelle's." I swallow the lump in my throat. "I just came from printing a picture of Isabelle, Jackson, and me baking at their house." My words come out just above a whisper as I will myself to keep the tears at bay.

"Why them?"

It takes me a second to calm my breathing before I look down at her. "I'm happy with them." I shrug. "Things that keep me happy are things I want to be sober for."

She tsks at me as she shakes her head. "Would you go ahead and just cry?"

I silently shake my head, the lump in my throat growing. "Just let it out," she voices gently. "It's okay to feel it."

Spinning on my heels, I rush out and head for my car. I don't drive in any particular direction, I just keep going and keep shoving down the pain.

It feels like I'm driving for hours, but as the house light turns on above me, I realize I'm in front of Jackson's place. I almost turn around, but the red light in his camera comes on and I know he already knows I'm here, so I climb out of the car.

With the red light from the doorbell still on, I know he's looking at me in the camera and I force a smile. "I would flash you, but I don't get naked on camera for free."

After a beat, his voice sounds through the camera. "You better be joking."

I bite back a smile as I hear his footsteps coming towards the door. When he swings the door open, he smiles down at me in his marvelous suit. His tie is absent and the first few of his buttons are undone. I take in his ruffled hair and it's clear he was working late.

"This is the part where you tell me you're joking."

"Are you shaming sex workers?" I slip past him and I smile to myself when I feel his heated gaze on me.

"Not at all." He walks beside me. "They can do what they want, but you won't be participating in the fun."

I halt my steps as I turn to him. "Until you step up to my brother and fuck me like you own me, I'm not doing a single thing you tell me to."

His eyes narrow as he watches me, and I quickly find myself regretting my words. He takes a step towards me, his eyes full of something dangerous. I take a step back and he stalks towards me until my feet hit the couch.

"Sit."

I'm sat without a word.

"Lean back." He nods for the back of the couch and I scoot back. A smile touches his lips as he rests a hand beside my head and slowly leans in. My eyes are on his lips until he tilts my chin up. "What was that about you not doing a single thing I tell you to?"

I scoff at his smirk. "That was for my benefit, JJ. Are you going to reward me, or should I go somewhere else?"

He cups my face before rubbing my bottom lip with his thumb. "Why do you look like you were crying, sweetheart?"

I try to move out of his grasp, but he holds me tighter.

"What happened?" He looks at me, trying to get something I'll never give.

"Are you going to give me what I want or not?"

He watches me carefully before placing a gentle kiss on my lips. It's soft and safe and not what I want, but he pulls away before

I can deepen the kiss. "You're clearly upset and I'm glad you're here. We can talk if you want to or we can sit in silence, but if you came to fuck out your feelings, it's not happening."

I move his hand away before standing. "Thanks for not wasting my time." I take a step, but he grabs my arm.

"Lisette, wait."

I pull my arm away but he steps in my way.

"Stay," he pleads.

"Jackson, I'm not staying if we're not having sex." I spell it out for him. "I'm not going to sugarcoat it for you and act like I came here for anything else. I think we can both agree we're too grown for the games and PG-13 shit."

His shoulders slouch in defeat. "Can you just talk to me?"

"I didn't come to *talk*." I snap, tears building in my eyes again. "I don't want to feel it, Jackson. I want to feel something else. That something is not here and that's fine. I'll see you for tutoring when I get back from my trip."

"What trip?"

"Sage has a fashion show, we're going to Paris." I register how monotone my voice comes out, but I'm too tired to care. I try to step around him, but he gets in my way again and I let my eyes fall shut when the tears don't stop.

I feel his arms wrap around me and I break. Everything in me shatters as a sob rips out of me. My knees go weak, but he doesn't let me fall. I cling to him as he lifts me into his arms.

We settle on the couch, and I wrap my arms around him before every thought spills past my lips.

"I don't want to do this anymore." I shake my head when the pain intensifies and he rubs my back before smoothing my hair.

"You're okay, I got you."

I cry harder and he holds me tighter. "I can't. I don't want to be here. I'm so fucking done."

I feel him go still before he pulls away. Holding my face in his hand, he wipes my tears. "What does that mean?"

I shake my head, but as I try to pull away, his grip tightens.

"I'm only going to ask one time," he starts gently. He seems to hesitate now before he pulls in a breath for courage. "Are you talking about killing yourself?"

I don't respond, but when the tears build in my eyes again, he pulls my head to his chest. "You're going to stay the night here and we can talk to your brother in the morning."

I quickly shake my head as I pull away. "No, I'm fine." Sniffling quietly, I rise to my feet. "I need to go."

I take a step, but he wraps an arm around me. "That's not happening, sweetheart."

I look between his eyes and he looks down at me like he's ready to tie me down.

Before I can object, he plants a soft kiss on my lips. "Please stay. Sleep it off and we can talk in the morning."

I nod in return and I suddenly feel numb as he walks me up to a spare bedroom. Slipping into the bed, I focus on the door as the tears start up again.

Jackson kneels in front of me before wiping my cheek. "Are you going to be okay in here?"

I know what he's asking and I only nod in return. He watches me before slipping into bed beside me. "I'll stay until you fall asleep." Wrapping an arm around me, he pulls my back to his front.

I let my eyes fall shut, but as tired as I am, I can't fall asleep as the memories of my bio mom assault me. I bite back a cry as I squeeze my eyes shut.

Tracing my steps back, I think of the last time I saw Sire. We were attempting to make tres leches for his girlfriend. He was happy, his smile comes to mind as we threw frosting at each other. I try to think of the last time I said I loved him, and when it comes to mind, I go through the rest of my siblings, checking them all off.

I need to say bye to Harmony. I can't leave things that way. I decided I'll see her one last time.

"Lissy?" Jackson whispers, but I keep my eyes closed. He lets out a soft breath as he soothes my hair. "You don't deserve this." He sucks his teeth before planting a kiss on my cheek. "I'm here for you, baby, just let me in."

He kisses my cheek before climbing out of bed, not knowing he's too late.

When the door shuts, he leaves me with nothing but the white pill in my pocket.

# Chapter Twenty-Six

## JACKSON

A SMILE TOUCHES MY LIPS as I walk into Sire's apartment and take in the full house. I hug Vidia before Isabelle races over to her uncle. I look around the room again and try to keep my smile intact when I notice Lisette is missing.

I haven't seen her since she came to my house Sunday night. I found her sleeping with Isabelle when I went to check on her in the middle of the night. Her nose was red and puffy, her pillow stained with tears. I felt like shit for not immediately calling her family, but when I woke up, she was gone. She texted me, asking me not to say anything, so that's what I did and I'm not so sure if that was the right choice. Then, she had a trip to Paris with her siblings this past week and I *just* want to see her.

"How are you doing, princess? I missed you." Sire scoops Belle into his arms before blowing a raspberry in the crease of her neck and she fills the apartment with her laugh.

"Hey." I walk over to August to dap him up before leaning over to hug his girlfriend. "How are you doing, Hazel?"

She hugs me in return before flopping on August's lap on the couch and telling me she's good.

Walking over to Sage, I pull her in for a hug. "Congrats on the engagement." I smile down at her new ring and she smiles brightly at her fiancé before kissing his cheek and thanking me.

I focus on him and I'm shocked they got engaged this past week. Sage is a ray of sunshine, wearing pink from head to toe while Liam is covered in tattoos and wearing all black with a glare that can kill.

"Don't mind him, he doesn't know happiness unless it's concerning Sage's happiness." Sire sends him a teasing smile, and when I look over at Liam, he's watching his fiancé and I notice the way his eyes soften when she smiles.

"Where's Lissy?" Belle asks the question that was on my tongue the second I walked in.

I glance at Sire for an answer but he only shrugs. "I told her to come over, but she said she was busy."

I hum in thought. "Ask her what she's doing," I say for my own convenience since she's also ignoring my messages. The only way I knew she was okay was because I kept discreetly checking on her through her siblings. "She canceled Belle's tutoring yesterday because she was also apparently busy."

She's clearly avoiding me. Something I said Sunday wasn't the right thing, and I wish I could've been more help that night.

"Lisette told me she was with you two yesterday." Sire looks between me and my kid, but I shake my head.

"No, she wasn't." I watch him carefully.

Sire glances over at the couch. I follow his gaze to August, who taps Hazel's hip urgently. She rises, letting him stand.

"I'll call her." Sage grabs her phone.

"I'll call Bay." August grabs his.

"I'll go to her house." Sire grabs his things.

"Woah." I look around the room. "What's happening?" I look between the siblings and they glance over at each other but no one answers me.

"Hello?" My voice raises although I don't mean to but the worried look on their faces puts a sick feeling in my stomach. "*What* is happening?"

"Nothing," Sire quickly answers as he takes something from Vidia's bag and shoves it into his pocket. "I'm sure she's fine, I'm just going to go check on her."

The look on his face tells me it's *not* nothing so I say, "I'm going with you."

"Jackson—"

"You said she's fine, why not let me tag along? Plus, I want to know why she lied and bailed on my kid."

He lets out a defeated breath before nodding for the door. "Okay, come on." He starts walking for the door and I quickly tell Isabelle that I'll be right back. When the twins confirm with a nod that they'll watch her, I turn for the door.

Before we can walk out, Vidia catches up to Sire.

"Hey." She gets on her tippy toes and steals a kiss. "She's fine. Call me if anything, okay?"

He kisses her forehead before taking her hand. "Come with me?" he asks in a hushed voice.

"Yeah, of course." They walk out, hand in hand, and I follow close behind.

Sire walks to his car way too fast for this to be *nothing*.

When he drives off, I glance at him in the rearview mirror. "Tell me what's happening, Sire. You're a shit liar and your stress is going to make me break out in hives."

He shakes his head at me as he zooms past a yellow light. "I just have a bad feeling."

"Do you think something happened to her?"

He doesn't answer.

I go still. "Do you think she did something to *herself*?"

He doesn't answer again and I notice Vidia takes hold of his free hand.

"Sire—"

"Yeah, Jackson. I think she relapsed, okay? She doesn't lie to me unless she's on drugs. Can you *please* stop?" Desperation seeps into his voice. "I can't answer your twenty questions and keep myself calm at the same time," he snaps, but I hear the fear in his voice.

I open my mouth to tell him about Sunday, but it falls shut, knowing that information does no one good right now. I sit back in my seat and my knee bounces in anticipation.

A minute barely passes before he's calling her, but it rings and rings and rings until we get her voicemail. He calls again and doesn't let it go to voicemail as he calls back more times than I can count. With every call she doesn't answer, the quicker he drives.

When he gets her voicemail again, he grabs his phone and brings it to his mouth. "Lisette Grace Allen," he bites out. "I swear to fucking God, if you don't call me back before I get to your house, I am going to hurt you and your nasty ass turtle. *Answer. The. Phone.*"

He hangs up before immediately calling back and my fear starts to set in. I prepare myself for us to walk in on the worst and I play every scenario in my head. Her bleeding out. Her overdosed. Her *dead*. I think of what I'll tell Isabelle, how the funeral will go. I think of all of that *twice* before we even make it to her place.

We race up the steps and Sire doesn't even bother knocking as he unlocks the door with his keys. I rush in after him, searching her living room, which is cluttered with dark red paintings.

"Lisette!" I call out to her as Sire and Vidia go straight for what I'm assuming is her room.

I walk in after them, but my steps falter as my eyes land on a half-naked man standing over her, shaking her frantically. He turns to us, fear in his eyes as he steps away from her. "I *swear* she was just fine." He puts a hand up in surrender before Sire pushes past him and kneels on the bed in front of her.

Vidia and I are close behind him as we examine her limp body.

"Is she breathing?" The guy behind us questions and I nearly pass out when I notice her concerningly shallow breaths and blue lips. I glance around at her nightstand and my eyes land on the powder, spoon, lighter, and a shit ton of a *mess*.

"Vidia, call 911." Sire sprays what I'm assuming is naloxone in her nose. I know it's supposed to take a few minutes, but it feels like an hour goes by before she takes a gasp of air.

She quickly sits up, frantically shoving Sire away from her as she tries to make sense of what's happening.

When I hear *him* start thanking God, I turn on my heels. "Who the fuck are you?"

"Ben." His scared eyes meet mine and I realize he's just as high. I let out a scoff as I turn back to Lisette.

I watch her carefully as she takes in her surroundings and slowly calms down.

She looks disoriented as she tries to get out of bed. Sire pushes her back down, but when she pulls the blanket off of herself, my eyes land on her tiny underwear.

Vidia's eyes land on my heated gaze before looking over at Sire who looks just as pissed. She turns to *Ben* as she pulls the phone away from her ear. "You should go," she warns him off before turning back to Lisette and checking her pupils for the operator.

"The pills..." Ben voices. "Can I get them before I go? They're kinda mine."

We all turn to him slowly and I let out a scoff before punching him in the face.

I've never been a violent person and I know that sounds like an oxymoron as I'm beating this guy's face in, but his words made me see red and I don't mean the blood on my hands.

"Jackson, enough." Vidia pulls my shirt, but I hit him one more time before grabbing his face.

"I swear on my daughter's *life*, if you come near her again, I am going to break every bone in your body." I shove him away before he collects his clothes and hurries out in less than ten seconds.

Leaning against the wall in front of the bed, I focus on Lisette and she still looks out of it as she looks around the room. When her eyes meet mine, she squints as if she can't understand me being here.

Before either of us can say anything, Sire holds her face in his hands. They just stare at each other and I can see Lisette's regret from across the room as she faces her brother's teary eyes.

"Don't," Sire cuts her off from whatever she's about to say and hugs her again. "It's fine. You're fine."

She's not though, and I can't tell who between the four of us is more scared to admit that.

# Chapter Twenty-Seven

## LISETTE

"**W**HENEVER YOU WANT TO LET go will be great." I tap Sire's back, but when he doesn't laugh, my heart somehow sinks further. All of my limbs are weak like I'm being weighed down by wet cement, but I muster up a smile anyway.

"Will it make you feel better if I say I didn't *mean* to overdose?"

He pulls away and looks at me, clearly trying to decipher if my words are true. "Did you?"

"Will it make you feel better?"

"Did you?"

I look between his eyes and he stares back at me, eyes red with tears, like his life depends on my answer. I shake my head softly and in the corner of my eye, Jackson and Vidia let out a breath of relief.

I don't bother asking how either of them are here and instead keep my gaze on Sire because I can't face Jackson. This was the one part of me I didn't want him to see. A couple of days ago, I so desperately wanted his lips on mine and now I want him to forget I exist.

"I don't have the energy, so don't fight me, Lis."

I look at my brother, my eyes widening as the thought of him admitting me crosses my mind.

"You're going to stay with me and Vid for a while."

I let out a breath of relief at his words. "No, I'm—"

"I just said we're not fighting." He stands from where he is on my bed. He glances over at my nightstand, his jaw clenching. "Since when did you start fucking smoking this shit?" He swipes everything off the table and I jump at his outburst, his voice nearly bouncing off the walls.

He runs his hand down his face as he calms his breathing. "The ambulance is on their way." He breaks the silence. "When you're discharged, you're coming home with me."

He doesn't let me reply as he storms out. "I need some air." He walks out and I decide to fight with him later.

Vidia pulls me in for a hug next, and when I hear her sniffing, I hug her back before whispering in her ear. "Tell him I'm sorry."

"He knows you are, baby." She holds me tighter, kissing my shoulder. "But you need to be the one to say it and you need to accept his help."

She pulls away and my eyes cut down to my bed sheets. Vidia takes my hand, but I keep my eyes low as she starts. "He's not going to sleep if you don't come home with us, Lis. If not for yourself, then do it for your brother." She squeezes my hand and I nod in return, knowing she's right.

I feel Jackson watching me, but I keep my eyes on my bed as I pull on a loose piece of thread.

"What happened?" Jackson asks so quietly that I almost don't hear him.

I glance over at him and the broken look in his eyes has me looking back at my bedsheets. "What do you mean?" I don't know why I whisper, but I do.

"I mean the last time I saw you, you weren't exactly doing well, then you just disappeared for a week, so I need to know what happened."

I see him shaking his head in my peripheral.

"Was it something I said? I tried to help, but I didn't know exactly what to do." He shakes his head as his eyes fall on the ground. "I should've called someone." He keeps his voice low and I swallow the lump in my throat. I glance up at Vidia and she gives me a single nod before standing.

"I'm going to go find your brother." She kisses my forehead before walking out.

I watch her go and glance at Jackson again before looking back down. It isn't until I hear my front door shut that I speak up. "It wasn't you," I quickly clarify. "Thank you for that night and thank you for not telling anyone, but I was just having a bad night. The need for this..." I glance at the pills on the floor before shaking my head at myself. "I slipped today because it felt like I had no other option, but I truly didn't mean for it to go this far," I say, trying to believe that myself.

The room is quiet for too long, so I look over at him, and he's still watching me.

"I wasn't lying."

I feel my brows furrow at his words. "What?"

"You have an escape with me. I'm not trying to be your knight in shining armor, but if I can offer you a few hours of bliss, why didn't you just come to hang out with me?"

I look between his eyes before shaking my head at him. "I didn't want to be a burden, JJ."

This time, he shakes his head at my words. "You're not."

"Aren't I though?" I gesture around the room, to what he just walked in on. "What are we doing, Jackson?" My voice is stronger now and his brows furrow.

"What do you mean?"

"No, what do *you* mean? You said you and Belle can be my reason to get out of bed, what does that mean? You'll be my friend? Because the jealous act you just pulled doesn't make me think that's what you want."

"And you never talk to me like friends is what *you* want." He pushes off from the wall. "Did he touch you?" His eyes darken as he studies me.

I let out a scoff at his words. "What does that matter?"

"It matters a great deal considering you were *unconscious.*"

I roll my eyes at what he's making this out to be and quickly clear the air before he gets my brother involved who is bound to drag our parents into this. "I invited him here for the pills. I was already wearing this and he went to shower, hence him being half naked. I smoked, and you guys walked in a few minutes later."

He watches me carefully. "So you just let strangers use your shower?"

"I never said he was a stranger." Ben is who I get my pills from. Yes, we've slept together in the *past*, but that's irrelevant. "Why do you care so much?"

"You're the one asking what we are," he shoots back. "Why ask if I can't know who you're sleeping with?"

"Because you shouldn't be here, Jackson," I snap.

He looks hurt, but I don't take my words back.

"Thank you for caring. Thank you so much, but look at your life and look at mine," I deadpan. "You and Belle can't be my reason to stay. I don't belong in your life, friend or not, and who I'm sleeping with is none of your concern because we're not together and shouldn't be."

He shakes his head before letting out a scoff. "Don't do that."

"I'm not *doing* anything."

"Yeah, you are. You're pushing me away when you don't need to."

*Yes, I do.* The last few weeks with Jackson have been bliss, but I can't do this; not when hurting them is inevitable.

I hear him let out a defeated breath before he closes the distance between us. "My kid *loves* you, and I've been told she's a brat, so you're stuck with her. We're kind of a package deal, so there's no pushing me away."

"You two shouldn't like me," I state flatly, desperately trying to get him to stop. To leave me before it gets uglier.

"Well, we do, so sue us. We have a great lawyer."

A smile touches my lips and I shake my head at him, but he holds my chin, dragging my eyes up to his. "Why is it so hard to grasp that you're likable?"

"I've been told overdosing on a Tuesday afternoon isn't a likable trait."

A somber smile touches his lips. "It's Wednesday, sweetheart." He sounds hurt as he tucks a hair behind my ear but I pull away again.

"What do you want from me, Jackson?"

"You. Just you." He reaches for my face but I don't let him.

"What does that *mean*?" I push. "Because you're looking at me like you want more than what I'm offering."

His brows furrow before his eyes fill with clarity, but I still say it plainly for him.

"I can't be a mom to her, Jackson."

He leans back. "I'm not asking you to."

"What would I be to her if we dated?" I go on before he can answer. "Or is the plan for us to be fuck buddies until her exam comes in December, then we go our separate ways?"

He lets out a scoff as he stands from the bed. "Is that *your* plan?"

"It's the easier plan," I force out.

"Is that what you think I meant when I said I wanted you?" He looks between my eyes. "You think *sex* is the reason I asked you out? Called out of work and moved all my meetings around just to spend the day with you? To get my dick wet?"

I know that's not why he wanted me around, but any other option scares the shit out of me.

When I don't answer, he goes on.

"So you don't want my kid in your life?"

"That's not what I said," I counter.

"It is though," he argues. "I would never ask you to take that responsibility, but don't sit here and act like my daughter is the reason you won't give us a chance."

"She is."

He takes a step back as if my words physically hurt him and I realize that came out wrong. "Fine."

"Jackson—"

"No, you've made yourself abundantly clear. I don't want to be with someone who doesn't want my daughter a part of their life."

"That's *not* what I meant." My shoulders sag.

"Well I meant it," he bites out. "I don't want you."

I let out a scoff at his anger. "Really?"

"Really."

"So why do you keep looking down at my underwear like you can't *fathom* the thought of me sleeping with the man you just threatened?"

Before he can reply, there's a heavy knock on the door. Jackson covers my lap with the blanket before taking a step away from me as the paramedics walk in with my brother.

# Chapter Twenty-Eight

## LISETTE

I KEEP MY EYES ON my iPad, ignoring the way my brother is staring at me from across the hospital room. In the corner of my eyes I can see Vidia tell him something, but with my headphones on, everything around me is perfectly silent.

She reaches for his hand, but he pulls away from her touch. My curiosity gets the better of me and I subtly press the button on my headphones, turning off the noise canceling.

"She's *not* okay, Vid." He shakes his head. "Please stop saying that. I know you're trying to help, but—" He cuts himself off.

I keep my eyes on my screen as I draw, trying not to let on that I can hear them.

"You haven't left this room since we got here," she says gently, and I can make out her figure in the corner of my eye as she crouches in front of Sire. The twins only just left, but he's against leaving the building.

"It's been three days, baby," Vidia continues. "I know you want to be here for her, but you need to be there for yourself. We'll be back in an hour tops. Please come home."

He covers his face with his hands, and when the guilt begins to eat at me, I turn my hearing back off.

It isn't until I finish my drawing that I notice someone shuffling in my peripheral. Looking up, my brother stands by the door talking to Jackson. I let out a defeated breath as I pull my headphones off.

"I'm *sure*," Jackson reassures my brother of something.

In front of them, Vidia seems to be holding her breath as she watches Sire. After a beat, he nods and her shoulders sag in relief.

"Thank you." She takes his hand before the three of them turn to me. Vidia smiles brightly as she gives Sire a light push.

He clears his throat. "I'm going to go shower and stuff." He watches me carefully. "I can bring you back some food. Just text me what you want."

I shake my head in return. "I'm not hungry."

Beside him, Vidia's shoulders slouch as she looks up at her boyfriend and I can see from a mile away as his worries come back.

"Actually, I'll have fries and a milkshake. It doesn't matter where you get it from."

A smile touches Sire's lips for the first time in days before he walks out with Vidia.

I watch them leave before I drag my eyes to Jackson. In one hand is a bag, and in the other he holds a bouquet. I don't need to see them to know they're not real.

"You're scared of hospitals," I remind him.

A smile touches his lips. "Yeah, well, there's a hot girl down the hall that I really needed to see. You happen to be rooming fairly close to her."

For what feels like the first time all year, I genuinely laugh.

He takes a step into the room, but I stop him from closing the door.

"It needs to stay open," I say, shame coating every inch of me.

His brows furrow as he turns to me.

"They're worried I'm going to... do something."

Understanding covers his face before he nods. "Does it need to stay open?"

A smile touches my lips at his silent question. I softly shake my head and he nods in return before shutting the door. He lifts the bag in his hand as he closes the distance between us.

"Our pottery stuff was ready." He sits beside me before taking out our vases, and they came out beautiful. "I was thinking we paint them here and I drop them off?"

I smile in return but only nod quietly.

He gestures to my iPad. "What are you working on?" He puts the vases away as I turn my drawing to him.

His eyes focus on the siren and pirate. "They look madly in love."

I smile. "This is like one of those projective tests." I shake my head as I look back down at the drawing and I can only see the siren's dark eyes and harsh webbed fingers wrapped around the man she drowns. I shift my head, trying to see it in the loving way Jackson does. I start to make out the way her lips on his neck might seem loving, although she's about to rip out his throat.

Shutting off the device, I tap the pen against the screen in thought. "You never updated me on Belle's school." I let my eyes meet his. "You know, after you yelled at them."

He visibly cringes. "I didn't *yell*," he attempts to correct me. "I called back and apologized..."

"Oh my god." I look up at the ceiling before meeting his guilty eyes.

"I also suggested I speak with their boss, and both Dean Carmen and Ms. Rose agreed to only call me for emergencies and update me on her progress at parent-teacher conference." He rolls his eyes and I smile at how much he reminds me of his daughter. "Hopefully, I won't be hearing from them again."

I nod in response before my gaze drops. "I wasn't expecting you to visit me." I keep my eyes on the bed.

He's quiet for a second, but I see him nodding in my peripheral vision. "I took a couple of days to think, then I decided I wanted to talk to you." He shifts beside me, and when I steal a glance at him, he sets the flowers aside before turning to me.

"I didn't mean it when I said I didn't want you," he starts. "I was hurt and offended, so I was being mean, but I didn't mean it. I apologize for losing my temper. You didn't deserve the way I spoke to you."

I bite my tongue as he continues.

"When you came over for pumpkin carving, and I told you I wanted you, there was not one single sexual thought in my mind, Lissy."

I turn to him now, my words flying out of my mouth. "I *want* your daughter in my life." I get straight to the point, voicing what I've been wanting to say for days now. "I just don't want to ruin this," I admit quietly. *I'm also scared of hurting her the way I was hurt by the woman who brought me into this shitty world.*

As he sits in front of me in a hospital room under my current circumstances, I realize not many men would show up for me the way he did even after the messy parts were on display.

I've lost countless relationships for what I am; an addict. A disappointment. A liar at times.

Jackson doesn't see that though. He's smiling at me right now and I know he doesn't see all the shameful pieces of me. Just the tiny ounces of good.

I don't know when it happened, but I realize now as I look into those gray eyes that I want to keep looking into them. I *want* to keep him around and the fear of that realization nearly makes me want to cry.

"So what does that leave us with?" His smile widens.

I shrug. "My mommy issues. My daddy issues. A brat I love and her hot dad."

He stifles a laugh and I smile at his one dimple. His big eyes settle on mine before his smile slowly fades. "We don't have to figure it out right now." He shrugs. "I just didn't want you to spend another day thinking you were unwanted. Especially by me."

His words mean more to me than he knows, but as I open my mouth, a pain settles in my stomach. Sinking into my seat, I cling to my abdomen, silently cursing the aftermath that comes with relapsing.

"What's wrong?" Jackson quickly rises to his feet.

I shake my head at him as I bury my face in the side of my pillow, waiting for it to pass. Pulling in a breath for strength, I shift in the bed. "The lack of drugs is just making my body hate me," I mumble, trying to be grateful that the throwing up stopped.

Another pain hits and Jackson shifts me so he can lay beside me. He wraps his arms around me and I bury my face in his chest as a groan escapes me.

"Is there anything I can do?"

I shake my head in response, suddenly hating that he's seeing this part of me. "You can go, Jackson..."

"I'm not going anywhere, sweetheart." He kisses the top of my head and I let him hold me.

# Chapter Twenty-Nine

## LISETTE

"LET ME OUT OF THIS damn house, Sire."

He sits on his couch comfortably while his guard dog does her job and literally guards the door at his command. "Athena, *heel*." I try to get her to move.

She looks over at Sire before looking at me and huffing in defiance. I reach for the handle but quickly pull away when she growls at me.

"I'm not scared of you," I whisper to her, but when she barks at me, I take an intuitive step back.

"What was that?" Sire calls out and I turn on my heels.

"I'm being serious, Sire. Like, I might actually start crying. I need to get out of here."

He turns in his seat to focus on me, but I'm not kidding. "Maybe you need to cry it out."

"I'd rather die, which you witnessed," I remind him and he flinches at my words. I let out a defeated sigh before walking over to him. "I'm sorry... that was fucked up to say."

His eyes meet mine and the look on his face only make me feel worse.

"I swear I'm not going to do anything," I promise him. "I just need air."

"So let's go on a walk together," he suggests.

I roll my eyes at what he's doing. I want to be alone and he knows that.

"You're going through withdrawals," he reminds me.

I don't answer him. Instead, I bury my face in one of his pillows.

"I'm not an idiot, Lisette. You want to get high and that's understandable, but you can leave next Wednesday. We agreed you'd stay for two weeks."

"Forget what I said at the hospital," I say into the pillow and if he understands me, he chooses not to answer.

While the withdrawals aren't as bad as they were in the hospital, my body is still angry with me and I feel like shit. The only upside to today is that the physical pain stopped. "I fucking hate oxy when I'm not on it."

My words only remind me how much better I'll feel on it and I sit up to look at Sire. "Please—"

"No, but thank you for asking nicely. I was really dreading the bitchy, scary, 'I want drugs' Lisette."

"Oh, I'm sure she'll come out to say hi later," I reply while flipping him off, and a smile grows on his face, but I'm too irritated to even attempt to smile.

I let my eyes fall shut when I feel my tears of frustration building.

"Can we stop fighting about our Thanksgiving plans? You're coming with us to Florida."

"Shut *up*, Sire. I'm not going over there. I don't even know Vidia and Hazel's family." My leg starts shaking as my irritation grows and he stops trying to convince me of the same thing he's been trying to convince me of all day.

He's leaving for Florida tonight since Thanksgiving is in two days, but I already told him I'm not going.

I remind myself that it's just the withdrawals pulling at my emotions and harsh attitude, but I can't bring myself to apologize, so we sit in silence.

When I hear the door opening, I look over and Vidia walks in with a smile. She looks over at Sire before smiling brighter at me. "How are you feeling?"

I stare at her for a beat before closing my eyes and choosing to use the last bit of patience I have to ignore her.

I've been here for five days and I only left three times, which was to go to a meeting with Sire, who's my new babysitter. I know he's worried. I *understand* that, but I can't breathe.

Jackson came over with Isabelle twice for our tutoring, but besides a hi and bye, Jackson barely spoke to me since my siblings are hovering like a fucking—

I cut off my thoughts as I feel myself getting mad.

*They're hovering like concerned siblings,* I tell myself and remember to be grateful that August and Sage *finally* decided to put an end to the three-day streak sleepover. I adore them, don't get me wrong, but I *hate* hovering, especially while my body feels like it's eating me from the inside out.

Then Harmony has been texting me off the fucking rails. I haven't seen her in a while, mainly because I was MIA from everyone and getting high, but I also don't want to hear her bullshit. I love her, I really do but I love *her*, not her mom and her sister. I just want to be left alone.

She keeps apologizing for the shit show and I told her countless times it wasn't her fault, but she's convinced that's the reason I'm avoiding her. It's not, I just can't face her and tell her I relapsed.

I take in a deep breath and use the next few minutes to meditate. Just as I start to appreciate how silent the house is, a phone starts ringing. I shake my head as I open my eyes and I realize it's my phone.

When I see Jackson's name, I feel my brows furrow. I grab my phone anyway and bring it to my ear. "Hello?"

"Hi, Lissy."

My heart *aches* at the sound of Isabelle's sweet voice. I open my mouth to greet her but have to clear my throat before trying again. "Hello, my sweet girl."

"Daddy said you're busy, so I took his phone because I *suspected* he was being a fibber since you're never busy for me."

I bite back my laugh. "That's very true. What's up, baby?"

"Daddy has a meeting and wants to cancel tutoring because you might not be feeling well. The meeting is here in our office and he can't drive me to you." She pauses and I imagine her rolling her eyes. "You can come here, right?"

"I sure can." I sit up in my seat.

"Perfect."

I hear Jackson call out to her in the background before he asks her if she's seen his phone. She stifles a laugh before speaking up again.

"Okay, hurry." She ends the call before I can reply and I can't help but laugh at her.

Sire looks over at me and is already shaking his head. "Lis—"

"Stop, Sire. Please, okay? *Yes,* I do want to go get high. You're right, but right now, I want to see Isabelle more than that, so I'm going to get ready and go read and maybe bake with her for the next three hours."

He studies me and I can see he wants to continue to hold me hostage here, so I continue to convince him otherwise.

"I'm supposed to be finding new coping mechanisms and getting back into my routine. Turning to healthy outlets when I get the urge to throw it all away," I remind him and I know he knows I'm right.

"Fine." He gives in. "But I'm dropping you off," he adds.

I roll my eyes at him but agree. "Fine."

"And picking you up."

"Oh, my god." I shake my head at him as I rise to my seat. "I overdose *once* and all of a sudden I can't do anything on my own."

I turn to him, waiting for him to laugh, but when he watches me with that *look*, I somehow just realize that's exactly what he's doing.

"Oh, my *god*." I keep my gaze on him and as if he just read my mind, his eyes cut down to the ground. "It was an *accident*. I don't need to be on suicide watch."

He doesn't say anything and him not believing me really does hurt.

"I swear it on the twins' life, Sire." I desperately try to get him to believe me.

"Okay." His eyes meet mine before he nods. "I'd still feel better if you let me drop you off."

I only nod in response and leave the room to get ready, no longer having the energy to convince him I'm fine.

THE ENTIRE RIDE TO JACKSON's house is silent. It isn't until we pull into his driveway that my brother turns to say something.

"I know you're hurt that I'm being overprotective. You feel like I don't trust you, but I think you can understand where I'm coming from."

I nod in response, and we sit in silence before I turn to him. "Just tell me if I broke all your trust." *Tell me if you lost all hope in me.*

He quickly shakes his head. "You didn't. I trust you, Lis. I'm just scared and being around you keeps *me* from relapsing."

I study him, trying to decide if I believe him.

"I swear it on the twins' life, Lis."

"Okay."

He nods and when his eyes get glossy I quickly look out my window.

"You know I'm sorry, right?" My voice is just above a whisper.

"I know, Applejack." His voice comes out strained, like he's struggling to keep it together. I almost tell him that I saw my bio mom and it nearly killed me, but a lump too big grows in my throat, so I remain silent.

"Can you please spend Thanksgiving with me and Vid's family?" He sounds beyond desperate now.

I nod in return, blinking away my tears. Pulling in a deep breath, I climb out of the car.

I don't hear Sire drive off and I know he's waiting until I'm inside. I try to convince myself that he always does this, and it's his way of being a good older brother. That he's not waiting to make sure I go inside because he doesn't trust me and thinks I'm going to leave to get high.

I ring Jackson's door and after a minute, he opens it. Our eyes meet and he looks surprised to see me.

"Hey, hot stuff." I slip past him and I don't miss the smile that creeps onto his face.

"Hey, I didn't know you were coming over." He shuts the door. "I misplaced my phone and didn't get to text you. I was going to reschedule tutoring. I have a meeting and didn't think you were up for driving."

"Sire drove me," I answer as I walk further into the house.

"Surprise!" Isabelle throws her hands in the air and behind her on the kitchen counter are balloons that read *feel better* and *get well soon*, along with a crocheted pot of flowers and what I'm assuming is an apple pie. "Did I surprise you?"

She's practically jumping with joy as she turns to get the crocheted pot of tulips. I turn to Jackson, but his brows are furrowed.

"We were going to take this to you tomorrow, but I guess I know where my phone went." He turns to his daughter who has a precious guilty smile on her face.

I stifle a laugh. "Yeah, you did surprise me." I don't need to fake my smile as I close the distance between us to take the gift from her. "Thank you, sweetie." I kneel down to give her a real hug and she almost knocks me over as she throws her arms around my neck.

Wrapping both arms around her, I dip my head in the crease of her neck and breathe in her sweet cherry scent. She squeezes me tighter before kissing my cheek.

"Well, you look like you feel better. When we went to visit you at Uncle Sigh's house, you didn't look so good." She shakes her head, her eyes slightly widened in concern and I break into a laugh.

"I really appreciate your honesty." I kiss her cheek before holding her tighter so I can stand while carrying her and she wraps her legs around me.

When I look over at Jackson, he's already watching us with a smile. He looks in awe as he watches me carrying his kid.

I quickly look over at the counter to the apple pie. "Did you make this?"

Isabelle nods excitedly. "The first one got burned. It was Daddy's fault, but I chose not to fire him."

I stifle a laugh, and when I glance at Jackson, he rolls his eyes.

"Well, thank goodness you're so forgiving. He really needs this job. I'm sure he would've been on the streets if you let him go."

Jackson lets out a loud laugh from beside us before taking a step closer and leaning over to kiss his daughter's cheek. He's so close, I can *smell* him. Fresh laundry and a smoky cologne engulfs me, but I don't step away. Not even when he stands at his full height and looks down at me. He just stares at me with a smile and I feel the corner of my lips tug upwards as he watches me like I'm all he wants.

There's a knock on the door and he rolls his eyes in annoyance before tucking a hair behind my ear. "She's right, you do look a lot better." He leans down and places the softest kiss on my cheek. He walks away before I can respond, and when I hear the door opening, a second later, a loud voice fills the house.

I rest Belle on the counter because she's getting heavy and before I can ask her about her day, a voice speaks from behind me.

"Well, *hello*," someone drawls.

I turn to see a man only a little shorter than Jackson. His hair is buzzed, and bleached blonde. I quickly realize he's Jackson's client. He's hot and looks young, which explains the bratty attitude Jackson is always complaining about.

He glances over at Isabelle before his smile lands on me. "You must be her mom." He goes on before I can correct him.

"Her dad told me you two weren't together." He closes the distance between us, takes my hand, and kisses the back of it. "I'm Rome, like the city."

"She doesn't care, like the rest of us," Jackson answers from behind him.

I narrow my eyes as I focus on him. "How old are you?"

A smile grows on his face. "I can be however old you want me to be." He takes a step closer.

I stifle a laugh as I pull my hand away.

Behind him, Jackson lets out a groan. "He's nineteen, but we're having him tested because he might've been swapped with a nine year old."

Rome glares at Jackson as if he just blew his cover.

"Well," I start. "I'm afraid you're fifteen years younger than I like my men."

His head snaps back to me, but I go on before he can open his smart mouth again.

"And I'm not her mom."

"Oh, well even better," Rome replies and I feel my brows furrow.

"Why would that be better?" Belle speaks up now. "Why doesn't anyone want to be my mom?"

I turn on my heels to face her. "*What?*"

Her shoulders are slouched as she looks between all of us and my heart sinks.

"Go to my office, Rome." Jackson shoves him out of his way before walking to Belle. "That isn't true, baby." He cups her small face in his hand and she looks up at him.

"Yeah, it is. I don't have a mom and Ms. Rose doesn't want to be my mom. Even *Mia* doesn't want to be my mom. Mia is great... What did I do?"

I have no clue who Mia is but I lift her into my arms again. "You're the best kiddo, Belle. If someone doesn't want to be in your life, it has *nothing* to do with you."

"Yeah," Jackson joins, kissing her head. "And Rose and Mia can't just *be* your mom, baby. That's not how it works."

"So how does it work?" She looks between us and when I look at Jackson, it's clear he doesn't have an answer, so I step in.

"Well, you already have a mom. Everyone has a mom because when we're babies, we're in our mommy's tummy, then we're born and we're here. So you have a tummy mommy, but she's not here and that's okay. If you get a second mommy, your dad has to get married and that'll be your mom."

It's clear this makes perfect sense to her as she lights up. "Daddy, you should marry Mia!"

Jackson stifles a laugh, and I *know* whatever this is wouldn't work. I know that and I don't want to explore whatever's pulling us together only to disappoint them, but still, jealousy begins to sprout within me at whoever this is.

Jackson takes his daughter from me to carry her. "I can't marry your ballet teacher, penguin."

I force a smile on my face as I ruffle her hair. "Your dad is also pretty ugly *and* smelly, so I don't think he'll ever get married."

Isabelle covers her mouth with her hand as she giggles.

"You don't need a second mommy." I kiss her cheek. "Your dad is all you need." I feel Jackson watching me, but I keep my smile on Belle and continue to convince myself that I'll never fit in their perfect picture.

# Chapter Thirty

## JACKSON

"**D**ON'T FLIRT WITH HER AGAIN." I shut my office door behind me and Rome tosses the paperweight in the air before catching it, a smirk playing on his lips.

"She's hot." He glances over at me, his smirk still present. "Nice tits too."

"Watch it, kid," I warn one last time as I walk over to my seat.

"She your nanny or something?"

I lean back in my seat as I study him. "Why is it so hard to believe that I take care of my kid on my own?" I ask, remembering his last assumptions of me only seeing my own daughter on weekends.

"Because you're a man," he deadpans.

"Men are more than capable of raising kids. Boys choose not to. Learn the difference and choose wisely which one you want to be." I gesture to the chair in front of me. "Sit."

He does before a smile lights up his face. "Before we start, was that Sire Griffin driving out of your driveway when I pulled in?"

I nod. "He's not going to watch you play until the charges for beating up Chase are dropped."

Rome sinks in his seat at that. I feel bad that this is happening to him, but I'm at the end of my rope here—there's been no good news since we last met.

"He'll watch you on TV though. He said he'll let me know if he has any tips after watching you play."

I see the bit of hope he regains.

"Is there any chance you can set up a meeting for him to tell me himself? If he has any tips, I mean."

I tell him I will before jumping into the meeting. "We need to do a major cleanup on your image. We tried getting your contracts back after releasing our statements, but there's too much damage done."

Rome runs his hand down his face before sulking in his seat. "I'm supposed to go to the basic needs kitchen the day before Thanksgiving," he says, monotone as ever. "It's something my sisters and I do every year in the neighborhood I grew up in. We relied on that kitchen for Thanksgiving growing up, so we give back. My sisters think I should post about it, but people are going to think it's just to look good."

"That's... really good of you." I watch him, surprised by his words since I thought he grew up rich but it's clear there's more to him than his spoiled attitude. "You should post a bit about it. There's always going to be people who think you're doing it for the press, but stay true to yourself."

I open my laptop. "Share your calendar with me. I have multiple other events you will be participating in and *these* are for the press, but we need all the help we can get."

He pulls out his phone.

"For the charity event, do not bring a date," I warn him.

"Why?"

"Because I don't trust your horny ass to not sneak off backstage or to the bathroom."

A smirk grows on his face, but he complies.

Before I can add more, a message pops up on my phone.

**Sire G**

Hey, my sister still there?

I feel my brows furrow at his text and rise from my seat. When I open my office door, Lisette's sweet laugh echoes through the house before my daughter's laugh follows. I smile at the sound of the happy house and respond to him.

Yeah. Why wouldn't she be?

Just making sure.

His text bubbles appear and then disappear. This happens
three more times before another message comes through.

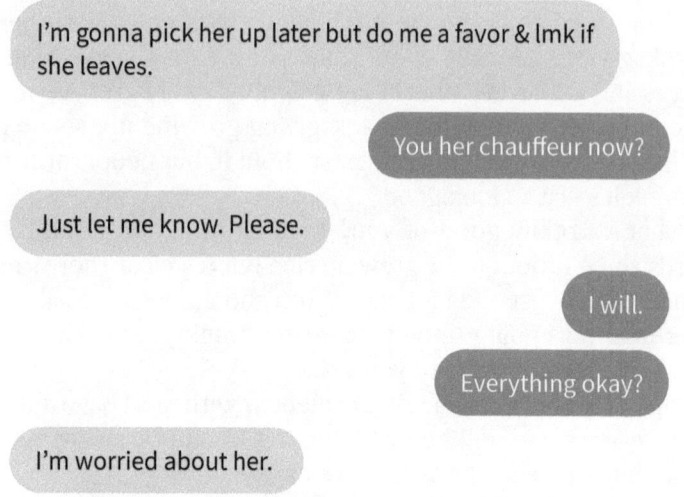

I'm gonna pick her up later but do me a favor & lmk if
she leaves.

You her chauffeur now?

Just let me know. Please.

I will.

Everything okay?

I'm worried about her.

His text bubbles disappear then come back.

Keep an eye on her for me. Let me know if she seems
off, zoning out and stuff. Joking more than usual
about being sad and shit.

A bad feeling settles in my stomach, but I only like his message.
   I walk back to my desk but as I look back at my laptop, I can't
think about anything else but that girl in my kitchen.
   *"You don't need a second mommy."*
   Was that her way of telling me she doesn't want this? My mind
trails back to our conversation in her room, the way she tried to
push me away from the hard part of her life. I know she doesn't
want my support, but I can't shake this overwhelming need to
help her. To do everything in my power to make sure every day is
a good day, one she can look back on when those dark thoughts
run through her mind.
   I shut the laptop and pull in a deep breath.
   "I'll call you to discuss the rest," I tell Rome. "Charity event on
Tuesday. Do not be late," I warn.

"Okay, Dad," Rome mumbles as he rises to his seat. He turns to look out to the backyard and nods to himself. "You have a really nice house."

He glances over to the side before nodding again. "You're a good dad, Jackson."

I'm thrown off that he called me *Jackson*, but I don't miss the sincerity in his words. I follow his eyes to Isabelle's newborn pictures.

"Thanks," I reply.

He nods in return before we walk out of my office. He keeps his head low as he walks for the door, but before walking out, he turns to me. "Thanks for this," he mumbles. "You can clearly afford a lawsuit from me and simply drop me as your client, but you won't."

"Yet," I add and his brows pull together. "This is my last resort, kid. The Red Sox put your contract on hold." I tell him the actual reason I needed him to come in today and I see the fear in his eyes.

"When?"

"They called yesterday, some bullshit about wanting to alter it, but I know how this goes. They're giving you time to fuck up. Making you a model citizen is my *last resort*. The Major League isn't just about hitting a ball and having a pretty face, Booker."

I can see his nerves skyrocketing as he runs a hand down his face. "I should've signed when you told me to." He sounds like he's about to cry and my dad heart practically bleeds for him. He's spoiled and bratty and doesn't care about much, but he's mine.

"We're going to fix this, but I need you to work with me."

He quickly nods in agreement. "I will. I swear."

I nod in return before opening the door and he thanks me profusely.

The minute the door is closed, Belle is screaming with a laugh and all of my worries and stress fades.

I walk into the kitchen but come to a stop when I find both girls *covered* in flour. Their laughs sober as they turn to me. Isabelle slowly drops her hand full of flour I'm sure she was about to throw. Lisette looks guilty as she stands in front of the counter in an empty attempt to cover the mess.

"She started it." Lisette points at my five-year-old who's jaw drops.

"I did *not*." She scoops up some flour before throwing it at Lisette's back and it covers the rest of her hair. "Liar."

A smirk grows on Lisette's face and I shake my head at the pair of them.

"I can't leave you alone for one minute, huh?"

"It's been five minutes." Lisette shrugs. "I never claimed to be a responsible adult."

She smiles and with a face like that, I couldn't be mad if the entire house was drowning in flour.

"Are we in trouble, Daddy?" Isabelle asks quietly.

Lisette lolls her head to the side, a mischievous smirk on her face. "*Are* we in trouble, Daddy?"

And there goes all hope of trying *not* to get hard in her presence. I shake my head at her before closing the distance between us. Her eyes grow with something like *excitement* as I stop in front of her.

"*You're* going to be in trouble if you keep on calling me that," I warn quietly and for once, she doesn't say anything in return. She tries, her mouth falls open but words are never spoken as her eyes land on my lips.

"How'd this happen?" I look up at Isabelle, desperately trying to distract myself from Lisette, who's still watching me.

"We were going to make our apple cinnamon cupcakes for Thanksgiving, but then *Lissy* started putting flour on my face."

I glance around the kitchen island and floor. "And that resulted in the entire bag of flour covering my floors?" I look back down at Lisette.

"She threw it back and I *may* have taken it a bit overboard."

I glance at my daughter who could be mistaken for a damn snowman. Lisette follows my line of sight and stifles a laugh.

"This doesn't look like it was a fair fight." I walk over to the bag of flour and there's surprisingly some left. Without thinking twice, I scoop up some flour from the counter and toss it in Lisette's face. Her jaw drops before Isabelle fills the kitchen with her laugh.

"That's because you clearly had an advantage on my kid." I grab more and throw it at her again. "And that's for the teasing nickname. Clean my kitchen."

A laugh bubbles from Lisette as she starts to scoop up flour from the counter.

"Don't even think about it, Lisette," I warn.

She raises her hand slowly.

"I'm *not* kidding. Don't—"

I don't get to finish my sentence as she tosses the flour at me. My eyes fall shut as their laughs fill my ears. I feel more flour being thrown at me and stand there with my eyes closed as they have their fun.

When I look down at myself, my black suit is now covered in white. My eyes meet Lisette's and as she looks down at my outfit her eyes slowly widen, as if she somehow just remembered I'm in a four thousand-dollar suit.

She chews on her lip nervously. "Why are you wearing that at home anyway?"

"I was in the office today," is all I say.

"It's just flour," she says, quieter now.

"Yeah, well, now you're in trouble." I stalk towards her and a smile grows on her face as she walks backwards. "Don't make this harder for yourself, sweetheart."

She takes off running into the living room with a laugh and I walk after her at a steady pace. My long strides quickly catch up to her as she corners herself.

"JJ, wait." She puts a hand up between us. "Your kid is watching, don't do—"

Her scream cuts off her sentence as I toss her over my shoulder.

"JJ!" She squirms in my arms, hitting my back and pleading to be let down.

I ignore her as I walk to the backyard while tapping a few buttons on my phone. I slide the back door open and Isabelle runs after me with a laugh as I watch the pool cover retract back.

"Don't you fucking *dare*, Jackson Jones," Lisette warns.

"What did I say about saying bad words?" I taunt, a smile creeping onto my face and she doesn't get to respond as I toss her into the pool.

Isabelle is hysterical beside me and I can't help but laugh with her as we watch Lisette in the deep end. Her arms flaunt frantically, but when she coughs, my laugh quickly sobers.

"Can you swim?" I kick my shoe off in a panic and when she screams for help, my other shoe is still on as I jump in for her. I quickly wrap an arm around her, but in a panic, she shoves me under the water.

When my head breaches the surface I hear her *laughing*.

"You fucking asshole." I throw water at her and she laughs up a damn storm.

"That's not funny, Lisette," I say more seriously and she simply rolls her eyes at me.

"I *could've* drowned. You didn't know I could swim. Now you know not to throw people into pools for fun."

With a hand on her shoulder, I shove her under the water again. A splash comes from beside me and I quickly turn to get Isabelle. Her head breaches with Lisette and they both laugh.

"Daddy, I don't need your help." Isabelle tries to push me off, but I keep a hand on her as I tread water.

"It's twelve feet, Belle. Let me help y—"

"I know how to swim."

My hand slips as she pushes me off and takes off swimming a few feet ahead of us. I stay close to her and when I turn to check on Lisette, a smile is on her face as she watches us.

"Such a helicopter parent," she teases.

"Call it what you want, but I'd rather she not drown." I swim a bit further from Lis to catch up with Belle.

"Oh, but to hell with me?"

"Apparently not since I'm in here with you," I shoot back.

Isabelle clearly gets tired as she swims back to me to cling to my arm.

"Quick break." She takes a few breaths before diving under the water.

"Okay, no." I pull her up before she can swim off. "Everybody out. We don't even have bathing suits on. Come on." I swim in front of Belle and she climbs on my back before I quickly make my way to the stairs.

I help her out before stepping out of the pool in a soaking suit. I shake my head like a dog in Belle's direction and she giggles while doing the same.

"We should get a dog." She lights up. "A big one, like Titi V's dog."

"Let's go change and finish baking." I distract her and she takes the bait as she walks off. I quickly grab her before she can leave a trail of water into the house.

"Uh uh, take your wet clothes off out here and grab a towel." I nod for the rack of pool towels we keep out here.

Isabelle walks over to them and when I turn to Lisette, I falter.

"Your pool is warm," she comments, her head to the side as she rings out her long hair.

My eyes land on her shirt, her *white* very see-through shirt, and I can tell clear as day that she's not wearing a bra since her nipples are on *full* display for me.

"Is it heated? Because that's another level of rich."

I take in the way they harden as a gust of wind blows past us and I know I'm going to be tortured by these images for the next few weeks.

"Why are you just staring like that?" Lisette looks down at herself and a light blush meets her cheeks as she sees what I do. "Take a picture, it'll last longer." She tosses her hair over her shoulder, standing proudly.

"No need," I mumble in response. I'm sure I suddenly gained a photographic memory because the sight of her wet hair clinging to her forehead in her soaked-through shirt and perky nipples will be in the front of my mind for a while.

I clear my throat and gain the strength to be the gentleman my mother raised as I look away from her.

"Come on, slow pokes," Isabelle says with a towel wrapped around her. She hurries past us, her clothes in a pile on the floor. "We have cupcakes to bake."

She disappears into the house, and when I look back at Lisette, my eyes instinctively go to her chest.

Rome was right. She has very nice tits. *Was he able to see her nipples through her shirt?*

I swallow my annoyance and walk past her for the towel rack. With my back to her, I quickly readjust the problem in my pants.

"I can see that, you know," Lisette whispers from behind me, her giggle touching my ear.

I feel my ears heat as I snatch two towels and hand one to her. She has a smile on her face but doesn't move to take the towel and *cover* herself.

"My brother is going to have a lot to say about this," she teases as she glances down between my legs.

*He'll have a lot more to say if I don't walk away right now.*

A groan escapes me when she smiles and I get harder. I move a hand to cover myself with my towel.

She finally puts me out of my misery and takes the towel from me. My shoulders sag in relief when she turns around. Just when I think I can walk away, she holds the towel between her legs and pulls her shirt off.

My eyes land on her bare back, and images of what she'll look like if she turns fill my mind. Without thinking, I close the distance between us. My front brushes against her back, and she remains still for half a second before tilting her head back to look at me.

"When are you going to stop holding yourself back and kiss me?" She turns to face me and it should be illegal how pretty this woman is.

My eyes trail to her nipples and I shake my head at myself as I look back up at her eyes and find them filled with need.

What she said in the kitchen rings in my head and as images fill my head of her kissing my daughter's cheek, calling her sweetie, and *carrying* her, I think about how easy it'd be with her and that's rare.

It's rare for me to take interest in the women in my daughter's life and it's even more rare for me to think they'll be an easy fit, but as I think of Lisette and my kid, deep down, I can see it working.

"Question," I say after a beat.

"Proceed," she replies, her eyes trailing down to the bulge in my pants.

"You said Belle doesn't need a second mom."

Her eyes meet mine.

"What's that supposed to mean?"

Her brows furrow as she studies me. "Why are you asking me that?"

"Because you're throwing me in for a loop with the mixed signals, Lisette. First, you let me believe you don't want her in your life, then you tell me you *do* want her only to literally turn around and say she doesn't need a second mom."

"Because she doesn't *need* one."

I throw my hands up in defeat. "I don't get you."

"I *do* want her in my life. Every damn day if you'll let me, but she should believe she's enough without anyone more than you," she tells me sternly. "Either way," she shrugs now, her eyes falling. "I'll ruin your kid."

My brows furrow as my gaze meets her worried one and it finally hits me. *She's scared.* "You must not know me if you think I'll let that happen."

Her head falls as she takes a step away, but I pull her closer and harder than I meant, causing her to crash into me. Steadying an arm around her waist, I quickly catch her.

When she looks back up at me, her eyes are on my lips but I grab her chin and force her to look at me. "I'm not going to let you hurt her, *ever.* You need to accept that maybe you *aren't* going to end up like your parents," I tell her, remembering the jokes she's made about having mommy issues.

Her eyes narrow, a hint of annoyance in them. "You have no idea what you're talking about." She pulls her face out of my grasp defensively.

I open my mouth to mend my words but she doesn't let me get a word in.

"You said we don't have to figure it out right now, so just drop it because I don't see this working out for a *while.*"

I let her go and it physically hurts my chest watching her walk away.

# Chapter Thirty-One

## LISETTE

MY BRAIN SCREAMS AT ME to turn around. To run back outside and tell him he's right. I *am* afraid of becoming the epitome of the woman I hate. I'm terrified I'm not strong enough to break the generational curse.

I don't turn around, though. Instead, my feet keep me marching forward, the fear of damaging his daughter is too big to overcome.

When I walk into the kitchen, Isabelle is sitting on the island, her wet curly hair falling around her face. She changed into a princess dress I'm certain is a pajama gown and she looks so damn precious.

"What took so long?" She pushes her hair out of her face as she cracks an egg into the bowl.

I don't answer her and instead take the hair tie from my wrist and tie her hair in a high loose bun. I kiss her cheek, purely instinctively, but I freeze as I recall what I just told her dad, and knowing I can't have them hurts.

"What do we have so far?" I muster up a smile. I adjust the towel around my chest as I look into the mixing bowl.

"One and a half cups of flour, two eggs, and half a tablespoon of salt."

My brows furrow as I look at her printed recipe sheet beside the bowl, the pictures making it easy for her to follow with help. "You mean *tea*spoon, right?"

She glances over at me before slapping a hand to her forehead. "*Shit.*"

My jaw drops before I erupt with a laugh. "Do not say that," I warn in a hushed tone. "Your dad will lose *his shit.*"

She shakes her head as she pushes the bowl away gently and slouches in her seat. "It's ruined now." She pouts. "That was all the flour we had left."

She looks around the kitchen filled with flour. "Can we use some of this?" She scoops up some flour from the counter, but I stop her.

"I don't think so." I see her eyes prickling with tears and roll my eyes at how dramatic she's being. "We can buy more flour, Belle." I bite back a laugh but go still at the sound of footsteps behind me.

I don't dare turn around and instead keep my eyes on Isabelle as she turns to her dad, tears threatening to spill from her gray eyes.

"What happened?" Jackson's tone takes on a sudden gruff protectiveness as he strides into the kitchen.

I force my eyes to stay trained on his kid as he brushes past me. In my peripheral, I notice a towel wrapped around his waist but not a trace of anything else.

"It's ruined." Isabelle points at the bowl, fighting back her tears.

"Penguin, we can make another batch. You don't need to get so upset."

She shakes her head, a single tear falling. "We don't have any more flour. I wanted it to be perfect for Abuela." Her voice breaks.

"We'll get more. It'll be perfect." Jackson shakes his head at her when another tear falls. "Oh my goodness, are you really going to be a *baby* over spilled milk?" He wipes a tear from her cheek.

"I didn't spill the milk and I'm *not* a *baby*."

A laugh escapes me and she snaps her head to me, her disappointment traded for anger. "Stop laughing! This is all your fault."

"Hey," Jackson warns, his voice strong. "Watch how you speak to her. There's no need to raise your voice. We can either go get more flour or you can sit here and cry then go to your room for the rude tone, and there'll be no cupcakes for anyone."

She doesn't respond and Jackson turns to me next.

"And you, stop laughing at her. It *is* your fault for throwing all the damn flour."

My eyes snap up to his and there's no trace of playfulness in his eyes. Just pure annoyance.

He lets out a frustrated breath, his eyes on the messy counter. "Clean my kitchen, *now*. Both of you." He turns before adding, "We can go get more flour when I finish getting dressed."

He sounds mad, but I know it has nothing to do with the flour.

"I think you're in trouble," Isabelle mumbles as she hops down from her seat.

*Yeah... I'm definitely in trouble.*

Not wanting to push his buttons, I do as I'm told and clean the mess I made.

By the time Jackson comes downstairs, the kitchen is as it was before I arrived.

"Here." He hands me a black shirt and gray basketball shorts. "I'll throw your clothes in the washer." He doesn't even look at me as he walks past me to grab my wet shirt by the sink.

Before he can walk off, I call out to him. "Wait."

He stops, his back still to me.

"I still have my shorts on." I'm not sure why my words come out mumbled, but they do.

He pulls in a breath. "Okay, just go change in the bathroom and drop it in the washer. The laundry room is upstairs. Last door down the hall, after the first left turn." He walks off before I can respond and I can't find the courage to ask for clearer directions.

I slip into the bathroom and shrug my wet pants off. My underwear falls next and I pat myself dry before slipping on Jackson's shirt. His scent quickly wraps around me and I find myself pulling in another deep breath.

His shirt falls somewhere between my thighs. The pants are a much bigger fit, but after pulling the drawstring and folding them, I make do.

Heading upstairs, I try to search my brain for where the laundry room was when Isabelle first gave me a tour, but I'm drawing a blank and the house is too big to even remotely remember.

I know he said something *last door*, but the last door I open at the top of the steps is what looks like another office. Closing the door, I make a right turn and walk to the end of the hall.

Opening that door next, I go still at the sight of Jackson's back. He's slipping a hoodie on and doesn't even flinch at the sound of the door opening.

"What's up, princess?" He turns and falters when he realizes I'm not Isabelle. "Yes?" he asks after I stare at him like an idiot.

"My bad, I can't find the laundry room."

"Last door to the *left*." He nods behind me. "Just follow this hall, the door is open."

I don't move as I try to decipher his tone. "Are you actually mad? Because I'll buy the flour and say sorry for *laughing* at her."

"I'm not mad." His clipped tone says otherwise.

"So what's with the attitude?"

"You're the only one who sounds like they have an attitude," he counters. "Watch it," he warns now, voice low.

"Don't tell me to *watch it*, Jackson. I'm not your kid."

"You're right. Neither of us are kids, so how about you lose the attitude and just say what your problem is?"

"I don't *have* a problem. I'm trying to figure out what *your* problem is. You're barely looking at me and clearly upset, so how about *you* say what your problem is?"

"I don't have a problem." He *rolls his eyes*. Like a *girl*.

"Do you want a tampon to go with that sass? Or are you a pad guy?"

His eyes narrow at me before he lets out a frustrated breath.

"See." I point at him. "Right there. The heavy breathing and eye-rolling. You're mad at me. Just say it and stop making it seem like nothing. I hate that."

"I'm not mad at you, Lisette. I'm mad at myself for letting you walk away," he nearly shouts, and I'm stuck in place.

He lets out another breath as he runs his hand through his damp hair. "You know what? No. I am mad at you for thinking this won't work."

I let out a scoff. "Right, because this is a prime example of a happy couple."

"People fight, Lisette. If you tried harder to *communicate*, maybe we wouldn't."

I roll my eyes at him. "Now I'm bad at communicating."

"You are," he shoots back.

Shaking my head, I point at him angrily. "*You're* the one who said we don't need to figure this out right now. Why are you so pissy? As if I need to make up my mind right this second. I can't give you that. Not right now."

"I didn't say this needed to happen *right now*. I know you have a lot going on, but don't stand here and say you don't see this working."

"I don't," I counter. "Why can't I feel that way and come back to it later?"

"Because I love you, Lisette!"

I go still and his eyes widen at his own words before he runs a hand down his face.

He shakes his head before his eyes meet mine. "I felt like I couldn't *breathe* when we raced to your house last week. In the back of my head I kept thinking about what I was going to tell Isabelle and how I'm going to lose sleep thinking about what we could've been had I not let you go to Paris upset. I want you, Lisette. All of you and this doesn't have to happen right this second, but it hurts hearing you don't see what I see when I *know* you do. You're just scared and won't tell me what it is that's scaring you and I can't *help*."

He sounds like he's exhausted.

I shake my head at him, that fear from before growing again. "You're not in love with me. You'll resent me eventually." *I'm too broken,* I don't add. "I'm the epitome of messy, Jackson. That's exactly why this won't work. Not right now at least."

"I said I love you." He seems to be correcting me. "If you give me a damn chance, I'd love to fall *in* love with you."

I feel my heart racing in my chest as the panic of the thought attacks me. "Just forget everything after we got out of the pool. I'll tutor your kid, cut back on calling you anything other than your name, and when she passes her next exam in a few weeks, we can go our separate ways." I turn without another word, discarding my clothes in the washer.

I'm reaching the steps when I hear a set of footsteps catching up with me. "Wait."

"Just drop it."

"No." He grabs my wrist, turning me to face him. "I don't want to pretend this never happened. I don't want us to go our separate ways after her exam."

"This is a disaster waiting to happen. Why can't you *see* that?" *Why can't you see how broken I am?*

He shakes his head, his eyes darting between mine, but he doesn't *say* anything; he just stands there.

"Why are you looking—"

His lips crash into mine and it only takes my brain one second to react as I melt into his touch. Wrapping my arms around his neck, I kiss him back harsher and *angrier* for confusing me and making me want him.

My tongue slips into his mouth as soon as he grants me access and I let out a moan as he pulls my hips to him, his fingers digging into my side like he's holding me for dear life.

In a sudden rush, he lifts me and I wrap my legs around him. He carries me somewhere I don't even care about because he starts pulling my shirt off and I can't care about anything else but his lips on me.

He settles me onto a bed, his hand slipping into my pants. I suck in a breath before he's pulling away. "Tell me you feel nothing else will come from this," he says breathlessly, his hand still in my pants. "Tell me you don't want to at least *try* to be a family with us."

I feel my face heat as I lay on his bed shirtless and gasping for air. I keep my eyes low as I move his hand. Rising to my feet, I pull my shirt on.

"Seriously?" He sounds *broken*, and I feel my face heat in embarrassment and anger.

I only shake my head, but as I try to walk past him, he steps in my way, leaning down to catch my eyes with his. "The only reason you don't want to *figure this out right now* is because you're scared and you're stalling. You're waiting for one of us to fuck up so you don't have to try."

I go still, a part of me hating how well he knows me.

He tucks a wet strand of hair behind my ear. "Just because you had a bad mom doesn't mean you'll be a bad mom." His words nearly shake me to the bone. "You're not her and you don't need a good example of a good parent to be a great one."

I blink my tears away, but he sees them and cups my face.

"I *know* you want us. I wouldn't be begging for you if I didn't think you did." He rests his forehead against mine. "Just say yes."

I open my mouth, but he plants a quick kiss on my lips.

"Please don't walk away from me again. Just say yes," he begs, his lips brushing mine.

This man is going to drive me to insanity, but I'll gladly give him the directions.

At the sound of a gasp, I turn and Isabelle stares back at us. Her brows furrow, but her dad pulls away, and then her jaw drops.

She seems to be going through every emotion as her face morphs from her wide eyes to her jaw-dropping.

"Were you just *kissing*?"

I look over at Jackson for an answer, but he looks to me as if I was supposed to know what the hell to say.

"Are you boyfriend and *girlfriend*?"

I glance over at Belle before looking at her dad who looks like a deer stuck in headlights.

"Oh my goodness." She slaps her hand over her face before she smiles at us. "Why didn't I think of this sooner? Daddy, you can just marry Lissy and *she* can be my mom." She smiles so damn big at us and you couldn't hold a gun to my head and tell me to walk away from this little girl.

I shake my head at myself as I turn to Jackson. *Say something*, I mouth.

A forced smile grows on his face as he turns to his kid. "Can you wait for us downstairs, please?"

"But are you getting married?"

"I don't think so," he answers casually.

"Mom?"

I go still as I stare at Jackson and his eyes widen as he takes a step away from me. "Um, no." He shakes his head gently. "Let's call her Lissy. Remember what we said about needing to be married to have a second mom?"

Her brows furrow. "But why were you kissing if you're not getting married?"

"We weren't kissing," he lies. "It only looked like that, but I was telling her a secret."

She looks confused as she looks over at me. "How about we negotiate you two getting married?"

"I need to go." I rush out of the room and Jackson calls out to me, but I ignore him. "I'm going to get the flour." I nearly run out of the house.

"Take my car," he calls out, and I grab his keys by the door before slipping out.

The minute I'm in his car, I call Bay.

"Where's the fire?" She has the nerve to *laugh* at my panicked expression.

"Jackson was in my pants," I blurt as I speed very far away from his house.

A smile grows on her face as she lays on her stomach, her phone against something on her bed. "Was it good or did you call it and he sucks like the majority of the male population?"

"That's not why I called." I steal a glance at her to check if she's still paying attention and she is. "His kid saw us kissing and called me the universal phrase for what children call the people who birth them."

Her brows pull together before she bursts into a laugh.

"It's not funny." I hit my head on the steering wheel when I get to a stop sign.

"Aww, she was just excited about the idea." She smiles, her freckles more prominent as if she sat in the sun all day. "What did her dad say about that?"

I let out a bitter laugh. "He told her not to call me that." I recall what he said about not introducing his partners to her and he looked just as scared as I felt.

"That's understandable." She nods to herself. "So you're dating him? What'd your brother say?"

"Who cares about my brother? That's not the point right now. He wants me to give us a *try*." I drive off again. "Like as a *family*."

"Well... he has a daughter, so if you date it will be a family setting." Bay watches me like she doesn't see the issue.

I shake my head at everything in my head.

"Wait, when was this?"

"A minute ago."

"And where are you going?" she asks lightly, but I don't answer. "You're *running*?"

"I'm scared," I shout now. "This is too much too fast and they scared me."

"Turn your car around right now." She keeps her voice strong, nearly threatening. "Name one bad thing about him."

I try to think but nothing comes to mind. "He's too perfect."

Bay says something under her breath. "You deserve him, Lis. You deserve to be happy and you love his daughter. Turn around and *try*."

I come to a red light and turn to her. "What if I fuck it up?"

Her eyes soften before she sucks her teeth. "Honestly? You probably will fuck it up, but," she quickly adds when she sees my face fall. "Not because you're an addict. You're *human*. Don't self-sabotage this. You just overdosed last week, you went out thinking you had no one, and today a great man wants to love you and raise his baby. That's a beautiful thing."

I feel my eyes prickling with tears as I pull over. "He said he loves me." I bury my face in my hands.

"Okay, that would scare me too. How long have you known him?"

I lay my head against my seat. "Technically..." I take a second to think. "A little over four years, but I've been hanging out with him and tutoring his daughter for a little over two months."

Bay nods in thought. "Yeah, that's a little quick."

"He said he loves me like how I say I love you. Not *in* love with me."

Her brows furrow now. "But we don't make out and fuck?"

I don't answer and her smile returns.

"I'm going to let you believe what you want since you look terrified. Listen." She brushes the L word aside. "He has no red flags. As long as you don't self-sabotage, this is going to be okay. It's going to be *safe*," she reassures me softly and I nod in return as my heart slows down.

"Go back and just go with the flow. One step at a time. When you get panicked, just remember you get to be happy. You've been through enough years of depression and heartache. Sober you is the best you and sober you will be a great mom. Either way, you'll have him to help you learn."

"Okay." I tuck my hair behind my ear as I drive off again. I stay on the phone with her as I get the flour.

I'm driving back to Jackson's house when I suddenly interrupt her rant about her roommate.

"Hey, have you heard from Erin?" I steal a glance at her and her face softens.

"You didn't hear?" Her voice softens and I feel my heart *sink*. "Winter was able to get her admitted into rehab."

I let out a breath of relief, my mind a true pessimist. "That's good." I nod to myself. "I was really scared for her after seeing her like that... she seemed so hopeless." I shake my head as I remember her emotionless eyes.

"Yeah." Bay looks off to the side.

"Did you ever find out what made her spiral?"

When Bay doesn't answer, I look at her briefly and she's watching me carefully. "You two weren't that close, were you?"

I shake my head in response. "I only hung out with her a handful of times besides when we all went to meetings together." I shrug. "We texted a bit but not about anything serious."

Bay nods in return. "She was in a custody battle."

My eyes widen as I glance back at her. "She has *kids*?"

She nods again before mustering up a smile. "We'll talk about her later." She pulls her curls into a bun before grabbing her towel. "She nor your mom are examples of what you'll become, so stop overthinking because I know that face." She gives me a pointed look as she steps into her bathroom. "Go take control of your happiness. Call me with updates later," she says before turning her shower on.

I pull in a breath, forcing myself to shake my thoughts of Erin for now.

When I knock on Jackson's door again, he looks surprised as he opens the door.

"Yes." I get it out before I can back out. "I'll try. Yes."

A smile so damn big grows on his face. He glances over his shoulder before planting a gentle kiss on my forehead. "We can't tell her about this."

I nod in agreement.

"I was incredibly reckless earlier." He shakes his head at himself. "You make me reckless and as much as I want to lose my mind with you, that can't happen again. I don't want her to get her hopes up. I want you apart of our family, but you said it yourself that you don't want to hurt her and—"

"I get it, Jackson," I cut him off.

He nods in return before kissing my cheek and as he leads me into the house, I don't miss the hopeful smile on his face.

# Chapter Thirty-Two

# JACKSON

W HEN LISETTE LEFT, A PART of me thought she was running away and never coming back. It's why I made her take my car, forcing her with a reason to come back, but she did and it was clear she just needed space to clear her head.

We're baking cupcakes in the kitchen, and while Isabelle hasn't called her mom again, I can tell Lisette is holding her breath around her. I'm still kicking myself for letting her catch us and I think I lied well enough, but I know I'm in for a hundred questions later.

It's not that I don't want her to know about us. I just rather burn alive than let my little girl get hurt. Whether that's her dreams being crushed or her physically getting harmed. Lisette is not in a good mental space right now and I'm aware that she just needs support, but I refuse to let my daughter get caught in the crossfire as we explore our feelings for each other. We need to be incredibly certain before she gets involved.

"Should we add the glaze to them?" Isabelle looks between Lisette and me.

I focus on Lisette and she watches the cupcakes like they're suddenly the most fascinating thing on Earth.

"Hello?" Belle waves her hand between us.

I answer her as I keep my gaze on Lisette. "I think we should wait until Thanksgiving and everyone can decide if they want glaze or not." In my peripheral, I see Belle nod in thought.

"What do you think, Lissy?" I ask.

"Uh-huh," she mumbles.

Stepping around Belle, I walk towards Lisette, but she backs away. "You seem distracted," I tread lightly.

"I'm not," she counters.

"You okay?" I dip my head to catch my eyes with hers.

She looks at me for a moment before nodding and I hold myself back from kissing her worried face.

"You sure?" I ask quietly. "Because if I pushed too far then—"

"You didn't." She shakes her head in return. "I need to stop standing in the way of my own happiness. I'm trying this." She seems to be repeating after someone, and I realize she must've called one of her girlfriends on her drive.

At the sound of the door ringing, I'm pulled away from her pretty face.

I'm not sure who I was expecting, but when I open the door to find Sire, I go still.

His brows furrow as he watches me. "Why are you looking at me like you've seen a ghost?" He steps around me and I change my face.

"I wasn't."

"You were. Is my niece okay?"

I pull in a deep breath as I watch him look around the house. "Yeah, she's great." I clear my throat and I feel so damn guilty now. All of a sudden Lisette *in my bed* is on the front of my mind as I watch her brother.

"You should have that housewarming party the twins were trying to convince you to do." Sire nods in approval as he gazes at my high ceiling.

"You know," he starts, a smirk on his face now. "Technically my talent is to thank for this house of yours."

I let out a scoff as I shove him and head for the kitchen. "You arrogant bitch," I mumble and he barks up a laugh from behind me.

"You're welcome for signing you as my agent," he teases.

"No, asshole, *you're* welcome."

He laughs from behind me again, and this time, I can't help but join.

Turning the corner, I enter the kitchen and Isabelle's entire face lights up as Sire whips around the corner behind me.

"Uncle Sigh!" She hops down from the stool and behind her, Lisette's brows furrow as she looks between me and Sire.

She focuses on me again, asking a silent question and I slightly shrug before turning to her brother.

He lifts Isabelle into her arms before throwing her in the air and clapping between each catch. It took me a very long time to not freak out when he does that, but Belle's smile eases my nerves. Their laughs fill the kitchen and I only feel worse because he's going to be so damn mad at me when he finds out my tongue was down his sister's throat while my fingers were in her.

Belle lets out a gasps, pulling me out of my thoughts as she squirms out of her uncle's arms. "I need to show you the turkey we made in school."

He lets her down and she takes a step before pausing, her finger in the air. "I need to use the bathroom first, then I'll show you my art." She runs upstairs, leaving us laughing behind her.

Sire turns to his sister. "Our flight leaves soon, we should get going. You still need to pack."

I look over at Lisette and I see the realization cross her face as to why he's here.

"I forgot to call you." She shakes her head at herself. "I'm not going."

Sire lets out a breath and I can't tell if he's disappointed or mad. "Lisette, can we stop fighting about this already? You agreed you'd come earlier. Why do you want to be alone for Thanksgiving?"

"It's not that I *want* to be alone." She shrugs. "I just really don't want to be around V's big family. I love her, but she made it seem like it's going to be a big party and I don't have it in me to smile for strangers."

He lets out a defeated breath and they go back and forth for a minute before I step in.

"You can spend Thanksgiving here." I shrug.

They both glance over at me, Lisette shaking her head. "That's okay."

"So you'll come?" I push.

She gives me a knowing look that I ignore. "Thanksgiving is a family holiday." She trails off, silently reminding me of my words from before, but Isabelle won't question her being here.

"It's family and friends," I correct her. I glance over at her brother for support, but his brows furrow as he looks back over at Lisette and I watch as his eyes give her a once over.

"Why are you in his clothes?"

I turn to Lisette and try to think about *anything* else to keep the blush off my face.

"She fell in the pool."

"I fell in the pool."

We speak at the same time, and Sire simply nods once before turning back to me. "You didn't need to invite her over, she can spend Thanksgiving with Vid and me." He shakes his head now, as if I'm doing him a favor, but it only reminds me of his worry for her and I know what he meant.

"I know I didn't." I shrug again. I almost add that I *want* to spend Thanksgiving with her and I'm sure that sounds innocent, but the guilt in the pit of my stomach is afraid he'll see right through me.

Sire looks like he's thinking before he shakes his head. "No, just come with us. I'm going to be gone until Monday."

"Although my depression doesn't let me do it often, I'm capable of feeding and bathing myself, Sire," she tells him, and I can hear the annoyance in her tone, although she clearly tries to conceal it.

"But—"

"Sire," Lisette deadpans. "We're not fighting about this. Especially not in front of him. I'm *fine*. I can be alone. I'm not going to do anything."

They watch each other, having a silent conversation.

"I swear it on the twins," she bites out and I can see Sire about to give in, but worry flashes through his eyes, adding to his hesitation.

"She can stay here until you get back," I suggest.

"What?" Lisette shakes her head. "No."

"Why not?" I turn my full attention to her, offended by her tone.

"Because I don't need a babysitter."

"What's with the attitude?" I ask, and she rolls her eyes at me. "Lisette," I warn.

"Don't *Lisette* me." She rolls her eyes again, turning to Sire with her arms crossed. "I'm going home and I'll be back here on Thanksgiving if I feel like it."

"*If* you feel like it?" I question before her brother can, disappointment seeping into my voice.

"I'd feel better if you stayed here," Sire voices, nodding in agreement with himself.

"I don't care how you'd feel," she counters.

"Stop being like that," he throws back.

"No."

I step in again. "Why are you being so difficult?"

"You're a man. You deserve no peace." She rolls her eyes before turning to her brother. I can see her anger growing and it's clear now this is more than her just sleeping over. "You said you trusted me. Making your friend watch me does not feel like that."

When I see a gloss covering her eyes, I feel my face soften.

"It was an *accident!*" Her voice breaks now and I go still.

"Lisette—" he tries to start.

"Whatever." She blinks her tears away, picking up her phone as she aimlessly scrolls. "I'll spend the night here until you get back, then I'll go to your house where you can watch me until Wednesday like we discussed. Have a safe flight."

I look over at her brother and he lets out a defeated sigh, his shoulder slouching. "Can you come outside so we can talk?"

"Have a safe flight, Sire." She turns on her heels, walking to the back of the house.

The room feels thick and when Isabelle walks in, she raises her brows. I have to bite back a laugh and shake my head, silently telling her to stop.

Her brows rise again before she shrugs. "I'll go check on her," she says as she pivots.

Sire lets out a defeated sigh as he runs a hand down his face. "She doesn't get it." He shakes his head at himself.

"Get what?"

"Everything." His eyes meet mine and he looks torn. "If she found me like that—" he cuts himself off before trying again. "I feel like I can't breathe when she's not near. My brain keeps replaying images from how we found her and it's *suffocating.* Having her in my sight is the only thing stopping me from looking for an escape at the bottom of a bottle."

I go still, knowing this is the first time he's ever opened up to me about his addiction. I realize now how badly this is really affecting him.

He takes in a deep breath and it's like he can breathe better with that off of his chest. "Sorry," he mumbles, running a hand through his hair.

"Don't apologize," I reassure him. "I think you two need to talk, but not tonight. Emotions are too high. I'll keep an eye on her, but if she says she doesn't need to be watched, then she doesn't need to be watched."

"You really believe that?" he nearly whispers.

I study him for a beat before shrugging, honestly not knowing what she needs.

"I'm not going to stand here and act like I understand what either of you are feeling, but I was there, too. While my relationship with her doesn't hold a candle to yours, I was scared, too, but when she was standing here a second ago with tears in her eyes, *begging* you to believe her, I did. If she says it was an accident, then that's what it was. I completely understand not trusting her. I don't think she's fine either, but you need to approach her in a different way because clearly this isn't working and you're only going to push her away."

It looks like a hundred thoughts run through his head as he lets my words sink in. After a beat, he nods, but he's clearly still lost in thought.

"Call me if anything."

I smile at his words. "Nothing is going to happen. I got her."

He smiles as if half of his worries were shaved off and there goes the guilt again because it was my selfish need to have her near that made me suggest she sleepover, *not* to put him at ease.

"I appreciate it, man." He closes the distance to hug me and I feel like the worst friend ever because the only thing on my mind is whether or not Lisette will be in my bed one of the next five nights.

"It's no problem," I force out.

Sire lets out a breath before he pulls away. "Let's go find the brat." He walks off and I follow behind, biting my tongue so I don't confess like a damn sinner.

*Calm down.*

*He trusts you with her,* the more rational part of me says.

I shake my head of my thoughts and follow Isabelle's voice to the backyard, where we find both girls with their feet in the pool.

"Hey," Sire starts gently and while Isabelle turns with a smile, Lisette keeps her eyes forward. "You can either hug me goodbye or get pushed into the pool."

Lisette doesn't answer until Sire takes a step toward her.

"If you push me, I'm drowning myself, and you will be going to jail."

A laugh escapes Sire and Lisette turns with a small smile before rolling her eyes. "I'm not hugging your ugly ass. Just go."

"Get up." He ignores her and their interaction makes me wish I had siblings.

"Sire—" She doesn't get to finish her sentence as he pulls her up by the arm and hugs her. She keeps her hands at her side as he wraps his arms around her head. After a second, he takes her arms and forces them around him before hugging her again.

He whispers something in her ear and I nod for Isabelle to follow me so we can give them a minute.

"Lissy said Uncle Sigh is an asshole."

I let out a defeated sigh and choose to ignore her, but I feel her watching me.

"Why is he an *asshole*?" She pushes her limits and I stop in my tracks as I look down at her. "I won't say asshole again," she says through a yawn, and I bite back a laugh when she isn't looking.

I follow behind her before she turns to me.

"I'm so excited for Thanksgiving." She smiles at me like her entire day is made.

I scoop her into my arms when I notice how tired she looks. I hug her close before kissing her. "So am I."

When she yawns again, I set her on the couch to watch a movie, knowing she'll fight her sleep if I send her to bed. I'm cleaning the kitchen when a set of footsteps sound through the house. When I look up, Sire has his arm wrapped around his sister's shoulder and she has her arms crossed like a brat.

"She promised to be on her worst behavior, so good luck," Sire announces before Lisette shoves him away.

"Leave before I piss you off."

Sire rolls his eyes at her before hugging her goodbye. He offers me his hand next for our handshake. When he looks for Isabelle, we find her falling asleep in the living room. I walk Sire out, and by the time I come back, she's somehow sleeping while sitting upright.

I pick her up and kiss her nose. "My sweet baby." I kiss her again and when I look up, Lisette is watching me with a smile.

"You're such a good dad." She shakes her head like she can't believe it.

"Why'd you say it like that?" A short laugh escapes me.

She shrugs. "There's not a lot of good parents in this world. I'm glad she landed with you."

Her words force a weight on my chest as I look back down at my daughter and I hold her a bit tighter. "I'll never understand how anyone couldn't be a good parent." I shake my head at the thought. "She's so easy to love."

When I look back up at Lisette, her somber smile is on Isabelle and I catch my words.

"I don't mean you weren't easy to love as a kid," I quickly corrected myself. "How your parents treated you isn't a reflection of you."

She smiles, but it seems forced now and I feel myself deflate.

"I'm sorry." I shake my head at myself and her smile seems genuine now.

"Let's ignore that last ten minutes and go back to the heated kissing."

I let my eyes fall shut, a smile growing on my face. "Did you say that so you weren't the only one who felt uncomfortable?"

"Woah there." She puts a hand up. "Too specific. How'd you know that?"

I break into a laugh before forcing myself quiet when Belle shifts under me.

I nod towards the stairs. "Let me show you where the guest room is."

She follows close behind me before speaking up again. "Aren't they all guest rooms?" she teases.

"Well, I have one reserved for my parents, but yeah, technically. You can pick any room you want, but they're not all fully furnished yet and I was going to give you the one with the fully stocked bathroom."

Lisette is quiet, and when I steal a glance at her, she's already looking at me. "Why can't I share a room with you?"

I face away from her compelling eyes. "Because we're not sleeping together."

"I said yes to you?" She sounds utterly confused as I set Isabelle in bed. I tuck her in before kissing her. Lisette steps beside me, kissing her cheek as if it were a habit, and I can't help but smile at my girls.

She turns to me, her brows furrowed and I'm drawn back to our conversation.

"I'm aware of that," I start again as I pull Isabelle's door shut and Lisette follows close behind me. "But Sire reminded me that you're not okay and I don't want to have sex until you're in a better head space."

She lets out a scoff. "You are aware that you nearly fingered me in the same *headspace*, right?"

I give her a knowing look. "I was thinking with my dick and proving a point. This is different and after you came here all sad and looking to fuck it out, it showed me you do that when you're hurt. I want to have sex with you when you aren't looking to escape."

We step in front of the room she occupied last time and she glances between the door and me. She watches me for a beat. "You're too much of a gentleman."

"Thank you?" My brows furrow at her tone and angry face.

"And too polite." She rolls her eyes.

I bite back a smile before turning more serious. "I think Belle will bring up marriage again if she knows you're sleeping here, so we need to figure out how we're hiding this." If she hadn't caught us, she probably wouldn't bat an eye since she loves sleepovers, but the idea of Lisette being her new mom is still fresh in her mind.

She shakes her head before her shoulders sag. "I can go home."

I stop her from stepping around me, the look on her face telling me she doesn't want to be alone. "I promised your brother you'd stay and I'm aware you don't need a babysitter, but just stop fighting us."

She rolls her eyes again.

Taking a step forward, I kiss her gently. "She has school tomorrow and we'll be out of the house before you're awake. We can just act like you're arriving early in the morning the next few days and you'll say bye to her when I put her to bed."

She lets out a scoff. "This is so dumb."

When she opens her mouth again, I shut her up with a kiss. "You don't want to be my dirty little secret?" I tease.

A smile grows on her face as she looks up at me. "I won't mind if I get to sleep with you and there was a secret worth keeping."

I give her a once over, but step away before I can change my mind. "Good night, reina."

She turns on her heels, but I notice the small smile she tries to hide.

# Chapter Thirty-Three

## JACKSON

LISETTE SLEPT IN MY HOUSE. Forty-eight hours with her in my space and I have no clue why I suggested this because every time I pass by the guest room she's occupying, her scent engulfs me and my senses are flooding with her.

Isabelle hasn't caught on and my plan for Lisette to act like she's arriving in the mornings has been working. With how obsessed my kid is with her, she doesn't even question her presence before pulling her around the house to play a new game.

"This is creepy."

I turn on my heels to find Lisette leaning against the wall, her arms crossed over her chest.

"You're just staring at my room." She nods towards *her room*. "Did you change your mind about your no sex rule or is the mess eating you alive? Because it'll be put together when I leave, and I will clean it right now if your OCD won't let you have sex in a messy room."

"We're still not having sex." I bite back a smile when she rolls her eyes. "I don't mind the mess." That was a lie. It was indeed eating me alive that her bed wasn't made and it was nearly 2:00 p.m. I take a step away from the door and she pushes off the wall.

The house smells like all of the food we've been cooking, but as she walks closer, all I smell is her. She used the soap I put in her bathroom, but her perfume is different—light and fruity.

"Isabelle just put her outfit on." She smiles up at me. "When I went home to pack, I got a dress like you suggested, but if you're matching her, then I'm going to be incredibly underdressed."

I let out a soft laugh. "She's just extra and needs to wear a prom dress for every occasion. Wear what you have."

"Well, I had no other option," she points out. "Unless you wanted me to wear nothing, of course," she teases.

"Nothing wouldn't be the worst outfit." I shrug, trying to keep my heart rate down and the blush off my face, but I know I'm failing when she smiles and my ears heat.

"I'll try the dress on and if I don't like it, nothing it is." She shrugs, walking past me to enter her room. I don't hear the door close and force my feet to *walk*.

I slip into my room. I change into cream slacks and a brown short-sleeved button-down. When I make it to Isabelle's room, she's looking at her white and peach dress in the mirror. There's a big bow on the back, and I watch as she fluffs the puffy ends.

I let her pick out her own outfits, especially for holidays, and I wasn't joking when I said it's mandatory to her that she's in an over-the-top dress.

"You look beautiful, baby." I smile down at her as I slip my phone out, but she quickly puts a hand up.

"No pictures. We need to do my hair." She's already walking to her bathroom and I follow close behind her. I hand her my phone and she scrolls through the album of hairstyles we put together.

When she settles on one, I get started by parting the front of her hair. Today's hairstyle is simple, two braids hanging in the front of her face with the rest up in a ponytail.

We're done in a few minutes and she turns her head in the mirror to examine it. "Perfect." She smiles to herself. "Okay, pictures now." She hops off her chair and puts a hand on her hip as she smiles at me. I stifle a laugh as I take a hundred pictures of her.

At the sound of someone laughing, I turn to the side and my breath gets caught in my throat at the sight of Lisette.

Unlike the clothes she usually sports, she stands in front of me in a dress. It's short, too short, but not too tight, at least the bottom isn't. The top hugs her boobs perfectly. It has long, flared sleeves, and everything about it looks perfect on her.

"Oh, I *love* this." Isabelle walks over to her, tugging on the sleeves. "You match Daddy." Belle looks over at my brown shirt and I smile down at her.

"We need a group picture." She walks over to her full-length mirror and I know better than to protest against a picture with this kid, but Lisette clearly doesn't because she stays where she is.

"I'm good."

Isabelle turns to her and I bite back a smile at her offended look. "We *need* a picture."

"We need food, water, and shelter. You *want* a picture," Lisette points out before looking up at me. "You didn't teach your kid the difference between wants and needs?"

I let out a low laugh but quickly wipe my smile clean as Belle turns to me. She's a little manic on holidays and I'm far from scared of my own kid, but I'm smart and I know how to pick my battles. This isn't one I am going to fight.

I simply give her a nod and walk over to Lisette. Wrapping an arm around her waist, I usher her to stand in front of the mirror with us. "Just make the kid happy so we can eat in peace," I grumble before smiling at the mirror, my phone pointed at our reflection.

I hear Lisette let out a sigh before she smiles and my smile quickly turns more genuine at the sight. I'm suddenly aware that my arm is still around her, but she doesn't seem to mind and Belle doesn't bat an eye, so I don't move as I take another picture of us.

As I look at us in the mirror, you couldn't pay me any amount of *anything* to believe *we wouldn't work.* I almost shake my head at her words. She fits with us better than a missing puzzle piece.

"Okay, now just me and Lissy," Isabelle instructs and I move out of the way.

Lisette looks miserable and Isabelle looks offended once again, but before she can voice a complaint, Lisette quickly forces a smile.

I snap a few pictures and my heart damn near explodes when Lisette squats to hug her for the picture. She kisses her cheek, and I quickly capture it in a picture.

"Let me carry you, baby." Lisette lifts her and I shake my head as I see Belle about to lose her shit.

"I'm not a *baby.*"

"Sure you are." She blows a raspberry in her neck and the room fills with Belle's laugh. "Such a cute baby," Lisette teases as she shifts her in her arms so she's cradling her like an infant.

"Aww, look at the baby," I join, taking a video of Belle.

"Stop it," she protests, but a smile is on her face against her clear efforts. "I'm a big girl."

"How old is she?" Lisette asks as she rocks Belle in her arms. "One years old?"

"Yeah, it *looks* like she's one." I squeeze Belle's cheeks.

"I'm five! Put me down right now."

Her bedroom fills with Lisette's laugh as I lean over to blow a raspberry in the crease of Belle's neck. She shifts frantically, and when I notice Lisette struggling to hold her, I step behind her and place an arm around both of them to support Belle from falling as she squirms.

"Look how cute the baby is when she's sleeping," I tease again and Belle shouts that she's awake, but we ignore her with a laugh as I point the video at the mirror. In my reflection, Lisette stares at me and my arms around them.

Her smile slips an inch before she looks down at Belle. "I love you." She moves one of her braids from her face, her voice full of so much admiration.

Belle looks very unamused as she watches us. "I would love you more if you didn't treat me like a baby."

Lisette stifles a laugh before kissing her forehead. "My sweet baby."

Belle groans, her eyes damn nearing rolling to the back of her head and we let out a laugh. Lisette sets her down just as the door rings.

"Abuela's here." Belle takes off running and I can see Lisette let out a defeated breath.

"I should go."

I quickly step in her way. "My mom will think it's rude or that something is wrong if you leave just as she got here. Just stay," I plead.

"No offense, but I don't really care what she thinks, JJ."

Surprisingly, I'm not offended.

"I told you I was leaving before they got here, and you've been stalling all day."

I grab her wrist. "Stop overthinking this." I quickly steal a kiss. "I told my mom a friend was going to be here. She won't think much of it. This isn't a meet my mom as my girlfriend thing."

A smile grows on her face as she rolls her eyes at me. "You kiss all your *friends*?"

"Only a handful," I tease before kissing her again.

Her eyes narrow on me, but I see the moment she gives in. "Fine. Whatever. It's just dinner." She walks past me and I am *way* too damn happy, but I try my hardest to keep the excitement off my face.

# Chapter Thirty-Four

## LISETTE

J ACKSON IS SMILING LIKE AN idiot, but I'm not delusional enough to convince myself it's my presence and not his parents that has him smiling like his entire day was made.

I do *not* want to be here. I didn't even want to sleep here, but Sire is a fucking headache, so here I am, playing house with his best friend. I should sleep with Jackson just to piss him off.

I get that he's worried. I *get it*, but his lack of faith in me hurts more than I'll ever admit. I'm fine.

Another thing I don't want to admit is that I've been *great* the two nights I've slept here. Not a single urge to run off and throw my life away for a small white pill.

It's *temporary*, my cruel mind reminds me.

*You always get an amazing week before it all comes crashing down. It's like clockwork. Inevitable.*

Images of Jackson's arms around me holding his kid push my dark thoughts away. He looked so happy holding us. I felt so happy letting him hold us, but there the thoughts went again, snatching away the hope he gave me.

My head keeps telling me this will never work but every smile he puts on my face makes me think otherwise. Like maybe he's right.

*He's not. You'll tarnish them.*

As I make it to the last step, my eyes land on his parents as Isabelle opens the door for them. My eyes land on the rings on both of their hands and I'm only reminded how different our lives are.

His parents are still married.

Me and my bio sisters have different sperm donors.

His parents are *present*.

Mine were absent addicts whom I haven't spoken to since I was a teenager.

They seem happy.

I wanted to die at the ripe age of ten, just a few years before I started using drugs to cope.

"And who is this lovely peach?" Jackson's mom's eyes light up as she looks over at me.

I force a smile and suddenly grow uncomfortable with both of his parents watching me, eyes wide in surprise and suspicion.

"This is Lissy." Isabelle beams. "I'm going to negotiate with Daddy that they get married."

Her grandma's face mirrors my shock. She hasn't brought that up since she caught us kiss, but hearing her words still shakes me to the core.

Jackson's mom looks behind me, and when I hear a set of footsteps, I know it's her son she's watching.

"What is this I'm hearing about getting married?" She raises her brows at Jackson. She looks over at me now, but she's still struggling to shake the shock from her face. When her eyes scan down to the scars on my leg, her eyes widen before she looks up at me again.

Now I really don't want to be here.

Jackson steps beside me, and since I'm still stuck in place at the end of his steps, he lightly pushes the small of my back, forcing me to walk with him. "Princess, we're not negotiating that. Lissy is very smelly and I don't like weddings," Jackson teases lightly and his daughter laughs at his jab at me.

"But weddings are so pretty." She begins to rant about one of the Disney princesses' wedding as her dad introduces me to his parents.

"This is Lisette," he says as he leans over to kiss his mom's cheek while whispering in her ear. "Ignore your granddaughter."

He forces a smile as he pulls away. "Lisette has been tutoring Belle and her plans fell through. She's joining us for dinner."

"And why does your kid think you're marrying her?" Jackson's mom says with something in her eyes I can't quite decipher.

"Stop it," Jackson mumbles. "She's a *friend*. The friend I told you was joining us."

She raises her brows like she's unamused. Jackson hugs his dad next as his mom turns to me.

"Well, I'm Ivy. It's nice to meet you, Lisette." She leans in, and I wasn't expecting a hug but find myself reciprocating it anyway.

"Hello," Jackson's dad starts, wrapping an arm around his wife while extending his hand to me. "I'm Jones. It's nice meeting you, Lissy."

I shake his hand before turning to Jackson, but he beats me to it. "Yes, I was named after him. My mom's dad is Jackson. It's really corny if you ask me, but just smile." He forces a smile before his mom playfully shoves him away.

"We gave your name a lot of thought."

"Did you though?" He teases her. "You just took it from the two important men in your life."

His dad laughs at him and I feel my chest tighten as I watch their smiles like a happy family.

"Oh, and you're just so creative, huh?" Ivy teases her son right back. "Where did you get Isabelle's name from?"

Jackson's smile slowly fades and his mom's eyes cut to Belle before she realizes an obvious mistake she made that I'm missing. I focus on Jackson again, but he simply forces a smile as he looks down at his daughter.

"Let's take a picture with Abuela."

Isabelle smiles up at them as she takes her dad's phone. Refusing to get in a picture with Jackson's *parents*, I quickly escape to the bathroom.

For safety measures, I hide out for a solid five minutes, which is a bad idea because with every minute that passes is another bad thought that enters my mind.

When I hear laughs filling the house, I assume the coast is clear, but can't bring myself to go back out. I feel so out of place here.

The first night was okay. The first morning was better. Jackson is off from work and it felt so easy spending the entire day with him as his daughter was at school. Last night was great as we watched princess movies. Today we were too busy cooking for me to even take a second to think. I was genuinely immersed in the kitchen as Jackson showed me how to make his favorite Puerto Rican dishes.

But *now*... now I feel like I stick out like a sore thumb in my cheap dress. I'm almost positive his mom was in cashmere and the money isn't the issue, I knew they had money, but it just adds to the fact that I don't belong here.

I jump out of my thoughts at the sound of a knock on the door. "Lissy?"

I let out a breath at the sound of Jackson's voice. "Yeah?"

He's quiet before saying, "You okay?"

"Peachy." I sink onto the toilet seat again, my shoulders slouching. I just want to crawl into bed. I hate all of those statistics for being right about depression rates spiking during the holidays, because my energy is suddenly drained, and I don't have it in me to smile for these people.

The door knob rattles, but since it's locked, he isn't granted access.

"Can you open the door for me?" His voice is soft and I shake my head at myself as I rise to unlock the door.

A beat later, he enters. Closing the door behind him, he leans against it and focuses on me. "What's wrong, sweetheart?"

"Drop the pet name, Jackson." My voice is so numb and the fear of an endless week of dark thoughts fill the pit of my stomach.

*I needed more time. I needed a few more days of peace before the weight in my chest returned.*

Pushing off the door, he closes the distance between us and gently tucks a hair behind my ear. "What's the matter? You were just fine. What happened?"

I shake my head, growing annoyed with myself because he's right, I *was* just fine. "Mood swings accompany depression." I smile up at him bitterly. "It's really the best of both worlds."

He doesn't laugh. He doesn't even smile and I don't appreciate the silence.

"Tell me what you need."

I shake my head at him, but as I drop my head, his fingers find my chin as he lifts my gaze back to him.

He watches me with certainty and stability as he says, "Tell me what you need so I can help, Lisette. Don't seclude yourself with your thoughts, it's not going to make you feel better."

*No, it's not, but I like torturing myself and sulking in the pain.*

"I want to go home," I whisper.

He watches me for a beat. "And do what?"

*Get high.*

I don't answer him and he simply nods like he just read my mind. "This is probably very inappropriate, but will a kiss make you feel better?"

A smirk grows on my face and a part of me hates how quickly he can alter my mood. "Taking advantage of me while I'm unstable and vulnerable? In the *headspace* I'm in? Shame on you, Jackson like your grandpa, Jones like your dad."

A laugh escapes him, and when his hand falls from my face, I try to hide my disappointment.

"You're right." He turns more serious. "That was inappropriate."

I quickly shake my head. "I was kidding. I'm not unstable."

"No?" He teases.

"Nope. Not vulnerable at all either." I rise to my feet and he doesn't move, keeping us inches apart.

A smile touches his lips as he tucks another strand behind my ear before cupping my face. "How about this," he starts, voice low. "You promise to stay for the entire night and keep the inappropriate comments to a minimum, for my parents' sake, and anytime you feel whatever you felt in here before I walked in, we can sneak away for one kiss."

I should *not* be this excited at the possibility of the waves of my sadness hitting, but I suddenly want them tenfold if it means getting a feel-better kiss.

"That sounds fair." I nod, realizing I would have agreed to anything he said if the ending of the deal was the same.

"Okay."

"Okay," I agree and he leans in, planting a soft, tender kiss to my lips.

As his lips press against mine, it's nothing like the hungry, rushed, wet kiss after the pool show. This one is slow and *safe*.

Before either of us can take this to the danger zone, he pulls away. "Better?"

I nod twice, not trusting my voice to come out strong enough.

"Good." Without another word, he takes my hand, guiding me to the dining room. "Found her," Jackson announces and Isabelle turns to us with a smile.

"Finally. Now we can start." She turns back to the table, and across from her are Jackson's parents, who, I don't fail to notice, look down at our clasped hands before sharing a look.

I feel my face heat in embarrassment and I'm not sure why, but I suddenly care a great deal what they think about me. My eyes land on the table, and in front of each of them are cookies along with piping bags of frosting.

"Turkey cookie decorating contest," Jackson explains. "Isabelle takes holiday games seriously, so for all of our sakes, *please* color the damn cookie and stick to the color palette. Do *not* mix them to make more colors, that's cheating and will result in a very early bedtime for *her* because we're not doing tantrums today."

I stifle a laugh at how tired he sounds and I'm intrigued to see what else she planned for today.

REMEMBER WHEN I SAID I was *intrigued?* Untrigue me. I'm not interested in another turkey-themed activity.

Being that Isabelle is the only child in the house, we're all stuck entertaining her. Pinning the feather on the turkey, making turkey paper headbands, turkey bowling with *turkey*-looking cups *that we made*, and a pumpkin for a ball. We're not even *eating* turkey today because she refuses to allow her dad to cook the *poor thing*.

I love the kid, but she's driving me mad.

"Why don't you have any thankful feathers on your turkey?" Isabelle glances at my bald bird that's supposed to have a feather for everything I'm thankful for, but mine is empty because I'm drawing a blank. I don't have anything I'm thankful for.

I know that sounds ungrateful, but I don't have anything in my life going on.

Her grandparent's turkeys are too far across the table for me to read, but they're full.

Isabelle's thankful turkey reads: Daddy, abuela, grandpa, KC, new house, new school! ballet, baking, my balising scils.

I feel my brows furrow at her last feather and lean closer. "What's this one?" I point at it. I helped her with the spelling, but don't recognize the last feather.

"My balancing skills. They're really important in gymnastics."

I smile at her as I take a new feather. "Let's try spelling that one again." I hand her a pencil instead of a marker so she can make mistakes. "Sound it out."

She does and I correct her.

"Ba*lan*cing. Not ba*lis*ing. Do you hear the difference? Ba-la-*ah*."

"There's an A in there?" Her face scrunches as if I'm the one who's wrong.

"Mhm." I sound it out for her again, and after another try and some help, she spells it right. "So smart. You should add your brain to your thankful turkey." I kiss her head before helping her spell skills. "Perfect."

She smiles as she takes a new feather and writes *Mommy*.

She steals a glance at me, biting back a smile as she glues her thankful feather to her turkey. "We're going to negotiate the wedding," she whispers. "Don't worry. I don't think you're too smelly for Dad."

I break into a laugh, and instead of bringing her hopes down, I take a feather and do the same, writing, *My baby Belle* with a heart.

Her brows furrow and I bite back a smile.

"That's not how you spell big girl," she remarks and I break into another laugh.

Her grandma distracts her as she asks about her upcoming ballet classes. They have their conversation in Spanish and it surprises me how fluent Belle is.

My smile fades as I turn back to my one-haired turkey. Stealing a glance at Jackson, his says: My daughter, my parents, our new home, my health, my job, my sanity.

I stifle a laugh at his last one, knowing these turkey activities are driving him crazy too. It's cute, but it's getting to the point where we need to stop.

Jackson steals a glance at me, and as he takes another feather and bites back a smile, he looks *just* like his daughter. Or rather she looks like him.

He finishes writing and I look over at his thankful feather.

*Lisette's kisses.*

I bite my cheek not to smile as he takes the glue and sticks the feather downside up so no one at the table can see what he wrote.

He grabs another feather, writing, *Lisette shirtless.*

I bite back a laugh as he glues that one downside up again.

The next feather says, *Lisette's smile*, and I break. My smile beams as he glues that thankful feather right side up.

"So cheesy," I mumble with an eye roll, but who am I kidding? Suddenly, I love cheesy.

"Add something to yours before you awaken The Holiday Monster," Jackson whispers as he nods to his daughter, his eyes slightly widened.

I force a laugh, but as I try to think of something I'm thankful for, a weight settles in my chest as I'm reminded I'm *not* thankful for anything I come up with. Not truly at least because deep down, I don't want to be here, fighting for happiness each day, forcing a smile.

A hand squeezes mine and I see Jackson watching me in my peripheral, but I keep my eyes on my one-haired turkey.

"Come help me get more paper," Jackson says loud enough for the table to hear as he pulls me to my feet.

As soon as we turn the corner, he pulls me into the bathroom and shuts the door.

"That look in your eyes is killing me, Lisette." He sounds like he's in pain, and I shake my head in response.

"This is what I meant, Jackson. My problems tarnishing you and your day. This is what you are signing up for."

He shakes his head at me and almost looks tired of my words. "Do you want your feel-better kiss or not?" He brushes me off.

Not being stubborn enough to say no, I climb on my tippy toes, planting my hand on his chest to steady myself.

He closes the rest of the distance, bringing his lips to mine, his hands on my waist. This kiss is harder, like he's punishing me for my words as he takes my bottom lip between his teeth.

A moan escapes me and he squeezes my waist in warning.

"Shh, sweetheart," he hushes against my lips before his mouth covers mine again, gentle this time. My tongue runs along his bottom lip and he's quick to open his mouth for me, capturing my tongue with his.

Pressing me against the door harder, one hand travels to my ass, riding my dress up as he squeezes. It's a battle to keep quiet but I do as I lift a leg to wrap around him, forcing him closer. When I feel the bulge in his pants, I shamelessly grind against him, one hand traveling up the front of his shirt while the other tugs at his hair.

Suddenly, the door behind me is pushed open, but with my weight against it, it closes. "Oh."

I quickly pull away, dropping my leg from around him at the sound of his mother's voice. Jackson buries his face in my neck.

"Sorry."

"One second."

We both say at the same time and I shut my eyes in defeat, silently cursing myself.

"Jackson?" his mom questions.

"Yeah, one second, Mom."

I look over at him and his eyes are on the door. A few seconds pass before his shoulders sag. "She's not leaving."

My brows furrow. "I'm not going out there," I whisper.

"I'm telling you," he starts again. "She's not leaving." He lets out a sigh as he slowly moves his hand from under my dress and politely fixes it.

When he opens the door, I step behind him, my face on fire.

"Stop looking at me like that," he tells his mom in a hushed voice as we step out of the bathroom. I keep my eyes low and try my best to hide behind him as he steps around his mother.

"Like you lied?" his mom counters.

"I didn't. We *are* friends, we just—" he cuts himself off and it sounds like his mom is waiting for him to finish, but he doesn't. Instead, a sigh takes the stead of his words.

"I hope you're not this friendly with all of your friends." She sounds like she wants to laugh and I never wanted to die more than I do right now. She *totally* heard me.

"Are we *really* going to do the whole Embarrass Jackson Thing right now? Really?"

There's a beat of silence before she says, "Lissy, dear, are you spending the night?"

"*Mom,*" he warns and he too sounds embarrassed. "What does that have to do with anything or concern you?"

"I'm not spending the night," I tell Jackson's back since I *still* can't bring myself to step around him. Either way, neither of them seem to be listening.

"Don't be rude, Jackson. I'm only asking so I know if I need to pack her some food."

"She's eating here and I told you that. You asked because you're a noisy, meddling mother and—stop doing that." He takes a step away from her. He bumps into me, but quickly brings his hand behind himself and catches me.

"You had some lipstick on your face."

*Please, God, let me die now. I'll get on my knees and beg.*

"She's not even wearing lipstick. Deja el relajo, por favor." His perfect Spanish pulls a smirk onto my lips. I knew he was half Puerto Rican, and with his mom's thick accent it's clear he speaks Spanish with her often, but I haven't heard him speak their native language and his accent is hot.

"You were right, happy? I lied. She's not my friend. *Enough.*"

I hear her *finally* walking off with a laugh and I silently pray to God to *take me out.*

# Chapter Thirty-Five

## JACKSON

When I turn to Lisette, her face is *scarlet*. A quiet laugh erupts from me and the blush creeps onto her neck.

"I will make an orphan of your daughter if you're laughing at me right now, Jackson Jones," she bites out and I quickly shut up before she turns to me, a fierce look in her eyes. "That's what I thought."

A smile creeps onto my face. "I thought you didn't care what she thought about you?"

"I never said I didn't care if she heard me *moaning* with your tongue down my throat like a whore," she whisper-shouts, hitting my bicep.

My smile disappears at her words. "Don't call yourself that," I tell her sternly. "She caught us kissing, not having an orgy, and if she had, you're still not a whore. Do not let me hear you say that again."

She rolls her eyes at me, cheeks still blushed. "*Do not let me hear you say that again*," she mocks. "You're such a dad."

She glances over my shoulder, shaking her head at herself.

With a smile, I rest a light hand on her waist before leaning over to kiss the mortified look off her face. "It's fine," I reassure her. "She's not going to bring it up. She just likes bugging me. She doesn't think any less of you, sweetheart."

"Stop touching me." She shoves my arm away, completely ignoring my words. "And no more kisses. And *do not* call me sweetheart in front of her."

A smirk grows on my face because earlier I had to drop the pet name altogether, but now I just can't use it in front of my mother. A *win is a win*.

I cup her face in both hands and kiss her all over her face. She laughs as she tries to push me away, but I keep her in my grasp as I plant a handful of rapid kisses on her lips.

"Feel better?"

"No," she whispers again, burying her flushed face in my chest.

With a low laugh, I cradle her head with one hand and wrap the other around her waist while she keeps her hands draped at her side. "You're just as dramatic as Belle."

I kiss the top of her head and she looks up at me with a glare.

"You're so beautiful." My voice deepens to a low whisper. I tuck a long hair behind her ear, a smile tugging at my lips.

"Stop looking at me like that." Her cheeks blush again and I never thought I'd see the day where nonchalant, carefree Lisette is *flustered*.

"Like what?"

"Like you *like* me," she says in something close to disgust.

"That's crazy. It's almost like I already told you I love—"

"Shh." She swiftly cuts me off while taking a step back and the disappointment seeps into me. I choose not to push her and take a step back to stop myself from kissing her again.

"I'll meet you in there in a minute," she mumbles and I nod in return as I slip back into the dining room, forcing a smile. "We should eat now," I announce and my parents look up from their thankful turkeys to agree.

I head into the kitchen and when I hear light footsteps behind me, I know it's my mom before she steps beside me to help serve the plates. "So," she starts and I fight not to let out a sigh. I don't bother asking why she didn't use the bathroom she caught us in, knowing she went looking for us.

"She's beautiful," she comments and I know she isn't talking about her granddaughter.

"Yeah, she is." I keep my eyes on the pot of rice and gandules as I serve Belle's plate.

"How long have you two been seeing each other?" She keeps her tone neutral.

"We're not *really* together, Mom," I tell her once again, honestly not knowing where I stand with Lisette.

She sets her plate down as she turns to me and leans against the counter. "So you're just sneaking off to bathrooms with her?" She bites back a smile.

"Actually, yes." I find myself confessing. "It's complicated right now. Her life is complicated."

I see the playfulness leave my mom's face as she realizes I'm not just saying we're not together to cover up the fact that we're together.

"Yeah, it seems complicated," she whispers now. "There are a lot of scars on her leg."

I feel my face fall as I turn to her. "Do not do that," I warn her.

She puts her hands up in surrender. "I'm not judging."

"That look on your face says otherwise," I whisper more harshly. "Do not look at her like that. You have no right to judge her."

"I'm *not* judging," she voices again. "If you're happy, I'm happy. She's beautiful." She shrugs and I roll my eyes as I see where this is going.

"You disapprove." I shake my head at her as I turn back to the food, stabbing at the pernil and plopping some onto Belle's plate.

She shrugs again. "Why are you introducing her to the baby if it's so complicated? You never bring women around her."

I hold back a sigh as I take note of how she didn't answer me. "I technically didn't introduce her to Isabelle. She met her years ago through Sire, she's his sister."

My mom nods as she puts something together in her head. "So she was Belle's tutor first... yet you still got involved?"

I don't answer her.

"I'm just confused because you don't get involved with people in her life. Not even that amazing ballet teacher of hers, who I honestly think you need to marry."

My eyes narrow as I remember my daughter also telling me that. "Did *you* put that idea in Belle's head?"

From the guilty look on her face, I know she did.

"Mom, stop talking about things like that around her. You put Mia in her head as a potential mother figure and she doesn't need to think about that, not with her *teachers*." I keep my voice more hushed now.

A somber look crosses her eyes, and I look back at the plate of food.

"I'm sorry, and I'm sorry I brought up the name thing earlier. I really didn't know where you got her name from."

"It's fine," I brush her off.

"I'm guessing Skye picked out her name?" she whispers so low I can just barely hear her voice.

I wait for that feeling in my chest to hit after hearing her name, like it's caving in on me but it never comes. Glancing over my shoulder, Belle is too distracted showing my dad how to take a Polaroid to hear us.

"Yeah... she did."

A small smile grows on my mom's face. "Has she asked about her again?"

I nod in return. "Just once."

She has a look on her face that tells me she has a hundred questions. "What did you tell her?"

I let out a tired breath as I run a hand down my face. "I didn't." I shrug. "She said she doesn't have a mom. Lisette was there and told her she has a *tummy mommy* like everyone else does, but that she didn't need a second one."

When I see my mom's face change before me, I wish I didn't say that because I know I just opened a whole other can of worms.

"Was that her way of telling you she doesn't want to be a stepmother to my granddaughter? Because Isa was just writing *Mommy* on her feather, so what does she plan on doing here?" She sounds so damn defensive and I quickly give her a look to calm down.

"That's not what she meant," I reassure her.

"Well." My mom thankfully moves on. "I know you're against it, but I think you should tell Belle about Skye."

"No."

"Jackson—"

"No, Mom. No." I feel myself getting upset and quickly rein it in. Taking a calming breath, I try again. "She's *five*."

"She's old enough if she's asking about her, Jackson. She deserves to at least see a picture of her mom and I think you should reach out to Skye."

"Oh, absolutely not," I snap, setting the plate down.

"She's her daughter."

"She's *my* daughter." I look between her eyes, my anger growing. "There is no reaching out to her. She lost that right when she left."

A sympathetic look crosses her face but when she reaches to touch me, I take a step back.

"Jackson, everyone makes mistakes. You need to—"

"I don't need to do anything." I force myself to keep my voice low.

"She deserves to see her kid," she says, her tone picking up strength.

"She doesn't deserve shit."

Her entire face morphs as if I just hit her. "Do not curse at me, Jackson Jones."

"We're not telling Belle anything until I want to, and we're not reaching out to Skye. If you go against my wishes, you won't be seeing her anymore."

"*Excuse me?*" she nearly shouts. "You're going to keep my grandbaby from me?" My mom keeps her fierce eyes on me and beside her, my dad steps in.

"What's happening?"

"She's *my* baby," I ignore him, keeping my gaze on my mom. "And that's final. Respect my boundaries."

"Respect your mother," my dad counters.

I open my mouth to reply, but he puts a hand up, quickly shutting me up like he used to do when I was a kid, and like muscle memory, I don't say a word.

My mom stares at me for two beats before walking into the dining room and kissing the top of Isabelle's head. "Happy Thanksgiving, beba. You be good for Daddy, okay?"

"Mom," I let out a defeated breath as I walk over to them.

"Are you leaving before dinner?" Belle looks up at her as she walks over to grab her bag.

"Mom, don't be like that."

She ignores me as she walks for the door.

"Honey, wait up." My dad tries to catch up to her fast pace.

"Ma, just—" I don't get to finish my sentence as the front door shuts.

# Chapter Thirty-Six

## LISETTE

I STEP INTO THE DINING room just as the front door slams. I feel my brows furrow as I look around the mostly empty room and it's just Belle.

"What'd I miss?" I ask as I glance out into the hall to where Jackson and his dad are having a hushed conversation.

"Nothing." Belle shrugs as she toys with a camera. "We finished our thankful turkeys and now we're going to eat, but I think Abuela left, so maybe we're waiting?" She shrugs again, her eyes still on the camera.

I glance back into the hall, and neither Jackson nor his father look happy.

"You better apologize," his dad bites out before walking out of the house.

Jackson's shoulders slouch as the door shuts and with no one else around, I walk into the hall with him.

"Please don't tell me that had something to do with me..."

When he turns to me, he lets out a tired breath. "It didn't," he mumbles and I can't decide if I believe him or not.

"Well, that tone was convincing," I tease, but when he looks at me again, he looks annoyed. "Who pissed in your turkey?"

The corner of his mouth lifts an inch before he shakes his head at me.

I close the distance between us before saying, "Don't say it didn't have anything to do with me if it did. It's like when you say you aren't mad when you are. I really do hate it and it just gets me in my head."

He looks between my eyes and a soft look covers his earlier annoyance. "It had nothing to do with you, sweetheart," he reassures me, his tone taking on that tired one again.

Before I can ask what's wrong, Isabelle walks in. "Hey..." She starts off gently, and a smile grows on my face when I see how clear it is that she wants something.

"What's up, penguin?" Jackson walks past me to her.

"So, I was thinking..." She looks between the two of us and nothing good comes to mind by that look in her eyes.

"Uh-huh," Jackson starts and he's biting back a smile as he watches her.

"I know we're having dinner soon, but can I *please* take just a little bit of pictures of Lola?"

I almost ask who Lola is before I remember she's her baby doll.

"I don't want her to feel left out and we didn't take any with her, but I think she'll love the camera Abuela got me." She holds it up with a hopeful smile.

"Okay," her dad entertains her. "But when I ask you to come down to eat, I don't want to hear you ask for five more minutes."

"Deal." She takes off running for her room.

When she's out of sight, his face drops again before he runs a hand through his hair.

"Since I love to make you feel worse, I want you to know you're failing my test." I shrug teasingly and his brows furrow as if he's actually worried.

"What test?" He searches my eyes frantically.

"I go through a field of studies after kissing a man. I have to make sure you're not a part of the ninety-eight percent of men who are horrible."

"And I'm failing? How many tests have you conducted? What happens if I fail?"

I stifle a laugh at his genuine worry. "If you fail, I'm running for the hills. Your parents just stormed out," I remind him. "It's not looking good for the momma's boy test."

"Momma's boy?" he repeats, a smile tugging at his lips.

"Yeah, you need to respect your mom, but not be a *complete* momma's boy to the point where she's a horrible mother-in-law and in love with you."

His brows furrow as he studies me. "What kind of men do you kiss?"

I tilt my head back with a laugh, but he watches me like he's concerned for me. I turn to him as my laugh sobers. "You gonna tell me what happened, or do I have to assume she's crazy and mad we kissed because she's in love with you?"

It's his turn to break into a laugh now. "I'm seriously concerned about the men you encounter." He shakes his head at me before letting out a sigh. "She's been bugging me for the last few months to tell Belle about her mom."

His words make me falter and a part of me is surprised because I didn't think there was anything to tell. "I thought she left you for another man? She wants you to tell your five-year-old that?"

"That's exactly what I said and she had the nerve to say people deserve second chances."

I feel my brows furrow. "Well, of course, people deserve second chances. What exactly happened?"

He looks frustrated now, but I'm too nosy to back down. This man is the definition of patient and understanding, but the mention of his daughter's mom sets him off. This is probably a bright red flag, but I'm too invested. I need to know what happened. Call it what you want.

He studies me, like he's thinking whether or not he wants to tell me. "How come when I ask about you, I get brushed off with a joke, but you want to know about this?"

I shrug. "Brush me off with a joke. If I laugh, you get a pass."

He doesn't even attempt. "Tell me what made you upset the night you came here before your Paris trip and I'll tell you about her mom."

I open my mouth to make a joke, but I'm assaulted with memories of that night. I feel myself break into a sweat at the thought of her, but before I can be sucked into my thoughts, I force a smile.

"We couldn't start small? Maybe how I became an addict or small talk like my emotionally absent dad? We can tie it to how I call you daddy because I have daddy issues. You know, that's why I like it when you tell me what to do. *Huge* turn-on." I give him a once over.

A smile grows on his face and it's clear as day that he's fighting off a laugh. "So many options," he teases.

"So many traumatic experiences," I add. "I don't think you have enough stories about her mom to acquire all of this information about me."

A snort escapes him now. "I'll have to give you a sentence for every traumatic story."

"This doesn't feel fair," I point out when I realize he actually wants to know all this stuff about me.

"Sorry, my dad didn't neglect me."

I break into a laugh so hard that my stomach hurts.

"Made you laugh," he points out with a chuckle. "I don't have to share."

"Yes, you do," I retort, turning more serious. "I'm nosy. Like incredibly nosy and I don't know what boundaries are. I will find her on social media so just tell me."

He shakes his head with a smile and I'm glad he thinks I'm joking.

"When Belle was a baby she got meningitis."

I feel my brows raise but hold my questions in for the end.

"It was really bad." He takes a minute before continuing and I can see the fear in his eyes. "We didn't think she was going to make it, and rightfully so, we were both really stressed. I was distant with her, I won't deny that, but when she went home to shower and get me a change of clothes, she came back to the hospital with a hickey on her neck."

My jaw drops and he nods at my reaction.

"It got really ugly and I caused a big show at the hospital. Again, I won't deny that. I was wrong for talking to her the way I did, especially around other sick kids and worried parents." A guilty look covers his face now. "I got escorted off of the property."

He looks back over at me as he continues. "She said she was sad and her friend just happened to be there." He rolls his eyes now. "But then Belle got worse, and it was *too hard* for her. The doctor told us she might not make it, and if she did, she might lose her hearing. She told me she didn't want to raise a sick baby alone and that we needed to work out our problems, but I told her there was no chance I was taking her back, whether our daughter made it or not. I made it clear I was sticking around for my baby, but she left. It was like Belle knew I needed her because she skyrocketed, and now she's perfect."

A smile touches my lips. "How long were you two together?"

"Three years before she got pregnant."

"Damn," I reply, disappointed now. "Did you love her?"

I don't miss the amount of seconds that pass as he hesitates. "She gave me my kid. Of course, I loved her."

My heart plummets.

"But I fell *out* of love with her a long time ago."

I nod in response, but my chest is still trying to recover.

His words about what he told me his mom said play in my head before I speak up again. "I think she might deserve a second chance."

Jackson's brows furrow and I quickly explain before he loses it on me.

"I'm an addict, Jackson. If I was sentenced every time I fucked up, I'd rot for life. Everyone deserves a second chance and I'll die on that hill."

"Okay, but—"

"*However*," I cut him off. "I'm not saying you need to get back with her. Isabelle should a hundred and ten percent get to know *something* good about her mom if she asks. She is a very curious kid, and her mom was mentally vulnerable when she cheated. Yes, it was wrong, but coming from someone who was abused because they had mentally unfit parents, people do unspeakable things when they're sad and mentally checked out. Does that mean I'm forgiving my bio parents? Fuck, no, they had a hundred chances with me, but she didn't fuck up big enough to lose her kid forever. She hurt you, JJ, not Isa."

He doesn't reply as my words sink in. "Yeah, okay," he mumbles, as he nods to himself, walking to the dining room.

I follow close behind him before he sinks into a seat at the table.

"Was that a 'yeah okay whatever bitch' or a 'you're right, but my feelings are hurt' yeah okay?" I ask gently and he forces a smile.

"The latter."

I nod in return as I sit beside him.

"I think it just hurts more because she moved on." He keeps his voice low, but I sit up in my seat.

"What?"

His eyes meet mine.

"Way to keep the best for last. The hell do you mean she moved on? You *followed up* on her?"

"Of course I did."

My jaw drops. "Do you have pictures?"

He shakes his head as he pulls out his phone. "You're too invested and not sympathetic enough."

"Sorry," I mumble. "You poor thing. Show me the bitch who broke your heart and left you with a kid you didn't even know about." I roll my eyes, but smile when I notice him smiling again.

He takes a second to scroll, and when he turns the phone to me, my jaw drops again. "Holy shit." I take the phone as I stare at what could be Isabelle's *twin.*

A beautiful woman smiles at the camera; she has olive skin and midnight dark hair. She's not what surprises me, it's the *kid* in her arms that can be Isabelle's carbon copy. The main difference is the eyes. Where Belle has gray eyes like her dad, this little girl has blue ones and she has pin-straight hair compared to Belle's curls.

"Holy. Shit," I mumble again. "Either Belle looks like her mom with your hair and eyes or her mom has a *very* specific type."

He swipes again and it's a wedding picture of a handsome blond man with blue eyes. He doesn't really resemble Jackson besides the complexion and hair color.

"How long ago was this?"

"They got married a year after she left. This is who she cheated with."

"No. Fucking. Way."

"Yeah." He takes the phone as he sinks into his seat. "I looked for her for Belle's first birthday and I found out she was pregnant. She said it was *too hard* to be in Belle's life because she felt guilty for leaving, but that she's happier. Good for her though, right?"

He doesn't sound sarcastic or bitter at all. He actually sounds genuine. Like he's forcing himself to be happy for her and his mom really did raise a good man.

"Well forget what I said. She got her second chance when you called her. Maybe she is a bitch."

Jackson shakes his head as he tucks his phone in his pocket. "Don't call her that."

And there goes my heart plummeting again. Of course, he defends her.

"My mom says that now that Belle is older and asking for her, I should reach out to her."

I feel myself go still. "Are you?"

He lets out a scoff. "Hell no."

I'd be lying if I said that didn't make me feel better. "You're better than me." I shrug. "I don't take back anything I said about second chances, but I'd hate her just a little bit."

"I can't." He shakes his head at himself now. "I tried hating her, but I can't."

"Maybe you're still in love with her," I tease but as the words leave my mouth, I'm immediately holding my breath as I wait for him to deny it.

"Maybe I am."

*Kill. Me. Now.*

A smile grows on his face as he studies whatever face I'm wearing. "That was a joke," he whispers and I force a smile on my face as my shoulders ease.

"Does being in love with my ex immediately mean I fail all your tests?"

I narrow my eyes at his teasing tone. "The ex is a whole other category of test and it isn't looking too good since you, one, have pictures of her and two, are still stalking her."

While it seems like I'm joking, I'm definitely not.

"I haven't stalked her in over two years," he counters.

"That doesn't make the pictures disappear from your phone."

He pulls out his phone before swiping a few times. After a minute, he sets it in front of me. "Gone."

I let out a scoff. "You did not."

"It's not like I need them." He shrugs. "The ones of her and Belle are still there in case I show her, but her alone or us alone are gone."

I don't move, but he nods to the phone and I'm too nosy to ignore an unlocked phone. Swiping it from the table, I look at the album name.

"Skye?" I glance up at him and he only nods. I look back at the album and my heart *aches* at pictures of them as a family. She really does look happy during her pregnancy. Her belly is huge and Jackson looks through the roof as he's holding a baby dress to her stomach.

I feel myself smiling at pictures of Isabelle as an infant in their arms. When I see one that looks familiar, I tap on it and realize it's from the newborn photoshoot Jackson has in his office.

I always assumed Isabelle had that photoshoot alone, but there are tons of pictures of the three of them in matching pastel pink outfits.

Pulling in a deep breath, I hand Jackson the phone back, deciding I've put myself through enough misery.

"Why didn't you marry her?" Nope. Not enough misery I guess.

He smiles, but it looks bitter. "She didn't want to get married." He raises his brows unamusingly. "Clearly, it was *me* she didn't want to marry," he mumbles.

All I hear is that *he wanted* to marry her, and I think I'm done for the night.

# Chapter Thirty-Seven

## JACKSON

T HERE WAS A SHIFT IN the air at some point while I was talking to Lisette, but I noticed too late.

We ate dinner with an awkward stiffness and I kept replaying our conversation in my head, trying to pinpoint what I said that made her walls go up.

My parents didn't make a return, which doesn't surprise me. I know my mom was too prideful to come back, so I'm going to have to go see her tomorrow or tonight if I value my sanity and don't want to hear a lecture from my dad.

I feel bad for losing my temper with her, and while I don't think I'm in the wrong for setting boundaries, I can't say that to her. If I want her to speak to me again, I'll have to accept defeat. It's not healthy, but it's how she is.

I only said what I said because I know her, and I know she'll go behind my back and find Skye. If she does, I meant what I said about keeping her away from my kid. I just can't tell her that either because she'll disown me or say I'm an ungrateful, disgraceful, and a thousand Spanish curse words of a son.

I shake my head of my thoughts as I focus on the story I'm reading Belle, but when I look down, she's fast asleep. I lean over to kiss her.

"I love you, princess." I tuck her in before planting one last kiss on her nose. "My sweet girl," I whisper to her as I kiss her cheek and force myself to leave before I carry her to my room. I'm aware I have an unhealthy attachment to my kid, but I don't care enough to do anything about it.

Walking past Lisette's door, I find myself stopping in front of it. I glance down and notice the light is off, but she might have a lamp on. Before I can talk myself out of it, I knock on her door.

"Yeah?"

I take that as a come-in and crack the door open slowly. Peeking my head in, she stares back at me from the bed in plaid shorts and a black sports bra.

"Hey," I greet as I lean against the door frame.

"Hi." She smiles over at me and my heart *flutters*.

"I'm not disrespectful to my mother or a momma's boy," I state and her smile widens.

"Thanks for the clarification." She nods appreciatively. "Seventy-three percent of my subjects fail that test," she teases.

A smile grows on my face at her words and I push off the door to be closer to her. "Was that what made you get weird?"

She shakes her head softly, but it's clear she knows what I'm talking about. "It's nothing."

"It's something." I stand in front of her, and when she looks down at her phone, I tilt her chin up.

"You were going to marry her."

I feel my brows furrow before it clicks. "I wasn't going to marry her. My parents pushed the idea on us after she got pregnant, and she said she didn't want to get married. I didn't even give it much thought," I tell her honestly, and while that sounds bad, I was more focused on becoming a dad. Skye didn't want marriage and I never pushed it. End of story.

"But if she wanted to, you would've?"

I let out a defeated sigh as I lay at the foot of the bed. "I would've given her anything, as I would *anyone* I love."

"This isn't helping your case." She looks back at her phone and I stifle a laugh.

"You're upset because I had a past relationship? It was *five* years ago and I was with her for *three* years. She had my baby. I think it's unrealistic for me to say I didn't love her and never once thought about the idea of marrying her."

She only nods and I bite back my smile as I grab her ankle. She tries to fight me off but I pull her harder until she's in front of me.

"This jealousy act is making me think you *also* L word me."

"Ew." She rolls her eyes. "I *like* kissing you and it's just becoming harder to do so when I hear you were engaged to the love of your life a few years ago."

I bark up a laugh at her fake annoyed face. "I was *not* engaged to her. Stop making up things in that pretty head."

"Notice how you didn't deny she was the love of your life?"

I shake my head at her. "She wasn't. I'm a sucker for romantics. My true love wouldn't have ended like that or at all for that matter. It was great until it wasn't. I moved on." I focus on her eyes for a moment before my gaze drops to her lips. "I'm crushing on this new girl. She's got a smart mouth on her, sarcastic as shit, and breathtakingly beautiful."

A smile grows on her lips. "So there's *two* girls I need to look out for?" She nods. "I'm a good fighter, so you better keep these bitches hidden."

I bite back another laugh before stealing a kiss. "Shut up." I kiss her one more time, more firmly.

"I didn't hear any traumatic stories," I remind her and her eyes fall to the side.

"I'm starting to think you lied about having a negligent dad. Do you simply call me daddy because it's a kink?"

She breaks into a laugh, and *everything* softens at the sound and sight.

"You couldn't catch me *dead* calling you daddy in bed."

"Is that a challenge?" I tease and she laughs again. "What if I begged for it?"

She moans and I bite back a laugh. "I *do* have a begging kink."

"Noted." I nod. "I'm assuming the daddy issues is where the praise kink comes from?"

She nods while biting her lip and I break into a laugh.

"No, I actually do have a praise kink." She turns more serious. "Tell me I'm taking it well and I'm a *goner*." She lets her head fall on the stack of pillows as I actually do take note of that.

"I really do want to know about your dad. Or about how you became an addict. Or these." I run my thumb along the scars on her thighs. "Whichever you want to start with, but if it's neither, then I'll wait."

Her eyes meet mine and she looks as if she doesn't understand me. "Why?"

"Why what, love?"

A smile creeps onto her face before she bites it back. "Why do you want to know?"

I study her, trying to decipher if she's just trying to push me away or genuinely doesn't know the answer to that.

"Because I want to know everything about you, Lisette. Your past doesn't define you, but it made you who you are and I want to get to understand that."

Her eyes dart down to the bed before she plays with the string of her pants. "It all sucks," she states matter-of-factly. "And it's going to make me sad, so I'm going to need a feel-better kiss after everything I share."

A smile creeps onto my face. "Fair enough."

Her eyes meet mine as she wears a smile of her own.

"Sounds like it's gonna be a lot of kissing," I voice.

"A shit ton," she adds.

I nod to myself as I reach for a pillow to get comfortable. "Okay. We're not having sex though."

Her brows furrow before a hint of disappointment flashes through her face. "I didn't mention sex. Do you not have enough self-control to kiss me without needing to attempt to impregnate me?"

A snort escapes me at her choice of words. "Trust me, I'm not getting you pregnant."

Another furrow pulls at her brows. "Don't sound so offended now."

I quickly correct myself at her tone. "I didn't mean it like that. Our babies would be adorable, but I don't want any more kids. Plus, I already feel like shit for kissing you behind your brother's back. I'm telling him about this before I sleep with you."

Her eyes meet mine, a smirk growing on her face. "Can you finally admit you want me?"

"Of course I want you." I steal a kiss. "How else would I test that daddy kink?"

She breaks into a laugh before tossing a pillow at me, but I catch it and rest it behind my head.

Her laugh sobers and when she realizes I'm waiting for her to open up, she starts to shut down. I give her a second but she doesn't look like she's planning to say anything.

I lean over and quickly capture her lips with mine. She immediately melts into me as I crawl on top of her, but before she can deepen the kiss, I pull away.

"That was a freebie." I kiss her nose. "You can share now."

A smile touches her lips before she pulls in a breath. "The dad thing isn't all that interesting. He was a drunk who only spoke to me if it was to pass him a drink or get out of his way." She shrugs as if growing up like that was the least of her worries.

"Then he left and in came a new man for my bio mom. This one liked to hit me though." She forces a smile. "I spent half my life seeking validation from older men to compensate for being ignored by the fathers around me, but I *am* really good in bed thanks to the experience."

Her face scrunches. "Not that I'm a whore or—"

I shut her up with a firm kiss.

She pulls away first this time and gets comfortable before toying with the buttons on my shirt. "Can we turn this into a strip confession? Lose a piece of clothes for everything I say?"

I steal a kiss while her eyes are on my shirt. "No, baby."

A smile lights up on her face as her eyes dart up to mine. "Don't call me that."

My brows furrow before I catch what I called her. "Why not?"

"Because it's too intimate."

"And *love* isn't?" I mindlessly brush a hair off her face as I focus on her long lashes.

"Love is hot. Baby is intimate, personal, *boyfriend*."

"God forbid I become that."

"Glad we're on the same page." She taps my chest twice before trying to move, but I pull her back down and pin her in place with my hips between her legs.

"Was your mom the same or is *she* great and named you after her?"

Her eyes dim as she goes back to playing with the buttons on my shirt. "That night I came here was the first time I saw her in over ten years."

I watch her throat bob as she swallows.

"She was so mean to me." Her eyes water and it crushes me. "I nearly drove off the road three times on my way to my AA center..."

I go still as I study her. She keeps her eyes on my shirt and I hate her mother for making her believe she's anything less than perfect. Leaning forward, I capture my lips with hers, kissing her with enough love for the both of us.

When I pull away, a somber smile grows on her face. "She hit me... a lot, and she used a lot of drugs when she was pregnant with me, so I was born already dependent on drugs." She shakes her head at her words like she hates herself. "She set me up for failure."

I tilt her chin up before catching her lips with mine. "You didn't fail though. You're doing great."

A smirk grows on her face as she rubs her fingers on my beard. "Say that last part again, but whisper it in my ear."

I bite back a laugh as I bury my face in her neck. I kiss her gently before biting her ear and she squirms under me.

Holding her tight, I plant a soft kiss on her cheek. "You were really upset after seeing her."

She lets out a scoff. "That's an understatement."

I nod to myself as I focus on her. "The overdose... was it an accident?"

Her eyes cut up to mine. She studies me before nodding. "I told you I didn't have the will to fight anymore, and that was true, but I didn't try to overdose last week. I wouldn't leave without saying bye to my baby sister."

I thought her answer would make me feel better, but it doesn't since she doesn't add how she no longer wants to die. Before I can push for more, she goes on with a teasing smile.

"I guess the sleeping with older men thing can count as a trauma dump." She shrugs mindlessly before pointing at her lips, and I kiss her gently.

When I pull away to look at her, she gazes at me before cupping my face in both hands and rubbing my beard. Her eyes travel down to whatever she's doing with my facial hair and I keep my eyes fixed on her as I count her lashes.

I noticed her beauty a long time ago, but as she's this close, I realize so many small details on her face I missed before. The scar above her eyebrow, the beauty mark on her eyelid and chin. My eyes scan the rest of her face, trying to memorize every inch of her.

"Do you care about how many men I've slept with?"

"No, sweetheart," I answer mindlessly, my eyes on her brows now.

"Really?" Her brows furrow and I kiss the crease in them.

"Is this another test?"

A smile grows on her face. "Maybe."

"Well, I honestly don't care."

"Do you wanna know what age I lost my virginity?"

"Nope." I kiss her again and she's biting back a smile.

"Why don't you care?"

I shrug.

"How many girls have *you* slept with?"

I bite back a smile as I see what she's doing here. "Somewhere in the triple digits," I lie.

Her jaw drops, and I fight with every fiber in me to hold back a laugh.

"Are you slut shaming me, little Miss Lost Her Virginity To a Man Twice Her Age in Middle School?"

She breaks into a laugh before shoving my chest. "I did *not* lose my virginity in middle school."

"But he was twice your age."

"He wasn't." She shoves me again with a laugh and I kiss the crease of her neck. "I was a willing victim, but he *wasn't* twice my age."

"*Willing victim?* Jesus Christ," I mumble and she breaks into a laugh.

I kiss her behind her ear gently. "Shh, you're going to wake up Belle."

She stifles her laugh as she wraps her legs around me, and I pull away to see her smile.

"I was fifteen…"

"Uh-huh."

"And he was nineteen." She watches for my reaction, like she's waiting for me to judge her or get upset, but I do my best to conceal my face.

"That's kinda cray cray…"

She throws her head back with another loud laugh and I can't help but join her.

"Did you lie about your age?"

She nods her head disappointedly. "You know me so well." She sighs and I kiss the somber look off her face.

"I can probably guess your body count," she says.

I shake my head at how persistent she is. I know she only wants to know if mine is higher so she can feel better, but she won't since I'm sure it isn't, which isn't a bad thing.

"Go ahead," I suggest, deciding I'll agree to any number she throws.

"Okay." She shifts under me as she gets ready. "Wait, how old are you and how old were you when you lost your virginity?"

"Seventeen and thirty-two."

Her brows shoot up. "You're *thirty-two?*"

"Yes..." I search her face for what the problem is, and she shakes her head disappointedly.

"You're *seven* years older than me, Jackson Jones. This isn't helping my track record."

A laugh bubbles in my throat.

"I thought you and my brothers were in college at the same time?"

"I took a few years off before going to college." I graduated the year before Sire and August, and I guess it worked out that I took a few years off to decide what I wanted to do because I definitely wouldn't be here if I went to college straight out of high school.

Her eyes narrow as she watches me. "Are you into younger women?" She looks intrigued now, but I shake my head.

"I'm into you." I steal a kiss, but she quickly pulls away.

"So yes."

"No," I counter. "But I'm into you." I kiss her again, and she tries to pull away, but I kiss her harder, pulling a laugh out of her.

"You should be *in* me."

"Alright." I sit up. "We're done. Thanks for sharing. You did great."

She fills the room with her laugh again as she pulls me back down on her. She kisses my neck with a quiet laugh and I let out a soft sigh.

"I should go to my room." I pull away because I really want to be inside of her and I meant what I said about us not having sex.

I don't miss the disappointed look on her face as I rise from the bed, and I've never caved so quickly.

"I'll stay five more minutes." I lay on top of her again and her smile returns.

"You could just sleep here," she suggests nonchalantly, but she watches my reaction like she cares a great deal. "You're just down the hall. No difference."

A smirk reaches my lips. "If there's no difference, I can sleep in my own bed."

She shrugs, but I see right through her. "If you want to leave, go ahead."

"Do you want me to sleep here?" I tread lightly.

"Yes, but I don't want us to sleep." She raises her brows twice and I break into a laugh.

"Enough," I warn.

"Okay, Daddy."

"*Lisette*." My eyes fall shut as I rest my head on the bed beside her face and I hear her giggling under me. I let out a defeated sigh as I stand from the bed and pull my shirt off.

She looks *way* too excited and I quickly shut down her feral thoughts.

"I'll stay if you behave," I warn her and a smirk grows on her face.

"Let's *negotiate*," she teases. "I'll agree to behave if *you* agree to sleep naked," she says, cheery as ever.

"Absolutely not." I don't admit that I don't have that much self-control.

"I had a feeling you were going to say that." She keeps her tone cheery and I laugh at her sarcasm. "My second offer is *me* sleeping naked."

"You seriously need to stop trying to seduce me. Are you ovulating or something?"

"Yes," she confesses and we're hysterical. I close the door when we get too loud, worried Belle will wake up.

When I turn back to Lisette, she's already gazing up at me with her pretty eyes.

"I'll sleep in my boxers and you can sleep shirtless," I offer and she smiles brightly before slipping her sports bra off and I immediately regret this negotiation.

My eyes fall to her breasts and I let out a content sigh.

"Don't try to get touchy with me." She rolls her eyes playfully as she climbs under the covers.

"Me?" I start as I slip my pants off and she watches my every move with great focus. "You're the one acting like a cat in heat."

She erupts with a laugh before burying her face in her pillow.

I slip onto the bed beside her and she immediately turns to face me.

"Hi." She smiles up at me.

"Hi." I smile down at her, leaning on my elbow.

"On a scale from one to ten, ten being most likely, how likely are we to have sex tonight?"

I turn my back to her and she stifles a laugh from behind me. She taps my back twice but I don't turn.

"Go to sleep," I mumble, fighting back a laugh.

"Answer me, JJ." She pokes my back again and I shake my head at her.

"Four."

"So I have a chance?" I *hear* the smile in her voice. "What can get me to a six?"

I let out a sigh and she pokes my back for an answer.

"If you were completely naked."

"Wow, just a six? What if I told you I just got waxed?"

"I'll tell you I don't care about body hair."

She's quiet for a beat before I hear her let out a content sigh. "He's a *man*, ladies, and disappointments."

# *Chapter Thirty-Eight*

## LISETTE

T HE SUN KISSES MY FACE, reminding me that I love the lighting most about the guest room Jackson gave me. The entire room is lit during the day, and as someone who needs sunlight in their depressed room, this place is perfect.

A smile touches my lips when I feel his gaze on me, and when I open my eyes, there he is, lying on his elbow, watching me.

"You're such a creep," I mumble before a yawn escapes me.

I've now slept here for seven nights, and he has been in this bed beside me for five of them. The first four times he came in just to talk to me, which led to kisses and then me convincing him to stay.

Last night, he just walked right in and slipped into bed with me like it has been his routine for the last ten years. No small talk, nothing. He just walked over, slipped his clothes off and crawled in next to me as I rambled on about something I can't even remember now.

It feels so *easy* being with him, but every time I step out of this room, there's a dark cloud looming over me, reminding me this is temporary and I leave today.

"You're so beautiful," he whispers, a smile tugging at his lips.

"I most likely have crusty eye boogers and morning breath. Nothing is beautiful about this."

His smile grows before he wipes the corner of my eye. "You do have eye boogers."

"Ew." I break into a laugh as I push his hand away when he reaches for my other eye. "You're getting too comfortable."

"I was *kidding.*" He rolls his eyes before trying to steal a kiss, but I turn my head and his lips land on my cheek.

"Morning breath." I cover my mouth, but he pushes my hand away and kisses me anyway.

"Your breath actually smells better than yesterday which proves my claim that it's beneficial to floss *and* use mouthwash, morning *and* night."

"Oh my god." I pull the covers over my face as he goes on with this argument again.

"I'm being serious."

"You're a *dad*, you're always serious."

He ignores my jab. "I'm surprised your teeth are so white for someone who doesn't floss and use mouthwash, let alone not brush their teeth at night."

"Wait until you find out I sometimes don't brush my teeth at all." I pull the covers off my face to see his mortified face and another laugh spills past my lips.

"You're joking." He watches me carefully.

"Is poor dental hygiene a deal breaker?"

"Yes," he answers so quickly, pulling another laugh out of me.

"Well, I'll go ahead and collect my things." I sit up in the bed and he still looks mortified.

"You're being serious." He sits up with me and I roll my eyes at how dramatic he's being.

"Calm down, it's only when I'm too sad to get out of bed."

His face changes now in understanding.

"No point in brushing my teeth if I'm just going to lay in bed and stare out into the abyss until I fall back to sleep." I shrug and his eyes soften.

"How often is that?"

"Depends."

"On what?" he pushes, and I let out a sigh as I crawl over to him and straddle his lap.

"Forget it." I lean forward to kiss him and he leans his back against the headboard before pulling away.

His hands land on my waist before they trail down to my thighs, his thumb trailing over the scars I marked myself with.

"I wanna know."

*I know, and I still can't understand why.*

His eyes meet mine and I force a smile. "I'm sitting on your lap shirtless and I can feel how hard you are, yet you want to talk about my depression? Are you a sadist?"

A smirk grows on his lips. "What gave it away?"

I roll my eyes at him and he turns more serious. Pulling in a deep breath, I decide to see where this goes. "It's pretty often. It's like spinning a wheel. Sometimes I'm sad enough to lay in bed all day, other days I need to drink or get high... sometimes this happens." I look down at my thighs and he rubs my scars again so tenderly.

"Can you feel which one is coming or does it just hit?"

"I can feel it most times." I nod to myself. "When I'm going to relapse, it's like this pull to drink, this urging need for it, and my brain justifies it until I give in. Same with getting high. Sometimes it's triggered, other times it's not." I shrug, and when my eyes meet his, he nods in understanding.

"The laying in bed with horrible dental hygiene is always a build-up. A few days of a weight in my chest, and when nothing brings me joy, I'm pushing through each day until I'm too tired mentally to do anything. Other times, it hits after I had a few great days."

"And this?" He squeezes my thighs gently, but I don't answer him. I keep my eyes on my scars, but I can't bring myself to form the words or even make a joke about it.

Jackson wraps an arm around my waist before gently flipping us so I'm on my back. My eyes meet his and a smile touches my lips when he leans forward to kiss me, and it truly does make me feel better.

Before I can deepen the kiss, he pulls away, leaving a trail of kisses from my neck to my chest. His eyes meet mine as he leaves a feather of a kiss on each of my nipples. It's so fast and soft, *innocent* even.

When he trails down my stomach I feel my excitement building because he's *still* opposed to sex, but he skips right past my pants and kisses my thighs.

I feel my throat tightening as he kisses *each* and *every* scar I put on myself. He takes his time getting all of them and I blink the tears out of my eyes. He turns to my other leg and a smile touches my lips before my vision blurs.

"Stop," I whisper, quickly brushing the single tear from my cheek before he can see.

"No." He continues and so do the tears. "If shame is holding you back from telling me, let me tell you, you have nothing to be ashamed of. You're stronger than your mind."

I shake my head in response and he simply kisses the rest of my scars.

"It makes me feel better," I confess. "I know how bad that sounds, I can recognize that, but when the thoughts are too loud and I can't feel anything else, I can feel *that*. When it hurts too much mentally, when I'm afraid I'll get high to distract myself, the cutting is a better distraction, and I would rather that than getting high. It's easier sometimes."

I watch him intensely, waiting for his face to change, for him to roll his eyes and tell me it's dumb and to *just stop* or *just talk to someone* like I've been told in the past, but it never comes. He simply crawls back over me and buries his face in my neck, wrapping his arms around me.

I hold onto him tightly, wrapping my legs around him as I force the lump down my throat.

"Call me the next time you want to hurt yourself," he mumbles into the crease of my neck and I let out a sigh, knowing that won't be happening.

"Why?"

He pulls away and wipes the tear from my face before kissing my cheek. "Because I'll give you something else to feel better about. I'll give you something else to feel in general, a different kind of distraction."

As I look into his eyes, I actually start to believe turning to him for help will work.

"Are you offering me sex? Because I might consider it." I let out a chuckle and he rolls his eyes before kissing my nose.

"I mean it, Lisette."

I want to make another joke to ease the heavy seriousness his words put in the air, but I can't come up with one as I'm suddenly mesmerized by the way he looks at me.

"I don't want to leave this room." I bury my face in his neck, letting out a defeated sigh. "I have no problems in here."

"You can come back whenever you want, but you made a promise to your brother and you need to talk to him."

I let out a loud sigh and he tries to pull away to look at me, but I hold him closer, my face still in his neck.

"You need to stop treating him like the villain. I know it's annoying you that he's being overbearing, but he *cares* about you, more than I've ever seen a person care about anyone."

I pull away, forcing myself to not get upset that he's on his friend's side. "That's not why I'm mad, Jackson. It's the fact that he doesn't trust me."

"Lisette, be for real for half a second," he deadpans. "He found you half *dead*. You were *barely* breathing. You *overdosed* when you told him you were *just busy*. If he didn't rush to you the second he did, you wouldn't be here right now. Do you seriously think he's going to get over that in a week and simply believe you when you say you're fine? You're not fine, baby. It's not that he doesn't trust you, he simply isn't believing your lies and you're mad about that."

I look off to the side, my cheeks heating. "Okay, but—"

"There are no buts, Lisette."

I keep my eyes off of him. I *hate* being called out when I'm wrong.

"I know you want him to trust you, but you've given him no reason to trust you, sweetheart. You have to see this from his perspective. I feel like you're just pushing him away and acting like this because you feel guilty which is *fine*. That's understandable, but stop ignoring his calls and treating Sire like he's such an unbearable annoying brother for simply caring."

I bite my tongue to stop myself from saying something I don't mean because he's right, and I just hate when I'm not.

"Fine," I mumble. Removing my arms from around him, I trail my eyes back to him.

He gives me a knowing look. "Be mad all you want, but don't give me attitude."

I don't reply, knowing it'll be with an attitude.

Jackson looks like he's about to say something, but a faint cry sounds behind the door.

We both go still before we sit up.

"She had a nightmare," he says as we climb out of bed.

"How do you know?" I quickly pull my shirt on.

"Because I know that cry." He pulls his pants on before rushing out of the room. I almost follow after him until I remember she isn't supposed to see me here. While I understand why we're not telling her about us, a huge part of me wants to skip to the part where I'm healed and get to be the one to run to her when she has a nightmare.

When Jackson appears at the door, his daughter is in his arms. Her head is on his shoulder as she falls back to sleep. "I'm going to go back to bed with her," he whispers as he nods towards his room.

"Okay." I muster up a smile. "I'm going to go soon," I whisper back although Belle is fast asleep.

His brows furrow, but I explain before he can protest.

"I'm going to talk to Sire."

A smile grows on his face as he closes the distance between us. Leaning down, he plants a kiss on my forehead. When he pulls away, I lean over to look at Belle. A smile touches my lips as I wipe her tears.

"Ugh, I love her so damn much." I take a hold of her little hand and kiss it gently.

When I glance up at Jackson, he watches me with a smile as he soothes her back. I kiss his chest before pulling him in for a hug.

"Thank you," I mumble quietly.

He kisses my forehead before wrapping an arm around me. "For what, sweetheart?"

I smile up at him. "For choosing me." I steal a kiss before soothing Isabelle's curls.

I'm not used to being chosen. Not by my parents, never by men, yet Jackson wants me—not just for sex, but to *love* and raise his daughter.

"I want all of my mornings to be like this, so I'm going to talk to my brother and get my shit together," I promise him.

A proud smile touches his lips and I kiss his daughter one more time before they go back to sleep, and I collect my things.

# Chapter Thirty-Nine

## LISETTE

M Y RELATIONSHIP WITH SIRE IS weird. When we were younger, it was a best friend thing with a mix of trauma bonding.

We turned to each other for *everything* until four years ago when he relapsed. I was being overbearing and trying to help, he said things he didn't mean, and the last four years were so weird for us. We stopped turning to each other when it came to our addiction, and it fucking sucked until he invited me here for breakfast and apologized.

Now I'm the one apologizing, and I don't like being on this side of the table.

When the bell rings, I look up and Sire walks in like he owns the damn building. I roll my eyes as he flashes his boyish grin at everyone who turns their head to look at him.

"What do I have to do to bring your confidence down ten notches?"

A smirk grows on his face as he slides into the booth across from me, leaning his arm across the back of the booth. "Either cut off my arm or my dick."

I break into a laugh and he kicks me from under the table when I get too loud. "Baseball and sex is where you get all your confidence from, huh?"

"Baseball and sex *with* Vidia is where I get all my confidence from."

"You didn't need to add that." I cringe and he laughs from across me. "How was Thanksgiving with her family?"

"Perfect," he answers sincerely. "I know I already won her mom over and I still try to kiss her ass, but it felt easy being with her family this weekend." He sighs now, a huge smile on his face as he lights up.

"They all sound like Vid when they speak Spanish. It's beautiful, and the *food?* Amazing. I made her help me practice my bachata for hours before going over and when I danced with Vidia in front of them, they said I'm Dominican by association. I love them."

A smile grows on my face at how obsessed he is with his girlfriend and her culture.

"Nice spot you picked." He looks around the room as if it's his first time seeing the place and I sink in my seat.

"I haven't been treating you fairly," I mumble.

"I agree." His eyes meet mine and I give him a knowing look.

"Don't make this harder for me." I roll my eyes before sitting back up and the words slip past my lips. "I've been lying to you. I'm *not* fine. I feel myself slipping, Sire. Every time I feel like drinking or getting high, I can *feel* myself caring less and less about the consequences. There genuinely feels like no point and I'm scared."

I feel my throat tightening at the confession, but force myself to keep a brave face on.

"Are you sober?" he asks gently.

"Yeah."

He watches me carefully, and I can see him hesitating to ask if I'm sure, but he never does.

"What are we thinking?" he asks. "Do we want to get professional help or—"

"No." I quickly shake my head. "I don't want to."

A sympathetic look covers his face, but I shake my head more firmly.

"I mean it. No rehab. No types of facilities or getaway camps." I quickly blink my tears away. "Going away means this is bad and out of my control, and I don't want to admit it's that bad. I don't want to go away."

He nods gently in return.

"I'm sorry for getting so mad about you caring," I start, Jackson's voice in my head. "I scared you and you don't trust me, and I get that. I was just mad that you didn't believe me when I said I was okay because I needed someone to believe me. I need *you* to believe I'm going to be okay."

He rises from his seat before slipping beside me. When he wraps his arm around me, I realize my tears haven't stopped.

"I believe in you," he whispers against my hair. "I know you're not okay *right now*, but I believe you're going to be okay. You're the strongest person I know, Lis. If you're not going to be okay, I may as well end it all now."

I break into a laugh before shifting in my seat so I can hug him back. We hold each other for a minute, and when I pull away, I'm glad we're in a very far corner and the diner is mostly empty.

"I need a temperature check," Sire starts with so much confidence like he has a full plan in his head. "How many days a week are you feeling down? How often are you thinking about using or hurting yourself?"

I wipe my tears as I think about it and the past week all of those numbers have been close to zero. It's incredibly unrealistic to say Jackson and Belle simply took away all my bad thoughts, but I haven't wanted to self harm *once* in the week I've been with him. Late at night I'll get sad, sure, but he'd walk into my room right on time. And I want to get high everyday, I'm an addict, but it's been a simple passing thought instead of the usual overwhelming need for it.

Sire is still waiting for my answer, so I cancel out this past week since it's an anomaly. "Sad everyday, but *concerningly* sad, four out of seven days. High everyday, but concerningly, two out of seven."

"Wait, that's actually so much better than I was thinking." He offers me a high five and I narrow my eyes at him.

"Were you hanging out with August this morning?"

I see his high energy deflate before my eyes as he slowly puts his hand down. "He slept over at Vid's mom's house with us Thanksgiving weekend," he mumbles.

"He's rubbing off on you."

"I'm hanging out with him too much." He shakes his head at himself.

"You could never hang out with him too much. It's August."

"True."

We both share a laugh before I turn serious again.

"I think I need a new environment." I share my idea from this morning. "My apartment makes me sad just thinking about it and it's not good for my mental health."

"I'll get you a new place," he says cheerfully.

"*I'll* get me a new place."

He opens his mouth but I stop him.

"You already paid my rent for the year. I'm not letting you get me a whole new apartment."

He rolls his eyes at me. "Don't be that girl in the movies that doesn't let the rich man help her."

"If you were a rich man who was trying to sleep with me, I'd let you buy me *three* houses," I state. "You're family and I know you don't mean it as a handout, but it feels like one, and when I'm depressed in my sad room, all I'm going to think about is how I'm a burden and can't do anything for myself because you bought the depressed room I'm crying in."

A smile touches his face, but I notice the somberness in it. "You're not a burden."

"I am."

"You're not."

"I am."

He lets out a defeated sigh. "Do you feel like that in your current apartment because I paid your rent?"

"Yes."

His entire mood plummets and I feel bad telling him after all these months, but it's true.

"I didn't mean it as a handout. We made a deal."

"And the deal was working great, but now I need something I worked hard for."

Sire nods in understanding. "So you're going to get a job?"

I let out a sigh as I rest my head on the table. "I've gotten too comfortable being unemployed. I don't want one," I whine and I know I probably sound bratty, but I didn't grow up rich, so it doesn't count.

"Marry a rich man," Sire jokes but his best friend pops into my head and the idea isn't the worst one I've had.

"I'm thinking of selling my paintings," I voice, picking up my head from the table.

"You mean you're taking my idea to sell your art."

"Shut up. It was my idea because I'm so smart and always have great ideas."

"You *never* have remotely good ideas. I actually think August has better ideas than you."

I ignore him. "Since I don't have enough pride to *not* ask for help, I'm going to ask these three, pretty famous, insanely rich, ugly people, if they can promote my art on social media."

His brows furrow before clarity passes through his face and he bites back a laugh. "Your paintings will sell out in ten minutes if you had *one* of those three, insanely rich, *beautiful*, people promoting them on their social media."

"Sage."

"Me."

We say at the same time and I break into a laugh. When I realize he is being serious, I laugh harder. "God, you're full of yourself."

The waiter comes to take our order, and when she walks away, I turn back to Sire.

"I have to talk to Harmony." I sink into my seat at the reminder. "I've been distant with her since I relapsed, but I invited her to breakfast with us, so please help me talk to her when she gets here."

Sire gives me a knowing look. "You need to do this on your own. You chose to get high, make it right with her."

"That's the thing." I sit up. "She doesn't know I relapsed. There's nothing for me to *make right*, but I know I have to tell her. I'm just scared she's going to hate me. Her mom is off on a bender every other week. I don't want to be like her."

"You're not." His tone is stern and I choose to believe him. We eat our appetizers in silence, but when I see Harmony make her way inside, my nerves damn near make me throw up.

She has a bright smile on her face, and with the bow on the top of her head, she reminds me so much of Isabelle. I shake my head at myself, the guilt eating at me for being a disappointment.

*You're going to disappoint Belle too.*

I'm snapped out of my thoughts as Harmony steps beside us. "Hey." She smiles at Sire shyly, and it takes me a second to remember they haven't met.

"Sire, this is my only likable kin." I gesture to Harmony. "Harmony, this is my least favorite brother." I pat the seat next to me. "Sit."

Sire laughs at my jab before asking Harmony about her day, and I let them talk as I build the courage to crush her soul. I feel my mood deflate with every minute that passes, but when Sire excuses himself to the bathroom and gives me that *look* I sit up straight.

"So." I shove her shoulder with mine. "I need to talk to you."

"Yeah." She turns to me, her eyes full of suspicion. "You've clearly been avoiding me all week and I hate the dry messages. I'm so sorry about Mom, but don't push me away because of her."

"I'm not," I reassure her. "It's not because of her."

She gives me a once-over before her eyes widen. "Oh my god, did Jackson get you pregnant?"

I slap her arm before glancing over her shoulder for Sire. "Jeez, I can't tell you anything. Shut *up*." I hit her again. "We haven't even slept together. Get your head out of the gutter and what new little boy is giving you hickeys?" I pinch her neck hard enough to deepen her mark.

She squirms away from me before pulling her sweater up. "This is abuse."

"Shut up." I roll my eyes at her. "Don't mention Jackson around my brother."

Her brows furrow before a smile creeps onto her face. "Oh, he doesn't know yet?"

I pick up my hand to hit her but she quickly inches away with a laugh.

"Alright alright." She puts a hand up in surrender. "So what's your deal if you're not hormonal or mad at me about Mom?"

I force a smile but when I open my mouth there's a knot too big to speak in my throat. I watch her face fall as she leans back to look at me, her eyes scanning mine.

"You're high?"

"No." I quickly shake my head.

Her shoulders sag in relief.

"But I was... I kind of overdosed two weeks ago." I watch her carefully as the disappointment covers her face. She looks down at the table, her head clearly running wild. "Can you say something?" I whisper before holding my breath as I wait for her to tell me she hates me.

She shakes her head, but when she turns to me, she only pulls me in for a hug. "Thank you."

I hold back a cry as I wrap my arms around her.

"Thank you for not letting me see you like that." She shakes her head, her voice breaking. "Mom doesn't have that decency so *thank you* for knowing you weren't okay and staying away until you got better. I want to be here for you, but I just can't handle seeing you like that, okay?"

I nod in return as I hold her tighter. "I'm going to get better," I promise her, forcing myself to believe it.

"I have an update on the cheater." She pulls away with a smile and I wipe her tears. After reassuring me that no one is pressing charges for wrecking her ex's car, she rambles on about the new boy who happens to be his best friend. When she mentions she's seeing him as revenge and he's in on it, I decide to give up on pointing her in the right direction.

# Chapter Forty

## JACKSON

"Thanks again for watching Belle." I keep my eyes on my mom as she puts a tray of lasagna in the oven.

"She's my granddaughter, you don't need to keep thanking me."

I hold back a sigh. While I came here to apologize the day after Thanksgiving, I haven't spoken to her since I left and I was naive to think she'd let it go that quickly.

"Ma."

She doesn't turn to me.

"I already apologized for what I said. I was emotional, like always when it comes to her mom and I'm not excusing my behavior or what I said. I *can* assure you it won't happen again. Can you stop punishing me for it?"

"You're a grown man, Jackson Jones. No one is punishing you."

Since her back is still to me, I roll my eyes at her use of my full name, as she has been using the past week.

"When are we going to stop fighting?"

She ignores me.

I throw my hands up in defeat. "I really don't understand why you're on Skye's side here. She left us. That was her choice. Why am I the villain for not wanting to give her a second chance?"

"Because everyone deserves a second chance, Jackson."

I shake my head at her words. "She hasn't said she wanted a second chance."

"And if she did?" She turns on her heels. "If she called you right now and said she wanted to see her daughter, would you allow it?"

I take a minute to think of my answer, but I don't know what I would do.

"No matter what, she's her *mom*, Jackson. She left when she was mentally vulnerable. She thought her baby was going to die and it was killing her. You reached out *once*, and I think if you pushed harder, Isabelle would have the mom she deserves."

I shake my head at her. "I thought my baby was going to die and it was killing *me*. I didn't go and cheat on her." I let out a scoff. "Her cheating actually wasn't the issue. She *left*. She heard our daughter might lose her hearing or die, and she *left*. I'm not going to beg her to have a relationship with that amazing little girl. She should want to. I'm not saying Skye is a villain. Maybe Isabelle is just too big of a trigger for her. Who knows, but I don't *care*. Isabelle and I are happy. *She's* happy. We don't need her, and I quite frankly don't want her around, especially not if the man she cheated on me with is going to sit here and play stepdad to *my* baby. I am not going to push harder for her to be a mother to a child she doesn't *want*. My daughter doesn't deserve her, she deserves more."

She crosses her arms at me. "And Lisette is more?"

My eyes narrow. "What?" I take a step back at her words. "What does Lisette have to do with this?"

"Stand there and tell me you think Lisette will be a better mom than her own mother will be. Reaching out to Skye won't kill anyone."

"Oh my god." I shake my head at her as I realize exactly what's happening. "You disapprove of Lisette and *that's* why you want Skye in the picture again, why you're pushing for me to go out with Isabelle's ballet teacher."

She doesn't say anything, but I can see the truth in her eyes.

"You're unbelievable."

"And you're letting a pretty face in a short dress cloud your judgment. Do you think her self-harm scars will just stop putting themselves there when you kiss her better? Do you think your father and I didn't notice how mentally checked out she was at Thanksgiving? The way you were pulling at nails to get her to smile and talk to us? She's severely depressed and has no business raising—"

"Don't," I cut her off before she could say something to upset me. "Isabelle is *my* kid. If I want to let wolves raise her with me, I will set up camp in the damn woods tonight. Lisette is an *amazing* person and your granddaughter is in *awe* of her. If you can take five seconds to get over her depression to see that, we could all move on because her scars aren't all she is."

She opens her mouth, but I cut her off again.

"You of all people know how protective I am of that little girl. We're keeping our relationship away from her."

She lets out a scoff. "Right, and inviting her over for Thanksgiving is keeping your relationship away from her. I was born at night, but not last night, Jackson. I'm aware she spent the night."

I go still. "That's different. She was there because—" I cut myself off from telling her Sire wanted me to keep her close, knowing that won't help Lisette's case. "Belle didn't know she spent the night. The idea of us is on her mind, yes, but she doesn't know we're dating and I spoke to her about that."

"So she's making you lie to your daughter? You never did that before."

"You're *impossible*," I snap, instinctively switching to our native language as my temper grows. "She's not making me do anything. I'*m* the one who doesn't want her to know about my relationship with her."

She nods condescendingly as she leans against the counter. "If she was so great, you would've told Belle."

"No, I wouldn't have and you know that. I don't just tell her about every girl in my life."

"But you go out of your way to lie about this one."

"I changed my mind." I give up. "I don't need you to babysit for me, but thank you." I turn on my heels to get my kid before she can say anything.

# Chapter Forty-One

## JACKSON

I TRIED CALLING SIRE, BUT my calls are going to voicemail for some reason. Not letting that stop me, I go to his house and Vidia opens for us.

"Hey, Jackson." She smiles up at me before I give her a hug.

"Hey, V." I kiss her cheek as Belle rushes past me. "Excuse me?" I turn to her as she searches for the dog. "What do you say to Titi?"

She quickly turns on her heels to hug her aunt. "Hi, where's Athena?"

Vidia laughs at her before kissing the top of her head. "She's taking a nap, beba, but you can wake her up. I need to feed her soon."

"Oh, I can give her a treat."

"Okay." Vidia laughs at her excitement. "You know where the treats are, but don't give her too many. She needs to have dinner."

She takes off to get the dog.

When Vidia turns to me, her smile falls. "You okay?"

I'm not, but I'm not about to tell her about my mother, so I nod in return. Stepping further in, she closes the door behind me. "Is Sire here? I was hoping you two could watch Belle for a few hours. I know it's last minute, but I—"

"Jackson, it's okay," she says with a laugh. "You can drop her off at any time without notice, you know that."

"Thank you." My shoulders sag. "I'm going out and I can pick her up later tonight, but she begged me to let her sleepover. I already have her bag since she was originally going to sleep at my mom's, but if you'd rather me get her, I can."

"Jackson, please stop." She laughs at me as she walks over to her couch. "Why do you act like she's never slept here every time you drop her off? *Of course* she can spend the night."

I smile at her as I sink onto her couch. "I just feel bad and I worry about her too much when I'm not around."

Understanding covers her face. "That makes sense, but I promise she's okay here."

I nod, knowing she's right.

"Are you going out with a girl or is this for work?" She smiles again as she glances over at my suit and I feel a blush meet my face.

"It's work."

She nods to herself as she picks up the remote and turns to her TV. "So I'm crazy and there's *not* anything going on between you and Lis."

My blush deepens and she turns to me with the brightest smile.

"I *knew* it." She nearly squeals.

"Does Sire know?" I glance over her shoulder but she shakes her head.

"He doesn't and he's not here," she reassures me. "I'm sure he has his suspicions, though. It was very obvious after you beat up that guy at her place." She watches me carefully but I rise from my seat before she can interrogate me.

"Thank you for watching Belle."

"Mhm." She rises to her feet. I call out to Belle and she comes out with Athena by her side, the huge dog nearly her height.

"Titi said you can spend the night, but behave yourself." I kneel to kiss her.

"I will." She kisses my cheek and tries to walk away, but I pull her in for a hug.

When I hug her for too long, she pushes me away. "Dad, just *go*, I'm fine."

"Don't be mean. I'm going to miss you." I smother her some more.

"It's *one* night." She tries to shove me away when I keep her close.

"Are you sure you want to sleep over? I can pick you up later and—"

"*Go*." She guides me to the door, pushing my legs. "I already know you're going to change your mind and take me back like *always*." She rolls her eyes dramatically and I have to bite back a laugh.

"You're not going to miss your dad?" I tease, but she ignores me. "You're hurting my feelings, Belle. Aren't you going to miss me so, so much?"

"Oh my fucking *goodness*," she mumbles.

I stop in my tracks before turning to her and her entire face drops at my glare.

"Watch it," I warn. "Who even says that?" I ask, knowing I've never said that phrase around her.

"Uncle Sigh," she trails off, her guilty eyes on me.

"Stop repeating people. You're not a parrot." I'm going to kick my best friend's damn ass. "Behave for Titi V. Your uncle will be back soon and do not ask him for sweets for dinner."

"Okay." She watches me carefully, but I decide not to ruin her night by sending her to bed early.

Beside us, Vidia stifles a laugh as she walks me to the door.

"I'm going to kill your boyfriend," I say, quiet enough for Belle not to hear.

"Not if he kills you first." She gives me a knowing look. "You're a good man, so I know Lis is being taken care of, but if this goes left, he won't even try to hear your side of things. His relationship with Lis is completely different from that of his other siblings. Don't hurt her."

I only nod as she opens the door for me, knowing I wouldn't dream of hurting her.

GRABBING THE BAG FROM THE passenger seat, I head upstairs, my excitement building. I know I saw Lissy yesterday when she left my house, but I haven't spoken to her since then, and while I'm fully aware that my attachment issues are latching onto her, I again, don't care. I like being around her, I like having her in my space with her laughs and messy room.

I knock on her door eagerly, and when Sire opens it, my smile drops.

His brows furrow as he looks back at me before he takes in the suit I'm in for the charity event.

"Hey." I force a smile.

"Hi?" He rightfully still looks confused.

"I'm taking your sister on a date." I rip the bandaid off. I'm not doing the whole *hide from her brother* thing anymore. The anxiety and guilt might kill me.

He looks even more confused before I see him putting the pieces together in his head. He lets out a scoff as he completes the puzzle he just made up.

"You're a fucking dirtbag." He turns away, and I was expecting him to slam the door in my face, so this is a *huge* win.

I follow him into the apartment and notice they're packing her art, but I don't question that as I focus on Sire.

"Before you get mad—"

"I'm not going to get mad, Jackson." He sinks into the couch, and I don't miss how tired he already sounds of this conversation. "I've spent enough energy being mad about Sage and Liam and it was for nothing because now I'm incredibly happy for them. You wanna take Lis out on a date? Marry her while you're at it. She's always wanted to marry a rich man. I'm sure her spiritual ass will say I manifested this."

I let out a scoff. "Okay, we both know you're not this supportive. August? Absolutely. You? Never."

He simply shrugs.

"You actually don't care?"

"Oh, I care. I'm just not going to waste my energy telling you how much I care since *you* don't and clearly don't have enough respect for this friendship to tell me, and don't say some bullshit like, *I just told you*. You only told me because I happen to be here."

He's not wrong about that last part.

"I *do* respect you as a friend. I felt like shit not telling you."

"Okay." He doesn't say anything else and calm Sire is scarier than angry Sire.

I open my mouth to say something, but he beats me to it.

"I trusted you to keep an eye on her because she was mentally vulnerable and you were moving in on her the whole time?" He lets out a scoff. "You're a fucking asshole."

I try to get a word in, but he doesn't let me.

"I really don't want to hit you right now, Jackson, so please stop talking to me."

I disregard his warning. "That's *not* what happened. You know I'm not that kind of man."

"Clearly," he mumbles, turning back to the painting he's packing.

"Sire—"

"Just drop it." He rises from the couch. "I didn't sleep last night for this girl. I'm not her dad, and this isn't worth me and Lis fighting over." He rolls his eyes like he genuinely does not give a single shit about me, and I think him not caring hurts more than if he was mad. It's as if I'm not *worth* his energy.

He walks into the kitchen as Lisette walks out of her room with a smile that can replace the sun and light up the Earth.

"I found him!" She holds up her turtle, and when I see the tear tracks on her face, it's clear she freaked out about losing him.

A smile reaches my face at how damn cute she is in her messy bun and oversized hoodie that I think belongs to her brother.

When she notices me, her face morphs into confusion. "Hi?"

"Hello." I close the distance between us, but I don't kiss her because I refuse to kick my best friend while he's already down. Instead, I hand her the bag in my hand. "Get dressed. You have half an hour to get ready."

If she was anyone else, I would've given her more time, but traffic was worse than I accounted for and I know she doesn't need much time to get ready.

Her brows furrow as she looks down at my outfit and the bag in my hand. "I'm busy."

"Yeah." I look around the room. "What's going on? Are you sending your art somewhere?"

"Yup." She lights up again and I think my new favorite thing is this woman's happiness. "You've missed *a lot.*"

"You can tell me all about it after getting dressed." I push the bag to her, but she doesn't take it.

"What do I need to get dressed for?"

"We're going on a date."

Her face is *dripping* in disgust and I try very hard not to be offended. She glances over at Sire, and when I turn to him, he shrugs.

"He told me. You can marry rich like I suggest and never work again." He sounds so monotone, that I'm actually concerned.

"Is he okay?" I mumble.

Lisette rolls her eyes. "We were up all night. He doesn't do well on zero hours of sleep." She waves him off before turning back to me. "We're not going on a date," she states so casually before walking to her room and I follow close behind.

"Why not?"

She turns her head to the side as if I should know the answer to that. "JJ."

I wait for her to add more, but that's all she says.

"Lissy," I say like she did, turning my head to the side.

She stifles a laugh as she walks over to her turtle tank and sets Piglet in.

"We're dating," she states. "I'm doing the trying thing. Belle thankfully hasn't brought up marriage since Thanksgiving and it's definitely too soon for that, but she's cute, so I'm letting it slide. *However*, we don't need to go on dates and do the whole romantic thing."

I roll my eyes at her fear of affection. "Get dressed. You have twenty-seven minutes." I sit on her bed.

"Where are we even going?" She holds up the white silk dress I got her.

"Charity event."

She lowers the dress to look at me. "The one you have with *Rome*?"

I nod. "This is a work event. Not a *date*."

"So you'll come."

"No." Her face scrunches in disgust again. "There's going to be a bunch of rich people there."

"I'm a rich person."

"My point exactly. I don't want to be around a bunch of yous."

I stare at her blankly as she bites back a laugh. "You have twenty-four minutes."

"It has not been three minutes."

"I'll buy a new watch since I'm so rich," I deadpan. "Don't make me tell you to get dressed again."

"*Don't make me tell you to get dressed again*," she mocks.

"You're such a *dad*," we both say it at the same time, me mocking her, and she breaks into a laugh.

"Go," we both say again, her mocking me this time and I bite back my smile. "*Seriously, Lisette,*" our voices sync, hers deepening.

I rise from the bed, and she takes off running into her closet with a laugh.

## Chapter Forty-Two

# JACKSON

I WALK BACK INTO LISETTE'S living room as she gets dressed, and I find Sire doing her pile of dishes.

He doesn't say anything as I walk into the kitchen. I lean against the counter as I watch him.

"What is she doing with her art?" I ask. While I want to hear it from Lisette because she seemed really excited, I'm simply trying to make conversation.

"She got the idea to sell them, and like every idea, she's going full send with it," he mumbles.

I glance into the living room, and with all the pretty packaging from pink bubble paper and thank you stickers she got, she definitely went full send.

I almost choose to leave him alone at his tone, but he speaks up again. "She's having a really high high day."

"High high day?" I push off from the counter, but he shakes his head like I shouldn't be concerned.

"She's sober," he reassures me. "That's just what we call it for, well, you know how she gets..." he trails off before pulling in a breath. "This one is just more manic."

I feel my brows furrow before I take a second to think of his words, looking back at her other good and bad days. "She's bipolar?" I voice as the thought enters my head.

His head snaps over to me. "Keep your voice down."

I glance over my shoulder for what he's looking at, but we're alone.

He lets out a sigh as he looks back at the dishes. "She has bipolar depressive disorder, but don't bring it up and *don't* mention the words bipolar or mania around her," he warns. "It's genetic and she hates that she got it from her. It's a huge trigger, so please don't tell her I told you. I thought you knew."

I nod in understanding, assuming he means *her* as in her mom.

"She has really low lows and really high highs," he explains. "I've been waiting for this one to hit after she relapsed. It's why I stayed up with her all night, keeping an eye on her and stuff. Waiting for her to plummet."

"What does she need?"

Sire glances over at me and simply watches me. "When did you start making a move on her?"

I falter at the sudden change in topic, but I guess he actually thinks I was moving in on her when she was vulnerable. "A few weeks before we went to the park with Athena. I was going to tell you that day."

He nods, clearly remembering.

"Is this the part where you apologize for thinking that low of me? As if we haven't been best friends for *seven* years?" I accuse, but he ignores me.

Instead he turns back to the last few dishes. "She just needs us close. She's extra impulsive and oblivious, and that mix can be dangerous. She just thinks she's having a good day and she is... only she thinks she's unstoppable. After we got breakfast yesterday, she was super happy with her ideas about moving and selling her stuff, talking about how it's the best day ever. It carried on all night into today. Nothing can knock her down, but the lack of sleep isn't good for her. I've been trying to bring her down to Earth, but she just thinks I'm kidding, so when she tells you about her plans, remind her to be realistic."

"I'm not going to take her joy away."

"I'm not asking you to. I just—" He lets out a breath. "Forget it."

"No. What is it?"

He sets down the plates in his hand before turning to me. "Bringing her down to Earth will help when she feels down in a few days. It won't feel like everything good is suddenly gone because it was never there. She's just seeing everything through rose-tinted glasses right now."

I simply nod in response because I don't want to agree. He said she needs us to stay close and keep an eye on her, so I'll do that, but if she's having a good day, we should let her.

Sire puts the plate into the cabinet and he really does look exhausted.

"You should get some sleep."

He doesn't respond and I don't add anything else.

A few minutes later, Lisette walks into the living room with a bright smile on her face, and Sire's words about her having a *high high* ring in my head.

"This dress is expensive as shit." She runs her hands on the silk. "I love it."

I stifle a laugh as I close the distance between us to steal a kiss. "You're beautiful." I pull off the tag I forgot.

The dress fits her frame perfectly as it drags down to the floor. Like I thought it would, it looks perfect against her blonde hair.

"How'd you know my shoe size?" She lifts her foot back, smiling at her YSL heel.

I kiss her pretty face again. "I looked at your shoe the other day. Are we ready?"

"Let me curl my hair and we can go." She turns before I can reply, but I follow close behind.

I sit on the toilet seat and watch her intensely as she rambles on about how she found Piglet. She sounds so happy as she speaks, jumping between topics rapidly and it's... weird.

I've seen her happy, but this is too happy, and I start to believe Sire is right and she is not *just* having a good day.

I don't say anything though, and when she finishes her hair, we pass by a sleeping Sire on her couch before heading down to my car.

I open the door for her, and as soon as I'm in the driver seat, Lisette turns to me. "Okay, I've been holding my tongue until we get in the car because I need your *full* attention," she exclaims and I bite back a laugh at how animated she is. "So I decided I needed to move. My apartment makes me depressed, *but* I need money, duh."

"Duh," I add and she rolls her eyes at me with a smile.

"So I decided I was going to sell my paintings. Now, I already had a Famoura account for my art and had like one viral video, *but*," she pauses for dramatic effect as she takes out her phone. "I told Sage I wanted to sell my art, so she reposted a few of my posts and told her followers my pieces were up for sale, and *look*."

She turns her phone to me and I look over at the stop sign. I scan her profile and she has nearly two million followers along with over six million views on her three pinned videos.

"Holy shit." I knew Sage was *insanely* famous and had a ton of followers, but that's a lot of people for something she simply reposted.

"Right?"

"When did she repost your stuff?" I turn back to the road.

"Yesterday morning." She's *literally* bouncing in her seat as she scrolls through her phone. "I've been getting *so* many requests. I already packed a shit ton of orders to send out tomorrow."

*That* explains why she started packing so many of them.

"This one guy offered me ten *grand* for a painting I did of a girl killing herself."

"*What?*" I turn to her again.

"I know right? Isn't that a lot of money for something I did in just *three* days?"

"No, I meant what to the painting. That's pretty graphic. When did you paint that?"

She waves me off. "It was a few weeks ago. It's not that bad. It's just her drowning. I actually love that painting and a few other people asked for it so I might go live and bid it off. I'm going to be rich by the end of the week."

"Okay..." My brows furrow at how excited she sounds. "I don't think you're going to be *rich* that quick." I try to bring her down a few notches like Sire suggested because it's clear now it's necessary.

"Are you worried I won't want you anymore when I have my own money?" she teases and I bite back a laugh.

"Yes. I like poor girls who are too depressed to brush their teeth."

She breaks into a laugh before shoving my arm.

"So what's the plan here? Are you going to make this a full-time job?" I ask, trying to get a feel for what's going on here.

She shrugs as she thinks. "I think it'll be cool. I don't want a nine to five and I like teaching, but I don't want to go back. I love painting, though, and I didn't think anyone would want *my* paintings, but they do."

A smile touches my lips. I've only seen a few of her pieces, but they're all incredible. "You should do it then. You need to make a plan and—"

"Ughh, you and your *plans*. Is that an OCD thing?"

I roll my eyes at her. "No, it's a me thing, *rude*."

"Hey, I was just asking." She rests a hand on my leg. "I like knowing all of your OCD tendencies. It's not *bad* if it was."

A smile touches my lips but then she lets out a loud gasp, I nearly stop the car.

"I could get an art studio," she exclaims, grabbing my arm in excitement.

"Okay, one step at a time, sweetheart."

"Oh my god. This is great, that way I can have more space." She gasps again. "What if I open an art store and sell my prints there? I can have the grand opening the week before Christmas so people can get *gifts*. It'll be a cute two-story place and I can even put my prints on like tote bags and—"

"Lisette," I cut her off. "How about you ship out the orders you got today first?"

I steal a glance at her and she rolls her eyes at me. "You and my brother are being such Debbie downers."

"I'm being realistic. I think it's great to have that goal for *some day*, but to have this up and running in *three weeks*? That's not happening, love."

"I can make it work," she says confidently.

"In three weeks?"

"I'm getting ten *grand* off of one painting," she says as if that explains enough.

"Do you know the logistics of opening a business or even renting out a space?"

She hesitates now. "Sire and August have a whole batting cage. If *they* can do it, anyone can."

"Right... and how long did that take them?"

"Well, I'm not going to have as many renovations as them."

"Okay, so let's say you find a space that needs no work, which is highly unlikely because I'm sure you don't want *white walls* in your art store. What's your credit score? Will you be approved for this space? You just said you want two stories, that's not a small space."

She doesn't answer.

"Do you know what kinds of permits you'll need for your store? You don't want to work all day. Will you hire staff? Do you even have enough paintings? Are you going to be able to make all these prints and tote bags to fill a two-story store in *three weeks*? Do you understand what an exit clause is? Will you hire someone who understands that and runs things with you? Who will you hire? How—"

"Alright alright, I get it. I'm not getting my art store." She sinks in her seat and it crushes me to break it to her.

I rest my hand on her thigh. "You can get your art store, reina. Just not before Christmas." I steal a glance at her and she's pouting.

Biting back a laugh, I squeeze her cheeks.

She rolls her eyes before turning to me. "Do *you* know what an exit clause is?" Her words come out muffled since I'm still squeezing her face.

I nod before stealing a kiss and turning back to the road.

"How about *you* do the logistics for me, and I make the paintings and sit with a pretty face at the cash register?"

My laugh fills the car. "It's a lot of logistics. Are you planning on paying me?"

"You're *rich*."

"You're not a charity case." I bite back a smile as I steal a glance at her and she's narrowing her eyes at me. "You're the one who said you'll be rich by the end of the week."

"I have ten grand. Take it or leave it."

I break into another laugh. With the way she plans things, she'd probably lose three thousand dollars every month at her store and see no profit, yet, I'll gladly run the logistics for her and fund this shit show if it'll make her this happy.

"If you find a space and find staff to help you run the place, I'll take care of the rest."

I see her sit up in her seat beside me.

"Really?"

"You have to hold actual interviews and find *good* people so you don't have to keep rehiring every three months."

"Deal!"

"But—"

"No, I already said deal."

"We're negotiating." I turn to her at the red light. "You need to have enough paintings and other merchandise to fully stock the store for two months and you have to get the money for that on your own. When you get all that, I'll loan you the rest and you can have your grand opening."

She looks like she's thinking. "So we'll basically be going half and half?"

"Sure." I let her believe that. "Everything will be in your name, though, unless you don't qualify for some reason, then you'll need a cosigner. I might not be able to since I just got my house and already own two other properties, but your brothers only own one and Sage doesn't have a house, right?"

She nods in response. "With the ten grand I'm paying you to do the logistics, I'm technically giving you the money you're loaning me to open the place."

"Sure." I also let her believe this is only going to cost that much.
"Deal."

We shake on it and another smile is on her face.

"This is the best deal ever. I'm basically paying nothing."

"Okay." I don't know what kind of math she's using, but she's happy and that's all that matters in life.

# Chapter Forty-Three

## LISETTE

A SWARM OF BUTTERFLIES TAKE off in my lower stomach as Jackson wraps his arm around my waist, holding me close as we enter the charity event.

The hall is flooded with men in expensive looking suits. Women in even more expensive looking dresses at their sides. There's a hushed piano being played in the center of the hall, but when I notice the art on the wall, I quickly turn to Jackson.

"The charity event is an *art* exhibit?"

"Yeah?" Jackson turns to me now. "I didn't mention that?"

"No, you didn't mention."

A smile touches his lips. "That's why I wanted you to come. Everything that's sold today is going to the All-American Sluggers. They have little league baseball teams in every state across the country and—"

"Sorry, I don't really care about the team," I whisper. "Who's the artist?" I walk over to a piece that first caught my attention and he follows close behind, stifling a laugh.

"Nice to see you care about my interest the same way I care about yours," he mumbles and I turn back to him, giving him a knowing look.

"You know I care about your interests, baby. Don't pull that, I listened to you talk about how baseball trades work for twenty minutes before you ranted about stocks. We both know you're not interested in a *little league team.*" A smile grows so big on his face, pulling my brows together. "What?"

He simply shakes his head. "Nothing." He nods to the painting behind me. "The artist is Alexander Sinn."

My brows shoot up as I turn back to the wall and just as he said, Sinn's signature is in the corner of his painting. "Damn." I nod in thought.

"Do you know him?"

"Are you kidding?" I let out a scoff. "Of course, I know him. Do you know how much controversy he is stirring in the art community right now?"

"No, tell me about it." He steps beside me as I marvel at the piece and ramble on about the artist.

"Jones."

We turn and Rome flashes a smile at us before he gives me a once-over.

"You brought the nanny." His smile grows.

"She's not—" Jackson shakes his head and I bite back a laugh. "Thank you for being on time," Jackson says accusingly.

Rome's brows furrow. "I *was* on time," he argues, and for some reason, I believe him.

"You're the one who was late, *Dad*," Rome teases and a laugh escapes me.

"I like you." I nod in approval and a smirk touches his lips.

"Well, thank you, honey." He takes a step towards me and Jackson swiftly stands in front of me.

"She's off limits," he nearly warns. "Go socialize and buy at least two paintings."

Rome's brows pull together again. "I don't want any of this?"

"I didn't ask you," Jackson argues, his voice hushed.

"So why would I pay"—Rome looks over at the painting behind me and his eyes widen before his mouth hangs—"Twenty-five *thousand* for"—He turns his head to the side as he tries to study the abstract piece—"What the fuck even is that?"

I break into a laugh but quickly quiet down when Jackson turns his glare to me.

I clear my throat, trying to be more serious. "Art is subjective. It can be what you want it to be." I try to keep a straight face, but I feel Jackson's glare still on me. When my smile breaks through, he rolls his eyes.

"The money is going to kids who can't afford to play baseball. I don't care what you buy or if you want it. Just buy something."

Rome rolls his eyes and Jackson doesn't look any happier. "Can't I just donate the money without taking the ugly art?"

Jackson walks away, pulling me with him and I break into another laugh.

"Stop encouraging him," he mumbles and I tease him with a pout.

"Aww, is Dad upset because his rich brat doesn't listen?"

He rolls his eyes again and I stifle a laugh.

"If he has enough money to afford these paintings, why is he trying to play baseball?"

Jackson turns his full attention to me. "Would you stop painting if you were rich?"

"Of course not."

"Okay, same for him. Baseball is his passion. He's not going to stop trying to achieve his goal to make it to the major league because he simply doesn't need the money."

"Touché." I nod in thought. When I feel my phone buzz in my dress pocket, I pull it out. My eyes scan the screen before I feel my jaw drop.

"What happened?" Jackson steps closer.

I turn my phone to him. "That guy who offered me ten grand for the suicide painting just *tripled* his offer," I whisper.

I watch Jackson carefully as his brows raise. "Wow." He nods like he's impressed as he reads the rest of the message.

I quietly squeal before hugging him. "My life is going *great*. I can't believe I wanted to die last week."

Jackson stifles a laugh, his arms around my waist. "Okay, I don't think your depression is *cured*. It's thirty thousand dollars." He keeps his voice low, but I still pull away to look at him, my brows furrowed.

"I didn't say it was. It's not the money, it's someone wanting what I created."

"Right, but one good day doesn't mean your life is going great."

I remove my arms from around him now. "Why are you being so negative?" When his shoulders sag, I know exactly what this is. "Sire spoke to you." I let out a scoff as I turn back to the art on the wall.

"Don't be like that." He tries to wrap his arm around my waist again, but I push him away.

"Stop touching me." I take a step away. "I'm not having a *high high* day. I know what those are, trust me, I'm the one with depression. I'm just happy."

"And I'm happy that you're happy."

I pull away when he tries to touch me. "What exactly did he tell you?" I watch him carefully, but he doesn't say anything. "Whatever." I walk off, his presence suddenly annoying me.

He calls out to me, but I keep walking, and since we're in a room full of people, he doesn't yell after me, but I hear his footsteps so I hurry mine. I walk into the first door I see which happens to be the men's bathroom.

Just as I turn to leave, Jackson quickly walks in after me.

"Move." I try to get around him but he steps in my way.

"I'm sorry, sweetheart," he coos and I roll my eyes at how damn sexy he sounds.

"You don't get to call me that when I'm mad at you. Why can't you guys just leave me alone? When I'm sad, you're both overbearing. When I'm happy, it's a fucking crime. What do you want?!"

"Lower your tone," Jackson says cooly, his voice low.

"No, you—"

I don't get to finish my sentence as he leans over, capturing my lips with his. His tongue slides into my mouth before his hand comes around my throat and I'm suddenly pinned against a wall.

I'm breathless as I kiss him back, but I make no move to pull away. Our tongues dance together as my arms come around his neck and through his curls.

When the kiss breaks, it's him who pulls away. "Are you done being a brat?"

I try to catch my breath and a smirk grows on his face, his hand still around my throat.

"I'm not being a *brat*. I'm making very valid points." I try to move his hand from around me, but as my hand touches his, I can't bring myself to push him away.

"You are making valid points but you don't have to storm off and yell to make them. I'm sorry for bringing your mood down. I'm happy that you're happy. I just don't want you to feel like all is lost in the world if you wake up tomorrow and you're sad."

I don't say anything because this is the part where I apologize for yelling and I don't feel like it.

He gives me a knowing look, but my eyes cut down to the floor. His hand tightens around my throat as he tilts my face up to meet his eyes.

"Say sorry."

Two words should *not* make my stomach dip the way it just did.

"No." I find myself saying, simply to push him and see where this goes. "How about you stop—"

"I don't want to argue with you, sweetheart."

"Oh, we're arguing, and stop calling me—"

His lips meet mine again and I feel myself smiling against him before his hand tightens around my throat again. A moan escapes me as I hold onto the hand around me, but he doesn't move to loosen his grip as his other hand pulls my dress up.

I pull him closer and when his hand finds my wet underwear, a breath of surprise slips past my lips. I'm practically *begging* for him as I spread my legs and as slow as humanly possible, he slips his hand in my underwear and rubs me in slow circles.

"JJ," I whisper.

"Apologize for the attitude."

"I'm so very sorry, Jackson Jones."

He pushes my head against the wall again, forcing my eyes to meet his. "That didn't sound sincere."

"Jackson." My eyes are on his lips as I mindlessly cover his hand with mine, guiding him to where I want him.

Painstakingly slow, he slides one finger inside me and I tilt my head back in pleasure just as his mouth lands on my neck.

"You're so pretty when you're desperate."

*New kink: Unlocked.*

"Apologize," he demands now and I will give this man anything he asked for if he asked in that voice.

"I'm sorry for yelling." My head dips, catching his lips just as he adds another finger and I moan into his mouth this time.

"Well, look at what we have here."

I pull away so fast my head slams into the wall. I squeeze my eyes shut as I rub my head and beside us, I hear Rome's laugh.

"Get out," Jackson bites out, rubbing my head gently.

"I'm in desperate need to relieve myself. Not like *you're* relieving yourself, of course."

I turn to him and when he glances down at Jackson's fingers, he nods like he's impressed. I feel my face burst into flames. Jackson holds his hand behind his back and Rome barks up another laugh.

"They like it when you lick your fingers after," he whispers.

*Oh my god.*

"I clearly don't need sex advice. Leave."

Rome ignores him and turns to me. "I was planning our wedding in my head, honey. You said you liked me?" He pouts and I break into a laugh as I bury my face in Jackson's chest.

"What was it you told me, Jones?"

I steal a glance at Rome and he leans against the door as he pretends to think. "I couldn't bring a date because you didn't trust my horny ass to not sneak off to the bathroom?" He shakes his head disappointedly. "I found *three* paintings that aren't entirely ugly. I just bought them and I was looking for you to tell you. Are you proud of me?" He smiles cheerfully. "All jokes aside, this is actually fun."

"Glad you like being a decent person."

"I hope you kids are being safe." He smiles at me now. "You look gorgeous, honey. I forgot to tell you earlier, but now that you're all flustered from having him—"

"Booker," Jackson bites out. "You have two seconds to walk out without another word."

Rome's brows raise in amusement, a smirk playing on his face. He pushes off the door, his hands in mock surrender as he flashes me a wink and leaves without another tease.

"If we get caught by anyone ever again, I'm going to kill myself."

Jackson turns his glare to me and I'm suddenly afraid to speak. "Do not say that."

I open my mouth but quickly stop myself from joking and simply nod. He keeps his eyes on me for a beat before turning to wash his hands.

"Come on." He nods for the door.

"Can we just go?" I get on my tippy toes to kiss him, but he leans away, his arm wrapping around my waist as he guides me out.

"We have to stay a little longer, reina."

I let out a disappointed breath as we walk out of the bathroom and I feel Jackson lean into my ear. "V has Belle."

I turn to him now, biting back a smile.

"At her house," he adds and my smile reaches my lips.

"Are you *sure* we can't leave now?"

"I'm sure, walk and watch the attitude." He nods forward and I roll my eyes as I turn around.

# *Chapter Forty-Four*

## LISETTE

I HATE SIRE.

Not actually, just for being right.
I hate Jackson for believing Sire.
Again, not actually.
I hate myself most of all.

# Chapter Forty-Five

## JACKSON

W HEN I TURN OVER, A smile touches my lips at the sight of Lisette in my bed. She looks so pretty in my shirt. Like she's *mine*.

"How long have you been awake?" I lean over to kiss her forehead and she simply shrugs as she stares off at something. "Your brother is bringing Belle in a few. Do you want to get up and make breakfast with me?"

She simply shakes her head before turning around.

I feel my brows furrow before I wrap an arm around her waist and bring her back to my front. "Are you still tired?"

I nuzzle my face in her neck and I don't feel her shake her head or hear her even acknowledge my question, so I pull away to steal a glance at her and she's watching my closet door.

"Are you okay, baby?"

She doesn't answer.

"Lissy?" I turn her face to me, forcing her eyes to meet mine.

"I'm fine," she mumbles, moving her face from my grasp. "I'm just tired." She turns again but her voice is lacking all emotion.

"Too tired for sex?" I tease, my hand crawling down her stomach but when she doesn't reply, my heart aches. "Are you physically tired or mentally tired, sweetheart?" I ask gently.

She lets her eyes fall shut as she gets more comfortable. "I said I'm fine. I didn't sleep the other night. I'm just tired."

I study her before choosing to believe her. "Okay." I kiss her nose before rising from the bed.

I brush my teeth and grab my phone before heading downstairs. Just as I enter the kitchen I get a message from Rome. I read over the post someone made about him being at the gallery. In the comments some people say he was there just to make himself look good, but the majority of the comments are commending him for *turning a new leaf* and how he seems sincere, which I guess isn't entirely a lie.

I watch his text bubbles but go still as I think of Sire on his way here. As images of him crashing his car with Belle in the backseat flash through my mind, I hold my breath as I rush to the front door. I tap it once, but when that doesn't feel right, I tap it three more times before I let go of my breath.

I wait a beat for the next intrusive thought, but no more come, so I turn back to the kitchen. My phone goes off and I swipe it off the counter.

**Rome B**

> ITS WORKINGGG

> WE'RE BACK IN BUSINESS BABY!

While he's constantly messing with me, I notice a change in his attitude. Like he really does want to be better and granted, it's because the alternative is losing everything but it's a start.

Tucking my phone away, I get to cooking.

I was going to let Lisette sleep longer, but something feels off and I don't think it's my OCD, so I head back upstairs with a plate of breakfast.

I walk in quietly, in case she's sleeping, but as I expected, she's awake. Her head is on the bed rather than the pillow and she stares off at something in the distance, lost in her thoughts.

When I get closer, I notice a wet spot next to her eyes.

I set the plate on the nightstand as I kneel on the floor in front of her and wipe her tears. "What's wrong, baby?" I whisper.

She shakes her head. "I'm fine." She sounds so distant, a weight settles in my chest.

"Remember when you said you don't like it when I say I'm not mad when I really am?" I wipe another tear. "Well, I don't like it when you say you're fine with tears in your pretty eyes. If you're not okay, that's okay, sweetheart."

She shakes her head again. "It's not okay."

"It is," I whisper, leaning forward to kiss her nose.

"I want to be okay."

"I know you do." I soothe her hair and my throat nearly closes as another tear trickles down her face. "Let's have breakfast." I kiss the tear off her face.

"I'm not hungry," she mumbles, voice vacant of any emotion.

"I know." I climb into the bed and pull her up so she's leaning her back against my chest. I grab the plate and hold a fork full of eggs for her.

"Don't make me do the airplane on you," I tease and she shakes her head before taking a bite. "Good job." I kiss the side of her face.

"Are you going to make me brush my teeth?"

"Yup." I kiss the back of her head before offering more food.

"Can I stay in bed after?" she asks, her mouth full of food.

"I'm going to ask you to come down when Belle gets here, but if you aren't feeling up for it, then you can come back upstairs."

She nods before taking the fork from me as I massage her back.

"What did my brother tell you?"

I know what she's asking, but I only kiss the back of her head. "Is there a reason why you didn't want him to tell me?" I ask gently, trying to figure out if she doesn't want me to know about her disorder because it's *me* or because of her own feelings.

She moves her food around, and when she takes too long to take another bite, I scoop up a fork full of food and bring it to her mouth. She takes a bite before leaning her back against my chest again.

"I share too many qualities with her," she mumbles and I know who *her* is. "I just really didn't want to have that too. I like to believe I'm just depressed and it's not *bipolar* depression." She says it like it tastes bad in her mouth. "Then days like this hit and I just hate it here."

I kiss her again as I hold her close. "You can share her qualities and be nothing like her, reina. Two things can be true at once. You're not your mother's daughter," I try to reassure her.

She remains quiet and I focus on her as she rubs the scars on her thigh. "I remember so vividly doing this the first time." She runs her finger along an older scar a few times. "I was sent to an alternative school to finish the end of fifth grade."

She shakes her head at something. "I got into one too many fights." She stifles a laugh now, but it sounds weird. "August and Sire purposely got into a fight for a week straight to be sent to the same school as me."

I bite back a smile as she shakes her head at her brothers.

"I was so happy to be there though. No one knew who I was." She shakes her head at something else now. "Everyone at our main school knew who my mom was. She was the neighborhood crazy lady and word got around quickly."

Her words are so emotionless now and I hold her closer as I let her get it off her chest.

"The new school was going well until she came to pick me up early. She was having a *good day* and picked me up for a mommy and daughter date." She pauses. "I remember being so anxious, I threw up all the lunch we had, and then her mood plummeted and she was back to her mean self."

She keeps her finger on her scars, pinching them until her skin turns red. "When I got home, I was so *angry* that she was my mom. I hated that I couldn't live with Kat and the twins. I cut myself to upset her. She hated the sight of blood, so I was going to leave a mess in the bathroom, but when the blade dug into my skin... it was almost euphoric."

When I hear her sniffles, I set the food aside and turn her so I can hug her. She wraps her arm around me and I plant a few kisses on the top of her head.

"Do you want to hurt yourself now?" I ask gently.

She only shrugs in return, so I simply hold her.

"How do I help on the high and low days, baby?"

She shakes her head. "Just be you." She looks up at me and I press my lips to hers. After a beat, she pulls away and I wipe her tears.

"Please don't shut me out." I kiss her cheek. "If you want to hurt yourself, we can find something else for that euphoric feeling, okay?"

She nods, but I can't tell what she's thinking.

I press my forehead against hers. "Just say PG-13 and I'll understand," I suggest, understanding that voicing otherwise might be too hard.

She nods again, a small smile on her lips. Turning around, she settles on my lap. She presses her back to my chest again as I finish helping her eat.

There's a knock on the door downstairs and I kiss her neck before getting up. "Go brush your teeth. I'll have breakfast with Belle up here." I kiss her nose before going downstairs.

When I open the door, a smile I don't even need to force reaches my lips as Isabelle leaps into my arms.

"Good morning, Daddy."

I hold her tight as I blow a raspberry in her neck. "Good morning, my sweet love." I kiss the top of her head as I hold her in one arm. Pulling away, I look over at Sire, who doesn't look happy to see me.

"Thanks for dropping her off." I shift my weight between my feet uncomfortably.

He turns to Belle and trades his glare for a smile. "Tell Daddy that joke I told you." His smile grows.

I turn to Belle, suspicion pulling at me.

She stifles a laugh as she clears her throat. "Knock knock."

My eyes narrow. "Who's there?"

"Lettuce." She laughs harder.

"Lettuce who?"

"Lettuce in. It's fucking freezing out here!"

Sire breaks into a laugh with her. I bite back my smile as I nod at the pair, taking this as my punishment for going out with his little sister.

"How about the other one?" Sire asks proudly.

"Knock knock." Belle laughs, barely getting her words out.

"No, I think we're done. Thank—"

"Who's there?" Sire answers.

"Cow says." Belle giggles.

Sire nods at me and I roll my eyes at him as I entertain his joke. "Cow says who?" I mumble.

"No, you fucking dumbass, cow says *moo*." Isabelle is hysterical in my arms and I can't help but laugh.

"Thank you for that, Sire." I set my daughter down and nod behind me. "I made breakfast, can you add whipped cream and syrup to our pancakes?"

She nods and kisses her uncle goodbye before heading off to the kitchen.

When Sire looks at me again, his smile fades. "Is my sister here?"

I nod slowly, trying not to give away just how bad she's doing because I don't want to worry him. He still looks tired from watching her the other night and I feel bad for leaving Isabelle with him, knowing she probably woke him up early.

"She okay?" He watches me carefully.

A smirk pulls at my lips. "She slept real good," I tease, hoping it'll distract him, and it sure does.

His jaw ticks. "Let's ask Belle to tell you one more joke."

"No more. Goodbye." I try to close the door, but he puts his hand up before his eyes harden on me.

"I'm not going to do the whole intimidating brother thing because outside of my family, you know me better than anyone." He watches me carefully. "I like you a lot." He seems to be giving up now. "Don't fuck this up because I would hate to make your daughter an orphan and lose my best friend."

I bite back my smile. "That's not going to happen. I told you I got her."

He watches me carefully before nodding.

"I didn't sleep with her," I reassure him, not wanting to be any more on his bad side than I already am.

He offers me his hand and a smile creeps onto my face as I do our handshake, accepting this as his silent approval.

After bidding him goodbye, I head to the kitchen for my kid and her sailor of a tongue.

"How was it with Uncle Sigh, other than the cursing?" I ask Belle as I lift her into my arms again.

"It was *great*. We made snowmen out of marshmallows, then ate them."

"Before bed?" I ask and she nods, watching me carefully for a reaction. "Whose idea was that?" I ask casually as I grab both of our plates, shaking my head at how much syrup she put on her plate.

"I can't remember." She shrugs, whipped cream on the corner of her mouth and a smile touches my lips.

"Can't remember, huh?" I tease, stealing a kiss on her cheek. "You're so precious."

"Why thank you." She smiles brightly and I kiss her again before heading out of the kitchen.

"Guess who's here," I whisper.

Her entire face lights up. "KC?" she says her best friend's name and I stifle a laugh as I tell her to guess again. She taps her chin before her brows shoot up. "Lissy?"

"Yup." I nod as we climb the steps.

"This is the perfect time for her to be here."

"Is that so?"

"Absolutely." She plays with my beard as she rambles on about needing Lisette to use her *art skills* to frost a cake for her. When we walk into my room, she kicks her shoes off before I climb in next to her and we eat as she rants about the cake she wants to make.

When my bathroom door opens, Lisette looks miserable, but when she notices Isabelle, a smile lights up her face and I choose to believe it isn't fake.

"Hi, my sweet girl."

And there goes my heart, *pounding* at a concerning rate. Nearly racing towards the woman in front of me who fits with us so perfectly.

"Good morning, Lissy." Isabelle stands on the bed and I hold our plates so the food doesn't spill as she runs across the bed to Lisette. "We have a lot to talk about. This cake I'm thinking about is just the bestest idea."

She leaps in the air and Lisette catches her right in time before nuzzling her face in Belle's neck.

"Oh, I missed you, baby." It looks like she squeezes her tighter and as I watch her holding my kid, calling her baby, my life feels complete.

"Want to hear a joke?"

I let out a defeated breath as I slap a hand on my forehead.

"Of course I do."

"Knock knock."

"Who's there?" Lisette answers.

"Cow says." Belle steals a glance at me, motioning for me to be quiet.

Lisette's brows furrow. "Cow says who?"

"No, you fucking idiot, cow says *moo*."

Her jaw drops before she breaks into a laugh. I shake my head at them but can't help but smile.

"That's a bad word." Lisette's jaw drops again as she turns to my defeated face.

"Yeah, that's why it's funny." Isabelle laughs harder. "You should've seen your face." She holds her belly as she laughs on the bed, and I can't help but join her.

"Oh." She suddenly freezes. "I need to use the bathroom!" She squeezes her legs together as she laughs.

"Did you just pee yourself?" I hold back a laugh as I glance between her legs.

She's hysterical as she climbs off the bed and I throw my head back with a laugh as she hobbles to the bathroom.

"Stop laughing," Lisette and I call out between laughs when I realize she's indeed peeing herself.

"I can't hep it." She runs off and Lisette breaks into another laugh before crawling onto the bed.

When our laughs sober, she scoots over to me. "Thank you for before." She kisses me gently. "I've had people leave me after finding me like that and you made me brush my teeth, so..." She shrugs. "We can do more romantic stuff because I really enjoyed our date."

A smile touches my lips and I quickly kiss hers.

"Daddy," my kid calls out from, I'm hoping, the toilet. "I *think* me and a little bit of the floor needs a shower."

Lisette laughs beside me as I shake my head with a smile.

# Chapter Forty-Six

## LISETTE

W HEN I WATCHED MOVIES WHERE the character went insane, I always thought to myself how that could never happen to me. They always seem unrealistically *mad*. I believed I had a grip too strong on reality for that.

I may have been wrong.

"Why are you whispering?" Bay voices on the other end, also whispering.

"Why else do people whisper, Bayla?" I bite out, covering my face with my hands.

"Wow, the full name is out. This is a crisis."

"No shit it's a crisis. I'm calling you from a *closet*," I whisper louder, and when she laughs on the other end, I can't help but join. I get half a second of happiness before my laugh turns into a quiet sob.

"Are you *crying*?"

"Yes." My cry turns into a laugh now because it's honestly funny that I'm falling apart so badly. My life is a fucking joke.

"I've been forcing myself to stay here all day because I know I'm going to relapse if I leave. It's so bad." I look around Jackson's guest room closet as I wipe my tears. The last few days I've been keeping myself around company, alternating between my siblings and Bay.

Jackson and I agreed I'd continue to only come over on tutoring days, not wanting to confuse his daughter, but while our tutoring session ended a while ago, I'm afraid of what I'll do if I leave the safety of these four walls.

"Have you gone to a meeting?" Bay asks and I can hear the sincerity in her voice now.

"I got in my car to go, then I saw the water bottle full of vodka in my cup holder and literally ran back inside Jackson's house. I actually have something to lose now if I fuck up, but a part of me doesn't *care*. Doesn't that sound bad?"

I bite at my cuticles until a copper taste fills my mouth.

"I'm going to skip past the lecture about having liquor in your car and assume you have that to *sit* in your car and drink. Not drink and drive."

I roll my eyes at her. "I'm an alcoholic, not a horrible person. Of course, I wasn't drunk driving." I let out a frustrated breath as I rest my head against the wall.

"I think it's amazing that you have something to lose now. It means you have something to fight for."

"But I don't want to fight," I whisper again.

"You think you don't," she reassures me. "It'll be easier to self-sabotage and give in to the voices. It's a *phase*, Lis, you know this. You have to fight past it and when it's gone, you'll realize why we fight."

I shake my head at her although she can't see me. "When I arrived today, he was doing a face mask with his daughter. A pink one."

She's quiet for a beat. "Okay, why are you saying that like it's a crime?"

"Because I don't deserve a man who does face masks and spa days with his five-year-old."

"Okay, so I'm actually not going to listen to the self-pity, I don't deserve him, sobs," she says, her voice dripping in faux cheeriness. "Literally cry about it. You deserve him and I'm not going to waste my phone battery convincing you of that. I forgot my charger at home."

"Fuck you." A bitter laugh escapes me but the weight in my chest only intensifies, yelling at me that I shouldn't be happy.

"You need to keep yourself busy, Lis."

"I *have been*," I force out. "I'm snapping a stupid rubber band on my wrist so I don't slit my fucking thighs. I'm swimming more than Micheal Phelps has ever swam, and I'm finally using my gym membership and working out, desperately trying to tire myself out so I can sleep rather than think of getting high. I'm. Burnt. *Out*."

"When you think you're burnt out you still have another mile."

"I just need one drink." My voice is barely audible now as I bury my face in my hands.

"It's never just *one* drink. You know that."

"I swear it'll be one."

"Lisette," she deadpans and she sounds worried now. "We don't get the luxury of one drink."

She waits for my response, but I don't give her one as my mind yells at me that one won't hurt anyone. I *know* it won't. I take one drink and the world is going to keep spinning.

"Call your brother," Bay rushes out. "Right now, call him while I'm on the line with you."

"No." If I call Sire, he'll help. I don't want help. I want a drink.

"Yes, Lisette. Call him."

"I'm fine," I lie, and when the tears stop, I know I made up my mind. "You're right, I have another mile." I rise from the floor before stepping out of the closet.

"Go get rid of the bottle in your car. I'll stay on the phone."

I nod to myself as I walk downstairs. With both Jackson and Isabelle taking a nap, the house is so quiet. I try to keep it that way as I tread lightly for the front door.

The walk down the driveway feels like those illusion hallways that get longer with every step you take. Dread pulls at the pit of my stomach with every move I make. When I finally reach my car, my vision is blurred.

"You there?" she asks.

I hum in response, not trusting my voice. Grabbing the bottle, I twist the cap off and my heart races in excitement.

"Just dump it on the side of the road. The ants will appreciate it."

My brain doesn't compute her words as I bring the bottle to my lips and take a slow swig. A burn courses through me followed by relief.

I let out a tired breath as I pull the bottle away and close the cap.

"Is it gone?" she asks.

I swallow the bitter taste in my mouth before lying. "Yeah, thanks, Bay."

She says something I don't fully grasp before hanging up.

I keep my eyes on the bottle, and I know I said I'd only take one drink, but *technically* that was one *sip*. The bottle is half empty, I'll just finish it and start with a clear mind tomorrow.

*Chapter Forty-Seven*

# LISETTE

I LIED.

# Chapter Forty-Eight

## LISETTE

I STARE AT MYSELF IN the mirror, convincing myself that I have everything under control.

"I'm not throwing my life away," I tell myself again. I nod in agreement before turning to leave. When I trip over something, I quickly catch my balance.

Glancing down at Isabelle's shoes, I blame that on my bad balance rather than the alcohol coursing through me.

"Belle!" I whip around the corner just as she does and she crashes into me so hard, I stumble back. "Woah there, tornado."

I steady myself before catching her. "Are we okay? Do we have all our limbs?" I pat her down before patting myself and she lets out a sweet laugh.

"You called?"

"I sure did." I hand her the shoes in my hand. "Didn't Daddy tell you to pick up your shoes?"

"Can't remember." She shrugs, snatching the shoes from me.

"Mhm," I hum. "Go put those away." I push her away.

"Can I go in the pool?" She smiles up at me and I can't say no to that face.

"Yeah, go change. I'll meet you downstairs."

She races off and as I walk downstairs, I hold onto the rail carefully.

It takes me nearly five minutes to compute how the retractable pool cover works. When Isabelle instructs me to the keypad on the wall in Jackson's office, I get the code right on the first try as I put in his daughter's birthday.

Sitting by the pool, I kick my feet in the water as I lay back on my elbows.

The last few days have been so peaceful. When I go out and waste the night by getting drunk, I wake up feeling like shit. But *now*, with just small sips to keep the thoughts at bay, it feels good. It feels good to have control.

Isabelle races past me and with my fingers in my mouth, I whistle at her like a lifeguard would. "Walk!"

She breaks into a laugh as she jumps into the pool and I watch her, a smile plastered on my face as she splashes about.

"You should get in."

"No, thanks, kiddo." I kick my feet to splash her and when she splashes me back, I don't even care about my favorite hoodie getting wet. Her laugh is too precious to care about anything.

*You should've stayed sober for that laugh.*

My smile slowly fades as the guilt seeps in.

*You've been drunk the last four days. You're going to scar her like your mom did you.*

I quickly rise from the pool edge, needing an escape.

"Watch my pirouette." Belle shows me her ballet skills and I watch with a forced smile before I need air.

"I'll be right back, babe. Stay in the shallow end." I rush into the house before she can reply. In the living room, I find the water bottle I've been refilling with the liquor bottle I bought and hid in my car.

I feel like I'm *dripping* in dirty shame every time I go out to my car to fill my bottle, but a few sips take it away. Now I feel disgusting as I stand in Jackson's house, *drunk*.

The tears prickle in my eyes and I quickly down the rest of the liquor before a lump grows in my throat. I gag after swallowing too much at once, but I keep it down.

Sitting on the couch, I wait for the liquor to drown the thoughts.

## Jackson

"I DON'T KNOW WHAT YOU want me to tell you, kid," I tell Rome, my phone pressed to my ear as I walk into the house.

"I would love for you to tell me the Hale brothers are going to be at my game this weekend."

"They're busy," I tell him for the third time, dropping off the grocery bags in the kitchen before heading to my office. "They've been watching you play on TV and—"

"I look better in person," Rome pleads.

"You sound like a teenage girl." I roll my eyes as I walk down the hall.

"How are they always busy when I have a game?"

"Maybe they're grown men with lives of their own? I'm sincerely sorry they're not waiting around for when they can watch you *play* the thing they do for a living."

He stifles a laugh on the other end and I roll my eyes at him with a smile of my own before walking around my desk and turning on my computer.

"Okay, here it is." I click on the email chain I had with his coach. "I was right, like I knew I was. You *don't* have a game this weekend, it's *next* weekend. I honestly tried my best to get him to fold, but you're still suspended."

Glancing behind my screen, Isabelle's smile catches my eye as she splashes in the pool. My brows furrow as I look over at the open keypad that controls the pool cover. Assuming Lisette guessed the easy code, I tap on the button on the wall and the window slides open.

"But Chase the assaulter gets to play? This is bullshit," Rome mumbles and I don't bother wasting my breath to remind him to steer clear of Chase.

"Don't forget the press conference this weekend," I remind him. "I have to go."

He bids me a disappointed goodbye and I quickly end the call as I walk over to the pool.

"Hello, my little penguin." I smile down at my daughter and I may be biased but she's the cutest damn kid.

"Hi, Daddy." She swims over to the edge and I lean over to kiss her nose.

Pulling away, I glance over to the patio and my brows pull together when I don't see Lisette.

"Did you get in the pool without telling Lissy?" I turn back to Isabelle. We spoke about this a hundred times but I keep my anger at bay.

"I did tell her. She went inside." She swims away before I can question her.

I rise to my full height but as I'm heading for the house, my paranoia gets the better of me and I turn back to her. "Sit here until I come back out, please."

She rolls her eyes dramatically and I give her a pointed look.

"You know you're not supposed to be in the water without an adult out here. I'll be out in a minute. Do you want to sit on the patio or in the grass?"

She doesn't argue as she sits in the grass, a few feet away from the pool edge. Stepping onto the patio, I quickly see Lisette on the living room couch, fast asleep.

This girl sleeps like the *dead*. Shaking my head at her, I slightly shift her on the couch so she doesn't fall, since she's barely hanging off the edge. Just as I move her, she jolts awake.

She looks disoriented as she looks up at me.

"Hi." I smile down at her. "You fell asleep while Belle was in the pool, but since you look so tired, I'm going to save the water safety lecture for later. Just a heads up, I'm mad, so it's going to be a long lecture."

I lean over to kiss her, and just as I do, I go still at the smell of liquor. I pull away as I study her features.

"Tell me you're not drunk, Lisette." I stand at my full height, and when the guilt covers her face, my anger grows so high, I didn't think it was physically possible. "Are you fucking kidding me?" My eyes land on the water bottle next to her. The one she's been drinking from all day and a part of me is mad at myself for not noticing.

"Jackson—"

"You left her in the *pool* as you sat here drinking until you passed out?" I try to keep my voice hushed, but I don't know how well I do at that. "She could've *drowned*."

Lisette flinches at my volume before she rises from her seat. "I didn't mean to fall asleep…"

I wait for her to add more, but she doesn't.

"That's *all* you have to say?"

She stays quiet and it only makes me angrier.

"I was gone for almost an *hour*, Lisette. How long was she in the pool alone?" I shake my head, rambling on before she gets the chance to respond. "You were just asking me yesterday if you can come over on non-tutoring days, and when I invite you to hang out with us, you're drunk? This is the first time I've left you alone with her and this is how it goes?"

"She's a good swimmer, Jackson." When she rolls her eyes, I lose my mind.

"I don't give a shit!" I bite out. "Pools are the highest cause of child fatalities. Did you know that? Nothing else compares to the danger of a body of water. She can drown in a fucking puddle. It doesn't *matter* that she can swim. It's the fact that she's unsupervised that I'm mad, Lisette."

"It was one drink."

I let out a scoff. "Get out."

She flinches as if I just raised my hand to hit her. I watch her open her mouth, but she doesn't say anything.

"Seriously, Lisette. Go home and get it together. I don't want you around her like this, especially if you're not going to take accountability or at the very least fucking apologize. I under-stand—"

"You don't understand anything so spare me." She turns to walk away, but I grab her arm.

"Don't walk away from me when I'm talking to you, Lisette."

She tries to snatch her arm away, but I keep my grip on her.

"Let go of me," she bites out.

I hold her gaze and maybe it's because I've never seen her this upset, but I don't even recognize her. I let her go and she storms out. I walk to the entrance, and when I notice she left her car keys, some hope remains.

Letting out a frustrated breath, I turn on my heels but go still when I see Isabelle staring back at me in a towel.

"I'm sorry I was in the pool without Lissy." She keeps her gaze low and voice hushed, and it *breaks* me.

"Belle—"

"You didn't have to scream at her... I was fine."

"Penguin, that's not why I was mad." I take a step towards her, but she starts walking towards the stairs.

"I'm going to shower. Sorry again."

"Baby, come here." I quickly catch up with her and kneel so I'm at eye level with her. "I'm so sorry for yelling and scaring you. I promise I'm not mad at you, baby. I'm mad at Lisette for something else. It's not because you were in the pool."

Her brows slightly furrow. "But I heard you. You said I could've drowned... I can swim. You didn't have to be mean to her, Daddy."

I let out a frustrated breath before kissing her forehead. "You're right. I shouldn't have spoken to her like that. That's not how we talk to our friends." I kiss her cheek now. "But I'm not mad at you. You're perfect and did *nothing* wrong."

She smiles at my words. "Promise?"

"Always." I hold my pinky out to her and she intertwines hers in mine.

"Do you want to swim with me?" She slowly lights back up and I force a smile as I tell her I do, but as I get in the pool with her, Lisette is the only thing on my mind.

# Chapter Forty-Nine

## LISETTE

I FEEL BAY WATCHING ME closely, but I don't turn to her as I keep my eyes on the painting I'm packing.

I haven't been active on social media the last few days, but after sending out the first batch of orders, I received a few more and I'm so glad I kept most of my art because I'm making a lot of money from stuff I did years ago.

In the corner of my eyes, I see Bay shake her head at something before she looks back at my phone. She's helping me sort through my messages. I'm still working on how to price my art, but she's been a big help.

In the corner of my eyes, I see her throw her hands up in defeat. "I've had your phone for *five* hours and he hasn't texted you once." She breaks the silence and finally brings up the Jackson thing.

"He isn't going to call." I try not to sound like I feel so bad about it, but I feel like shit and the only reason I'm not drowning in liquor is because she's here.

"It's been two *days* and he hasn't called."

"He's not going to. I fucked up, why would he reach out?"

She shakes her head as if that's the most unbelievable thing. "I'm not saying that your sobriety is in his hands, you know I always try to take accountability, but I couldn't be with someone who doesn't call me after a fight. Especially if that fight was regarding my sobriety. You could be getting high and overdosing right now. Does he not care?"

I bite my lip as I think of her words and another dark cloud seems to loom over me. "You don't know Jackson... he's *incredibly* overprotective with his daughter and *so* particular. It's probably the OCD, but she has to sleep at a certain time, she needs to eat certain foods in specific portions, only certain people are allowed to babysit her, and even more specific people are allowed nights with her. I wasn't just drinking, I was drinking while supervising his child. Maybe he doesn't care about anything concerning me because he thinks I don't care about his daughter."

"But you do," she counters and maybe it's just how dark and blue her eyes are, but they're almost filled with as much heartache as I feel.

I let out a long breath before flopping on the couch beside her, popping the bubble wrap between us. "I do care about her... I think that's what hurts the most. I never wanted kids, but now I can't imagine not having her in my life. I *love* his daughter more than I thought it was possible to love someone."

*And yet I still got wasted in their home.*

A weight settles in my chest as I lean back, soaking in all the bad feelings and thoughts.

Beside me, Bay turns so she's facing me, bringing one of her legs onto the couch. "He didn't say he wanted to break up with you, right? He just wanted you to leave..." She cringes as she says it out loud again.

"That genuinely makes it worse." I bring my legs onto the couch, hugging my knees to my chest.

When my phone starts ringing, I slightly sit up in my seat. I turn to her, but when she frowns I sit back in my seat.

"It's Harmony," she says, just as disappointed as I feel.

"Just text her and tell her I'm on the phone with you and that I'll call her back." I sound miserable and I'm glad she doesn't comment on it.

My phone immediately starts ringing again and I roll my eyes as I turn to Bay, but she sits up, her eyes wide.

She turns the phone to me and the picture Jackson, Belle, and I took on Thanksgiving stares back at me as Jackson calls.

"Talk about speaking him into existence," Bay mumbles, but I'm stuck in place as I watch my phone ring.

"What do you think he wants to talk about?"

"Girl, I don't know. Answer." She holds the phone out to me but I don't take it.

"What if—"

"Oh my god. We're not doing this." She swipes her finger across the screen, answering his call.

I open my mouth to yell at her, but Jackson speaks up before I can.

"Hello?"

I look up at Bay and she mouths something I can't understand.

"Hey..." I speak into the phone before taking it from Bay.

"Where are you?"

I feel my brows furrow as I glance around my living room. "Home?" I glance over at Bay and she shrugs before leaning forward to listen better.

"It's a tutoring day."

"Yeah... I know."

Bay mouths something again as she moves her two pointer fingers around each other.

"What?" I whisper.

"He wants to see you," she whispers back.

"Are you with someone?" Jackson pulls our attention.

"Um..." I look up at Bay and she shakes her head. "No?"

She quickly shakes her head again before imitating cutting her neck.

"Yes? No, no, I'm not."

Bay slaps a hand on her forehead and I throw a hand in the air, completely lost.

"Okay." Jackson sounds just as confused as I am. "Nice to see we're lying to each other now," he grumbles.

"What? No, Jackson—"

"In case there was some sort of miscommunication, we're not broken up, so I hope for both you and your *friend's* sake that your *friend* is a girl."

I bite my tongue not to laugh. "I didn't think we were broken up, but thanks for the clarification, caveman."

He lets out a sigh and I can't tell if it's one of relief or frustration, but either way, my smile slowly fades.

"Jackson, about the other day..." I take him off of speaker and bring the phone to my ear as I stand from the couch. "I have no excuse for what happened, but I need you to know that I care a lot about your daughter. I love her and I would *never* put her life in danger. I know you feel like I did, but—"

"I don't *feel* that way, Lissy. You *did*. Anything could've happened in the blink of an eye and you weren't there. Not mentally at least, and I *understand* that. I know you think I don't, but to a certain extent, I do. I just need you to be honest with me, reina. This isn't going to work with secrets. I don't *care* that you drank—"

He lets out a frustrated breath and I settle in the kitchen, chewing at my nails impatiently.

"I do care, I just mean that's not why I was mad. I would never be mad if you came to me and said, 'hey, I'm having a really hard day and I slipped up.' Do you understand that?"

I nod in return before clearing my throat to respond. "Yes. I do."

"Are we going to be honest from here on out?"

I feel like a child in trouble, but I force the self-sabotaging part of myself to shut up for once. "Yes."

He's quiet for a beat before he speaks up again. "Were you just drinking?"

My eyes fall to the ground before a warm blush meets my cheek. "I wouldn't get high while supervising your daughter, and I really was not that drunk..."

"Okay."

I stop biting my nails as I stand a bit straighter. "Do you believe me?"

"I'm choosing to, Lisette."

I hold back a sigh before asking, "Would it have changed anything if I was high?"

"No," he answers quickly, making me believe him. "I would've been just as upset, but also as forgiving."

My brows furrow at his last part.

"You're an addict, Lisette, that's the reality. It doesn't make me love you any less and I'm not an idiot. I'm fully aware that you're going to struggle and possibly relapse. I'm not going to hold that against you, but don't mistake this for toxic forgiveness. I'm giving you a chance, but they're not limitless. This is your opportunity to earn my trust back and make this work because I want to be with you, but don't think for a second I'm going to ever put this relationship above my daughter."

His words sting, but I think it hurts more that I can't be angry at him. Of *course*, he isn't going to put me above his daughter.

"I understand that. I don't want you to put me above your daughter. I want this to work, too, but I need you to remember what I said before we started this."

"Don't do that," he warns. "If we're doing this then we're all in. I know you *think* you can't be a good mom, but don't use that as something to fall back on to say you told me so when you fuck up. If you're not ready, then I understand and we can put this on pause, but my daughter loves you, so there's no half-assing this. I don't plan for you to step into the mom role for a while, but I know she'd love that more than anything. I'm not forcing that responsibility on you, but I know deep down you want her to call you mom."

I do... I want her for the long haul. I'm just incredibly scared that I'm going to fuck this up beyond repair and neither of them deserve that, especially not that little girl.

"Okay." I nod to myself, convincing myself I'm capable of not ruining everything nice I have.

"Do you feel like you want to put this on pause?" He sounds like he didn't even want to ask, but I immediately shake my head.

"No, I don't want to. Trust me, I don't." I hate how desperate my words come out, but there's no taking them back.

"Okay." He lets out a breath I'm choosing to believe is relief. "Are you coming over for tutoring?"

I quickly agree before I can change my mind.

Ending the call, I let out a long breath, my head falling to the ground.

"That bad?" Bay voices from behind me.

I turn on my heels, shrugging mindlessly. "He's so perfect and forgiving." I shake my head at myself and hold back from saying I don't deserve him because I know what she's going to say, I just need to believe it.

# Chapter Fifty

## LISETTE

WHEN JACKSON OPENS THE DOOR for me, I'm surprised he looks so happy to see me.

"Hey," I smile up at him before stepping inside. "Where's my star student?" I look around for her, my excitement building. I know it's only been two days, but I miss her.

Before I can walk off to find her, Jackson pulls my hand, dragging me back to face him. He looks between my eyes and it's clear he wants to say something.

"I want to talk to you about something before she comes downstairs."

He watches me carefully and I hate the fear in the pit of my stomach as I think of him ending things.

"I know I already spoke to you over the phone, but I wanted to say this part in person."

"Okay..." I look at him, my heart rate picking up.

His shoulders sink and so does my heart. "I need to put my daughter before all else," he starts. "You told me you were scared of hurting her and I said I wouldn't let that happen... I meant that."

I nod in return. "I know."

He nods slowly. "So... I think we should limit the time you spend with her."

I go still, forcing myself not to react, my pride refusing to show an ounce of my hurt.

"We should go back to you only coming over for our regular tutoring schedule. As for staying for dinner and stuff... we should cut back on that. When your tutoring sessions are over, that'll conclude our day together." He hesitates now, "I'm also not comfortable with you supervising her alone."

I nod, forcing the lump down my throat. "That's fair." I rapidly blink away my tears.

He looks between my eyes. "We can still hang out. I'm not trying to punish you here, sweetheart. I don't want you to hate yourself for relapsing." He takes my hand, but it's too late for that. I'm beyond hating myself.

He goes on, trying to make me feel better with his explanation. "I wouldn't forgive myself if I turned a blind eye on this. It was... a wake up call, and I don't think you're incapable of being alone with her. That's just something we have to work towards again. At the end of the day, she's my *baby*, Lissy."

"Got it." I step away.

He pulls me back to him. "Please say something."

I shrug. "I can't be mad at you, JJ. You're just being a good dad. You don't trust me and that's understandable." I force a smile before quickly wiping my tears and his face falls. "I know I'm here to tutor her, but why tell me to come over if you want to put more space between us?"

"She knows it's tutoring day and asked for you. When you were late, she said it was because I yelled at you and I don't want her to think I didn't apologize to you." His eyes scan my face. "I think I had every right to be upset, but I'm sorry for raising my voice the way I did."

I nod in return, but when another tear falls on my face, he tilts his head to the side before wrapping his arms around my head. I swallow my cry, a few silent tears falling on my face.

He kisses the top of my head and I wrap my arms around him. When he pulls away, I keep my eyes low as I wipe my tears.

"Are *we* okay?" he whispers.

I pull in a deep breath before turning to him. "Do *you* want to put this on pause?" My voice breaks and I want the ground to cave in under me, swallowing me whole.

"No, mi reina." He takes my hand, squeezing it gently.

A broken smile touches my lips at his name for me as I shrug in return. "So... I guess we're good."

He nods gently before kissing my hand four times.

"I'm going to use the bathroom." I pull my hand away.

He looks like he feels like shit, but I don't say anything because there's nothing more to say.

I walk over to the bathroom and take a minute to get myself together. I splash some cold water on my face before looking at my puffy eyes in the mirror. I stare at my reflection, but my vision begins to blur again.

Pulling out my phone, I sit on the toilet seat and I FaceTime Bay.

On the first ring she answers, and her face falls when she sees me. "Do you want me to pick you up?"

I shake my head, turning the water back on to drown my cry.

"What'd he say?" She watches me carefully. "If it was out of line, I can get my cousins to kick his ass."

I squeeze my eyes shut before shaking my head. When I feel another sob coming, I bite down on my tongue.

After a minute or so, I force the lump down my throat and get my breathing together. "He—" I hiccup. "He thinks I–I should spend less time with her." I look up at the ceiling, biting my tongue again.

On the other end, she lets out a sigh. "He's not enabling your behavior. That's good."

I nod, trying to see it that way.

"I know it hurts, Lis, but *feel* it. You get five minutes to feel it, and the next time you want to drink around his little girl, you'll feel these five minutes first."

I bury my face in my palm as I soak in the disappointment. This is my fault and it hurts more that I can't blame this on him. I try to remind myself that he's *not* punishing me. He's putting his baby girl first and I wouldn't have it any other way. Him being right doesn't make it hurt any less though.

"Alright," Bay says over my cry. "Your five minutes are up."

I blink my tears away and stand from the toilet to rinse my face off. When I dry my face, I grab my phone and she looks back at me, a knowing look on her face.

"Get your shit together so you can be a good mom," she voices the words I once said to her.

I nod in return, pulling in a deep breath. "Thanks."

She smiles in return before I hang up. Stepping out of the bathroom, I hear a gasp.

"Lissy," Isabelle calls out to me and it mends the broken pieces in me as she races her way down the steps.

I make my way to her, and when she has three steps left, she leaps off the stairs and into the air. My heart gets lodged in my throat when she lands wrong and tumbles to the ground.

"Jesus." I hurry to her, but she stands to her feet just as fast as she falls.

"I'm okay." She smiles up at me before her face falls. "Oh, were you crying?" Her brows furrow before clarity fills her face. "Are you feeling a little sad?" She pats my hand gently.

I let out a laugh as I kiss her head. "I'm feeling a lot sad, sweet girl," I admit.

She pouts before opening her arms out to me. "Come here."

I waste no time lifting her into my arms.

She cups my face before staring into my eyes. "Is someone mind being mean to you?"

I shake my head gently. "Just my own mind."

"We should kill it with kindness." She holds my head. "I love you very much. You're the bestest, most beautiful mind ever!" She seems to be telling *my mind* and I break into a laugh when she kisses my forehead. She hugs me and I hold her tighter as I blink my tears away.

I can feel Jackson come up next to us, but I keep my eyes closed. He wraps an arm around me and kisses my head. "I love you," he whispers into my hair. "I'm sorry." His voice is so quiet against my hair, I almost don't hear him.

I don't trust my voice to be strong enough to speak up, so I only nod.

Hugging Belle tighter, I let out a contented sigh at the smell of her cherry scent and bury my face in her neck. I kiss her cheek and keep her in my arms as I walk into the kitchen. "Do you want to eat before we start working?"

I rest her on the counter and stand between her legs as she passionately tells me about her breakfast that she apparently did not enjoy. I turn to look for Jackson and he looks like he's about to say something, but his phone starts ringing. He pulls out his phone and his brows furrow before he looks back over at us.

"This is important..." He glances down at his phone before shaking his head. Looking back at me, he meets my eyes for a long moment. "Are you sure we're okay?"

"Yeah."

"Are *you* okay?"

I only nod, desperately trying to be okay.

He tilts his head to the side. "Promise?"

"Yes, Jackson," I voice stronger. His phone starts ringing again and he lets out a frustrated sigh before pecking the back of my hand four times. "Let me take this, then I'll make lunch."

"I can cook," I suggest.

He sends me a teasing smile. "I doubt that." He answers the call, but my jaw drops at his jab.

"Yes, I can."

"Don't burn my house down, Lisette," he calls out before saying something into his phone and walking out.

I let out a scoff as I turn to Belle. "I can cook," I tell her and she nods in agreement.

"You can do anything you put your mind to."

I smile at the encouraging words of a five-year-old. "Fuck yeah, I can."

"Fuck yeah, you can." She holds her hand up for a high five and I let out a defeated breath as I shake my head at myself.

"Please don't tell Daddy I taught you that." I give her a high five before turning to the fridge.

"Sooo," she says from behind me.

I bite back a smile as I look through the meat Jackson must've seasoned earlier. "So?"

"You and Daddy..." she starts again.

I grab the container labeled 'chicken sandwich' before turning to her and she has an innocent smile on her face.

"What about us?" I ask casually before grabbing what I need to fry the chicken.

"He said he only wants to be your friend, but I watched a movie yesterday and they were friends first then got married, so I think maybe we can plan something like that for you."

I turn to her, studying her small frame. "When did he say he only wants to be my friend?"

She shrugs. "Like the other days ago."

I feel my shoulders sag as I turn back to the stove, my mind running wild.

"I just think the wedding will be really nice so maybe you and Daddy can think about it because I'll love it if you were my mom." Her voice grows quieter at the confession.

I turn back to her and she watches me carefully for a reaction. "Yeah?"

She nods, her smile growing.

"Are you sure?" I genuinely ask, afraid shitless that I'm going to fuck this up further. "What if you don't like me tomorrow? Or in a week? Or in a year?" I voice my fears to the *child* in front of me and she laughs as if everything I'm saying is unrealistic.

"But I love you." She shakes her head at me. "Why wouldn't I like you? You're the best."

I smile at her words.

"Do *you* want to be my mom?"

My heart aches as I close the distance between us to kiss the top of her head. "I really do," I admit.

Her eyes light up. "Perfect." She wraps her arms around me. I hold her close but she quickly pulls away, humming in thought. "Maybe we can write a proposal for Daddy, then negotiate with him."

She proceeds to tell me the plot of the movie she watched with great detail about the wedding. Stopping mid rant, she comes to join me. "I can help." She reaches for the stove, but I catch her hand before she can turn the fire up.

"I can do it."

I move her aside. "You can help putting the sandwiches together."

I flip the chicken before glancing at her and she looks offended. "But that's the easier part."

"That's why you're going to do it."

Her brows pinch together further and I bite back a smile. "Daddy lets me cook."

"Daddy does not let you use the stove," I correct her, knowing him too well to know that isn't true.

She hums in response. "Well, no, but Uncle Sigh let me make pancakes and eggs."

"On the stove?"

"Yup, he carried me and I did it all on my own."

Now *that* I don't put past my brother. "Well, pancakes are easier. The oil and the chicken are too hot. Let me do it."

She takes a step towards the stove to inspect it. "It doesn't look hot, the fire isn't even up enough." She reaches for it again, but I pull her hand away.

"Trust me, it is. The oil gets hot fast and the fire needs to stay low. Back up while I do this next one. It's going to pop."

I take the perfect golden chicken out before grabbing the next one.

"Trust *me*, I can help," she says again and as I set the chicken into the pan, the fire bursts in front of us.

We both let out a scream as she starts to adjust all of the nobs. "Stop it!" I whack her hand away before turning the fire down and she bursts into tears.

"Are you okay?" I turn to her in a hurry and she holds her hand to her chest. "Are you burned? Let me see." I pull her hand away to inspect it.

"What's wrong?" Jackson hurries into the kitchen before scooping her into his arms and rushing for the sink. "Did she get burned? What happened?"

"She-she hit me," she cries into her dad's arms and he pulls her hand out of the water, his brows furrowed as he looks between us.

"What?"

I roll my eyes at her dramatic reaction. "She put the fire up when I told her not to and—"

"And you *hit* her?"

I go still when I register the fury in his voice. "I barely touched her. I just slapped her hand away from the stove. I think the fire scared her more. It grew really big and—"

"I don't care if she burned the house down," he bites out. "Don't *ever* put your hands on my kid."

I open my mouth to respond, but nothing comes out and he storms off before I can think to say anything. I'm stuck in place before my shoulders slouch.

I feel my cheeks burn in embarrassment, feeling like an idiot simply standing in his house. I turn back to the stove and take the chicken out of the oil before turning the fire off and leaving.

When I get into my car, I throw my bag in the passenger seat, frustrated with myself. Everything in my purse spills onto the ground and I look up to the roof of my car, silently collecting myself for a moment.

I feel like all I've been doing is messing everything up recently. I feel my mood plummeting and quickly force myself out of this rabbit hole. Letting out an exasperated breath, I lean over my console to grab my things. As I'm putting everything back in my bag, my eyes land on the small mint box on the ground.

I go still, contemplating my entire life as I stare at the small box.

*Don't, Lis.*

Deep down I want to listen to that voice. I want to leave that box where I strategically placed it for a rainy day.

"It was one fight, Lisette. This isn't a rainy day," I remind myself.

My eyes remain glued on the mint box, and when my brain starts making a pros and cons list, I know I'm fucked.

I grab the box and lean in my seat as I rotate it in my hands a few times.

*You don't need to kill yourself over this, stop being dramatic.*

I roll my eyes at my thoughts. "I'm not going to fucking overdose." I open the cap and stare at the white pills. My heart races and I quickly place the top back on.

"I don't need it."

*No, but you want it.*

I shut my eyes, focusing on my breathing, but the box in my hand is nearly shouting at me.

*You can take one and be fine.*

"I'm going to want more..."

*No, you have self-control. Just take one.*

I open the mint box again and stare down at the pills. Slowly, I pick one up, rolling it between my fingers.

I just want a few hours without this fucking feeling.

My vision starts to blur and how emotional I've been recently pisses me off more. I quickly drop the pill and take off driving. I almost go to see Sire, but Sage is closer. I'm in front of her apartment complex, the pill on my lap.

I stare down at my kryptonite as I weigh my options. I should go upstairs and let her help.

*You can take one then go upstairs and let her help.*

I shake my head at myself and a tear lands on my cheek. A lump grows in my throat as I grab one of the pills, and I quickly swallow it before I can weigh the right choice.

# Chapter Fifty-One

## LISETTE

W HEN SAGE'S DOOR SWINGS OPEN, I'm surprised when my eyes land on her fiancé.

"Hi." I stare up at him and his glare settles on me before he steps aside. I stifle a laugh as I decide to fuck with him. "You know," I start before leaning against the door frame. "I really love this Frankenstein's monster thing you got going on. Big, scary, only talks in grunts."

Liam looks like he could die of boredom as he watches me.

"What exactly did you do to make my sister fall for you?" I ask, genuinely curious considering Sage is a ball of sunshine compared to this man.

"Why do you care?"

I smile at his grumpy tone. "I like you."

"You've mentioned." He steps further aside. "Are you coming in or not? The door doesn't stay open if I let it go, and I don't think Sage will appreciate me dropping it on your face."

"So if she didn't care, you'd drop the door in my face?"

"I certainly wouldn't be standing here holding it for you. Are you coming in or not, Lisette?"

I shrug. "Maybe I want to stand here."

"You have fun with that." He slowly lets the door go so it gently stops at my foot.

He walks away and I stifle a laugh as I follow after him.

"How's your day going, Liam Walker?"

He doesn't answer me.

"Did you get a new haircut?" I pick up my pace and get on my tippy toes to ruffle his hair.

"Don't touch me." He quickens his steps and I catch up before linking my hand to his. "Get off of me." He tries to pull away but I hold him tighter as we walk into Sage's makeup room.

Liam is as stiff as a board as we stand behind my sister with my finger threaded through his.

In the vanity, Sage smiles before turning to us. "Lis, hey." She has setting powder under her eyes but still looks gorgeous, her dark skin literally glowing. Her bright green eyes cast down to me holding her fiancé and her brows pull together. "What's that about?" She looks over at Liam and stifles a laugh at how uncomfortable he clearly is.

"Get her off of me, please."

I rub his arm and he literally inches away from me like I'm infected.

"Please, Dory. *Get her*," he begs and I break into a laugh as I release him.

He lets out a breath before walking over to Sage. "Ask her to leave," he whispers before kissing her dimples.

She breaks into a laugh and I flip him off before settling on the couch.

"Funny you're here. Sire is on his way." Sage types something into her phone before giving me her attention.

"Ugh, no, tell him not to come. My life is horrible and I just need girl time or I'm going to kill myself." I let out a tired breath as I let my eyes fall shut, but when the room remains quiet, I look over at Sage who's watching me like she could cry.

"Not actually, Sage." I roll my eyes at her. I say that casually all the time and she never picks up on my lack of seriousness.

*Maybe because you mean it half of the time...*

I let out an annoyed breath before apologizing. She looks like she feels better as she turns back to her mirror.

"You sound upset, did something happen?"

I chew my lip in thought, and since I don't have the balls to tell her a great high is about to kick in, I resort to my lighter issues. "Did Sire tell you about me and Jackson?" I watch her reflection as her brows furrow.

"Which Jackson?"

"The only Jackson we mutually know."

She still looks confused and I have my answer. "What about you two? I only knew you were tutoring Isa and you spent Thanksgiving there."

"I kissed him," I blurt. "Well, first he kissed me. Then he saw me shirtless and then he kissed me a lot more and slept with me.

We didn't fuck, although he did finger me, but we literally just fell asleep together a few nights. Now we're dating, but it's weird because we keep fighting and I told him this wouldn't work, but now I'm in too deep because I love his damn kid and she loves me. Apparently, Jackson loves me, but I'm sure he hates me now since I hit Belle and he wants me to see her less. I didn't even *actually* hit her. I just whacked her hand, but he was so pissy about it."

I let out a breath before focusing on Sage whose jaw is dropped with a lip liner pen held to her bottom lip.

She blinks twice before turning in her seat to focus on me. "You—" She shakes her head. "Jackson—*what*?"

"I literally just caught you up. Get over the shock and help me."

She shakes her head again before waving her hands as if we were swatting a fly. "Sire let Jackson take you out? That is *not* fair. He gave me hell when I mentioned he was cute. Why do you get to date his best friend?"

Liam slowly turns to her. "Why do you sound so damn disappointed?" he grumbles from beside her and she turns to him as if just remembering her fiancé was sitting there.

"I'm not..." She smiles at him but his glare doesn't budge.

"Sage." That's all he says and Sage stifles a laugh.

She leans forward to kiss him, but he doesn't kiss her back. "Don't be like that. I was only pointing out that Sire is more overprotective when it comes to who I date, but Lis doesn't get that treatment. Jackson *is* adorable with his perfect little girl, but I don't want him and never saw him like that." She kisses him again, and when he rolls his eyes, she pulls away.

"Is that an attitude?"

"No, ma'am." He finally kisses her back and I bite back a laugh at how Sage clearly has this man on a leash.

"I didn't think so. Apologize for the eye roll."

"I'm sorry, beloved." He kisses her again.

A smile grows on my sister's face before she turns her focus on me again. "I actually haven't spoken to him about that," I say. "Jackson told him when he was running on no sleep."

Her face scrunches. "He's horrible with no sleep."

"Yeah." I lay back on her couch, setting my feet up. "I'm waiting for his true reaction to come out, which is why I've been avoiding him, but that doesn't matter right now. You're the only one in a happy relationship. Help me."

Her brows furrow as a smile grows on her face. "That's not true, Sire and Vidia are madly in love."

"Yeah." I raise my brows unamusingly. "But I can't go to Sire. Either way, do you not remember what they went through to get where they are? Sue me, but I don't want to hate Jackson for four years before we get our happily ever after."

Sage cringes now before something comes to mind. "Hazel and August are happy," she points out.

"They're either too happy or fighting like cats and dogs. Why would I ask them for advice?" I roll my eyes at how grossly in love they are.

Sage shrugs as she turns back to do her lip liner. "What do you need help with?"

I throw my hands up in defeat. "I need you to turn your fish brain off for me, Sage. I just told you we're fighting because I hit Belle."

"Why would you hit her?" She turns back to me like I just appeared from thin air.

"Stop looking at me like that!"

"*Okay.*" She turns back to her vanity.

"I didn't *hit* her, I just smacked her hand away from the stove because she made the fire fucking huge. It wasn't even hard, but Jackson blew up on me."

Sage chews her lip in thought but takes a beat before responding, beside her, Liam shocks me as he speaks up.

"Maybe because you hit his daughter?"

I focus on him before he shrugs.

"I don't know the guy, but if you hit my kid, we would've had an issue and you're the kids' aunt. Don't touch people."

"Okay." I lean back, offended as fuck. "Who the hell asked you?"

Liam puts his hands up in defense and Sage answers before he can defend himself.

"I wouldn't yell at her if she *whacked* their hand away from danger. That's not abuse."

Liam shrugs again. "I'm not letting anyone hit my damn kid. I don't care if they burned the house down, they're *kids.* I'm going through too many hours of therapy to be a good dad for her to come out of nowhere to do something I would never do."

Sage focuses on him, a hint of a smile on her lips.

Liam turns to me again. "Like I said, I don't know the guy, but why was your first reaction to hit her?"

Sage's eyes soften as she watches me, and I feel my face heat in embarrassment as it dawns on me that my first reaction was to hit her. I shake my head at myself before burying my face on the couch.

"I'm going to be a horrible mom to that little girl." I feel my eyes prickling with tears. "I can't do this," I whisper to myself, silently wishing I had taken more than one pill.

"You want to be her mom?" Sage sounds like she's smiling, but her words only make me feel worse because I *wanted* to.

No one says anything, and when I'm able to keep the tears at bay, I lift my head from the couch, but Sage reads right through me as she rises from her seat to sit beside me.

"I think you're going to be an amazing mom."

"Bullshit." I let out a scoff as I lay my head on her shoulder. "I got hit for talking too loud during my dad's basketball games, for not passing him a bottle quickly enough, or for hiding my mom's drugs so she wouldn't get high. That's all I know, and I know it's wrong, but look at how it was *instinct* to *hit* her."

My chest begins to hurt as I realize for the hundredth time, I'm too damaged.

"That stuff isn't genetic and I think if you try hard enough, you can not only break the generational trauma, but heal your inner child by raising Isa."

I let out a defeated sigh, but as she goes on listing all of my redeeming qualities, a warmth engulfs me before I feel my limbs start to loosen. Relief rushes through me as I sink into my seat.

"Oh, you okay?" Sage voices, and I nod in return as I lay my head on her lap. I keep my gaze on her pretty smile as she plays with my hair. She blurs in and out of focus, and for a split second the conscious part of my brain begins to panic before that goes quiet too.

"I'm so sorry," I mumble, reaching forward to touch one of her braids, but I think I miss.

"What?" Sage looks confused as she focuses on me. "Did you say you're sorry?" She gives me a once-over before shifting in her seat.

I nod in return, blinking slowly.

"Lissy?" She moves again. "Lisette, did you take something?" She shakes me harder and I let out an annoyed breath as I open my eyes, shaking my head no.

"Babe, help!" She moves me again before Liam stands over me. They sit me up and I try to shrug them off but Liam grabs my face.

"What did you take?"

"Nothing." I shove his hand away from my face before leaning my back on the couch again.

He's about to say something, but there's a knock on the door and Sage rushes out.

"Lisette, open your eyes," Liam nearly yells and I open my eyes again to glare at him.

"I'm awake. I'm fine."

"Where is she?" Sire's voice fills the room and I shake my head at myself.

He kneels in front of me, holding my face in his hand. "What did you take?"

I shove his hand away, forcing myself to sit upright. "Nothing."

"Bull fucking shit, Lisette." Sire looks frantically at me before patting me down. "How did you take it? Did you smoke it again?"

I let out a scoff, a smile tugging on my lips. "Do you want some?"

His eyes snap up to mine, anger written on his face. "Is this fucking funny to you?" He grabs my face again and it's no use pushing him away. "This is getting out of hand, Lisette."

"Don't do this in front of them," I warned him.

"You chose to do this in front of them by coming over here like this," he countered. "Maybe an audience will work. Why didn't you come to me? Bay called me and I know you were drunk all of last week. What the hell are you doing? Where did you even get the pills from? Jackson warned Ben to stay away. Is he a fucking idiot or are you?"

I don't answer him, and as I try to look away, he forces me to face him again.

"Answer me, Lisette."

"Do you think it's easy?" I snap, pushing his hand away from my face.

"No," he retorts. "I know exactly how hard it is, and I know how much harder it's going to be if you choose to get high again tomorrow and the day after that. Look at what you are doing.

Hiding away with Jackson instead of sticking to our plan isn't going to help."

"You two," Sage voices gently. "Stop yelling."

"Don't blame this on, Jackson." I rise from the couch and I feel myself stumble, but I hold myself up on the arm of the couch. "This has nothing to do with him."

"I think it has some part to do with him. You don't need a relationship right now, Lis, you need *help*."

"Maybe I don't want help!"

"Maybe that's the fucking problem!"

"Well, if I'm such a problem, then maybe you should've let me overdose!"

Sire goes still and my chest heaves as my anger boils.

"You don't mean that. Take it back," he warns, but I don't make a move to do so. "Take it fucking back, Lisette." He charges for me.

Liam steps between us, and it isn't until he pulls Sire away, that I realize how close we are. "Back up," Liam warns.

"Stay out of this, Walker." Sire shoves his hand from his chest and Liam surprisingly remains calm.

"*Sage* asked me to separate you two, so chill the fuck out," Liam bites out. "I don't give a shit if you two kill each other, but my fiancée has tears in her eyes, so both of you stop fighting *now*."

Sire lets out a defeated breath before turning to Sage, but I don't look at her. Sire tries to move past me, but I step in his way.

"Maybe I—"

"Don't say something you're going to regret, Lisette." Liam tries to cut me off, but I ignore him.

"Look at how you react." I point to Sire, my heated gaze on him. "Maybe I don't come to you because this is what you do."

"Don't give me that bullshit. I'm *always* so supportive and you know that, but it comes to a point where it's frustrating, Lisette. I know you know how I feel because you were there for me time and time again. Whenever I fucked up and lied about being sober, you were being *ten* times as irritating as I am right now. You just hate the roles being reversed, but guess what? You're stuck with me."

He shoves past me to Sage and I storm out of the room. I'm nearing the door when my vision blurs again, but I use all my strength to stay focused on my exit. My movements feel sluggish, like I'm walking through quicksand, but I keep going the last few feet. I hear footsteps from behind me, and I think it's Sire, but Liam steps beside me, grabbing my arm when I tilt to the side.

"You can barely walk. Where are you going?"

"Why the hell do you care?" I grab the door, but I can't get it open. I let out a defeated breath and keep my gaze on the door.

"Sage cares," he corrects me. "She asked me to not let you leave, so that's what I'm doing."

"You let her walk you like a damn dog. Grow a pair and mind your business." I try to open the door, but with one of his hands on the door above my head, it doesn't budge.

"You're the only one of her siblings who I genuinely like," Liam says and I feel my brows furrow as I turn to him. "I don't know shit about addiction other than how bad it is for you. You have your entire life ahead of you, Lisette, and you probably feel like you have nothing right now, but considering how torn you were moments ago about Jackson and his daughter, I think you have a thing or two to fight for."

I keep my gaze on his and I'm surprised to see his eyes soften.

"Sire is insufferable, but he cares. He's a family man and it's his only redeeming quality, but it's a hell of a good one to have. You can let him help you or you can leave and run to get even higher, but you hitting Isa will be the last memory she has of you because you're either going to kill yourself or Jackson simply isn't going to let you near his kid with a ten-foot pole in this condition."

I flinch as his words hit me so damn hard they physically sting. Taking a step away, my eyes fall to the ground and I turn on my heels, too embarrassed that my dirty laundry was aired out to a man I barely know.

Wanting to change the topic, I turn on my heels. "Why are you in therapy?"

His brows furrow before he realizes I don't want to be the only one who's uncomfortable. "I have a bad temper and I don't want to end up like my dad."

I nod in return and before I can ask him to elaborate he speaks up.

"That's all you're getting. I barely even know you."

I bite back a smile and I really do like his attitude. "Sire was wrong about you."

"And he's going to continue to be wrong about me. I'm not the same asshole I was in college. I genuinely care about Sage, so much it fucking hurts, and by default, I care about everyone who shares her last name."

A bitter smile touches my lips. "I'm not a Hale."

"Like hell, you're not."

We both turn to face Sire and his anger is void of his expression.

"Let me catch you saying you're not one of us again, and I'm kicking your ass," he warns before closing the distance between us.

I try to bite back a smile, but I'm sure I'm failing. I take a step away, but he catches me and wraps his arms around my head. "You're killing me." He sounds like he's in actual pain as he holds me close.

"Let me help you, Lisette. You deserve the support. You deserve to be loved, to see the sunrise tomorrow. You're *not* a burden. You're a fucking headache, yeah, no shit, but you're my headache." He kisses the top of my head and I look up at him, tears threatening to spill from my eyes.

His eyes soften as he kisses my forehead.

"I take it back," I force out and more tears spill before he pulls me closer.

# Chapter Fifty-Two

## LISETTE

"**J**ACKSON DOESN'T WANT TO HAVE sex with me." I pull away from Sire's hug, wiping my tears. "I have no clue what he's waiting for because he's clearly attracted to me. There's no way all that is just morning wood and—"

"You know," Sire starts, his eyes shut as he pinches the bridge of his nose. "I really don't need the details from your high ass right now."

I stifle a laugh and he doesn't look pleased as he looks back over at me. I know what that face means and I roll my eyes before walking to the living room.

"Can we talk about him instead of my high ass?" I know I have a few minutes left in me before my brain crashes and I'd rather not spend the next few hours of my high talking about my high.

"Fine, but we're going to talk about this later."

I nod in return before my weight drops on the couch. I feel the drugs taking over every ounce of me, and before I can soak in the euphoric feeling, he forces me to sit up. "I'm not letting you enjoy this. Stay awake."

I let out a sigh as I force my eyes open.

"When did you two even start... that?"

"*That* as in dating or me feeling his amazingly impressive morning wood?"

"Jesus Christ," he mumbles and I bite back a laugh. He turns to me, remaining serious and I appreciate that he doesn't look too disappointed in me. "What are you two doing?"

I almost make another sex joke, but decide to get this over with. "Dating... I think?" I reach for his face, wanting to touch the scar on his nose but he pushes my hand away.

"You think you're dating? What's confusing about it?"

I can see the protective brother coming out from a mile away and quickly rein him in by telling him about the mess from the drunk pool incident to the fire hitting.

His brows are raised by the end of it all. "Yeah... you're fucked."

"No..." I let out a groan as I rest my head on his shoulder. My heart sinks because he knows his best friend way better than I do.

"He is so fucking anal about his kid, Lis. He almost cut off his mom because she hit Isa a few years ago. It was a huge fight. Hitting and who gets access to babysit her is on the top of his list."

I shake my head at his words. "Do you think he's going to break up with me?" I hate how worried I sound, but he's right. I'm fucked and it has nothing to do with Jackson's anger. I'm fucked because I'm falling for him and I'm screwing up the one thing I have going for me.

"He honestly might." Sire is quiet for a beat. "But maybe he won't?" He tries to mend my heart. "The fight with his mom was way worse. She actually hit Isa with a shoe or a hanger? I can't remember, but it was messy. This is different, though."

That surprisingly makes me feel a bit better, but not enough to make me feel bad about getting high. "Why does life have to be so hard?" I lift my face to focus on him and he watches me like he knows exactly how I feel.

"It won't always be this hard."

"That's the thing though." I shake my head at his words. "It's been this hard for a year now. I'm so tired, Sire, and I'm so tired of not being able to just drink. I feel like a failure every time I simply want one, you know?"

"I do."

"Like, how ridiculous is it that I can't get into a fight with my boyfriend without wanting to relapse? It's pathetic."

He gives me a knowing look and I shake my head at my words.

"Don't say it."

"I'm not saying it because I hate Jackson. I'm not saying you two shouldn't be together because I'm an asshole or because I'm a protective older brother. If I wanted to get high every time Vidia and I fought, we would both decide being together wasn't a good idea."

"So you're going to break up with her the next time you go through a rough patch?"

He lets out a defeated breath. "No, that's not what I meant. It's different when you're already in a relationship. Starting one isn't the best idea. You know how hard it is making it a year sober. We shouldn't get attached to people during that time. *That's* why I didn't want you and Jackson to go out. You need to focus on yourself. You need stability."

"He's the only stability I have," I surprise myself by admitting.

"And *that's* the issue, Lisette. He can get hit by a damn truck tomorrow. You need to be able to stand on your own two feet without him. Getting into a relationship, healing *with* him without knowing how to heal on your own is such a bad idea, I know you can see that."

I shake my head at his words, refusing to admit he's right. "Him and Isa are the only things keeping me happy and I know," I quickly go on before he can repeat himself. "I know I need to know how to heal on my own before he heals me, but maybe I just want a family, Sire. Maybe I want to take the easy way out for once in my damn life and let them put me back together."

"That's not their responsibility. Don't be selfish."

"Do I not deserve to be selfish?"

"That's not what I meant, but you—Isa is still so young, Lis. She doesn't deserve that. You being in and out of it like this." He gestures to me. "Bailing on her recitals because you're drunk, sleeping past picking her up from school because you're high. I'm not saying you'll turn into our surrogates, but you know what we're capable of if we go down that path. Look at what you just did while she was swimming," he reluctantly adds. "If you want to be in her life, you need to be ready."

I blink my tears away as I focus on my bleeding nails. "Isa said she loves me." I swallow the lump in my throat. "She tells me she loves me time and time again, and that voice in my head, the one telling me I'm not lovable, it just disappears. She tells me she misses me and that weight in my chest from feeling like a burden for simply existing, it's gone when she hugs me."

I turn to Sire just as a tear falls on my cheek. "She wants me to be her mom. I never wanted that, Sire. I never wanted kids, but I want her so damn bad. I want her smiles, her sassy fucking attitude, her mess, her obsession with pink, baking and taking selfies." The lump in my throat grows so big it hurts to speak, but I plead with him anyway. "I'm losing faith in myself and they're the only thing I'm clinging to."

Sire pulls me into his embrace and I instantly wrap my arms around him. "I have faith in you."

"I don't, though." I bury my face in his chest and he holds me tighter as a sob rips through me. "I just want one day, Sire. One day to let go, to feel like my worries are floating away. The closest thing to a high I can get is them."

Sire is quiet before something hits him. "You love him."

I don't admit it, but my silence is answer enough as he soothes my hair.

After a minute, he pulls away with a gasp. I sit up and when I hear an airplane passing, I quickly rise to my feet.

"I call it." I wipe my tears and we run onto the balcony and I almost trip over myself, but he steadies me as we make it outside, searching the clouds for our form of a shooting star.

When I see the plane I smile to myself before closing my eyes.

*I need something to tell me which way this is going to go because I don't have much more fight in me. I wish for hope.*

# Chapter Fifty-Three

## LISETTE

**M**Y HEAD IS POUNDING AND I try to sit up, but my entire body feels weighed down. I press my palms to my eyes as I suck in a breath in pain. I try sitting up more slowly now as I look around the soft-lit room. I scan the room carefully and this isn't my house. I try to retrace my steps, and when I notice the emerald couch I'm on, reality hits me like a truck.

"She's awake."

I go still at the sound of August's voice and glance out at the balcony. For a split second, I contemplate making a run for it, but I won't make that jump, and dying in order to avoid this talk is too dramatic even for me.

I lay back down as August comes around the couch, a huge smile plastered on his face. "Good afternoon." He hands me a cup but I don't take it.

"Is Sire here?" I whisper and when he nods I close my eyes in defeat.

I hear a few more footsteps before the couch dips a few times. Forcing myself to get this over with, I sit up and look around at the twins and Sire. I expected more people so I'm choosing to be grateful this isn't an actual intervention.

Sage smiles over at me, her eyes glossy with tears. "You scared me."

I shake my head at myself. I fucking hate making this girl cry. "I shouldn't have come here, Sage, I—"

"No," she quickly cuts me off, sliding down to take hold of my hand, and I hate how affectionate she is, but I let her hold me. "I'm glad you came here. You can always come to me."

"You know," August speaks up and I turn my attention to him next. "I'm a bit offended I was the last to hear about this, but this isn't about me, so I'll suck it up." He puts his hands up in surrender and a smile tugs at my lips.

"*This* as in me relapsing or me dating Sire's best friend?"

His brows furrow before he turns to our brother. "Since when have you been calling Jackson your best friend?" He doesn't let him respond. "*I'm* your best friend."

I glance over at Sire and he shakes his head at him. "This isn't the time for this, August. We—"

"No," August objects. "This is the time. Are you seriously going around telling people Jackson is your best friend? You've known the guy for what? *Seven* years? I've been here since you were still wetting the bed."

I stifle a laugh, but pretend to cough when Sire glares at me.

"We're brothers, August. Besides you, he's my best friend."

August's jaw drops. "You can't have two best friends. That's why it's called *best*."

Sire's eyes narrow on him. "You're seriously going to make me pick between you two?"

August folds his hand over his chest and Sire mumbles a curse.

"You're not going to say anything about Lis dating him?" He tries to turn this to me now but fails.

"That is not what we're talking about. If she's happy then I'm happy, and if he hurts her, then we'll hurt him, but you need to tell me right now if he's your best friend."

"You're unbelievable," Sire mumbles.

August's jaw drops. "You're really picking him?"

"Of course not, August." Sire rolls his eyes at our brother. "I'll always pick you. I didn't think calling my closest friend my best friend would be an issue since we're *brothers*, but I guess I was wrong. Can we go back to what this conversation was supposed to be about?"

A smile grows on August's face.

They all turn to me and I feel my mood plummet but hold it together.

"Let's get this over with."

Sage gives me a knowing look, but I don't apologize for the attitude. I don't like being cornered and I want to get out of here.

August sits on the coffee table in front of me, his usual light-hearted expression gone. "We're worried about you, Lisette."

"I'm—"

"Don't say you're fine." He sends me a weak smile. "We've been through too much together. We know you too well. You're not fine, but that doesn't mean it's the end of the world. We just want to help you."

"Okay, thank you. Is that all?" I try to stand but go still when Sire lets out a scoff, a smile tugging at his lips. "Is something funny?"

His eyes meet mine and a bitter smile is on his face. "I told them we were going to have to do this the hard way and they wouldn't listen."

I glance around the three of them. "What's the hard way? Because I'm not going to rehab and you're not—"

"We're not going to force you there." Sage takes hold of my hand again. "If you don't want to go, then we won't force you."

I focus on her before pulling my hand away. "So what's the hard way?" I push.

Sire leans his elbows on his knees as he focuses on me. "Let's skip the ultimatums, Lis," he starts. "You're going to be on a cute little house arrest for the next few weeks, rotating between all of our houses until we decide you're okay on your own. We'll go to meetings like a happy family and you'll start therapy. In three months or so, you'll be so happy you decided to listen to us."

I let out a laugh, but when none of them smile, I realize he's being serious. "You're joking." My laugh sobers as I look between all of them.

"I wasn't asking." The weight of his words hang over me and I shake my head at him before standing.

"I don't need a babysitter."

"You do," he counters.

"I don't need *therapy*."

"You need to be *severely* medicated if you actually believe that." He rolls his eyes at me.

"Sire," Sage bites out as August shoves his arm.

"You two are just as delusional." He turns to the twins. "You're both too damn nice and this isn't going to *work*. We can't kill her addiction with kindness and I'm honestly getting tired of this shit."

I open my mouth to tell him to fuck off, but I go still at his words. "You're getting *tired* of me?" I let out a scoff and he runs a hand down his face as he leans back.

"Not of *you*, Lis. I'm tired of *them* thinking this nice approach will work."

"You said you had faith in me," I remind him of his lie.

"I do. I have faith that this plan will work if you let us be your crutch. You don't have to do this alone. Stop torturing yourself." He stands from his seat but I take a step back before putting a hand up between us.

"I don't want to be cornered, Sire. I don't want to be monitored and hovered over. You all shouldn't have to stop your lives to do that for me."

"We want to," August starts gently, rising from his seat and my panic rises as both boys walk closer to me.

"Stop!" My scream bounces off the walls and they both freeze. "Do not come closer."

"Lis." Sage stands from the couch next. "I promise you, we're not going to take you to rehab."

"So stay where you are." I take another step back. "We don't need to talk two feet away from each other and you don't need to touch me." My heart pounds in my chest as I look between the three of them frantically. Slowly, August takes a step back, but I watch Sire as he stays standing in place.

"Let me leave," I plead.

"Absolutely not." He shakes his head once before I make a run for the door. Just as I reach for the handle, his arms come around me.

"Let me go." I claw at his arms, fighting for my life.

"Don't you see how ridiculous this is?" Sire keeps his grip on me as he walks back to the couch, but I keep fighting him off. "Who's point are you proving right now, Lis? Mine or yours?"

"Get off!" I kick him again and he drops me on the couch as he stands over me.

"You look like a crazy person."

"Thanks for that, but this isn't the drugs." I roll my eyes at him as I stand, but he shoves me back on my ass.

August steps beside him. "No, it's the lack of them, which is even more concerning," he says gently.

"Yeah," Sire starts. "And you're a fucking asshole when you're going through withdrawals, so now that the kicking and screaming is out the way, let's come to some kind of agreement." He glances down at the scratches on his arm before shaking his head at me.

"I don't need you."

He lets out a humorless laugh and I grab a pillow before chucking it at his face.

"I mean it," I bite out.

"Oh yeah?"

"Yes." I sit up taller and he focuses on me for a beat before nodding.

"Fine." He takes a step back and I feel my brows furrow as I watch him. "If you can last more than a week sober, I'll leave you alone to get better on your own. If you fuck up, you're on a rotating house arrest and I'm calling Mom."

I bit my cheek to stop myself from agreeing, but my pride is a bitch and even if the withdrawals currently eating at me want to get high, I'll last seven days just to prove him wrong.

"Fine." I rise from my seat.

"Fine." He takes another step back. "But you need to see me every day. If you miss one of my calls, I'm going to assume you're high."

I let out a scoff. "So much for believing in me." I shove past him before grabbing my phone. "Fuck you, Sire. I'll check in with the twins, you can go to hell. Don't call me."

"You're really going to be like that?"

I hear him walking after me, and just as I reach the door, he grabs my arm, forcing me to face him.

"You just want to check in with the twins because they won't be able to see through your lies."

"Get off of me." I try to pull away but he doesn't let me.

"Where are you going to go?"

I don't answer and he shakes his head at me.

"You really want him to see you like this?"

"Shut up." I shove him but he doesn't move an inch.

"Look at you, Lisette. You're itching for another hit. You're seriously going to run to Isabelle like this? Like your mom—"

I slap him across the face before he can finish his sentence, and a gasp breaks the air as the twins stare at us in shock.

"Don't compare me to her," I warn, and when he doesn't say anything, I shove his chest. "Don't *ever* compare me to her." I storm out, and I think it hurts more that no one stops me.

After a solid half hour of searching for my car, I find it in front of a fire hydrant. Walking towards the windshield, I snatch the bright orange ticket and rip it twice before dropping it onto the ground. It isn't until I pull on the handle that I realize my keys are sitting on Sage's couch.

My head drops onto my window before a defeated sigh escapes me. "I fucking hate it here." I'd rather lay in the middle of the road behind me than go back to that apartment.

I walk for a few blocks and every step feels harder than the last. Sire's voice plays on a loop in my head, and the sight of Sage's tears remains in the front of my mind. The shock on August's face when I hit Sire flashes through my mind before Sire's words yell at me.

*I'm just like my mother. Guess everything they said about the apple and the damn tree is true.*

A knot grows in my throat and I blink my tears away as I pull out my phone and order a car to a liquor store.

# Chapter Fifty-Four

## JACKSON

I WATCH ISABELLE THROUGH THE window as she dances her heart away in her ballet class. She can dance circles around every five-year-old in there, and I'm too proud to act like she isn't the best in the class. My kid's a star and it feeds my Dad ego.

My phone rings in my pocket, and I step away from the door before looking down and a picture of Isabelle on Sire's shoulders lights up my screen. A smile touches my lips at the sight of his contact picture and the joy on my daughter's face as Sire smiles up at her like he'd go to the ends of the earth for my kid.

I slide my finger across the screen before bringing it to my ear. Just as I open my mouth, he's already speaking up.

"Is Lis with you?"

"Hello to you too. I'm great, thanks for—"

"Yes or no, Jackson?" he rushes out, his voice wavering.

I feel my brows pull together as I step further away from the other parents. "Is she okay? What's wrong?"

A loud sigh sounds from the speaker. "She turned her location off, and I don't know where she went." The panic seeps from his voice and straight to my bones.

"I haven't spoken to her. We got into a fight and—"

"What fight?"

I ignore his question because while he was my friend long before I started dating his sister, I don't like telling people about my relationship issues, and I don't doubt for a second that he'd hurt me for his sister.

I flip the conversation back on him. "What happened? Why would she turn her location off?" I listen carefully as he recites what I told him to who I think is August.

"Call me if she calls you." He ends the call with that and immediately I feel my nerves eating at me.

I've been calling Lisette since yesterday's fight, but every message I sent went unanswered and something in my gut tells me something is wrong. Now Sire's call just confirms my worries.

"She's so big."

I look up as a mom from beside me voices. We've both been bringing our girls here for years and I always forget her damn name.

"I know, right?" I tuck my phone in my pocket.

"Who are we watching now, Jane?" Another mom comes beside me and I silently thank her for reminding me of Jane's name.

"Jackson's baby." She nods towards Belle as she spins on her tippy toes.

"She's a natural."

I smile at her praise.

"She must take after her mom. Was she a dancer?" the new mom asks, and I don't miss the way she glances down at my left hand.

"Nope, but I like to think I'm rubbing off on her just a bit."

I turn on my heels at the sound of Lisette's voice and I let out a breath of relief at the sight of her. She tugs at her sleeves and I feel my brows pull together at how tired she looks. Like she hasn't slept in weeks.

"Hey, JJ." She smiles up at me and a smile of my own grows on my face at how pretty she is. She looks a hot damn mess but she's still gorgeous.

"Hi, Lissy." My eyes scan her tired face. "Do you have a tracker on me?" I tease but her sour mood doesn't shift.

She looks over my shoulder and takes a step beside me as she watches Belle twirl around in her pink tutu. "I remember you mentioning when she had ballet practice when you showed me videos of her dancing." She shrugs. "This was the most expensive studio closest to your house."

She turns to me now, worry pulling at her brows. "I know you wanted me to stay away from her and I'm sorry for showing up, but I want to talk to you."

"No, it's okay," I reassure her, mainly because she looks sick to her stomach. "I've been calling you."

She nods as she turns back to the window of kids dancing. "Is that the ballet teacher she wanted you to marry?"

I bite back my smile as I follow her line of sight to a woman who doesn't hold a candle to her. "You sound jealous." I keep my voice low although the moms around us took their seats again.

"Should I be?"

I feel her watching me carefully and I look back down at her to answer her unspoken question. "We're good." I take her hand and I don't miss the breath that escapes her.

"I overreacted," I start. "I know you didn't hit her with ill intent. We should talk, but we're good."

She nods in return before kissing my hand. "We really do need to talk."

I feel my brows furrow as I try to decipher what that means. "Okay..."

She smiles, but it's clearly forced. "Can we talk now? Before she's done. I don't want to wait until tonight when she falls asleep."

I nod at the seriousness in her tone and guide her out of the building. She's quiet the entire time, and it isn't until we're in my car that she turns to me.

"I have a lot to say so please don't interrupt me, and if I cry, just ignore me. I'm drunk."

I go still at her words, but she rambles on before I can question her sobriety.

"I was abused growing up," she starts and she watches me carefully, but I keep my reaction at bay.

"I always thought my household was normal. Sire lived next door with a worse life. It wasn't until we visited the twin's house that our world got turned on its axis. I remember August spilling juice and I flinched when Kat let out a gasp. I prepared for her to hit him and yell at me for the request, but she didn't. Sire and I were so damn confused by how nice everyone in that house was."

She shakes her head at herself as she leans against the door to focus on me. "I hit Isabelle out of pure instinct and it wasn't with ill intent. I didn't do it because I was mad or to hurt her, but that was my first reaction, and I'm not telling you this sob story to excuse myself but—" she cuts herself off as she tries to find the right words. "I'm not going to go around hitting your kid. I don't want to. It's just all I know, you know? It's built inside me. I know your parenting style is different, and I'm not trying to change that. It was just my initial instinct and at first, I didn't see anything wrong with it because I'm wired that way. But I don't want to hit her, and I won't."

When she remains quiet I realize it's my turn to respond. "You're drunk?"

Her eyes dart between mine and a spot over my shoulder before she picks at her nails.

I take her hand but she pulls away, shaking her head as she focuses on the console between us. "We're not talking about that right now."

"I think we should."

She shakes her head again before biting her nails. "Can you just reply to what I said?" Her eyes meet mine and she looks... skittish.

I keep a careful gaze on her before giving her what she wants. "I don't expect you to know how to react to everything Belle does the first time. I've been raising her for five years and she still does shit that makes me question my entire existence."

She stifles a laugh and I bite back a smile before continuing.

"She wants you to be her mom and I want that too. That means eventually you're going to be responsible for disciplining her and under no circumstance are we hitting her. She can be a sassy brat at times, but she's far from a bad kid and hurting her will never solve anything. I know you whacked her out of pure fear. There was a lot going on and I'd like to believe you wouldn't hit her as a form of discipline if you had a clear mind. We'll work around the wires your parents screwed up."

Another smile grows on her face, but when I notice her picking at her cuticles, I know she wants to add more. We sit in silence and I watch her work up the nerve before she turns to me again.

"I'm probably proving you right, aren't I?" She looks torn and it truly puts a pain in my chest. "About needing to spend less time with her."

I shake my head at her. I didn't mean for my words to hurt her so much. I knew there was no easy way to put it, but it needed to be said. Even if she wasn't struggling right now, I never introduce my partners to Isabelle. Especially not as early as I did this time, and I'm aware this was different since she already knew my daughter, but we're moving too fast and Isabelle is getting too excited.

"I didn't want to be right, love." I rub her leg, feeling the need to touch her. "I *desperately* wanted to be wrong. I wanted you to prove I was overreacting. I wanted to grovel my ass off for even suggesting it." I let out a frustrated breath, angry with myself now. "I'm sorry if that's what pushed you to drink, Lisette. I have no idea what I'm doing here, so I need you to tell me how to go about these things. When and how to share bad news. How to comfort you."

She forces a smile now. "Is that your way of saying you've never dated an addict? Am I taking your V card?"

I don't laugh, needing her to genuinely help me here.

Her smile falls in the silence. "This is the worst time in my life, Jackson," she confesses, and I hate how defeated she sounds. "I've dealt with my addiction and depression my whole life, but this is the only time where I felt like giving up for *this* long. It usually goes away, but it's not, and I really shouldn't be in a relationship right now."

My heart sinks, but I nod in return, putting on a brave face as I force myself to be supportive in any way she needs, even if that removes me from the picture.

"We shouldn't be together."

I hold my breath so I don't speak.

"But I want you more than I want to get high." Her eyes meet mine and I let out the breath I was holding. "I want to read with Isa every night instead of getting drunk. I want to wake up in bed with both of you, not hungover with a guy whose name I can't remember. I feel so lost when I leave your house and I know that sounds pathetic, okay? I truly want to die knowing I'm the girl that's clinging onto a boy, but I'm holding onto the possibility that maybe you're not a phase. Maybe it's not just sexual tension. I shouldn't look for myself in a man, but I'm really fucking hoping you're not *just* a man, JJ."

"I'll be anything you need me to be."

"I need solace." She lets out a bitter laugh, tears building in her eyes.

I take both of her hands and kiss each of them gently. "Then I'll be that. I'll be your anchor and Isabelle will be your headache."

She lets out a laugh and I smile at her before pulling her over the console and onto my lap. I bring my lips to hers and hold her close as she straddles me.

"I can feel your dick getting hard."

I let out a defeated sigh as I bury my face in her neck. "You're full of so much shit." I roll my eyes at her and she laughs from on top of me as she squirms. "What are you doing?"

"Trying to wake it up. Your car is perfectly tinted for car sex."

"Jesus Christ," I mumble before pulling away. "Why do you end every vulnerable conversion with the topic of sex?"

She shrugs innocently. "I'm sorry my daddy issues made me into a whore? Damn, no need to make me feel like shit about it." She's clearly teasing and I bite her neck, causing her to squirm in my lap again.

Her laugh sobers before she looks over at me again. "One more question."

I almost think she's going to ask if we can have sex but she turns more serious.

"Do you really see a future with me?"

I study her for a beat, but she's being genuine as she continues.

"I know Belle wants me to be her mom, but those are forever. I'm not her biological mom, so I'm not actually stuck here, but—"

"You're stuck here," I interrupt her with a kiss. "My daughter loves you." I hold back from telling her I love her, knowing she's afraid of those three words. "I still think we need to take things at a slow pace with her, but you're stuck here."

"What do you want?" She bites her lips and I realize she's nervous.

"You." I kiss her again but she pulls away.

"For how long?"

I shrug in thought. "What's your expected lifetime?"

Her brows furrow. "I don't know. I think my grandma lived until she was eighty."

"Then I want you for the next fifty-five years. At eighty-one, get the fuck out."

She breaks into a laugh and I smile into the crease of her neck, kissing her gently. I take in a breath of her, but at the faint smell of alcohol on her, I let out a quiet sigh as I hold her tighter.

"Can we talk about your sobriety?" I kiss her neck gently before pulling away.

She keeps her eyes low but I lean over to catch her gaze. "I want to get high."

"Okay..." I watch her carefully but she won't meet my eyes. "Let's call your brother. You can—"

"No." She shakes her head and I feel my brows pull together at the sudden rage she takes on.

"You should go to a meeting," I point out.

"So I'll go to one, but I don't need him."

As I watch her, it's obvious I missed something. "What happened, Lisette?" I lean back in my seat as I focus on her, taking in the bags in her eyes and the way her hair clings to her sweaty forehead.

She bites at her nails again as her eyes dart between everything but my face.

I pull her hand away from her mouth before holding her face in my hands. "Are you also high?"

She shakes her head and tries to pull away, but I keep her hand in my grasp.

"Use your words and look at me," I tell her more sternly.

Slowly, her gaze meets mine. "I missed your calls..."

"I know, I was worried."

"I *was* high." She watches me, waiting as if I'm supposed to explode at the news.

I falter before reining in my reaction. I nod slowly, holding my breath so I don't sigh, not wanting her to think it's a sigh of disappointment or frustration because I don't feel either of those things.

"Where are the rest of the pills?"

She looks back down at her nails and as she picks at them again, they start bleeding. "I got rid of them."

I scan her face, trying to figure out if she's lying or not, but I can't tell and I hate that I'm out of my element here.

"I'm going to call your brother and—"

"No." Her eyes meet mine again, burning with fury. "I'm fine. Do you not trust me? I just told you the truth. I messed up, okay? But I came forward and told you like I said I would. Doesn't that count for anything?"

I sink further in my seat. "You're right. I'm sorry, that does count for something, but he's worried about you."

"Did he call you?" Her eyes scan my face now like she's in trouble and I suddenly don't trust her.

"You need to tell me what happened, Lis. You're scaring me."

She lets out a frustrated breath as she rolls her eyes. "We got into a fight." She pushes the hair from her face before leaning against the wheel. "He wants me on stupid house arrest, but I don't want to be monitored."

"He's trying to help."

"Stop taking their side!"

I go still as I watch her blow out another angry breath. "I'm not taking sides... who's *they*?"

She rolls her eyes again as she bites at her thumb. "The twins and *him*." She shakes her head at something she thinks of. "Just *don't* fucking call him."

"Okay," I start, more bass in my voice. "I don't know where this attitude came from, but drop it. *Now*."

She hesitates, her brows pulling together and she opens her mouth to say something, but quickly shuts it at my warning look. When she settles back down, I nod to myself, and I don't know jack shit about drugs, but I think she's going through some sort of withdrawal. That or she's a really mean drunk.

"You need to get this together." I gesture to her frame and a warm pink flushes her face. "I'll support you however you need me to, Lissy. If you don't want to call Sire then fine, I won't mess with your family drama, but what you're *not* going to do is mess with my family. If you want to see my daughter, you'll see her sober. Understood?"

She quickly nods, and when tears start building in her eyes, I immediately regret taking the rough approach.

"I'm sorry." Her voice breaks before she breaks into a sob. I wrap my arms around her as I hold her close.

"I just want to see Belle," she pleads.

"You will. Just not like this." I kiss the side of her head as she keeps her face buried in my neck. "I can have my mom pick her up from ballet, and after we get you sobered up, we can spend a few hours with her tonight."

She shakes her head. "I don't want to inconvenience your mom..."

"You're not inconveniencing anyone," I reassure her, but at the mention of her, I feel myself growing annoyed at the reminder of how my mom feels about Lisette and I'm definitely going to have to lie about why I need her to take Isabelle.

Like always, when we fight, she's acting like nothing is wrong. Instead, she's been giving me the cold shoulder and sending me food. I'm honestly glad for it because I don't care to fight with her about Lis, although I'm sure she'll bring it up soon enough.

Pushing those thoughts away, I kiss the top of Lisette's head. "She'll love to see her granddaughter and I want to help you get cleaned up. It'll only be a few hours." I recall Belle mentioning how she missed my mom, so it honestly works out for everyone.

She nods in my neck, sniffling quietly. After holding her for another few minutes, she pulls away and I hold her face in my hands as I wipe her cheeks.

"I can get better," she says, and I'm not sure who between the two of us she's trying to convince.

# Chapter Fifty-Five

## LISETTE

THE WARM WATER OF MY shower sprays on my head, mixing with my tears. I hug my knees as I chew at my pinky nail, desperately trying to get the screaming out of my head.

I envision Isabelle's smile, the sound of her sweet laugh, and the smell of her cherry shampoo. I keep her on a loop in my head as I fight the tug pulling at me, willing me to say fuck it for another escape.

"She can't see you like this," I remind myself. "He won't let you near her." I force my eyes shut, hitting my head with the palm of my hand.

"You're fine," I whisper to myself on repeat. Again and again, but when the lodge in my throat is too big to speak, my blurry vision lands on the razor in front of me. I sniffle quietly as I grab it and dismantle it to get the blade out.

I just need to feel something else other than this. I can't get high... Jackson will see right through me and I want to see Belle too badly. I can't drink either. I need to be sober, but I need to feel anything other than the pain in my chest. The banging in my head. The nausea from the damn drugs leaching at my will to fight.

I wipe my tears on my shoulder as I trace one of the scars on my thigh. I bite my lip to conceal my cries and a copper taste fills my mouth as I watch the red fill the tub and trail into the drain, taking a bit of me with it.

"Lissy?" Jackson's heavy knock sounds on the door and I jump in surprise. The blade digs deeper into my skin and I suck in a breath as I drop it, pressing my palm to my leg to slow the rushing bleeding.

"Fuck." I soak in the pain for a beat but when too much blood fills the tub, I curse myself again.

"I can't find your turtle, are you sure he isn't in there?"

"He's not," I choke out as I lean over to grab my towel.

"Why do you sound like that? Are you okay?"

I let out a groan as I press the towel to my leg and shut the water off. "I'm fine."

The door swings open, and I quickly pull the curtain back before he can see the mess.

"You don't sound fine."

I let my eyes fall shut as I lean my head against the shower wall.

"Why are you sitting in there with the water off?"

"I'm meditating." I take in a shaky breath before pulling the towel away from my leg, but the bleeding doesn't stop.

"Do you normally meditate naked?"

I let out a pained laugh. "Do you want to meditate naked with me?"

He quiets and another smile tugs at my lips.

"Is that blood?"

I look up and notice the red stains on the side of the tub from when I grabbed my towel. I bite my lip, silently hoping he'll just ignore it and let me deal with this on my own.

"Please tell me you just got your period, Lisette." The curtain is pulled back before I can reply and I keep my eyes on my leg, not having it in me to face him. "Jesus Christ." He immediately pulls me into his arms.

I suck in a breath of pain as he lifts me out of the shower.

"What the hell are you—" he cuts himself off, shaking his head.

He rests me on the bed gently and I use some of the towel to cover myself but there's no point since his focus is on the blood coming from my thigh. "Let me see." He reaches for it, but I push his hand away.

"It's not that bad. I just cut myself shaving and—"

"Don't fucking lie to me right now, Lisette." He looks between my eyes with restrained anger before his gaze softens. "Just let me help you."

My eyes dart down to the ground before I pull my hand back. He lifts the towel before quickly covering it again, pressing the cut hard. I suck in a sharp breath before grabbing the shirt I laid out, quickly throwing it over myself.

"You need stitches."

"No, I don't."

"Don't—" he cuts himself off as I shove his hand away to pull the towel back and the bleeding slows, but the cut is deep. When it starts bleeding heavier, he moves my hand and applies more pressure.

I bite down my tongue as I grip the bed sheets. "Do you have a blood kink? Because we can totally take advantage of this." I smile up at him, but he doesn't even look at me.

My smile slowly disintegrates and just as I'm about to look away, his gaze meets mine.

"I was right out here. Why didn't you call me?"

I shake my head at his words. "Why do you and Sire keep saying that? Every time I drink or get high or cut myself, it's always 'Why didn't you call?' You can't help."

He shakes his head at me, his eyes searching my face. "We can't if you don't let us." He brushes a hair behind my ear before holding my face gently. "Nothing we say to you is going to work until *you* believe you can be helped."

"I'm too far gone." I shake my head out of his grasp but he holds me tighter.

"You don't believe that."

"It's true."

"So we don't need to go see Isabelle."

My brows furrow as I look between his eyes.

"If you believe you can't be helped, if you *truly* don't plan on fighting, then don't give her false hope. Don't let her fall in love with you if you're going to leave her. She doesn't need to gain a great sense of humor from you leaving."

I blink my tears away as I try to move my face, but he remains holding me.

"Tell me right now what's it going to be. Are you going to fight for your future or are you going to give up, because I'll call your brother and he can fight this battle for you. You don't need to do this alone, but decide now what's it going to be because I love you, but I refuse to let you hurt my kid."

I bite my tongue to hold back a cry. Squeezing my eyes shut, I shake my head silently.

"What does that mean?" he whispers.

"I don't want to fight," I choke out and a beat passes before he lets go of my face, but I quickly grab his hand, looking back up at him. "But I do." I hold his gaze, desperate for him not to leave me.

He nods a few times before leaning forward and pressing a soft kiss on my nose. "Do you have anything I can stitch you up with?"

"In the kitchen."

He nods slowly, but I can see all of his gears turning as he glances down at the rest of my scars.

"You can change your mind, you know."

His eyes meet mine.

"About what you said in the car," I clarify. "About how long you want me."

He rolls his eyes before kissing me. "I'm not changing my mind. All you get is fifty-five years. You still need to get the fuck out at eighty-one. Your sob story won't work on me."

A genuine laugh erupts from me before he wraps his arm around me. I bring my arms around his neck, pulling him back on the bed with me and he hovers over me, keeping pressure on my cut.

"I know you said you were waiting until I'm mentally stable before we have sex, but how long are you willing to wait?"

His head tilts to the side as his eyes scan my face. "I don't care about sex, Lisette. I'll wait forever."

A somber smile reaches my lips. "Forever or fifty-five years?"

He bites back a smile before kissing me. When he pulls away he turns more serious. "When you're sober and not self-harming, I'll fuck you however you want." He kisses my neck before sitting up and I smile over at him.

"Well, that's all the motivation I needed."

He rolls his eyes playfully before stepping out.

I slip my underwear on, and when he makes it back with the stitches kit, I start to wish I had taken something for the pain when he wasn't looking.

# Chapter Fifty-Six

## LISETTE

"Y OU'RE ACTING LIKE A LITTLE bitch."

My loud gasp fills the air as I pull away from hugging Isabelle. I'm still carrying her as I turn to Jackson to see if he just heard that. The sun has already set, but I can see his glare with the way his headlights illuminate him.

After napping together, we spent the day waiting for the alcohol to leave my system. As much as I want another drink, I'm glad I get to hang out with Isabelle for a few hours. We just got back from picking her up from her grandparents' house and I stayed in the car as Jackson went to the door, but I didn't miss the judgmental look his mom shot at me through the window. I have no idea what I did to that woman, but that's for future me to feel like shit about.

I bite my cheek not to laugh at Jackson's glare. I turn back to Isabelle and a smile grows on her face when she sees *my* smile.

"That's funny?" Jackson focuses on her and I raise my brows at Isa when she looks at me. "We'll see how funny it is when you have to go to bed straight after showering."

I raise my brows further and try to keep a straight face, but when her brows furrow, I need to bite my tongue harder.

"Today is movie night," she counters.

"Today will be movie night for only me and Lissy if you curse again. Cut it out already or you can cancel your sleepover with Uncle Sigh tomorrow, too."

"But—"

"Faith," Jackson warns and they have a stare-off for before Isabelle turns to me.

"He's so mean to me. It's just a *word*." She rolls her eyes and I can *feel* Jackson's glare from behind me.

"Come here."

I stifle a laugh as I hurry into the house with her before Jackson can yell at her. "Stop making him angry." I kiss her cheek before snuggling my face in her neck and her laugh fills the air as she tries to push me away.

"Why are you kissing me so much?"

"I missed you." I hug her tighter and she lets out an exaggerated groan.

"You're crushing me!"

I'm not, but I hold her tighter before pulling away. She acts like she can't breathe and I let out a laugh as we settle on the couch. Her dad walks in after us and drops my art supplies on the ground by the entrance of the living room. We decided I'd paint with Belle until she needs to go to bed, and as much as I want to sleepover, I don't set myself up for disappointment by asking him.

"Daddy." Isabelle looks over at him with a smile.

Jackson looks over at us, his bored look set on her. "Don't ask me for anything. You were not behaving nice in the car ride here and I don't appreciate that."

She raises one brow dramatically as she holds her chest. "I don't appreciate the attitude."

He shakes his head at her as he walks over to me. I expect him to take her from me, but he instead, brushes a hair behind my hair. "You hungry?"

I bite back a smile as I shake my head. I can feel Isabelle watching us and I slowly turn to look at her.

"So..." she smiles at me, and it's clear as day she wants something.

"Leave me alone." I stick my tongue out at her before tossing her aside and climbing off of the couch. She laughs from behind me as Jackson flops beside her.

That familiar feeling tugs at the pit of my stomach and as I try to push it away, a wave of heat flashes past me. My heart races and I try to calm my breathing as I walk to the kitchen, desperate for a minute alone to collect my thoughts.

I pace around the kitchen island twice as I weigh my options, silently fighting a mental battle to stay here with Isabelle rather than running off.

"Hey."

I jump out of my thoughts, turning to Jackson, who's leaning against the island, watching me carefully.

"What's with the pacing?" His eyes narrow as he scans my face.

I shake my head mindlessly, pulling my hand away from my mouth to answer him. "I'm fine." I muster a smile but the concerned look on his face only deepens.

He closes the space between us and pulls my fingernails away from my teeth. "I'm going to ask you again, and I need you to answer me honestly this time." He looks into my eyes before he nods.

"What's with the pacing?" he asks again, his tone just as gentle as before.

I shake my head as I bite at my nails again. "I really thought I could do this, Jackson." I press my palms to my eyes as my heart rate quickens again and I can feel myself nearly drowning in sweat.

"I thought seeing her would help, and it *did.* I swear it did. I just—" I cut myself off as I take a step away from him, but he grabs my hand before I can put more distance between us.

"You're going through withdrawals." He nods in understanding and I let out a breath of relief for not having to admit it.

"I just need to shut it up." I nod quickly at the idea. "I'm just going to step out to get my head on straight." I lean forward to plant a kiss on his lips. "I'll be right back."

I force a smile as I move to go around him, but he steps in my way.

"Can you promise me you're going to come back sober?"

I go still and I feel him watching me, but I keep my eyes on his shirt. All of my emotions are being pulled at once and I settle on anger as I look up at him.

"Do you think I won't? Because you said you'll be my solace and this doesn't feel like that," I bite out.

I wait for him to fight back and give me an excuse to leave, but his face remains neutral. "This is the withdrawals, so I'm going to let the attitude slide, but if you don't lower your voice, we're going to have a problem."

I open my mouth, but it quickly falls shut at the sight of his glare.

He nods once as he continues. "Withdrawals or not, nothing you need to say needs to be said over the volume I'm currently using. Do you understand that?"

I roll my eyes at his *Dad tone*, but as I try to walk away, he steps in my way again.

"Remember the reason you came here," he whispers before kissing the top of my head.

Everything in me wants to fight and push him away so I can escape for another high, but before I can think about that option, he wraps his arm around my head, pressing my forehead to his chest.

I let my eyes fall shut as I breathe in his scent.

"What do you do when you normally feel like this?"

The first few things that come to mind are none he'll let me do.

"Paint." I settle on. I nod to myself as I think of my healthier coping mechanism. "I listen to music and paint."

"Okay." Jackson pulls away to kiss the top of my hair. "So let's listen to music and paint."

I nod in response and after another minute of collecting my thoughts, he takes my hand and pulls me into the living room. Isabelle sits beside me as her dad sets a playlist on and we get to painting.

The first half hour is torture, but eventually, I drown my feelings in the acrylic paint and bleed my pain onto the canvas.

"You should add—"

"Don't." I move Belle's brush away from my canvas. "I'm not adding to yours. Don't add to mine."

Her brows pull together as she looks over at me and I silently curse myself for the harsh tone.

"You don't want my help?"

"No thank you," I voice more gently before pinching her cheeks

She studies me as if she can't understand English. "Why not?"

I look down at the monstrosity on her canvas. Jackson stifles a laugh before pinching my waist and I bite my tongue as I choose my words wisely. "I just want to do this one on my own, but we can do one together later."

She shrugs in return before turning back to her painting. When I finish mine, I lift it to get a better look.

"How do you pick what you're going to paint?" Jackson questions from behind me.

"I kind of just start and whatever I'm feeling ends up on the canvas."

He's silent as we study the girl in my painting, curled up on a bed with a dark, large figure crawling towards her, nearly consuming her.

I let out a tired breath as I drop my canvas onto the table. I feel a tug on my shirt, and when I turn to Jackson, he nods for me to get closer. I almost tell him I'm fine, but instead of lying, I sit beside him.

He wraps an arm around me as I lean my head on him.

"How's your leg?" He keeps his voice hushed, although I'm sure Isabelle isn't paying us an ounce of attention.

"Honestly... my other leg wants a matching scar." I gently run my finger along the bandage.

He squeezes me tighter and I pull in a deep breath before laying my head back and turning to him. He took his shirt off a while ago and I keep my focus on his chest.

"In case you wanted to skip a workout day, I prefer dad bods." I trace his abs and in the corner of my eyes, I can see his smirk.

"Well then, I'll be sure to get rid of the gym downstairs."

I bite back a smile before leaning forward to kiss him. My lips press against his hungrily, and just as I deepen the kiss, he pulls away. He glances to the side and I remember Belle is still here, but she keeps her back to us as she paints.

I nod in return as I lay back again and a bitter feeling fills my mouth. I can sense the waves of anger and sadness pulling at me in every direction and I'm starting to become spread out too thin.

"Can we go upstairs?" I ask quietly as I trace his lower abdomen.

His stomach dips and I bite back a smile as I look up at him but he shakes his head. "Not for what you want, reina."

My shoulders sag. "Please? I need to feel something else, Jackson. I need a different distraction."

He shakes his head gently, his eyes full of sympathy as he watches me. "You know that's impossible with her here," he nearly whispers.

"I can't be here." I give up.

He nods in return as he takes my hand, kissing the back of it gently. "I'm not letting you leave."

I let out a frustrated breath, but as I try to stand, he wraps his arm around me. "You can stay or call one of your siblings, but you know you shouldn't be alone, and I know you want to go upstairs, but I don't feel comfortable sleeping with you like this."

I shake my head at him as I rub my temples.

He leans over for the markers. "Here. Draw something else."

I bite my tongue, holding back on a chain of curses he doesn't deserve.

Opening the markers, I mindlessly draw on his ribs. After a few minutes, Isabelle pulls up a chair to sit in front of us. I expect her to start drawing on her dad like I am but she turns to me instead.

"What happened here?" She rubs the scars on my thighs before her eyes land on my other leg and her brows pull together. "Are you bleeding?" She cringes as she looks at my bandaged leg and Jackson stops her from reaching for it.

"Not anymore," I reassure her.

"Did that hurt?" She sits back down as she rubs my scars gently.

"Yeah, a little."

She inspects every scar I put on myself and Jackson reaches for her again, but I push his hand away before he can stop her.

"I like how this feels." She nods to herself as she rubs her tiny fingers along my leg.

"You think so?" I touch my leg and they feel horrible, every bump reminds me of the pain that made me cut as deep as I did time and time again. "I think they're turning ugly," I admit quietly.

She shakes her head gently before picking at one of my bigger scars. "I have a scar too." She points at a faint line on her knee. "Daddy says scars are reminders of how strong we are." She opens one of the markers mindlessly and draws a star around one of my scars.

A soft smile touches my lips and I feel my throat closing as she traces a rainbow on another scar before adding more stars. I watch her with teary eyes as she adds a piece of herself to the ugliest part of me.

"You're so precious." I quickly wipe my cheek when a tear falls. Mustering up another smile, I tuck a loose hair into her bun before holding her chubby face in my hand.

She smiles up at me before doing a double take. "Does it hurt?" She lifts the marker from my leg, but I quickly shake my head no.

"I just love you so much."

She looks like she doesn't understand me as her brows furrow. "You don't have to cry, I'm right here."

A soft laugh escapes me as I pull her onto the couch with us. I hug her close and her body goes limp as she lets out a groan.

"Ugh, too many hugs today."

I stifle a laugh before kissing her cheek.

"Ugh, so many kisses. Stop being a little bitch."

My cry mixes into a laugh as I bury my face in her neck. She taps my back gently and after a beat, I collect myself and pull away to look at Jackson who's on his phone with a glare.

He starts calling someone on speaker and after a few rings, Sire answers. "Hey, did Lis call you?"

I feel my brows furrow as I pull away from Isabelle, but Jackson ignores him as he looks at his daughter. "Isabelle just canceled her sleepover with you."

"No, I didn't," she counters, reaching for the phone, but Jackson keeps her back.

"How come?" Sire asks on the other end.

"I didn't cancel Uncle Sigh."

Jackson puts a hand up and she crosses her arms on my lap as he talks to my brother. "She keeps cursing so there won't be any sleepovers."

Sire is quiet and I watch as Jackson gives his best scold to Isabelle.

"Did she call you a little bitch?" Sire asks and I can hear the smile in his voice.

"Yes," Jackson bites out and I need to hide my smile from him as I imagine the kick Sire is getting out of this.

"Well, she's sorry so—"

"She's not sorry," Jackson counters.

"I am," Belle says, and I step in when I realize she's about to cry. "She's sorry. Stop it, JJ."

"Don't start crying now." Jackson keeps his eyes on her and my heart crushes as I pull her into my arms. "Put her down."

"No." I glare over at him. "She's sorry and she's having her sleepover. Stop it." I hold her tighter and before Jackson can voice a complaint, Sire speaks up again.

"Is that my sister? I told you to call me if you heard from her. Are you two home?"

It sounds like he's moving around on the other end. I shake my head before Jackson can answer. He opens his mouth but nothing comes out as he decides whether or not he's going to lie for me.

"Hello?" Sire voices when no one says anything.

I snatch the phone from Jackson before moving Isabelle so I can stand.

"I'm fine."

The rustling on the other end stops and Sire is quiet before he responds. "You scared the shit out of me, Lis. Turn your location back on."

"I don't see why you need it." I walk further into the house as I listen closely and I catch the sigh he lets out.

"You're angry," he states more than asks.

I let out a scoff at his words. "Let me tell you you're just like your mother and see how much joy you'll be filled with."

"I only said that because—"

"Because you wanted to hurt me," I finish for him.

"Because you needed to hear it," he counters. "You want to get high right now, don't you? You're probably pushing Jackson away. Picking fights and barely tolerating Isabelle. They don't deserve that and you're going to hate yourself for hurting them when you're sober. Come stay with me."

"You don't know what you're talking about." I shake my head at his words. "I'm not taking it out on Belle and I'm not *tolerating* her."

"Not yet you're not."

*He's right.*

The doubt yells at me and I hang up on him.

# Chapter Fifty-Seven

## LISETTE

WHEN I WALK INTO THE studio, I immediately regret agreeing to this bullshit.

Christmas music plays from somewhere, and for some reason, it smells like horrendous gingerbread cookies. The chatter of my siblings grow louder with every step I take. Whipping around the corner, my eyes land on all of their Christmas sweaters.

*Jesus Christ.*

"Lis." Sage throws her hands up as she smiles over at me. Her red dress looks stunning on her and practically makes her glow as she glides over to me. She quickly pulls me into a hug and no amount of my hatred for Christmas could make me a bit annoyed by this girl.

"This was supposed to be casual." I pull away to study her designer heels.

"This is casual." She looks down at her dress before a smile touches her lips. "You all didn't want to wear a dress, but that wasn't stopping me. Plus, Hazel is in a skirt." She shrugs before her eyes practically light up. "I brought your Christmas sweater."

"Great." I force a smile. "Burn it," I add cheerfully before kissing her cheek. Her jaw drops and I rush off before she can object.

Her twin meets me next and flashes me a bright smile. I shake my head at the Christmas tree on his bright red shirt. "Who coordinated these outfits?"

August's brows furrow as he looks down at himself. "They're cute."

So this was his idea.

He breaks into a laugh at whatever face I'm making and I bite back a smile at his contagious laughter.

Sage comes up next to us and the minute she opens her mouth, I interrupt her. "I'm not wearing reindeer ears."

Her brows furrow as she touches the ears on her head. "I like them."

I stifle a laugh at her cute pinched brows. "They're cute on you, but I'm not doing it."

She agrees and behind her, Liam wraps an arm around her waist before kissing her cheek. "Come finish eating, Dory."

A smile touches my lips at how in love with my sister he is. "How do you do, soon-to-be Mr. Hale?"

He drags his eyes to me slowly and I bite back my smile at his unamused look. He doesn't say anything as he takes Sage's hand and guides her away.

"Great talk as always!"

Beside me, August stifles a laugh when Liam shakes his head at me.

Walking further into the studio, I find Hazel and Vidia who are also in Christmas sweaters. "At least you two aren't wearing a tree."

A smile grows on Vidia's face as she pulls out a sweater from the bag beside her. "This one is yours." I study the white sweater with nearly twenty trees going around the chest and back.

As I'm about to voice a protest, Sire walks over. He keeps a straight face as he studies me and I truly try not to roll my eyes at him, but before I can stop myself, I'm already looking away in annoyance.

"So we're still fighting, nice to know." He nods once as he sits next to his girlfriend.

"Thanks." I take the sweater from Vidia before turning, but I take one step before Sire speaks up.

"Can we maybe act like a family for this photoshoot?"

I keep walking as I respond. "I'm here for the twins. We don't need to speak to stand beside each other in a picture."

"Are you sober?"

I go still at his question and the rest of the room falls quiet. A scoff escapes me as I whip around to him and all I see in his eyes is that patronizing look.

Hazel puts a hand up before I can fight back. "We're not doing this with you two today." She glares between the two of us. "We're taking family pictures to send to our parents. You're going to wear the cute sweater my boyfriend picked for you and neither of you is going to fight about your sobriety."

She turns to Sire now. "She's here and that's what counts. It doesn't matter if she's drunk or high—" She points at Sire when he opens his mouth. "It doesn't matter *right now*."

She keeps her glare on him before Vidia takes his hand. "You two have been at each other's throats all week. I know you're both exhausted from fighting. Give it a rest."

I look around at them and let out a defeated breath because they're right and the last thing I want to do is ruin this.

"Fine," Sire and I speak at the same time and a smile grows on Vidia's face.

"Good." She sits up straighter before focusing on me. "Now that everyone is here..." She watches me with a smile that rings an alarm in my head.

"Do you want to share with the class who Santa wrapped in a cute bow for you this year?" I bite back a smile and she breaks into a laugh at me. "You're blushing."

"Shut up, V." I roll my eyes at her and beside her, Sire bites back a smile.

"Wait, you're seeing someone?" Hazel looks intrigued now. "You talk about boys like you hate them?"

"That's because she's not seeing a *boy*. He screams man." Vidia shoves Hazel's arm as she raises her brows at me and I feel my face flush.

"Oh my god." Hazel's jaw drops. "Who is this guy?"

I shake my head at Vidia's obvious excitement and I'm surprised August hasn't told her. "You're so annoying." I try to play it casual as I sit across from them and toy with a loose yarn in the sweater.

"One hint." Vidia holds Hazel's hands. "DILF."

Hazel's brows furrow before her jaw drops again. Her head whips to me and I bite my cheek so hard I can taste the blood in my mouth.

"Jackson?!" She watches for my reaction and I nod once before they both squeal.

"You're both so irritating." I stifle a laugh at the pair.

Hazel sits up in her seat as she watches me like a telenovela. "How's the sex?" She keeps her tone hushed although right beside her, August's brows furrow.

"I beg your *finest* pardon?" He looks between the three of us before focusing on his girlfriend. "Why on Earth would you care?"

"Hush." Hazel waves him off as she focuses on me. "I don't care about any dick other than mine. This is standard girl talk."

August opens his mouth before his brain catches onto what she just said and he bites back a smile as he sits back in his seat.

Vidia pipes in from beside them. "He seems like he's good." She nods like she's impressed.

"How the hell does he *seem* like that?" Sire asks next.

"Because he walks around with your confidence minus the cocky ego." Vidia rolls her eyes at him before turning her attention back to me.

Sire stifles a laugh and like the whipped bitches my brothers are, neither of them speaks up against their girlfriends. Both girls are waiting for my response, but I don't give them one.

"Can we get these pictures started? I have things to do." I rise from my seat before pulling my sweater on.

"Things to do or a person?" Vidia taunts me and my cheeks are on fire.

"*Things.*" I roll my eyes at her and she squints her eyes at me. "I'm going to the bathroom. When I get back can we start?" I look around the room and Sage nods in agreement, her cheeks filled with whatever Liam is feeding her.

Escaping to the bathroom, I immediately let out a breath of relief when the door shuts behind me. I stare at myself in the mirror, convincing myself no one can see through me.

If Sire asked if I was sober then I look sober... right?

Taking a step closer to the mirror, I study my reflection before deciding I don't look drunk. Turning on my heels, I take a step to exit, but at the sound of my family's laughter, the guilt begins to seep in.

Shaking my head at my entire life, I pull out the water bottle from my bag and take a few small sips. I let the burning numb the pain and guilt. Letting my eyes fall shut, I pull in a deep breath for courage and hurry out of the bathroom.

Just as I turn the corner, I bump into Vidia.

"My bad." She quickly catches me before bending over to grab my water bottle just as I reach for my bag.

"Thanks." I take the bottle from her as she wipes her hand on her shirt.

"I think it's open."

I quickly close it, but as she takes a whiff of her fingers, her brows furrow before her entire face is covered in disappointment. "Lis..."

"Save it, V. Just run off to Sire." I try to move past her, but she places a gentle hand on my arm.

"I'm not going to run to him." She pulls out a piece of gum from her pocket before handing it to me. "You're here and that's all that matters. You two can fight tomorrow."

I look down at the gum in her hand before looking back up at her. "He's going to be mad at you for hiding this from him."

She shrugs before pushing the gum into my hand. "Fighting with you is hurting him and if dealing with his anger means he can have a good day with his sister then I'll take it."

I nod to myself as I take the gum. "I shouldn't make you lie for me..." I shake my head at myself as I recognize I'm slowly burning my bridges.

*You're spiraling.*

I shake my head of my thoughts, forcing the gum back into Vidia's hand.

"I don't need you to cover for me."

Her brows furrow as she looks between the gum and me. "I know you think you're undeserving of all shapes and forms of help, but that's not true." A somber smile covers her face before she drops it in my hand and walks off.

I look down at the gum and quickly eat it, sparing myself from the headache that'll accompany me if anyone knows the decision I made.

When I walk back into the main room, my eyes land on Sage talking to the photographer.

She directs all of us on where to stand and as Vidia makes her way back in, she squeezes next to Sire. I glance around at my siblings and their significant others, each of their smiles pulling at my heartstrings.

*I wish Jackson was here.*

"That's my foot," Liam grumbles, and I stifle a laugh as I step away from him.

"Oops." I flick the Santa hat he's wearing and considering he's over six feet, I need to reach quite a bit. Settling back on my feet disrupts my balance and I bump into Vidia.

"You okay?" She steadies me and I turn to her, a smile on my face as I focus on her.

"I'm going to sit." I nod in agreement with myself as I settle on the ground.

"You're covering the banner, Lis." Sire watches me carefully, but before he can ask me anything, the photographer speaks up.

"No, that's perfect." She snaps away and I turn to the camera, the alcohol painting a genuine smile on my face.

# Chapter Fifty-Eight

## JACKSON

I STEP INTO MY ROOM from the bathroom quietly, but as I turn to my bed, Lisette is already awake, a smile on that pretty face.

"This is a great sight to wake up to." Her smile grows as she gives me a once-over.

I bite back a laugh as I adjust the towel around my waist. "Did I wake you?"

She shakes her head, her eyes still on my frame.

After I put Isabelle to bed last night, I called Lisette and within the first few minutes of talking to her I knew she wasn't okay. I invited her over just to have her near and talk, but I'm glad she slept over because I genuinely like waking up next to her, and she looks like she feels better.

A smile touches my lips as I close the distance between us. I lean over and plant a soft kiss on her lips. "Beautiful."

As always, she rolls her eyes at my affection before snuggling into her pillow again. I quickly steal another kiss before grabbing the clothes I laid out on the bed.

"You can get dressed out here." She stops me as I'm about to walk off to the closest.

I turn to her and she watches me carefully as I set my clothes back down on the bed. I wait for her to look away or at the very least act like she's not watching me, but she shamelessly keeps her gaze on my half-naked body.

I reach for my towel and still, she doesn't look away. "I'm not wearing anything under this."

She nods slowly. "I was hoping you'd say that."

I stifle my laugh as I pull my towel off. I watch her carefully as her eyes trail to my lower half. I suddenly feel my body heat as she watches me, but I refuse to show her just how shy she makes me.

Instead, I walk over to the bathroom door to hang up my towel. I can feel Lisette watching my every step as I walk back to the bed and tug my boxer briefs on. At the sound of her soft sigh, I bite back a smile as I steal a glance at her.

She leans on her elbow as her eyes trace my frame. "Can I have another kiss?"

I smile over at her as I apply my deodorant. "You can come get one."

She clearly bites back a smile and I nonchalantly grab my lotion as she crawls over to me. She kneels on the edge of the bed and a second barely passes before she grabs the hem of my briefs and pulls me to her.

She looks up at me through her lashes like she's waiting for something. "I'm here."

"So kiss me."

Her eyes narrow as she sits up and reaches for me. I don't lean over and with our height difference and my low bed, she struggles just a bit. I let out a low laugh as she sets her hands on my shoulder to climb me.

"You're so needy." Giving in, I lean over and catch her lips with mine. Wrapping my arms around her waist, I lift her from the bed and she quickly wraps her legs around my waist.

My phone starts ringing and Lisette lets out a sigh as she drops her head onto my shoulder. "Please send them to voicemail."

I stifle a laugh as I reach for my phone. When I see it's Vidia, my brows pull together because she never calls me.

"Hey," I say into the phone and Lisette's brows pull together as she watches me.

*Who is that?* She mouths, but I shake my head as I wave her off.

"Hey, Jackson." Vidia hesitates on her end.

I try to set Lisette on the bed, but she shakes her head, tightening her grip around me.

"Is Lis with you?"

I glance over at Lisette. "Yeah, what's up?"

"Well..." Vidia starts again. "I just didn't want you to be ambushed, but Sire is on his way. Lisette was drinking yesterday at the photoshoot and I just told Sire... he's pretty mad."

I go still and Lisette mindlessly cups my face, running her fingers along my jaw and beard. I scan her face and she doesn't look hungover. My mind trails back to yesterday and I don't pick up on any signs that she could've been drunk.

"Are you sure?"

"Yeah." Vidia lets out a quiet sigh. "He should be pulling up soon, but it's going to get messy so I just wanted to let you know in case Isa was home."

I nod to myself and Lisette leans forward to kiss me, but I turn my head away. "Thanks for the heads up."

We end the call on that and I toss my phone aside before looking down at Lisette.

"Who was it?"

I scan her face, watching her reaction carefully. "How was your photoshoot yesterday?"

Her brows slightly pinch before she shrugs. "Fine." She tries to kiss me again, but I turn away.

"I'm trying to talk to you. Can you stop kissing me?"

A furrow grows between her brows as her eyes narrow on me. "Who was that?"

"How was the photoshoot?"

"*Who* called you, Jackson?" Her temper quickly grows and I shake my head at myself for not seeing it.

"When you came from your photoshoot I asked you if you were okay and what did you tell me?"

We both stare at each other, her eyes filling with guilt and anger as I force mine to remain understanding, but I'm so mad at myself. I thought she was only tired yesterday because that's what she told me and that's what I excused her slurred words for. Tiredness. That's the main reason I asked her to sleepover.

"I asked you a question."

She tries to climb off of me, but I keep her in my arms.

"Let me down."

"Answer me."

Her eyes meet mine and I prepare for her harsh words, but she surprises me when I see the tears in her eyes. "I lied."

I nod in return as she blinks her tears away. "It was just so hard." Her eyes drop as a pink blush covers her face. "I couldn't face my siblings, but I needed to be there, or they'd know I wasn't sober."

I nod in response before setting her on the bed and we both remain silent as I finish getting dressed.

I'm putting my deodorant and lotion back in their place when she speaks up behind me.

"Are you mad at me?"

I shake my head in response as I reorganize the top of my dresser three more times. When a sense of ease passes through me, I speak up. "I wish you hadn't lied."

"But are you mad?"

I turn to her and when I see her picking at her nails, I close the distance between us and cover her hands with mine. "No, sweetheart."

Her eyes meet mine and she doesn't look like she believes me for one second.

I lean over and kiss her gently. "I promise, mi reina." I kiss her more firmly before lifting her into my arms.

She wraps her arms and legs around me before I lead us out of my room.

"We can't continue like this, Lisette."

She buries her face in my neck as she holds me closer. "I know. I'm going to get better."

Rubbing her back gently I kiss her cheek. "You keep saying that, sweetheart, but what are we going to do to make sure you get better?"

She's quiet the entire way downstairs. When I get an alert on my phone, I know my camera just picked up Sire's car pulling in. Heading for the door, I quickly open it before he can knock and wake up Isabelle.

"Lis, can you get down for a minute?"

"Why?" She runs my hand in my hair as I drag my eyes up to her brother.

He shakes his head at us before his eyes settle on Lisette. "Just put her in my car."

I feel Lisette go still before her grip tightens around me.

"Lissy, get down so you can talk to your brother."

She shakes her head and I pull away to look at her. She looks between my eyes frantically before kissing me. "Let's go back upstairs."

"Look at me," Sire demands and I feel my brows furrow at his tone.

"Okay," I start when I feel the shift in the air. "I know you're mad that she was drunk yesterday, but my daughter is sleeping upstairs and this neighborhood is way too quiet for either of you to cause a scene."

"We're not going to make a scene because Sire is leaving." Lis hugs me close again as she rests her chin on my shoulder.

In front of me, my best friend shakes his head at us before walking around me to look at Lisette. "I knew it."

"Stop it, Sire." She shifts to hide her face from him.

"What?" I turn to look at him, but he grabs Lisette's face, forcing her to look at him.

"Tell him or I will."

She tries to move her face from his grasp, but he keeps a firm grip on her jaw.

"Get off of her." I move his hand and replace it with my gentle touch as I hold her. "Tell me what?" I look at her and she starts tearing up as she rests her forehead on my shoulder.

"He already knows I'm not sober. We're working on it, Sire."

He runs a hand down his face before looking up to the sky and taking in a slow breath.

"Lisette, please get off of him."

She shakes her head in response before clinging to me like her life depends on it.

Sire takes a step toward me, but I take a step back. "What is going on?"

"She's high, Jackson. That's what's going on. Put her in my car, please."

I turn back to Lisette, cupping her face in my hands. She gazes up at me, tears in her eyes, but I don't see it. "Is it true?"

"No." She shakes her head and beside me, her brother throws his hand up in defeat.

"She's a liar. You're seriously going to believe her over me?"

"You're an addict too," Lis points out.

"Hey," I warn, but they both ignore me.

"And which one of us is sober?" Sire counters.

"Get off of your high horse." Lisette turns back to me, rubbing my jaw gently before kissing me. "Don't listen to him."

I scan her face, torn between who to believe.

"This is fucking ridiculous," Sire lets out a scoff. "She has you so damn pussy whipped, Jackson. I can bet my life on this. I *know* her and she's high."

"No, you don't," Lis bites out before hugging me again.

I shake my head at his words. "I was with her all night, Sire. How?" I look back over at Lisette now, searching my brain for something I could have missed.

He shifts his glare to Lisette and she turns her face away from him. "She probably tried to sober up after the photoshoot, fought *all day* and after she did, she felt good, but then she couldn't sleep. She climbed out of bed, and said she needed to use the bathroom."

My heart sinks as I watch the tears build in her eyes as he recites exactly what happened yesterday.

"She got high, but most likely woke up a few hours ago and just needed one more. Then she woke up this morning with the prettiest smile on her face."

I feel my shoulder slouch. "Get down, Lissy."

She shakes her head repeatedly as she buries her face in my neck again. "Please," she pleads.

"Get down so we can talk." I drop my hands to my side, but with her grip, she remains around me. "Lisette." I tap her hip and she picks her head up, tear tracks on her cheeks and my heart nearly breaks.

"Okay."

I nod gently before hugging her again.

"Jesus Christ." Sire covers his face with his hands before he snaps. "It's crocodile tears, Jackson. Isa pulls this shit on you every other week and you don't see it with her either. She's an addict. She's *lying* to you and those aren't real tears."

"Shut up, Sire!" The anger in her voice is almost unrecognizable. When she turns to me, her eyes are soft again and her tears are back. It's like watching two different people.

"I want to stay with you." She leans forward to kiss me, but I lean away.

"Why?"

"What?" Her brows furrow and as she rubs my facial hair, I move her hand.

"Why do you want to stay with me?" I ask again.

She sniffles quietly as she kisses my hand. "I don't want to fight. I'm tired of fighting."

Sire opens his mouth, but I put a hand up as I respond. "He doesn't want to fight with you."

She keeps her eyes low and I hold her chin, tilting her head up to me. "I'm happy here with you," she confesses.

"You've been high and drunk here with me," I correct her.

Her eyes drop and it's clear her mind runs with a hundred different things. She lets out a sigh before her eyes meet mine. "You're right." She nods gently as she cups my face and runs her thumb to smooth out my eyebrow. "I just needed one day of quiet, but I'm done." She looks between my eyes and I want to believe her. So badly that I nearly do.

"I promise, JJ." She meets my eyes and I can feel myself slipping. "I don't have any more pills with me. I took the last one this morning. You can dump the rest of the alcohol I have and I'll stay here with you. I won't leave and I'll get sober. I'll be better for you. For Belle."

When I see the tears building in her eyes again, I force my eyes shut and weigh my options.

"I just—" Her voice breaks and there goes my heart, *shattering* at the pain I can hear. "I just need someone to believe in me."

"I believe in you," Sire says from beside us.

When I look back at Lis, Sire reaches for her face, but she moves away from his touch. He shakes his head before he drops his hand.

"Why don't you want to come with me?" He sounds torn as he keeps his eyes on her.

"I want Jackson."

"I never said you couldn't come back. Why are you so opposed to coming with me?"

She doesn't answer him.

Sire leans over to catch her eyes with his, but she looks away before resting her forehead on me again.

"You and I both know I can get you sober, Lis. You just don't *want* to get sober."

I watch them carefully, but at the sound of Isabelle's faint call for me, we all turn to the house. Lisette is quick to climb off of me, but as she steps for the door, Sire grabs her arm.

"Give me five minutes," he pleads.

She tries to pull away, but I step in her way.

"The deal was you see Isabelle sober," I remind her. "You broke that deal, so give him five minutes or you need to leave."

Her eyes drop to the ground as she takes a step back to face her brother. Stepping away, I call into the house to tell Belle to give me a minute.

"Winter is worried about you." Sire keeps his voice hushed as he leans over, trying to get her to look at him, but she refuses. "Bay is scared too. Why won't you answer their calls?"

"Is this what you want to waste your five minutes on?"

He's quiet as he watches her. "Call me when you're ready, Lisette. It doesn't matter the time or how drunk or high you are. When you go back in there and take out your anger on that little girl then feel like shit for not coming with me when you had the chance, call me."

"Daddy?"

Lisette turns on her heels and as I open the door, she scoops Isabelle into her arms, rushing off before she can greet Sire.

I let out a tired breath as I turn back to my best friend.

"She's lying to you," he states, his voice monotone and tired.

"What?"

"Lisette." He nods towards the door. "She didn't take her last pill. She's still hiding some in your house somewhere."

I shake my head in return, refusing to believe that show she gave me was just that. A show. "How do you know?"

"Because I was her, Jackson," he deadpans. "Did she ever tell you about our fight? The one we had a few years ago and didn't truly resolve until earlier this year?"

"No..."

He nods as he glances over at the house. "I relapsed right before I signed you as my agent. I wasn't on vacation that summer, I was in rehab and when Lisette tried to help me, I threw her suicide attempt in her face. I said something that was unforgivable because I didn't want to be saved. That's what she's doing now. Pushing me away, being cruel."

He looks torn as he continues. "She's not doing that with you because you're her escape. She knows I can help so she's pushing me away. She knows she can get away with murder with you so she's manipulating you. The same way I used to manipulate August. We're addicts, Jackson, and we can be your worst nightmare."

"I'm not going to force her out."

"And by doing so you're enabling her."

I open my mouth to defend myself, but he beats me to it.

"I'm going home because she needs to *want* to get sober. She needs to see she has nothing before she fights for something and as long as you continue to forgive her, she's going to continue to fuck up and beg for your forgiveness that she knows she already has. She's going to tell you it was just one drink. Or her last pill. She's going to yell at you and then pretend to cry. When you threaten to call me, she's going to confess one small thing. She'll sit there, high as a kite, and tell you she only had one drink. She's going to make you think her small confession counts for something so you can think she's being honest. She's going to manipulate you and tell you to keep her secrets because she needs someone in her corner. She's going to ruin your relationship, Jackson."

He digs into his pocket before handing me a small nasal spray. "I'm really hoping you won't have to use that and I'm wrong." With that, he walks away, leaving me stuck in place.

# Chapter Fifty-Nine

## JACKSON

WALKING BACK INTO THE HOUSE, I find the girls in the living room. Lisette sits on the ground as Isabelle braids her hair.

"Good morning, princess."

Belle looks up from the couch, a bright smile on her face. "Good morning, Daddy. I'll have waffles for breakfast with some mango."

I stifle a laugh as I close the distance between us and almost immediately her hug eases the pain in my head. I take a deep breath with my nose in her hair before scrunching my face. "Yuck."

She stifles a laugh and I kiss her before setting her down.

"Someone is in desperate need of a shower." I ruffle her hair and she smells the ends of it before smelling her underarms.

"It must be you, Dad."

I open my mouth, but nothing comes out and Lisette lets out a quiet laugh from behind us.

"I just showered. It's you, little piggy." I squeeze her cheek before guiding her big head out of the living room so I can talk to Lisette. "Go get ready for a bath, I'll be up in a minute then we can have breakfast."

"I can shower myself." She seems to be reminding me.

"I'm aware of that, but—"

"So you're aware that I'll do it by myself like a big girl." She sends me a pointed look and I am truly not ready for her to be a teenager because she has enough sass to last two damn lifetimes.

"Please go pick out your outfit and I'll be up to help you shower."

"I don't need help." She walks off, but I call out to her.

"I want to make sure you're okay. Pick out your outfit and wait for me before you get in the shower, okay?"

She remains quiet and I know she's plotting to fill the bath to the brim with water and enough bubbles for three showers.

"Faith. *Carter.*"

"Okay, Daddy," she drags out and I can just imagine her eye roll.

"Watch the attitude, little ma'am."

I can hear her sigh and I take a step after her, but stop short at the sound of Lisette's laugh. Letting out a breath I walk back into the living room to find Lisette smiling at me.

"You two are so entertaining to watch."

"Don't encourage her. She turned five and is just plain fucking *rude* sometimes. I have no idea where she gets it from." I roll my eyes at her and Lisette only laughs harder.

"You look just like her when you do that."

"She looks like me." I bite back a smile when I catch myself rolling my eyes again. Pushing aside my incredibly sassy child, I step in front of Lisette.

"Come on." I hold my hand out to her and she takes it as I pull her up.

"Where are we going?" She smiles up at me and she looks so damn precious, but I remain strong.

"You're going to get rid of the alcohol and pills then hang out upstairs until your high wears off."

She takes a step back, but I speak up before she can.

"The deal was you see Isabelle while you're sober," I remind her slowly. "You're not sober so you can stay upstairs. You don't get to go get high and do what you want. Our agreement remains."

She lets out a scoff as she looks off to the side. "So I need to sit in timeout upstairs?"

"It's hardly timeout," I point out. "There's an arcade up there along with a movie room. You can also go downstairs to the gym if you'd like or out by the pool. The house is big enough for all of us. Go where you'd like, but you don't get to go near Isabelle."

"Whatever." She tries to walk off, but I step in her way.

"No, it's not *whatever.*" I lean over to catch her eyes with mine. "You lied to me and I have yet to hear you take accountability for that. I refuse to enable you and I have every right to be upset, which I am," I point out.

Her eyes dart to mine before they soften. Her shoulders slouch as she takes hold of my hand. "I'm sorry... I just—"

"Uh uh." I pull my hand away gently. "Don't apologize after I point it out. Like it's an afterthought. I don't deserve that." I stand up straighter as I step away from her. "Bring the alcohol and pills down then go back upstairs. We can talk tonight."

She nods in return before her eyes prickle with tears. I look away, knowing I'll give in if I see her cry.

"I'll wait here." I walk over to the couch, my heart physically hurting as I hear her walk off.

I'm pacing the living room as soon as she's out of sight. Sire's voice is on a loop in my mind and I force myself to keep that same voice in the front of my mind, preparing myself to catch any signs of her manipulation. As much as I want to believe her, he knows her better than I do and I looked right past her when he noticed she was high within a few seconds.

When I hear her making her way back downstairs, I take my seat again. Turning to the entrance, she walks in with a water bottle and a half-empty bottle of Tito's.

"This is it." She turns for the kitchen and I follow after her. Leaning against the counter, I watch her spill it down the drain. At the sight of the pink blush crawling up her neck, I close the distance between us.

Remaining behind her, I set my hands on either side of her before kissing her cheek gently. "You have *nothing* to be embarrassed about."

She shakes her head in return before wiping her cheek. "Really?" Her voice breaks. "Because being told to *go upstairs* by my boyfriend is pretty embarrassing and degrading. Don't speak to me like I'm a fucking child."

Moving my arm aside, she storms past me.

"Lissy."

"I get it, Jackson. I'm high, I lied, and you're mad. You've made that clear."

"Lisette."

"What?" She spins on her heels and my eyes drop to the ground.

"The pills."

She remains quiet and as I drag my eyes back up to her, she shakes her head. "I don't have any more."

I watch her carefully as I try to decide if I believe her. "Sire said—"

"Of course, you believe him over me." Her eyes fill with anger. "Lis—"

"I don't need you either."

I take a step back at her words and I know she doesn't mean that. I remind myself she's just high, but the anger in her eyes still hurts.

"You said you'll be my solace, but it's clear that was a lie, so I'll just go." She storms off and I quickly follow after her.

"Lissy, wait."

She storms upstairs and I hurry after her.

"Where are you going to go?"

She ignores me.

"Do you want to go to a meeting?" I suggest, but when she rolls her eyes, my shoulders slouch because I don't know what the right thing to say is here.

She pulls her hoodie on before turning her angry gaze on me. "You said I can't be near Belle if I'm high. I'm doing as you wish." She snatches her phone from the bed before getting her bag and heading for the door.

"Don't flip this on me and do not bring her into this," I warn, but she storms out of the room. "Please stay so we can talk."

We reach the top of the stairs when Belle calls out to me.

"Dad, can you help me? I can't reach my new dress!"

I stop between Lisette and my daughter's room. When Lisette goes down the steps, I take a step after her, but Isabelle calls me again.

"Fuck, Lisette. *Please* just wait one second."

"Go to your daughter, Jackson." She turns to me at the bottom of the steps. "I just need space. I'll be back tonight."

"Do you promise?" I look at her, struggling to determine which way this is going to fall. "Promise me you'll be back."

She turns without a word and I almost go after her, but at the sound of something loud coming from the bedroom, I rush for Belle.

"I slipped." She stifles a laugh as she sits on her rug with a pile of clothes around her. "I'm okay. Can you help me get that one?" She points behind me and I help her get her outfit together with a pit in my stomach.

# Chapter Sixty

## LISETTE

**JJ**

> I know you want space but can you please share your location with me?

10:37 AM

> Your brother keeps asking me for you. I'm going to tell him you left...

11:04 AM

*3 missed calls from Biggest Loser*

12:22 PM

**Biggest Loser**

> Jackson just told me you stormed out? Please don't do this right now, Lisette. We don't have to fight but call one of us.

12:24 PM

> I don't care if you're high. It doesn't matter who you're with. We're not angry, just answer someone's calls.

12:25PM

**Viddy**

> Hey, Lis. Sire is worried about you, babe. He's going to a meeting right now. Please meet him there. Or don't, you can come to my place. I'll be home all day <3

12:40 PM

**Winter AA**

> Dear, your brother is here at the center. He's worried sick and we'd love for you to join us today. I'll be here all day if you want to visit. We don't have to talk.

1:32PM

**Biggest Loser**

> You have until 5 PM.

1:58PM

**Harmony**

> heyy, i feel like we haven't spoken in forever! are you free today? he who shall not be named texted me…

2:05PM

*2 missed calls from JJ*

2:13PM

**Bay**

> Listen here you bitch, if you don't reply to one person today, I will kill your turtle. I'm at your house and I'm not above drowning this little shit.

2:28PM

*4 missed calls from Bay*

3:41PM

> I was joking Lis. Please call me

3:50PM

**JJ**

> You're still coming over tonight, right?

4:11PM

**Harmony**

> i was talking about my ex by the way, not sure if that was obvious but i didn't reply to him.

4:17PM

> can i come over tonight?

4:18PM

*17 missed calls from Biggest Loser*

5:02PM

**Sage**

> Hey, wanna come over and help me take my braids down?

5:07PM

**The better brother**

> Hey Lis! I'm going to get a gift for Hazel, wanna join?

5:20PM

**Hazel**

> Lis, your brothers are going to call your parents if you don't respond to someone.

5:31PM

*1 missed call from Mom*

5:44PM

**Mom**

> Call me or your father is sending his team to look for you.

5:47PM

# Chapter Sixty-One

## JACKSON

M Y KNEES ARE STARTING TO hurt as I scrub the kitchen floors. As I see the pantry in the corner of my eyes, I rise to my feet. Slipping my gloves off, I head for the door and when I flick the light on, my panic only grows.

We haven't heard from Lisette in a week. I can't think of anything else but her and it just feels like everything is going to shit, especially with the way the pantry looks right now. Everything is a mess from making breakfast this morning.

I start reorganizing the food, but I suddenly feel like I can't breathe in the small closet. Taking a step out, I catch my breath before rushing back and taking as much as I can hold. Setting it on the counter, I hold my breath before running back inside, making more trips than I can count to empty the pantry.

I'm scrubbing the floors and walls in there too and my nerves begin to settle, but as I step outside, the kitchen is a mess again. My breath quickens as I take a step back. Trapping myself in the pantry, I sink into the ground. I tap my head in a smoothing beat, but when the intrusive thoughts are too loud, I pull out my phone.

I call Sire and he answers on the first ring.

"Did Lis call?"

"Sire." I take a calming breath as I collect my thoughts. "I need you to go pick up Isabelle from school and bring her here." I shut my eyes before pulling my knees to my chest.

"What? Why do you sound like that? What—"

"Sire," I snap, my voice scaring me. "Please go pick up my daughter, okay? I need her with me. I need to see with my own eyes that she's okay."

There's something shuffling on his end. "Okay, but I'm not on her blue card anymore. Call them and tell them I'm going to get her."

I nod in return and focus on that small task.

They give me a bit of pushback when I call, but they tell me they'll release her to Sire when he gets there. Hanging up, my eyes land on my therapist's emergency number and with shaking hands, I hit her number.

After a few rings, she answers. "Hi, Jackson. What's going on?"

I rest my head against the wall as I hold my phone tighter. "There's been no news from Lisette." I shake my head as I glance at the door and it's as if it's going to eat me alive if I open it and let the mess in here.

"Are you in a safe space?"

I nod in return before shutting my eyes. "My house is a mess. Everything is a mess. I can't *fix* anything and I just need to get out of here."

"Everything is not a mess," Julia tries to reassure me. "Think of something you have control over and focus on that."

I shake my head in return as nothing comes to mind. "I'm trapped." A lump grows in my throat. "What if she's dead?" I tap the floor beside me, grasping for something to bring me comfort.

"Jackson, what do you see right now?"

I glance around the tight space. "My pantry." I choke out. "I emptied it to clean, but now the kitchen is a *wreck*. I can't open the door. I'm stuck here."

"Okay, okay," Julia's voice is calm and I try to focus on that, knowing this isn't that bad if she's acting so calm. "Jackson, you're having a panic attack. Breathe in as I count. In one, two three—"

"I need to wash it away, but I can't get out of here."

"Jackson, breathe with me." She counts again, but with every intrusive thought that enters my mind, my body pulls me to complete a compulsion, but I'm fucking stuck in here and I *can't*. I can't wash my hands, I can't tap the front door or the kitchen counter.

"She's dead, isn't she?" I feel my eyes prickling with tears and when my phone falls, I hear Julia's soft voice, but I can't answer her.

Covering my ears, I voice all of the good things to block out the bad ones.

"Isabelle is on her way, she's fine."

*Sire will probably crash on the way here.*

"He's a good driver. He'll keep her safe. They'll be here soon."

*Belle probably choked on those grapes you gave her for lunch. They're probably giving her CPR right now.*

Images of her blue face come to mind, but I shake my head and pull my hoodie off, shaking the thought out.

"She's fine."

*Lisette overdosed.*

"She's fine." I shake my hoodie out harder.

When the door swings open, I go still at the sight of my daughter's smile.

"Daddy, we were knocking forever. We had to use the emergency key. What are you doing in here, silly?" Her face softens as she sees my tears, but I quickly pull her in for a hug. Squeeze her tightly, I hold my breath as I rush past the mess in the kitchen.

"Jackson..." Sire watches me carefully, but I pass him and Vidia and rush out of the negative thought-infected house. Grabbing my car keys, I sit in the back seat with Belle.

"Dad, what happened?" She sits on my lap as she wipes my tears with her little hands.

I kiss her gently as I muster up a smile. "Nothing, I'm better now."

Her eyes narrow as she watches me. "You're still crying." She wipes my tears again before hugging me. "I know exactly what will make you feel better." She pulls away with that smile of hers. "Ice cream."

I stifle a laugh as I pull her back in for a hug. "Are you just saying that because *you* want ice cream?"

She shrugs, a guilty look on her face. "I'll go make you a banana sundae." She reaches for the door, but I stop her.

"No, don't go in there." I glance out at the house and there's too much I can't control in there. We're safer in the parked car.

She looks between me and the house before shrugging. "Okay, we can have Uncle Sigh make it for us. My foot still hurts."

"Why?" I glance down at her feet before gently pulling her shoe off. I inspect her foot as she opens the door and yells out to Sire who goes off to make her the sundae.

"I just sprained it during recess."

"How? The school didn't call me." I move her foot around and watch her carefully, but she doesn't wince.

When Sire comes back out with two bowls of ice cream he watches me carefully. "Here you go, princess." He hands her the bowl, but his eyes are on me. I avoid his gaze and after a few seconds, he walks off.

I remain in the car with Belle as we eat and she rambles about everything under the sun. After a while, Sire comes back outside with his girlfriend beside him.

He knocks on the car window before slowly opening the door. "That's the twins and my parents." He nods to the car pulling up. "Do you want to come back inside?"

I glance over at the house, but Vidia speaks up before I can object. "We put everything back in the pantry," she voices gently. "It's probably not how you like it, but it's pretty organized."

I let out a calm breath as I turn to Isabelle. Kissing her head, I nod in return before scooping her up and sliding out of the car. I kick my shoes off before entering the house and everyone behind me follows suit.

Gazing into the kitchen, I feel at ease as I take in how clean it is. "Thank you," I say as I turn to Vidia and she nods in return.

When Isabelle asks for a refill on the ice cream, I let her have a few more scoops before grabbing her tablet. I slide the backyard door open and sit her on the couch. Putting her tablet on her lap, I kiss her gently.

"Watch something out here while I talk with the grown-ups." I slip her headphones on.

She nods mindlessly as she puts a movie on.

Shutting the door behind me, I turn to the living room where I find Lisette's family.

Sage sits beside her fiancé, her eyes red with tears as she holds his hand. Beside them Hazel sits on August's lap, hugging him close. I glance over at the entrance where a man with the twins' green eyes and dark skin stands talking to a woman with tight curly hair. Their parents, I remember from the handful of times I've met them.

Sire walks over to me, Vidia's hand in his. "Sorry for the ambush," he whispers. "My dad wanted to tell us something, but I needed to bring Belle here and didn't want to wait. I figured you also wanted to hear so I told them to meet me here."

I nod in return before thanking him for bringing Belle.

"You okay? What was—"

"I'm okay." I nod and he watches me carefully before handing me my phone. I quickly text Julia to let her know I'm fine.

At the sound of someone clearing their throat, I look up at Isaac, Lisette's dad, who steps into the center of the living room.

"My friend thinks they have something but I'm just waiting for his call."

Beside him, his wife shakes her head before sitting beside Sage.

"What is it?" Sire looks between his parents. "Mom?" He turns to Kat.

She looks over at her husband who silently shakes his head.

August sits up from the couch, a panic in his eyes. "I've seen that look before. Don't withhold stuff from us like we're kids. What happened?"

Everyone turns to Isaac and I bite my nail nervously.

He fixes his tie before walking over to August. "I don't want to worry you all before we know for certain." He rests his hand on his arm. "Let's just wait for his call. He'll be there soon."

"Be where soon?" Sage's voice breaks as she takes her mom's hand. "What aren't you telling us?"

"Dad," Sire starts, his voice wavering. "Just say it." He shakes his head gently, tears building in his eyes.

A pit grows in my stomach as I turn to Isaac.

"There was a body reported that fit her description."

I take a step back but my back hits the glass. Sliding to the ground, I rest my arms on my knees as the room erupts into chaos.

There's crying, yelling, and pure panic, but it all meshes together in my head and all I can make out is the soft laughing from behind me. Looking over my shoulder, I focus on Isabelle's smile as she lays there, ice cream smudged on her face and hysterical over a movie she has watched a hundred times.

"How am I going to tell her?" My voice is just above a whisper as I bury my face in my hands.

The room gets louder with every second that passes. I think Isaac and Kat try to get their kids to calm down, but nothing works.

"How did she *fit* the description?" I make out Sire's voice from the crowd. "Half the LA population is white and blonde. She has tattoos all over her left arm. Did they check?"

"Was she in pain?" Sage asks next. "How did it happen?"

"She's *fine*," Sire rushes out. "It's not her."

"Sire," Vidia says gently and when I look over at them, she takes his hand. "You need to prepare for the worst, mi amor."

"No." He takes a step away from her. "Don't think like that." He turns to August now who's watching his brother with tear-filled eyes.

"Sire." He shakes his head gently.

"She's fine, August." His voice breaks now.

I watch Isaac carefully as he pulls out his phone. He brings a hand to his mouth before the twins rush over to him. I hold my breath as I sit up.

Sage looks over at his phone first and it must be a picture because she breaks into a sob as she turns to Liam's chest.

I go still.

August shakes his head next and when he hugs his mom something in me breaks.

"No." Sire shakes his head and he's still across the room, but at his siblings' reaction, his knees go weak. My vision blurs as Vidia tries to hold him up and they both end up on the ground.

"Is it her?" I choke out, but no one answers me. "Is it her?"

Hazel rushes over and leans over to see the phone. Her shoulders sag before she shakes her head. "No, it's not."

Sire picks his head up and you would've thought Lisette just walked into the room from the relief on his face.

I press my palm against my eyes as I try to catch my breath. I keep telling myself she's fine, but countless thoughts storm my mind, convincing me she's not okay.

When a scary one comes into my head, I rush to my feet. Walking into the kitchen, I tap the counter in a soothing beat before letting out a breath.

I look back into the living room and everyone sits in silence, but I can't take another minute with my thoughts. Pulling out my phone, I look through the album I made of Lisette.

I've been looking at it every day since she left. Swiping through the entire album is a new compulsion and it brings me the most peace.

I focus on the first picture of her where she's reading to a sleeping Isabelle. I smile as I remember how immersed into the children's book Lisette was that she didn't notice her fast asleep.

A few pictures down is one Belle made us take together as we baked for her class. Lisette offered to frost the cupcakes for her and they all look like flowers. I smile at the shock on Isabelle's face. Lisette spent that entire night teaching her how to frost flowers and I remember how surprised we both were by Lisette's artistic side.

When my eyes land on the picture of us from Thanksgiving, I find myself staring at her for several minutes. She's carrying Isabelle in her arms and as she throws her head back with a laugh, Lisette stares down at her, a perfect smile on her face as she gazes down at my daughter. Her brown dress hugs around her perfectly, her long hair draping down her back. Beside her, I'm staring down at her in awe.

My heart sinks as it hits me just how long I've been in love with this girl... not long. *I wanted so much more time.*

I finish swiping through the album before calling her. A part of me knows she won't answer, but I need to at least hear her voicemail.

"Hey, JJ."

My brows furrow at her cheery voice. I rush to my feet as I hurry into the living room. "Hey, Lisette." Everyone turns to me and I put it on speaker when they all gesture for me to do so.

"What are you up to? Do you want to get lunch?"

I look over at Sire and he nods before mouthing, *she's high. Just agree.*

"Yeah, do you want to come over and I'll cook?"

There's a honk on her end. "I'm going, calm down."

"Are you driving?" I look over at Sire when I see him shaking his head. He closes the distance between us and puts the phone on mute.

"If she is, don't scold her for driving intoxicated. Don't put any blame on her. Just go along and find her."

"Of course, I'm not driving." Lisette pulls our attention back to my phone. "I found a perfect parking spot in front of my apartment, I'm never moving it. Listen, I'm shopping right now, but I'll be at my place in an hour. Can you meet me there?"

I'm still trying to shake off the shock of hearing her voice after processing that she was dead, but Sire taps my arm and I snap back in. "Yeah, sweetheart. Of course."

"Okay, can you just do me a favor and tell Sire I'm okay?" Her voice is quieter now and when I look over at Sire, I can see the hurt he's drowning in. "Don't tell him you're going to see me. I'm going to see him tonight, but I just want a few more hours before I get yelled at. I blocked all of them a few days ago and I'm in for a headache. Harmony has also been asking a ton of questions and I just need a few more hours of peace."

I shake my head at how care-fucking-free she sounds, but I keep my anger aside. "Okay, reina. I'll see you in a bit."

I hang up and when I turn to the room, everyone looks just as shocked.

"God, give me the strength." Kat looks up to the ceiling before burying her face in her husband's chest.

I glance over at Sire. "What do I do?"

He takes a minute to think before running a hand through his hair. "I'll handle it."

"What?" I grab him as he tries to walk off. "No, I want to help."

"Jackson—"

I cut him off at the sight of that look in his eyes. "Don't you dare say this is a family matter, Sire. I'm coming."

He watches me for a second before nodding. "Fine, but you need to do exactly what I say."

# Chapter Sixty-Two

# JACKSON

"**T**HIS IS GOING TO GET ugly." Sire keeps his eyes on Lisette's door and I know his words are for me, but I don't respond. "If you want to leave, you—"

"I'm not leaving. I already told you, I'm all the way in."

He gives me a single nod and leaves it at that as we watch the door.

After a few minutes, a phone dings. We all turn to Sage in anticipation.

"That wasn't Liam..." She gives us an apologetic look before typing something into her phone and after a minute it dings again. She shoots up in her seat and I quickly stand with her.

"That was him, she's here." She walks into the bedroom where Vidia and Hazel are and her twin follows close behind her.

Sire stands behind the door and I lay back on the couch, trying to look like I'm not hiding all of her loved ones in this apartment and about to bombard her. I try to get my facial expressions together, but a key is put into the door and I don't have time to get shit together.

I pull out my phone to look casual, but I'm sweating.

The door opens and I wait a second before looking up. When I do, I notice the bags under her eyes, but I can't tell if they're tired bags or if she's high.

She keeps her eyes on her phone as she steps into the apartment and Sire softly takes a step in front of the door.

When she finally looks up she seems to falter, but quickly catches herself and offers me a smile. "Hey." She closes the distance between us and leans over to kiss me.

"Sire gave me your key, I hope you don't mind that I let myself in." I pull away and study her for a beat. "I haven't heard from you in a while." I grab her hand and she leans in to straddle me.

My hands instinctively land on her ass. When I steal a glance behind her, Sire only shakes his head at us before rolling his eyes and I try very hard not to laugh.

Lisette lets out a breath, pulling my eyes back to her. "I'm sorry... I was upset that you believed my brother over me so I was ignoring you, but I know you were trying to help." She quickly steals a kiss. "I'm okay though."

I feel a smile touch my lips at the sincerity in her voice, but behind her, Sire waves for my attention. He points up to the ceiling, signaling that she's high, but when I look back at her, I don't see it.

"You promise me you're okay?"

She looks at me for a moment before stealing another kiss. "Yes, JJ." She climbs off my lap before rustling my hair. "Let me feed Piglet then we can grab food." She walks to her room and I quickly stand.

The minute she opens her door, she goes still. "What the hell are you all doing here?"

I keep my eyes on her as she looks around her room.

"Hi, Lissy bear." Sage's voice seems to break, but Lisette quickly turns on her heels. Her head whips to the door and when she notices Sire slouched against it, a panic grows in her eyes.

"Are you fucking kidding me?"

Sire pushes off the door, but she puts a hand up to stop him.

"We're not doing this." She shakes her head at him.

"We are." Sire nods for the couch, but when August rests his hand on Lisette, she looks just about ready to lose her shit.

"Don't touch me!" She takes a step back before putting her hands up. "No one touch me."

"Okay." August puts his hands up in surrender. "No one is going to touch you."

Everyone descends from the room and Lisette continues to back away from them before she ends up in the kitchen.

"An intervention?" She looks around the room before her eyes land on mine and she looks so betrayed... just like I knew she would be. "I told you I was okay." She shakes her head softly and I quickly take a step towards her.

"I want you to believe you, Lissy, I do. But can you look me in the eyes and tell me you aren't high right now?"

She looks hurt at first... then her anger settles. "Let me leave." She keeps her voice low, almost as if she were warning us.

"I appreciate that you asked nicely." Sire smiles over at her before pulling a chair and sitting in front of the door. "But you know we aren't going to let that happen."

"I *genuinely* hate you, Sire."

I feel myself flinch, as if her words were thrown at me, but he only puts a hand on his heart in mock pain. "You wound me, Lis." He turns more serious. "Do you want to tell anyone else you hate them or can we start this?"

"Yeah, I do actually." She turns to the group and I desperately want to look away, but I force my eyes to stay on her. "If you all don't let me leave then I also hate all of you and will *never* forgive you for this."

Sire laughs softly and it seems to piss her off more. "We don't care for your forgiveness, Lisette. In a few months, it's going to be you asking for our forgiveness."

She starts to pace the kitchen as she realizes she's trapped.

"Lissy..." Sage starts softly as she slowly makes her way to the kitchen. "We just want to help you and—"

"I don't *need* help," she snaps.

Sage turns her head to the side and I can't see her face, but I'm sure she's close to crying. "You do." Sage sniffles before wiping her cheek, but Lisette looks as if Sage just threw up on her favorite shoes.

Navi steps forward. Sire called their AA Chair and she sent her to hold this all together.

"Lisette." She smiles over at her and Lisette must've just realized her because she looks as if she appeared from thin air.

"Who the hell are you?"

"I'm Navi." She offers her a smile.

"Get the hell out of my house, lady." She turns back to Sire. "Who the hell is this?"

"She's Navi," Sire answers and I keep my eyes on Lisette, but I can hear his smile.

"Yeah, I got her damn name, dumbass. Who is she?"

Navi takes a step forward. "All of these people are here because they care about you."

I keep my eyes on Lisette as something seems to click in her head. "You're going to facilitate this." She lets out a scoff before looking back over at Sire. "I *never* intervened you—"

"I'm counting you sending people in one by one as an intervention so yes, you have. Four times to be exact."

"Not like this!" She takes a sharp step forward. "I never *ambushed* you or brought in some-some fucking stranger." She shakes her head as she gives Navi a once over before looking back at her brother. "This fucking hurts."

"I'm not doing this to hurt you, Lis." Sire's voice takes on a more serious tone. "We just needed extra support and—"

"I know how this works." She paces the kitchen again. "I've been a part of these for friends. I know—"

"So you know we're trying to help," Navi says softly.

"I know that you're *just* here to facilitate." She glances back at us. "Which one of you is going to take charge? Who's going to woman the fuck up and say something to me? Huh?"

I feel everyone's eyes on my back, but I don't say anything.

"It's not going to be Sire." She turns her head to the side. "That's too predictable. I'm sure you all canceled him out and guessed I won't listen to him." She turns to her other siblings. "It's not going to be the twins, they bruise like fucking peaches."

"Lisette, we—"

"Stop talking, Navi." She rolls her eyes before glancing behind me. "My guess is Vidia." She shrugs. "You've got tough skin, care about my brother. Go ahead, V. Open the meeting, give it your best fucking shot."

But Vidia doesn't say anything.

"Lisette," I say gently.

Her eyes meet mine and she must read right through me because she shakes her head softly.

"Please just listen to us."

She looks at me before she lets out a scoff. "Fine," she mumbles before brushing past me. She flops onto the couch with us. "I have shit to do so let's just get this over with. Let's go around in a circle and share what we love about Lis." She crosses her arms as she leans back in her seat.

I glance over at my best friend and he shakes his head at her before getting up and sitting with us.

Navi is last to sit as she glances around all of us. "Let's open the circle by—"

Lisette starts to laugh and I glance around the room, but she only laughs harder, so damn hard it seems genuine. "Open the circle? Wow, straight out of an NA meeting huh? This is going to be so much fun. Go ahead, Facilitator. Continue."

Navi doesn't acknowledge her outburst. "Let's start by sharing what we did today."

I glance at Lisette and she suddenly looks uncomfortable in her seat.

"I'll go first," Sire starts. "I went on a walk to clear my thoughts of how this will go because I really want it to go well."

Lisette rolls her eyes before looking down at her nails.

"Jackson," Navi turns to me. "Why don't you go next?"

I swallow the weird taste in my throat before turning to Lis, but then I quickly remember Navi told me not to directly address her the entire time so she doesn't feel attacked. I turn to Sire instead. "I dropped Isabelle off at my mom's house."

In the corner of my eye, I can see Lisette's head snap up to mine.

"She gave me a hard time and was crying. She overheard that we were coming to see Lissy. She misses her, but I told her she had nothing to worry about." I turn to Lisette and her eyes are still on me.

"She doesn't."

I nod. "I know that."

She keeps her eyes on me and I desperately want to hold her, but I stay in my seat as everyone shares about their day. It mostly entails things around Lis since we spent the day worrying about her, but they're subtle about it and no one mentions how we thought she was hurt.

"What'd you do today, Lissy?" I ask when Sire signals at me, but she looks back at her nails before picking on them.

"Nothing much." She shrugs.

"Everyone else shared." Sire watches her. "I think you can do better than that."

"What do you want me to say, Sire?" Her eyes snap to him with so much rage.

"I want you to share about your day." He remains calm.

I look back over at Lisette and she glances around the room before shaking her head.

"Nothing much," she voices again, clearly refusing to admit to every person she loves that she was out getting high.

"Okay." Sire leans back in his seat. "You know why we're all here, Lis—"

"Because you love to make my life miserable?" She sits up in her seat before he can respond. "I can't get over the fact that you *organized* an *intervention* for me. This is so fucking low."

"I'm not doing this to hurt you and—"

"*Yes*, you are."

Every other person seems to flinch as she raises her voice.

"All I wanted was one fucking week. Just one with no responsibilities and—"

"We don't get that luxury. We don't get to call a timeout on our addiction, Lis."

"You're impossible," she mumbles before sitting back in her seat.

Sire opens his mouth, but she beats him to it.

"Fuck you."

"Oh, fuck me? How about—"

Vidia takes his hand as his volume starts to rise and he takes in a deep breath. This isn't supposed to be a fight. It isn't supposed to be us blaming her or putting responsibility on her, and I can see Sire remembers that as he looks back over at his sister.

"None of us are here to hurt you, Lis."

"I don't care."

"We care about you," he continues.

"I *don't* care."

"You do." I step in, but she keeps her angry eyes on her brother. "You may not care in this moment, but we know you care about us and you saying you don't isn't going to push us away. I'm sure you also care a great deal about Harmony... or maybe Isabelle."

She looks over at me now and it's as if she's never been angry a day in her life. "I know *you* and the girls care about me, JJ." She sinks into her seat as she hugs herself. "My siblings don't."

"That's not true," August starts now. He's sitting next to her and moves to touch her, but quickly catches himself. "I care about you, Lis. Without you, who's going to piss Sire off at every chance?" He leans over with a smile to catch her eyes with his, but she turns away.

"I love you, Lisette. A lot more than you know," he almost whispers.

"You complete our family," Sage continues. "When the universe trapped me with a boy for a twin they also gave me the sister I always wanted." Sage quickly wipes her tears as she focuses on her.

"Lis—" Sire attempts to voice how much he loves her.

"I don't care what you have to say, Sire."

He only nods before leaning back in his seat. "Good thing I don't care about what you care about."

"Of course, you don't. You planned an intervention and—"

"You mean everything to me, Lis—"

"No, I don't."

"You *do*, and nothing you say is going to change that. Nothing you say is going to take away your title as my favorite person and you know that, which is why you're picking on me, but guess what, Lis?"

She turns away from him and he gets up to crouch in front of her.

"Hurt people hurt people. *You* told me that."

She turns her head to the other side again, but he grabs her face and I swear my heart gets lodged in my throat at the sight of tears in both of their eyes.

"You told me that. You forgave me for saying things to you that *no one* should've ever thought so if you want to be mean, go right the fuck ahead because it's not going to stick. You told me you were losing faith, but I never doubted you for a minute and I know you're going to be fine."

Sire stands before gesturing to the rest of the group and Hazel and Vidia share how much they care about her before it's my turn.

"The minute Belle's mom walked out on us I decided it'll just be us."

Lisette glances over at me now.

"I didn't want to bring anyone else around her. I didn't want to give anyone else the power to hurt her or leave her."

She avoids my eyes and I quickly catch myself.

"That was until you, Lisette. You haven't hurt her and I don't think you will. I still want you to be a part of our family... I still want you to be her mom and you can, you just need to get better first, but you need to let us help you."

She wipes a tear, but it's clear she isn't going to look at me.

"Isabelle couldn't be here, but she wrote something for you." I keep my eyes on her as I pull out Isabelle's letter. She keeps her head turned, but I can see her trying to steal a glance in the corner of her eye.

"Do you want me to read it to you?"

She shakes her head softly before quickly wiping another tear.

"Here." I lean forward in my seat before stretching my hand out to her. "You can read it yourself."

I watch her carefully as she swallows and turns to me.

"Did she spell it all right?"

I offer her a small smile before shrugging. "I haven't read it." I lift my hand and she takes it, but simply rests it on her lap.

I sit back in my seat and Navi signals for the next step, explaining to her how she hurt us. Sire explained how she can't argue with facts and how we feel, so rather than telling her her actions aren't good, we're going to tell her how *we* feel about them.

It barely lasts five minutes before she's up and pacing and when I see her break into a sweat, I realize she really is high, but she's clearly coming down from it.

Sire warned me that this would get ugly, but when it does, I don't recognize her.

"Let me out! Let me out! Let me out!" She bangs on the kitchen counter before walking around it a few more times, screaming her mantra.

"Keep sharing," Navi whispers and Vidia nods softly before speaking over Lisette's screams.

"You hold a special place in our hearts and it hurts seeing you like—"

"Would you stop?" Lisette finally stops yelling. "I don't get why you're even here, Vidia. I'm sure when you get angry with me in the future you're going to turn around and use my addiction against me the same way you did with Sire."

The room goes still.

"I hold a special place in your heart? Fuck off. You're not special. The only reason my brother is with you is because your mom is a hotshot coach."

Vidia forces a smile. "That's not true and—"

"It is. You're the idiot for believing otherwise and, Sire"—she turns her fierce eyes to him—"You're even dumber for forgiving her after outing your addiction. Who even does that?"

"Shut up, Lisette."

I steal a glance over at the couple, but Vidia is walking to the bathroom. I have no clue what she's talking about, but I think all my questions about why Sire and Vidia broke up in college were just answered.

"Who's next?" Lisette scans the room for her next victim. "Sage, just go now. Your tears are no help and take August with you."

"I'm not—"

She quickly cuts him off. "You're useless, August. An absolute pushover. You covered for Sire his entire teenage years because you *felt bad.*" She rolls her eyes before Hazel speaks up.

"Being mean isn't going to do any good, Lis," she starts gently, taking August's hand when his shoulders slouch.

"Shut the fuck up, Hazel," Lisette starts and my jaw slightly drops at how ruthless she's being. "I care less what you have to say than anyone else here."

"I don't care about what you care about," Hazel replies carelessly. "But I do care about how you talk to my man so watch your mouth. We're trying to *help.*"

Lisette lets out a scoff. "You know." She tilts her head to this side. "I think this bitchy thing you got going on is just an act. You're so much bark and no bite."

A smirk grows on Hazel's face. "Oh, you want to see how much bite I got?" She takes a step forward, but August holds her back. "I love you, Lis, but if you need some sense slapped into you, I'll gladly volunteer."

"Hey," August speaks up. He steps in front of his girlfriend, towering a full foot over her as he forces her to look at him. "This is not what you came here for. I told you she would do this. I need your temper in check."

They watch each other before August nods behind her. "Go find Vidia." He leans over to kiss her and Hazel spins on her heels without a word.

"You can go too, August." Lisette just doesn't quit, but it's clear now that she's trying to get everyone to walk away from her. "You're the reason Sire almost overdosed in that alley and—"

"Lis," Sire warns. "Stop talking," he bites out.

"Aww, what's wrong, Sire?" She turns her head to the side. "You don't want everyone else to know that you're worse than me?" She lets out a soft chuckle before looking around the room, but not a single soul is laughing.

"You all think I'm bad now, but you haven't seen bad because Sire is the worst of them all."

"No one thinks you're bad, Lisette."

She ignores Navi. "Since we're all sharing how hurt you all are when I'm high, let's talk about how Sire hurt us."

"This is about you, Lisette."

"Stop talking!" She screams so loud that Navi takes a step back.

"No one gave Sire an intervention when he forced August to pass a drug test for him the first time, then that second time, then *again* when he went missing for days and let his poor brother find him nearly dead in an alley. Or *again* in college so he could sign with the Dodgers."

Silence.

"Not a single fucking soul ambushed Sire when he said—" She pretends to think. "What was it? Something along the lines of throwing my suicide attempt in my face? No, that was *fine* because Sire is just a mean drunk, and boohoo because his childhood was so hard."

"Did that make you feel better, Lisette?" Sire gets up from his seat now. "I can see the oxy is nearly out of your system since you're being a fucking *bitch*."

"Sire—"

"No, Jackson, she wants to be mean. We can play the mean game. Fuck you! You want to have a screaming match? WE CAN SCREAM!" He takes a step towards her, but August quickly steps in his way. "I already told you, Lis, be mean all you want, but nothing you say is going to stick. I'm! Not! Going! Anywhere!"

When no one says anything else, Lis walks for the door. It swings open, but Liam is there before she can take a step out.

"Wow." She lets out a scoff before turning back to Sire. "You must've been really fucking desperate to call this guy."

"Beloved?" Liam has his eyes set on his fiancée. "Do you want to step outside?" He keeps his voice soft, but when Sage shakes her head no, he looks down at Lisette.

"Go back inside." He tries to grab the door, but she doesn't let him.

"Get out of my way."

Liam looks up at Sage and when she shakes her head, he *pushes* Lisette into the apartment and slams the door on her face.

"Open the damn door!" She bangs on it so hard I think she's going to break her hand. "LET ME OUT!" She keeps screaming, over and over again as she bangs on the door and pulls the handle, but it's clear Liam is holding the other side because it doesn't budge.

After maybe five minutes of screaming bloody murdering and throwing herself at the door, she must get tired because she leans her head against it before slouching and falling to the ground.

"Let me out," she whispers and it fucking breaks me.

I take a step towards her, but she grabs Isabelle's letter from her pocket and Navi puts her hand up to stop me.

We watch her carefully as she reads the letter and when she breaks into a sob and hugs the paper I push past Navi.

"Her spelling is getting so much better." She wraps her arms around me before breaking into another sob. "Why did she add a cupcake recipe?"

I let out a soft laugh, but quickly bite my tongue as I feel a cry bubbling in my throat.

"JJ..." She pulls away before holding my face in her hands. "I want to be her mom. I want to be with you and be a family with you."

"I want that too, Lissy." I rest my forehead against hers.

"So let's leave." She voices softly... too softly.

When I pull away she keeps her eyes on me and all that rings in my head is Sire's warning. She's going to say every and anything she can to get out. That she was going to pick on everyone and manipulate me.

"Do you really want to raise Belle with me?"

"Yes." She wipes her tears before planting a soft kiss on my lips.

I take hold of her hand as I pull away. "You need to get clean if you want to do that, Lis."

"I will," she quickly agrees and I let out a breath of relief. I look over at her siblings with a smile, but Sire's glare doesn't budge and Navi still watches her as if we need this to go on for longer.

*What the hell am I missing?*

"Let's just go, JJ." She turns my face back to her before grabbing my hand, almost in a rush.

"Let's talk about that plan, Lisette." Navi walks over.

I turn to look at her, but Lisette turns my face to hers again. "We don't even know that lady, JJ. Please, let's go and we can be a family. We don't need anyone else."

"You plan on running away with them?" Sire lets out a scoff. "If you want to get clean, why cut off your family?"

Her family. The people who are going to notice when she's high... when she's lying.

I pull away from her, but she grabs my hand again. "I meant what I said, I swear. I want to be in Belle's life."

I pull my hand away harder as I stand. "So you need to get clean. You need to get clean *first*," I emphasize.

She scans the room, but turns back to the door as Sire walks over.

"There's a bed waiting for you at one of the best rehab facilities."

She keeps her eyes on the door.

"You just need to give it ninety days, but we'll all visit you. Jackson will take Isa to see you, right?"

"Yeah..." I lie. I'm not bringing my kid anywhere near her like this. I love her and it hurts thinking about keeping her away, but absolutely not. If hearing my lies will get her to comply then I'll voice them, but Isabelle noticed she wasn't well the last time she relapsed and I'm not putting her through that again, whether she fully understands or not.

"Fine." Lis keeps her eyes on the door. "I'll go to rehab."

I let out another breath and Sire has a small smile on his face.

She sniffles quietly before wiping her tears. She walks over to her room and I follow behind her. She heads for her turtle first and feeds him before a somber smile touches her lips.

"I'm tired of fighting." She shakes her head, her palms pressed to her eyes. "Can someone pack my bag?" She cries quietly as she sits on the edge of her bed.

"I can do it," the twins voice in synchrony before rushing off to her closet.

Sire steps beside her and kisses the top of her head. "You're going to be fine." He seems to be promising her.

She nods before she cries harder. "I'm so sorry." She looks around the room, but no one is angry with her. "I love you all. You know that, yeah?"

"Of course we do." Sire wraps an arm around her.

She nods quietly before sniffling, but her tears don't stop. "I just need a minute." She walks off to the bathroom and we leave her be.

Sinking into her bed, I bury my face in my hands. "That was torture." I glance at my watch and we've been at this for a fucking hour.

"The hard part is over," Sire replies. "For us at least."

I nod in return and we sit in silence as we wait for Lisette to come out of the bathroom. After a few minutes, the twins come out of her closet with a bag.

"I packed her a lot of socks so they don't make her wear those grippy ones they gave her last time," Sage voices quietly. "She hates them."

August smiles at her words before hugging his sister, but the sound of someone falling has us all turning to the bathroom.

I don't hear anything else and quickly rise to my feet. "Lisette?" I knock on the door softly, but I don't hear a response.

At the sound of choking my heart nearly stops. I shove my arm into the door, but it doesn't give. Sire bangs on it beside me and we're all trying to get it open before I kick it down.

Rushing in, we nearly trample over her. I feel my eyes widen as I take in her limp body on the ground, vomit near her mouth.

Sire calls out for someone to call an ambulance, but all I hear is a buzzing sound as I drop to my knees and cradle her head.

A few people push past me as we all try to fit in her small bathroom and the buzzing in my ear gets louder.

I think I hear my name, but when I look up, I can't make out what Sire is telling me. He looks like he's yelling, but I can't hear. As I look down, I'm nearly moving in slow motion as he checks my pockets for something.

He shakes my shoulders and my hearing suddenly comes back.

"I don't *know* if she's breathing," Sage cries. "Just send some-one." When I turn to her, she's on the phone, but turns to the hall and screams out for her fiancé.

"The naloxone I gave you, Jackson." Sire shakes me again, his eyes drowning in a fear that scares me all over again. "Where is it?"

I shake my head as I look down at Lisette and Vidia pulls her away so her head is on the ground.

"I don't have it."

# PART II

**To Be Continued...**

# *Acknowledgments*

First and foremost, huge thank you to all of my sensitivity readers. Each and every one of you was a huge help in shaping the struggles of both of my characters. I appreciate the insight you all gave me and the time you put into working with me.

To my readers, with every book I release, I get ten times more support than the last, and I wouldn't be here without my circle—which seems to grow every day.

To all of my girlies from the private story, you've been here since the first rant and continue to support me through every step of this process. I adore each of you immensely.

To my readers who relate to Lisette in any shape or form—I see you. Everyone, of course, has a different experience when it comes to their mental health, but I hope I was able to represent these real-life struggles well enough. I wrote this book during a time when I needed a Jackson in my corner. Instead, I wrote down all the things I needed to hear. Out of all of the Hale siblings, Lisette holds a special place in my heart because she healed a piece of me. On every bad day I had, I grabbed my laptop and poured myself into this book. I hope you all found a way to appreciate Lisette's imperfections. I know I certainly love her enough for the both of us.

Honorary mention to my love, Chelsea. Your help with certain aspects of this story was so important. You helped me see things through different lenses. Thank you for caring enough about these characters to share those parts of your life with me.

To my parents, words will never be able to express just how much I appreciate both of you. Every time I called you to rant about how I wanted to come home, you were so supportive. And when I finally threw in the towel, you both had open arms. Sometimes, you really just need a hug from your mom, and my support system made this book possible. So, Mom, thank you for being the Kat to my Lis.

To my brother, who isn't going to read this — you're not a reader by any means and probably have no plans to read my books, yet anytime I had an update, you were all ears — from the plot to my cover reveal. It took me three books to admit it, but here it is: thank you for the inspiration for my characters. Anytime you make a joke or do something to make me laugh, I say, "I'm writing that down" — and I actually do. If it's not in this book, I wrote it in the outline for future stories. While it was unconscious, the bond I have with you and the boys wrote itself into the Hale siblings. I love you, losers!

The best for last, Ash. You're my go-to person for everything book-related. We're three books in now, and I'm afraid you're stuck with me. Thank you for being my sounding board to bounce ideas off of. Thank you for threatening me to take breaks and pick up one of your never-ending recs (I'll read them all one day). Most of all, thank you for being you.

# About The Author

Janiah Benitez is a twenty-year-old hopeless romantic from New York City. When she's not writing, Janiah is trying to complete her never-ending TBR or planning for her dream bookstore.